THE MOTHER'S CONFESSION

Part 6
of
The Windsor Street Family Saga

By

VL McBeath

The Mother's Confession
By VL McBeath

Published by Valyn Publishing.

For more about this author please visit
https://valmcbeath.com

For permission requests, write to the author at:
https://vlmcbeath.com/contact/

Editing services provided by Susan Cunningham at Perfect Prose Services
Cover design by Books Covered

ISBNs: 978-1-913838-26-3 (Ebook Edition)
978-1-913838-27-0 (Paperback)

Main category - FICTION / Historical
Other category - FICTION / Sagas

Legal Notices

Explanatory Notes

Meal Times

In the United Kingdom, meal times are referred to by a variety of names. Based on traditional working-class practices in northern England in the nineteenth century, the following terms have been used:

Dinner: The meal eaten around midday. This may be a hot or cold meal depending on the day of the week and a person's occupation

Tea: Not to be confused with afternoon tea or the beverage of the same name, tea was the meal eaten at the end of the working day, typically around five or six o'clock. This could either be a hot or cold meal.

Afternoon tea: Taken at around four o'clock, this would typically consist of sandwiches, cakes, and a pot of tea.

Money

In the nineteenth century, the currency in the United Kingdom was Pounds, Shillings and Pence.

- There were twenty shillings to each pound and twelve pence to a shilling.
- A crown and half crown were five shillings and two shillings and sixpence, respectively.

For further information on Victorian-era England visit:
https://vlmcbeath.com/victorian-era

Previously in

The Windsor Street Family Saga

Part 1: *The Sailor's Promise*
Part 2: *The Wife's Dilemma*
Part 3: *The Stewardess's Journey*
Part 4: *The Captain's Order*
Part 5: The Companion's Secret

Set in Liverpool (UK), *The Windsor Street Family Saga* was inspired by a true story and it is **recommended that the books are read in order.**

For further information visit my website at:

https://valmcbeath.com/windsor-street/

Please note: This series is written in UK English

CHAPTER ONE

Liverpool, November 1884

Thick grey clouds shrouded the sun as Nell Riley stepped onto the deck of the SS *Arizona* and rested her arms on the rail overlooking the Port of Liverpool. The last of the passengers were trudging down the gangplank into the throng of people on the landing stage, and she scanned the faces looking up at the ship. *You knew there'd be nobody here.* She turned to the stewardesses who'd been her companions for the previous nine months.

"This is it, then."

"It is for you. I'll be here again next year." The older of her colleagues stood with her back to the wind, holding her hat. "Are you sure you won't change your mind?"

"I am. I'm ready to stay at home and see what that brings." Nell stared down at the growing crowd. "Will either of you have anyone waiting?"

"My mam will be here." A young blond-haired stewardess waved to the crowd. "Not that I can see her."

The older woman sighed. "There'll be no one here for me, only my sister, when I reach her house."

"That's what you get for being so rude to the stewards." The younger girl continued to search the crowd and missed the scowl on her colleague's face.

"Being overfriendly nearly got you into a lot of trouble, and you'd be as well to remember that."

"I'd rather that, than still be a spinster when I'm your age…" She stopped when the head steward interrupted them.

"Are you ready to leave, ladies?"

Nell nodded. "As ready as we'll ever be."

"If you'll follow me, I'll escort you from the ship."

Nell was the last down the gangplank, and she stepped to one side as a second steward followed with their luggage.

"Good day, ladies. Have a good Christmas."

The young stewardess bounced on her toes and waved as an older version of herself headed towards her. "There's me mam. I can't wait to tell her about the trip." She grabbed her bag and, with little more than a backward glance, disappeared into the crowd.

The older woman picked up her case. "She'll be someone else's problem now. Thank goodness. I couldn't cope with her for another year."

Nell smirked. "You don't know who you'll get to replace her yet."

"Don't say that. These young girls think they're coming on the ship to look for a husband, not to work. If you ever change your mind, you know where we are…" She offered her hand to the steward. "Farewell until next year, sir. Goodbye, Mrs Riley."

Once they were alone, the steward smiled at Nell. "It was a pleasure working with you, Mrs Riley."

"And you too, sir. Thank you for everything." She glanced around the immediate area.

"Are you looking for someone?"

She feigned a smile. "More in hope than expectation. Everyone will be at work this morning."

"Did you say you were going to Toxteth Park? I'll find you a carriage, if you like. It's a long walk with your bag."

Nell fingered the coins in her pocket. "Why not? I don't treat myself very often."

"Give me a minute." He left her where she was, but she stepped backwards onto the bottom of the gangplank as the crowds closed in on her, only relaxing when the steward jumped out of a carriage on the other side of the road.

"It's all yours." He handed her luggage to the coachman. "Have a safe journey."

She settled into her seat, still studying the crowds as the carriage pulled away and headed along the dock road. *So, that's it. No more leaving home.* She sighed and closed her eyes. *Time to start again. Forget Ollie. And Mr Marsh. Although he'll probably want to forget me...* She rubbed her hands over her face. *What a mess I've made.*

She closed her eyes as the carriage bounced over the cobbled streets but opened them when they turned from Windsor Street into Merlin Street. *Here we are. Let's find out what's been going on.*

Unusually, Maria wasn't waiting in the window when the carriage pulled up outside, and Nell peered across the street to her sister Rebecca's house while the coachman rolled down the steps. *Where is everyone?*

"When you're ready, madam." He offered her a hand.

"I'm sorry." She reached into her pocket and pulled out a shilling. "Is that enough?"

"More than enough. You can have some change." He handed her a selection of coins before retrieving her bag and placing it by the front door.

"Thank you. I'll take it from here."

The house was quiet when she stepped inside, and she strode to the back room. "Is anyone home?" She leaned on the table to peer through the window. *The washing's out. Where are they?* "Maria? Alice?" She walked back to the hall. "Are you upstairs?"

When there was no reply, she headed across the road to Rebecca's. After a brief knock, she let herself in. "Rebecca?"

"In the kitchen."

Leah jumped down from her seat at the dining table. "Mama."

Nell swept her up in her arms. "What are you doing here?"

"Alice and Aunty Ria have gone out."

"Where to?"

The smile disappeared from Rebecca's face. "To Betty's. She lost the baby she was carrying. It was a couple of months early and didn't survive."

The blood drained from Nell's face. "Not again. When did this happen?"

"On Monday of this week. Alice has been sitting with her ever since, but Maria doesn't like her walking there by herself. They go together once Elenor's at school, but Maria usually comes straight home. She'll probably pop in for a cup of tea and to collect Leah."

Nell squeezed her eyes tight. "The poor girl. She'll be distraught."

"The doctor's given her some laudanum, but it's no use when she has baby Albert to take care of. Alice has been a godsend."

Leah released her hold of Nell's neck. "I want to see Albert."

"Perhaps we will when Betty's better. You sit there with Florrie while I have a cup of tea." She sat her daughter at the table. "I'll walk up there myself when she's ready for visitors."

Rebecca raised an eyebrow. "What will you say?"

"I don't know. Sometimes it just helps being there." She let out a deep sigh. "Have I missed anything else?"

Rebecca creased her lip. "I don't think so. How was the trip?"

"Good. We made it into New York. The captain knew the ship would be half empty on the return, so decided we could do the cleaning on the return journey."

"That was nice of him."

"It was. We had a young stewardess with us who was thrilled about going to Central Park. She reminded me of myself when I first went ashore."

"You don't seem so excited now."

Nell's shoulders dropped. "The novelty had obviously worn off." *And the memories are still too vivid.*

Rebecca poured the tea as they sat with their daughters. "Have you thought about what you'll do now?"

"I've thought, but I've not come up with any answers. I

won't need to work now George has his foreman's job, but I won't need to be a mam either when Leah starts school."

"It's come around quickly. We'll have to go to the park again."

"Have you finally got rid of Mrs Pearse?"

Rebecca huffed. "I have, thank goodness. I can't believe I put up with her for so long..." She paused as the front door closed and Maria joined them.

"You're home! I'm sorry I was out." Her face dropped. "Did Rebecca tell you?"

"She did. How's Betty?"

"Not well. The baby was fully formed, a little girl, and she had to go through all the motions." Maria sat down and helped herself to a cup of tea. "All I can say is it's a good job she has young Albert. He's the only thing keeping her going."

"How's Jane?"

"Managing for Betty's sake, but it's not easy."

"I'll call on her as well." Nell took a sip of tea. "Rebecca doesn't think I missed much else."

"Did you tell her about Vernon?"

"Gosh, no, I forgot."

"What about him?"

"He's getting married."

Nell nearly choked on her tea. "Who to?"

"Miss Ally, the young lady he's been walking out with."

"He's not known her long. Three months, perhaps?"

Maria shrugged. "I suspect it's longer. He just didn't mention her to us."

"Has she been to tea?"

"She has now, although they'd already announced they were getting married by then. She's nice enough."

"He doesn't waste any time, does he? Have they set a date?"

"The fifteenth of March."

"Gracious. She's not..." Nell pointed to her stomach "... you know."

"No, she is not!" Maria plonked her hands on her hips. "My son wouldn't do anything like that."

"All right, calm down. I only asked."

"Well, watch your tongue. That's how rumours spread. Besides, the wedding would be next week if she was."

Nell suppressed a smile as she took another mouthful of tea. "I'd better finish this. I need to get my washing done and on the line."

"There are a couple of letters for you at home. Alice thinks one is from Mrs Cavendish."

Nell's smile returned. "Hopefully, it's telling me she's had her baby. It was due while I was away. Who's the other one from?"

"She didn't recognise the handwriting."

"Mrs Robertson?"

"No, she said it's a man's writing."

Nell's heart skipped a beat. *Oh gracious. That can only be one of two people.*

CHAPTER TWO

The letters were behind the clock on the mantlepiece, and Nell picked them up as soon as she'd taken off her cloak. One was definitely from Mrs Cavendish, Clara, but Nell studied the writing on the other. *Mr Marsh?* Her pulse quickened as she sliced open the envelope and sat down to read it.

My dear Mrs Riley

I hope you had a good summer sailing to New York and can look forward to spending time with your family over Christmas. For my part, I took several voyages to South Africa, but by the time you read this letter, I'll be somewhere between Liverpool and Australia

Nell glanced at the date on the letter. *First of November. Three days after I left Liverpool for the last voyage. He'll be halfway there now.* She huffed and continued reading.

I looked out for the Arizona *whenever I was in port, but alas, fate determined we were not meant to meet again this year. God willing, I'll return to Liverpool in March next year, and I hope you'll be ashore when I arrive. Not that I'll call uninvited. I understand that life may be different for you than it was when we met.*

Still, I live in hope that one day we'll take another walk together. If you expect to be home in March and would be happy for me to escort you to the park, write to the White Star office so the letter will be waiting for me.

If I don't hear from you, I'll understand you don't want to see me.

Merry Christmas to you and the family.

Yours truly

Thomas Marsh

Thomas. I didn't know that was his name. She stared at his handwriting until Maria disturbed her.

"Who's it from?"

"Only Mr Marsh. He's working on a ship to Australia."

"You didn't tell me you were still in touch with him."

"I wasn't, but we bumped into each other on the landing stage at the start of the year."

"Why write now?"

Nell shrugged. "For something to do, I suppose." She picked up the other letter. "Let's see what Clara has to say... Ah, I was right. She was delivered of a healthy baby boy on Wednesday, the twenty-second of October, at six o'clock in the morning. That was a few days before I left on the last voyage. Both she and the baby are doing well, and they've called him Edward after Mr Cavendish."

Maria smiled. "It's taken her long enough. I bet she's relieved to have a boy."

"She doesn't say, but I imagine so. Oh…" Nell fell silent, tears forming as she read the rest of the letter.

> *The best news is that Lady Helen is also with child and expects to be delivered next month. We have so much in common, and having our children so close together…*

So, he's done it. The room blurred as an image of Ollie with his shirt open at the neck, the image she'd tried so hard to forget, filled her mind. *He lay with her.* She squeezed her eyes tight. *What did you expect? That's why he married her … to give the family an heir.* She dropped the letter onto her knee and wiped her eyes. *But he wanted me…*

"What's the matter now?"

"Nothing. Look at the time. I'd better be going for Elenor." She gathered up the papers and pushed them into their envelopes, but as she did, she took a final look at Mr Marsh's neat handwriting. *The least I can do is write to him.*

The clouds were a deep grey as she arrived at school with Leah and Rebecca, and Alice looked up from her place by the wall as they joined her.

"Aunty Nell." Her eyes lit up. "I didn't expect you to be here. When did you get home?"

"A couple of hours ago." She gave her a warm smile. "I believe you've been to Betty's. How is she?"

"She's out of bed now, but she's overcome with melancholy. She said it was a terrible ordeal."

"I'm sure it was. Will you visit again this afternoon?"

"No. Aunty Jane arrived as I was leaving and so she'll stay with her until Mr Crane gets home."

"I hope he *does* go home and not to the alehouse like he used to."

"He will. She said he's been very good."

"I'm glad to hear it. Next time you call, ask if she's happy for me to visit, too."

"She'd love to see you."

Nell glanced around at the faces in the playground. "Do you both usually pick up the girls?"

Alice chuckled. "Why wouldn't we?"

Nell shrugged. "No reason, except it would save time if only one of you came."

"What else would we do if we didn't come here?" Rebecca rolled her eyes. "Walking to and from school is the highlight of my day."

"Really?"

Alice grinned. "You can be like the rest of us now. Thanks to Dad there's no need for either of us to work."

What joy. "Is he enjoying his new job?"

Alice nodded. "He seems to be..." She turned as the school bell rang and a procession of girls filed out of the double doors. "Elenor." She waved to her cousin. "Look who's here."

Nell bent down, her arms outstretched, as her daughter sauntered over to them.

"When did you get home?"

"This morning. Aren't you pleased to see me?"

"Are you going away again?"

"No, she's not." Leah bounced on the spot as she clapped her hands.

There was no smile as Elenor reached for Alice's hand. "Why did Leah see you first?"

"Because you were here..."

Alice tugged on her arm. "Come on, you're being silly."

"I'm not. She always sees more of Leah."

Nell took a deep breath. "Don't be like that. Leah was at home, but she'll be at school soon, too."

"It's not fair. You should have picked me up before you went home."

"All right. If I go away again, I will."

"You said you weren't going..."

"I'm not, but if I do..." Nell shook her head as Isobel joined them. *Is this what I've got to look forward to?*

Once dinner was over, Maria collected up the empty plates and carried them to the kitchen. "One of you can pour me another cup of tea."

Nell snapped from her trance. "I'll do it."

Alice tutted. "Sit down. You look like you don't know what day it is. You must be tired if you were working this morning."

"I am. I'd hoped to have my washing done by now but didn't get round to it. Would you mind taking Elenor to school this afternoon, so I can peg it out while it's light?"

Elenor pouted. "Why aren't you taking me? You would if Leah was with us."

"It wouldn't make any difference."

"You don't like being a mam."

Nell gasped. "Of course I do. I've given up my job because of you and Leah."

"But you still went away. No one else's mam did."

"Well, I'm not going again. Now stop this. Why can't you be happy like Leah?"

"Because she's silly."

Leah hit her sister's arm. "I'm not."

Maria rejoined them. "I'd leave the washing until tomorrow. It will be dark by about four o'clock."

Nell sighed. "I suppose I've nothing better to do in the morning."

Maria scowled at her. "I hope you're not going to skulk about like this all winter. I can give you plenty to do."

"I won't. I'm just not used to being at home, that's all. Perhaps I'll call and see Jane this afternoon."

Alice tutted. "I told you earlier, she arrived at Betty's when I was leaving, so she won't be home until teatime."

"I'm sorry, I forgot." Her shoulders slumped. "I've several letters to write. I'll do that. They'll take my mind off things." *Or drive me to despair.*

Once she was home from school, Nell lifted out the writing set and dipped the pen into the ink, before staring at an empty piece of paper. *Write to Mrs Robertson and ask if she's receiving visitors. That's easy enough, and if she is, it should fill up a few afternoons over the winter.*

Once the letter was written and in its envelope, she reread the letter from Clara. There was an extra sentence she hadn't read before dinner.

We'd love you to come and stay with us for a few weeks.

Nell pinched the bridge of her nose. *What on earth do I say? I can't go. She's bound to invite Ollie, and Lady Helen won't be there, given her condition. Does she think I've forgotten what happened?* She glanced at Leah, who was drawing a stick lady on a small blackboard. *I've told them I won't leave again, so that's what I'll tell Clara. After being away for so long, I can't leave them so soon.*

The pen scratched as she wrote, but her hand trembled when she sent her congratulations to the Hewitts. *Did he move anyone else into the London flat?* She let out a deep sigh. *It's nothing to do with me.* A second later, Maria's knitting needles stopped clattering.

"There's a lot of sighing going on over there. Have you nearly finished?"

"It's not easy. I need to think what to say, and I've a lot to tell Clara."

"She won't have time to read a long letter with a baby to care for."

"She has a nanny, not to mention the staff who do everything else."

"It's all right for some."

Nell let out another sigh. *It certainly is.*

"Is that the last one you're writing?"

"There's one more, but it can wait. I'll make a cup of tea as soon as I've finished this."

Maria jumped up. "I'll put the kettle on. The sooner you put that away, the better."

I don't know why. We've nothing else to do.

Once she'd finished, she blotted the ink and folded the

paper into the envelope. *I'll write to Mr Marsh tomorrow. There's no rush if he's on his way to Australia.* She glanced at Alice, who was doing some mending by the fire. "I'll walk to the postbox with these once I've had my tea. Would you like to walk with me?"

"And me?" Leah smiled up at her.

"Of course, you. We can all go, if you like."

Maria shook her head. "Not me. These feet are worse than when you were last here, and walking up to Betty's hasn't helped."

"Sit down, then, and I'll pour the tea. Is there any cake?"

"I've lifted it out."

Nell disappeared into the kitchen, returning seconds later. "I've not asked. How's the money situation now George is working?"

Maria glanced at Alice.

"You can talk in front of her. The household budget affects all of us."

"I wasn't hiding anything. Alice has been doing the bookkeeping while you've been away, so she'll know better than me."

"Don't tell Dad."

Nell grinned. "Your secret's safe with me. Are we managing all right?"

Alice nodded. "As long as Mam's not extravagant at the shops and we watch how much coal we put on the fire, we'll be fine."

"That's a relief. I know from experience my money won't last forever."

Maria shifted in her seat. "I hope you meant it when

you said you're staying this time. You don't need to have money of your own."

"It's nice being able to look after yourself."

"Not as nice as having a husband to look after you. I've been thinking, and it's about time you were settling down again."

Nell stared at her. "Where's that come from? I've told you I don't want another husband."

"I don't care whether you want one or not. You need to think of those girls. They need a father figure in their lives."

"They have George."

"You know perfectly well George doesn't get involved with them. They need someone who knows how to discipline them before it's too late. You're only storing up trouble for yourself."

"I'm doing no such thing."

"So why does Elenor answer you back all the time? She needs a firm hand, not indulging."

"I don't indulge her, but she's missed me. Now I'm home, I'm hoping she'll settle down."

"Well, don't come crying to me if she doesn't."

CHAPTER THREE

Nell woke the following morning as Leah bounced on the bed, and she yawned as she led the girls into the living room. George, Billy and Vernon were at the breakfast table, and she checked the watch on her chain.

"It's earlier than I thought."

Billy laughed as he helped himself to a piece of bread. "I'm surprised you can even see the face of that, looking as tired as you do."

"Less of your cheek. I'd be up and about by this time on the ship, but I couldn't sleep last night. It must be because I wasn't being tossed about by the waves."

"You'll get used to being on land soon enough." George stood up. "You can sit here. I need to be going. It really wasn't a good idea to get a job at the dock furthest from the house."

"At least you enjoy it when you're there." Maria held the door open for them. "Have a good day."

Vernon flicked his cap onto his head. "I'll need to be

quick with tea tonight. I'm picking Miss Ally up at half past six."

Maria gasped. "Where will you go at that time of night? It will be dark."

Vernon grinned as he followed George out of the door. "We'll find somewhere."

Nell turned to Billy, who was still at the table. "Don't you go with them?"

"Sometimes, but it doesn't take me as long to get to work, so I thought I'd have another cup of tea and be sociable. Have you really finished going to sea now?"

Nell nodded. "I have. I didn't enjoy being on this ship as much as the first one ... even though I didn't realise I enjoyed being on the first one at the time."

"It was probably the novelty."

"I expect so." She buttered a piece of bread for each of the girls. "What can you tell us about this Miss Ally that Vernon is walking out with? I was surprised to hear he's getting married."

"It surprised us all. I only met her when she came here for tea. She's the sister of one of the blokes he works with."

"Would he go to the house of other workers?"

Billy shrugged. "He must have done. She wouldn't go to the alehouse."

Alice interrupted. "The brother is part of the gang Vernon goes out with on a Sunday afternoon, and he met her when he called to collect him."

"It still seems out of character. I'm surprised he's interested at all at his age. What about you, Billy? Shouldn't you be settling down before him?"

Billy laughed. "I won't find anyone before March." He stood up from the table, leaving the cup of tea Maria had topped up for him. "You'll need to wait a bit longer for that. I'll see you tonight."

Nell grimaced as the front door closed. "Did I touch a nerve there?"

Maria shrugged. "Why would you?"

"Because he left rather abruptly."

Alice lowered her voice. "He's shy with women."

Maria frowned. "Why would he be? He's used to us being around him."

"That's different."

"I don't care what you say. He's plenty of time yet, and I don't want both of them leaving home and taking their wages with them."

Nell nodded. "We wouldn't need to buy so much food if he did."

"We'd still need the same amount of coal."

"All right, that's enough being miserable." Nell paused as the letterbox clanged. "The postman's early." She went into the hall and picked up the solitary letter. "It's from James." She hurried to the dining room, where Maria sat expectantly.

"Let's hope he's on his way home."

Nell opened the envelope and smiled. "He is. He posted this when they arrived at their last port, so he should be here next week." The smile fell from her lips. "Oh."

"What's the matter?" The colour faded from Maria's face. "Is he all right?"

"He's fine, but he'll only be home for five days."

"That's not long when he's been away for two months. It means he won't be here for Christmas."

Nell's shoulders dropped. "There must be a reason. Don't have a go about it when you see him."

"But he could ask to miss a trip for once."

"And sit around earning no money for two or three months? Don't be daft. It's his job, and he has to do what the company wants. It's not for us to choose."

Maria took a deep breath. "I wish he'd stop this travelling altogether. He's the one who should settle down, but he won't meet a young lady while he's on an all-male ship?"

"That's rich. You didn't want me going near any of the men when I was away."

"That's different, and you know it."

"Not for the women involved, it isn't. All the stewards are someone's son."

"All the more reason for him to stay in Liverpool, then. Will you speak to him? He's more likely to listen to you than me."

Once Elenor was at school for the afternoon, Nell bid farewell to Alice and Rebecca and headed towards Betty's new house.

She knocked on the front door and let herself in. "It's only me."

Her niece sat in a chair by the fire of the only downstairs room, but she didn't manage a smile. "When did you get back?"

"We docked yesterday. I'm so sorry to hear about the

baby." She bent down to pick up Albert, who had crawled towards her.

"I don't know how it happened. I could feel it kicking and wriggling and then it stopped." She ran a hand over her eyes. "I can't stop crying. It was horrible, Aunty Nell ... and the things the doctor did to me. I don't think I'll walk properly again."

Nell grimaced. "It's vivid now, but it will get easier. Trust me."

"It's all I can see when I close my eyes..."

"There, there." Nell placed a hand on Betty's shoulder. "Have you seen much of your mam?"

"She's here most days, and she's been very good with Albert. She said she'd call this afternoon."

Nell steadied the child, who was struggling in her arms. "You be a good boy. Granny will be here soon."

"He constantly wants attention, but I can't give it to him." Betty struggled to move as Nell set him on the floor near the fire. "You stay where you are. I'll put the kettle on."

"Thank you. Mam's been cooking tea for us while she's here. I'm not sure if it's a blessing or a curse having our own house. At least in the boarding house, the landlady provided all our meals."

"If you were still in the old place, you wouldn't be able to have so many visitors. Alice said she's been calling, too." Nell disappeared into the scullery.

"She has, thank goodness. I don't know what I'd have done without her and Mam."

Nell stepped back into the room as the door opened and Jane joined them.

"Good afternoon, Nell. I didn't expect you to be here. You should have told me you were coming."

"I only decided a couple of hours ago. How've you been keeping?"

"I can't complain. Well, I could, but there'd be no point. My troubles are nothing to Betty's. Or Tom's. Have you seen him since you've been home?"

"No. I only got back yesterday. What's up with him?"

"He's a terrible cough and keeps getting pains in his chest."

"Has he seen a doctor?"

"What do you think? This is our brother we're talking about. He won't pay for anything, besides..." Jane rolled her eyes "...Sarah reckons there's not much up with him. She's sure he's exaggerating so he can get out of work."

Nell cocked her head to one side. "He never used to need an excuse. Is he still going to the alehouse?"

Jane laughed. "What do you think? He's not that ill."

"So other than a cough that's pulled something in his chest, there's nothing up with him?"

"Now you put it like that, no."

"If he's not at church on Sunday, I'll call and find out what's going on."

Jane picked her grandson off the floor. "When are you going back to sea?"

"I'm not. Now George has his new job, Alice and I can stay at home."

Betty managed a smile. "I'm glad. Alice is pleased, too."

"And Maria." Jane settled herself in a chair.

"They may be, but I don't know how I'll fill my time once Leah starts school. I'll be bored again by Easter."

Betty grimaced as she shifted position. "You can always come and keep me company."

"Let me see how I get on at home, but I may take you up on that."

CHAPTER FOUR

Tom leaned forward in his chair, gasping for breath as his body convulsed, a series of coughs rattling the fluid in his chest. His wife, Sarah, rushed into the room with a cup of water.

"Here, get this down you."

Tom tried to speak, but the coughing began again.

Nell perched on the edge of her seat. "Shall I come back?"

Tom shook his head as he finally managed a breath. "Give me a minute."

She looked up at Sarah. "Jane said he had a cough, but I'd no idea it was so bad."

"It isn't usually. You obviously called at the wrong time."

"This cold air won't help."

"It's that ... warehouse." Tom took a mouthful of water. "It's only fit for the rats..."

Sarah put a hand on his shoulder. "Calm down, you'll set yourself off again."

He rested his head on the back of the chair, his narrow eyes studying Nell. "What brings you here?"

"Jane told me you were ill, so I thought I'd call. Has she seen you like this?"

He shook his head. "Nobody has."

"You need a doctor..."

He started to laugh, but the cough returned as Sarah folded her arms across her chest.

"You know very well we don't have the money."

"I'll pay for him..."

"No." Tom's windpipe squeaked as he spoke. "It's not right..."

"Why are men so stubborn?" Nell glared at him. "What about cough syrup? Do you have any?"

Sarah answered. "He finished it a couple of days ago."

"Which is probably why he's coughing so much now. At the very least, let me buy some for you."

"We can manage..."

Nell raised her voice. "Tom Parry, stop being so daft. Just because I'm a woman doesn't mean I can't help you out. I've got the money..."

He sank into the chair, his energy gone. "If you must."

"I'll get the strongest they have, but I still think you should see a doctor. Jane said you'd been having pains in your chest, too."

Sarah looked at him. "Is it any wonder, coughing like that? He's probably done himself some damage. If we could stop the cough, he'd be fine."

Nell nodded. "As long as you're sure. And if you need anything else, tell me instead of struggling."

"We don't want your pity." Sarah straightened the chairs around the table.

"It isn't pity. I'm trying to help while he can't work. Is that so wrong?"

"He works when he can and Len's earning now. We're not desperate."

Nell bit her lip. "Is Ada still taking in sewing?"

"She is, and she earns enough to help with the bills."

"Have you been too busy to buy more cough syrup, then?" Nell glowered at her sister-in-law. "Why does it upset you so much that I have my own money?"

"It's the way you got it. You should never have gone away. Those poor girls... If Grace ever left my granddaughter like that, there'd be trouble."

"That's not likely with Sam working and them having no one else to look after. In our house, someone had to work, and it was the only job that would pay me a decent wage..."

"Enough..." Tom tried to stand up, but sat back down as another bout of coughing doubled him up.

"Don't worry, I'm going." Nell glared at Sarah. "I'll be back in ten minutes with the medicine. You can thank me later."

Maria was spreading jam onto the top of one half of a Victoria sandwich cake when Nell got home.

"When did you last see Tom?"

Maria shrugged. "Last week. Before you came home. Why?"

"Have you any idea how ill he is? It sounded like he was

about to cough his lungs up. I went and bought some cough syrup for him."

"You shouldn't be doing that."

"I had no choice. Sarah was giving him nothing but water. I offered to get the doctor, but he wouldn't hear of it."

"And I'm very glad about that. You'll have spent all your wages before Christmas at this rate."

"He's your brother. Don't you want to help?"

"He's done nothing to help himself over the years, all that skiving off work and losing his job."

Nell started to tidy the table. "I know you're right, but he's not well. Hopefully, the cough syrup will sort him out."

"It's to be hoped he doesn't become addicted to it or you'll be buying it forever more."

"Don't exaggerate." Nell studied the clock. "I've time for a cup of tea before I pick Elenor up. Are you nearly finished?"

"I will be by the time the kettle's boiled."

Nell had just set it on the range when the front door opened and closed. "Who's that at this time of the day?" She stepped into the living room as her nephew James pushed open the hall door. "What are you doing here?"

He grinned as a smile split her face. "That's a nice welcome."

"You know what she means." Maria appeared from the kitchen. "We weren't expecting you until tomorrow, and you're always home mid-morning when you arrive. What made you so late?"

"I needed to call at the office, and it took longer than I expected." He kissed his mam on the cheek. "Is that the kettle boiling?"

"It is." Nell took his kit bag from him. "Let me put this out in the washhouse and you can sit down. Have you eaten?"

"I grabbed a couple of penny pies on my way here, but a slice of cake would be nice."

Maria admired her newly finished creation. "You need to wait for this. The old one needs eating first."

Nell rolled her eyes at him. "I'll see what I can find."

James was by the fire when she returned, his ginger hair disturbed where it rested on the chair.

"How was the trip?" She handed him a meagre slice of sandwich cake.

"Very good. This route to Brazil certainly pays better than any of the others I've worked on. It's easier, too."

"So, when do you go back?"

His eyes flicked to his mam, and he gave a slight shake of the head. "I'm not sure yet. Where's Alice?"

"At Betty's."

"That's nice. She seemed much happier last time I was home, not having to work."

"The girls are too. Betty not so much." She glanced at the clock. "I need to go for Elenor shortly, but your mam can fill you in on the news once I've gone."

"Don't you want me to walk with you?"

"You can if you like, but I thought you'd want to rest your legs after being out all day. Besides, I go with Aunty Rebecca."

He sniggered. "All right, I know when I'm not wanted."

"That's not true. I'll only be twenty minutes and you're not allowed in the playground, anyway."

"All right, you've convinced me."

The following afternoon, Nell accepted James' arm as they left the house on their way to Princes Park. She looked up at the pale grey clouds.

"You've brought nicer weather with you."

James laughed. "I'd hardly call this nice. I'm freezing."

"Are you going to tell me when you leave again? You were rather vague yesterday."

He said no more as they continued walking.

"Are you up to something?"

He took a deep breath. "Vernon told me he was planning on getting married last time I was here."

"What's that got to do with anything?"

"It started me thinking."

Nell smiled up at him. "Are you going to settle down too?"

"No, nothing like that. The thing is, he's seven years younger than me, and yet he'll be leaving home and making his own life."

"You have your own life."

"Not really. I've worked as a steward for years, but month after month, I come back here and hand over my money. I should do what I want. Not what Mam wants me to do."

"Will you get your own house?"

"Not exactly."

"What then?"

He took a deep breath. "I've told you before how much I like Brazil, so I've decided I'd like to stay there for longer."

"How much longer?"

James pursed his lips. "I've not accepted it yet, but one of our regular guests has offered me the position of manservant in his house."

Nell stopped, her mouth opening and closing. "So, you wouldn't be coming home?"

"I would, just not so often. Once a year, perhaps."

"But ... you can't..." She stared after him as he continued walking.

"If that's how you react, what will Mam say?"

"I'm sorry. I don't mean to stop you doing what you want, but it's such a shock."

"It's what I want to do. There's nothing for me in Liverpool."

"You don't know that. You could get a job in any number of smart houses with your experience."

"But look at the weather." He stared up at the sky.

"It's not always like this."

"It is more often than not. When did you last see blue sky?"

Nell paused as they approached the gates to the park. "Will you take the job?"

"If I can. I went to see someone in the office yesterday to ask if I could work the outbound voyage but not the return. They're looking into it."

"When will you find out?"

"Later in the week, hopefully."

"And would that be it? You won't be home for a year?"

He carried on walking but said nothing.

"And there was me and your mam disappointed you wouldn't be here for Christmas."

"I'm sorry, Aunty Nell, really I am, but I won't get a chance like this again."

Nell squeezed her eyes together. "When will you tell everyone?"

"Not until it's a done deal. I can't face the arguments. It's ridiculous. I'll be thirty next year, but she still wants to run my life for me."

"She does that with me."

"It's different for you."

Nell shook her head. *No, it's not.* "Not really."

It was as if James hadn't heard her. "When she was talking about Vernon yesterday, she was dropping hints that I should give up going to sea and settle down. Well, for her information, I will be. It just won't be in Liverpool."

"You've met someone in Brazil?"

James' cheeks coloured. "Not exactly. I meant I won't be working on the ships any more."

"But is there a chance you'll meet someone out there?"

"Who knows?"

Nell studied him. "Don't you ever want a family of your own?"

He shrugged. "I have friends. That will do for now."

CHAPTER FIVE

Nell looked over at James as she set the table for dinner.

"You're very quiet."

"I'm thinking, that's all. How long before we can eat?"

"Ten minutes or so. As soon as Alice arrives home with Elenor. Are you going out?"

"I need to go to the office."

"Have you heard anything?"

He put a finger to his lips as the back door opened and Maria rejoined them.

"Would you like to walk with me to the Pier Head this afternoon?"

"That would be nice. We could drop Elenor at school and keep going."

"Ah. Actually, I was hoping to go earlier than that."

Maria poked her head through the door. "What are you up to?"

"Nothing, I just need to go into the office." He stood up and went to the door. "I won't be a minute."

Maria carried the bread to the table. "What's up with him? He's been in a strange mood this week."

"Something to do with work, but I don't know the details." Nell turned to the fire and threw on a couple of pieces of coal.

"If he won't tell you, what chance do I have?"

Nell bit her lip. "You need to give him some space. He's old enough to look after himself."

"I'm his mam. I worry about him."

"And we've told you to stop worrying about us all. Let people live their own lives."

Maria's eyes narrowed. "You know what's going on, don't you?"

"Only that he's not happy."

"Why isn't he? He said this job going to Brazil is the best he's had."

"I know, but..." Nell breathed a sigh of relief as the front door opened and Leah ran to her.

"We're home."

Nell stroked her head. "Let's take your cloak off and you can wash your hands."

"They're clean." She pushed them forward, the palms face up.

"You can still wash them. Elenor needs to do hers, too."

Leah groaned and stomped to the hall as James rejoined them.

"They're here. Good." He took his seat at the table as Maria hovered over him.

"When you get home tonight, you can tell me what this is all about. You've not been yourself this week."

"There's nothing to tell."

"I think there is."

"Mam! That's enough. Can you get this dinner served? I'm in a hurry."

"All right, I'm going."

Nell patted his hand as the girls thudded down the stairs. "Go without me this afternoon. We can talk tomorrow."

James said nothing as the door burst open and Leah ran in, thrusting her hands at Nell.

"They're shiny now."

"There's a good girl. You sit down. James is in a hurry."

She scrambled onto her seat as Maria put a plate of oxtail stew in front of him.

"Get that down you. Hopefully, it will put a smile on your face."

Nell recoiled at the look on his face as Maria disappeared back to the kitchen. "Take a deep breath."

"I wish it was as easy as that." He scooped up a forkful of mashed potato. "At least I'll be on my way again soon."

Nell pulled her cloak tightly around her as she left the house and hurried across the road to Rebecca's, letting herself in.

Rebecca appeared from the kitchen. "You're early."

"I was at a loose end and hoped the company might be better over here than at home."

"Oh, heck. What's she done now?"

"It's not her. James isn't happy, but he won't speak to anyone. Maria keeps having a go at him, which only makes things worse."

"I'd have thought you'd want to stay with him."

"He's not in. Nobody is. Alice has gone to see Betty, and he went to the shipping office after dinner and hasn't come back."

Rebecca pulled her face. "It shouldn't have taken him that long."

"Exactly." Nell looked at the clock. "Would you mind walking to school now? I'm half-hoping we'll meet him on the way there."

Rebecca sighed. "My cloak isn't as warm as yours."

"It's not that cold. Come on. We can walk quickly."

The night was already dark as Rebecca's daughter Florrie ran ahead of them and through the school gates, but Nell stopped, staring at a shadow under the gas lamp a little further along the street. "You go in. I'll join you when the bell goes."

"Where are you going?"

Nell nodded to the lamp. "I think that's James."

Rebecca hesitated but disappeared as Nell strolled towards the light.

"Aunty Nell. I hoped you'd see me."

"I nearly didn't. What are you doing here?"

"Waiting for you. I'm leaving in the morning and won't have a chance to talk to you properly before I go."

"Tomorrow! Why are you going so suddenly?"

"A steward pulled out of the voyage at short notice, and they asked me to cover … if I wanted a favour from them."

Nell put a hand to her mouth. "You're not coming back?"

"I am, but after this trip they've said they'll arrange for me to do an outbound voyage only in March."

"When will you tell your mam and dad?"

"I'll tell them over tea that I leave in the morning, but..."

"You're not going to mention your other plans, are you?"

"Not yet."

Nell rubbed her hands over her face. "How am I going to keep this to myself for another few months?"

"I'm sorry. I shouldn't have told you, but I thought you'd understand."

"And I do..." She took a breath. "But I'll miss you."

He put a hand on her shoulder as the school bell rang. "I'm not going yet. I'll be here in March." He walked her to the gate. "I'm off for a quick pint, so I'll see you at home. Don't tell anyone you've seen me."

Elenor was already in the playground when Nell arrived, and she stamped her foot on the ground. "You're late again."

"Less of your cheek. I'm not. You've only just walked through the door. I saw you."

"Why was Aunty Rebecca here, but you weren't?"

"Because I had to see someone. Now come along. I don't want to hear another word."

Rebecca waited for the girls to run on ahead.

"Was it James?"

"Erm ... no. No, it wasn't. Just a dad waiting for his daughter."

"That's unusual."

"Yes. He ... erm ... he said his wife was ill, but he couldn't go into the playground."

"Who was it? I didn't notice any of the girls on their own."

"I didn't ask. He looked embarrassed to be speaking to me. I'd forgotten men round here aren't used to it."

"No, they're not, and you'd better start remembering quickly. You'll be making a name for yourself."

Nell snorted. "You sound like Maria."

"Because I agree with her. You need to be careful."

"And I will be. If working on the ships taught me anything, it was that."

Elenor had let herself in by the time Nell arrived home and was sitting at the table with Alice.

"You're back." Nell hung up her cloak. "How was Betty?"

Alice puffed out her cheeks. "She's not in so much pain, but she's still struggling."

"It will take time for everything to sort itself out, but it will."

"I hope so. I hate to see her like that."

Nell peered into the living room. "Is James here yet?"

"No. I've not seen him since dinner."

"That won't put your mam in the best of moods."

Maria shouted from the living room. "What are you two whispering about?"

"Nothing, I was only asking if James was home." Nell followed Alice to the table and took a breath to steady her voice. "He's probably called in to the alehouse."

"I wish he wouldn't... Is this him now?" Maria darted to the hall. "Where've you been? I thought you were only going to the office."

"I didn't realise I had to get your permission to do anything else."

"That's not what I meant. It would just be nice to know what time to expect you."

James' face didn't soften. "You needn't worry about it after tomorrow."

"Tomorrow? You're not leaving...?" Maria glared at him as he took his seat at the table.

"They needed someone to fill in for a steward who can't do the trip."

"They could have given you more warning."

James shrugged. "They didn't have much themselves."

"I'd hoped you'd delay going back, not go early."

"I'm sorry, Mam, but you knew I wouldn't be here for long. Besides, I don't think I should be here when everyone has a couple of days off work."

"Why not? Your dad's pleasant enough with you nowadays."

"Only because he doesn't see me."

Maria's shoulders dropped but her eyes suddenly widened. "You will be here for Vernon's wedding?"

"As long as nothing crops up."

CHAPTER SIX

Christmas was a distant memory as Nell took a deep breath and rapped on the door knocker of Mrs Robertson's house. The housekeeper welcomed her with a smile.

"Good afternoon, Mrs Riley. I wasn't expecting you so soon after your last visit."

"I'm afraid I've very little else to do during these winter months. Not that that's the only reason I call, but you know what I mean."

The housekeeper chuckled. "I know exactly. Still, it's nearly the end of February. It won't be long before Easter's here, not to mention the spring flowers."

"You're right. I really should have brought a more positive attitude with me." She followed the woman up the stairs, but stopped in the doorway of the large, mahogany-panelled living room as Violet toddled towards her.

Mrs Robertson stood up. "Good afternoon."

"Good afternoon." Nell bent down to the child, but she

ran in the other direction as Mrs Robertson offered her a chair by the fire.

"Is everything all right? You don't look happy."

Nell huffed as she sat down. "I'm feeling sorry for myself, that's all. I miss James when he's not around and the weather doesn't help."

"What's the problem?"

She shook her head. "I didn't call to burden you with my problems."

"Nonsense, that's what friends are for."

Nell sighed. "I had a letter from Clara, Mrs Cavendish, this morning. She sounds so happy."

"You can't hold that against her."

"Oh, I don't. I'm delighted for her after what she had to put up with at her parents' house."

"What is it, then?"

"It's the contrast to the life I have now she's gone; I can't help envying her."

"The weather will be warming up soon enough. That should cheer you up."

"And it will..." Nell stared at her lap.

"But?"

"You know she's friendly with Mr Hewitt and his wife, Lady Helen? Well, Lady Helen gave birth to a baby boy just before Christmas."

"And that's what's upsetting you?"

"I can't shake the image of them cooing over the baby together..."

"So, you still carry a torch for Mr Hewitt?"

Nell bit her lip. "I wish things could have happened differently."

"What do you mean?"

Nell sighed. "I could have had a life like hers. Well, not exactly, but similar, and I walked away from it."

Mrs Robertson's eyes glistened. "Now you have to tell me what happened."

Nell gulped as the housekeeper brought in a tray of tea and she waited for her to leave. "Promise you won't repeat a word of this."

Mrs Robertson put a hand to her chest. "Who would I repeat it to?"

"All right." She took a deep breath. "When I was at Mr Hewitt's wedding, he asked me to move to London so we could be together."

Mrs Robertson's forehead creased. "At his wedding?"

Nell nodded. "He hadn't been married twelve hours..."

"There must be more to it than that. A man doesn't just ask a question like that out of the blue."

"No." She stood up and wandered to the bay window. "We'd been dancing, then he took me out onto the terrace. It was rather dark by then..."

Mrs Robertson gasped. "And you let him?"

"It's not what you think. When he asked me to move, I ran away. I was frightened that if I stayed, I'd succumb to him."

"Then you should be proud of yourself, not full of remorse."

"I am–" *sometimes* "–but when I get a letter like I had this morning, it brings it all back to me. Can you imagine the life I would have had if I'd stayed?"

"Well ... no. I don't think I can."

"It wouldn't be the same as living here. He offered to get

me a flat and buy me a whole wardrobe of new clothes. I expect he'd have taken me to the theatre, perhaps even dinner parties. He told me I'd want for nothing..."

"But what about your daughters? You must know you made the right decision."

Nell squeezed her eyes tight. "I do, but on days like today..."

"Come and sit down and I'll pour the tea."

Nell strolled to her chair. "The most exciting thing I do at the moment is walk to and from school twice a day."

"That's more than I do." Mrs Robertson handed her a cup and saucer.

"Today, maybe, but you're going on a voyage with Captain Robertson soon. What do I have to look forward to?"

"Something will crop up. Did you ever write to Mr Marsh?"

She shook her head. "No."

"I thought you'd grown to like him."

"I did, but for some reason, I kept putting it off. He doesn't need me in his life, the way I've treated him." *And the way I still feel for Ollie.*

"He may be the distraction you need."

"Is that a good enough reason to contact him?"

"From what you told me of the letter he sent, I think he'd be happy to see you, whatever."

"Perhaps. It would give me something to do, too." She tried to recall Mr Marsh's slim features and neatly greased hair, but all she could picture was him lying in the hospital bed, his beard unshaven and his unkempt hair splayed over his forehead. *He always had a twinkle in his eyes when I visited him.*

Mrs Robertson smiled. "You may actually find you enjoy his company."

The walk home was slow, and the light was fading as Nell pushed open the front door. Elenor and Leah were at the dining table with Alice when she joined them.

Leah grinned when she saw her. "Where've you been?"

"To see baby Violet. Do you remember her?"

"Why didn't you take me?"

Elenor banged her elbows on the table. "Or me. I've never even met her."

"You were at school. I'll take you when it's the holidays."

"I bet you don't. You never take me anywhere."

Nell clenched her teeth. *Is it any wonder...?* She popped her head into the kitchen where Maria was stirring a pan. "That smells good. Do you want me to do anything?"

"No. It's ready. I'm just waiting for the men to come in."

"That sounds like them now." Nell stepped into the living room as the front door slammed. "Is that all of you?"

Billy was the first to appear. "Vernon's on his way. He stopped to talk to someone, and Dad didn't want to wait."

"He'd better not have gone to the alehouse." Maria carried the teapot through.

"He's seeing Miss Ally later, so he wants to be quick."

"At least she keeps him to time. I'll say that for her."

George strode into the room and took his seat. "We

needn't wait. I told him we wouldn't if he was more than a minute behind us."

Maria returned to the kitchen. "It sounds like he's here."

"Let me help you." Nell followed her, and by the time they carried the last of the plates through, Vernon was in his seat. "Have you had a good day?"

Vernon beamed. "I have." He nudged Billy. "You know that house I was telling you about? It's mine."

"What!" Maria almost dropped her dinner. "What house?"

"I won't be living here once I'm married, so I've paid a week's rent to the landlord of a house I like. I can move in when I'm ready."

"But the wedding's a month off..."

"I can't wait until the week before to get something sorted out. There might be nothing I want by then."

George looked up from his food. "Was that the landlord you met outside?"

"It was. I said I'd call round to see him, but he was looking out for me."

"Where is it? Local, I hope."

"Only on Park Street. It took me ten minutes to walk there the other day."

Maria pushed her food around the plate. "This is it, then. You're the first to leave."

"I'm not. James has been gone for years."

"That's different. This is still his home and when he gives up going to sea..."

Nell choked on a piece of potato. "I'm sorry." Her cheeks reddened as Maria glared at her. "It went down the wrong way."

Vernon rolled his eyes. "Mam, he won't give up stewarding or move back here. He only comes home to keep you happy."

"Don't talk nonsense." Maria coughed to level out her voice. "He'll stop sailing one day."

"When we're dead and buried." George shovelled in a mouthful of stew. "Certainly not while I'm alive. He wouldn't give me the satisfaction."

"I'm sure that's not why he keeps working." Nell gave George her best smile before looking at Vernon. "When will you move?"

He shrugged. "I might as well pack up my stuff tonight when I come home."

"Tonight?" The high pitch of Maria's voice returned. "But you'll need more than clothes. You'll need blankets ... and pillows ... food..."

"Ah, yes, I've been thinking about that. If I carry on paying some keep, can I come here for tea between now and the wedding? I can't cook for myself ... and it would save Lydia having to come to the house and do it for me."

"Lydia." Maria spluttered into her tea. "She can't be there with you before you're married..."

Vernon held up a hand. "That's why I want to come here. If it's all right with you."

George nodded at Maria. "As long as he pays for more than he eats. He needs to contribute to the coal as well."

"You'll have to manage without my money when I'm gone."

George glared at him. "And you'll have to eat before you're married. Give your mam half your usual rent, if you want feeding."

"Will I get my washing done for that?"

George pointed his knife at him. "Don't push your luck. You can sort it out with your mam, as long as she's not out of pocket."

Maria shook her head. "I don't know how we'll manage without your wage."

Nell patted her hand. "We'll cope. It will be spring soon." *And I'm assured everything will be fine by then.*

CHAPTER SEVEN

Nell was the last downstairs for breakfast and Maria put a bowl of porridge in front of her.

"Why've we got this?"

"Because it's cheaper than coal."

Nell's forehead creased. "What's coal got to do with it?"

"It might be March, but it's still cold outside. If we eat something warm, we won't need to use so much of it. Now we're not getting Vernon's money..."

"We're not that short..."

"And I'd like to keep it that way." Maria paused as the letterbox clattered. "This had better be from James." She hurried to the hall and returned with a letter that she thrust towards Nell. "It looks like it to me."

"I'd say you're right. May I finish this first, while it's hot?"

Alice reached over for it. "I'll read it."

Dear all

I hope everyone is well, and the weather is improving.

It's lovely in Brazil and the thought of coming back to the cold and rain isn't very inviting.

Still, by the time you get this, I should only be a couple of days away. We leave two days after the mail ship I plan to send this on. I hope it will stop you panicking about whether I'll be with you for the wedding.

I must go. Someone's calling me.

See you soon

James

Maria huffed as she stood up. "That was short and sweet."

Nell glared at her. "At least he'll be home soon. Can't you see some good in anything?"

"When he's not seen us for months, you'd think he'd spend a bit more time writing."

"It takes time. You know that from when I write. In fact, you've reminded me. I need to send a letter this afternoon."

"Who to?"

"I never responded to the letter Mr Marsh wrote while I was away. I probably should."

"That was months ago."

"I know, but there was no rush to reply because he was on his way to Australia, but he's back sometime soon. As a courtesy, I should have something waiting for him."

Alice tutted. "You'd better get it done before James arrives. You won't have much time once he's home." She stood up from the table. "Time to go to school. Who's coming?"

Leah jumped from her chair, but Elenor stayed where she was.

"I don't want to go."

"You're going." Nell stood up and pulled her arm. "I don't know why we have this argument every morning. Don't you want to read like Alice? She didn't learn how to do that without going to school."

"Nobody will write me letters."

"You don't know that. Now get a move on or you'll be late. You won't like it if the teacher's cross with you."

Elenor skulked to the hall. "You've got to come too, then. The girls at school don't believe you live with us."

"Why not? I come with you most days."

"Because you're the only mam who isn't in the playground every time."

"Just because I'm not there doesn't mean I'm not at home."

"They think it does."

"Well, you should tell them."

Alice sighed. "She has, but they still tease her. Perhaps you should take her on your own for a few weeks."

Nell groaned. "This is coming from the mothers, not the children. I doubt they even notice."

"It's Ruth's mam."

Nell looked down at Elenor. "Mrs Pearse?"

She nodded.

"That explains it. She's determined to make me out to be a bad mam. I'll just have to show her I'm not."

The table had been cleared by the time she got home, and Nell lifted out the writing set before Maria joined her.

"Did you see Mrs Pearse at school?"

"I did, but she was with half the mothers in the playground. I'm sure all this with Elenor is because I split up her cosy arrangement with Rebecca. I don't know why, though. She seems to have enough friends."

"Some people just want what they haven't got. I wouldn't worry about her."

"I wouldn't if it only affected me, but I don't like her upsetting Elenor. I'll have to see if I can catch her on her own later."

Once Maria had disappeared into the backyard, Nell pulled Mr Marsh's letter from her handbag. *Why does he bother with me, after everything I've done?* She dipped her pen into the ink.

Dear Mr Marsh

How nice to hear from you, but what a surprise that you've travelled to Australia again. I hope your reason for such a long journey was a positive one.

I've finished my time on the Arizona *and have no plans to go to sea again. If you'd like to write when you get to Liverpool, I'll be at home, and would be happy to take a walk.*

She read it several times. *Does that sound too brazen? Maybe, but is there another way to say it? No. How do I sign off?* She studied the signature on his letter. Thomas Marsh. *Mrs Riley will be too formal. I could use my full name, like he did.* She took a deep breath and dipped her pen in the ink again.

I look forward to hearing from you.

Yours sincerely
Elenor Riley (Mrs)

Once she'd sealed the envelope, she looked at the clock and walked into the yard. "I'm going to take this to the postbox before I forget. I'll pop in and ask Rebecca about Mrs Pearse, too."

"What about the beds? You're supposed to be doing them today."

"I'll do them this afternoon. I'm not doing much else."

Rebecca was sweeping around the fireplace when Nell called, a patch of soot on her cheek.

"What happened?"

Rebecca rolled her eyes as she sat back on her heels. "I'd no sooner finished cleaning when a clump of soot fell onto the hearth. It's everywhere."

"I can see." Nell stared at the black dust covering everything. "Last time that happened to us, it took days to clean up."

"I don't have days. I need to have the place spotless by the time Hugh gets home."

"Surely he'd understand. It's not your fault."

"He'd blame me for not dusting inside the chimney." She huffed. "If I keep going, it will be fine by this evening. I won't relax until it's done." She got back onto her hands and knees.

"Is there anything I can do to help?"

"You could take Florrie over the road with you. She's a habit of slowing me down."

Nell stared down at her niece. "I'll clean her up first. Maria won't be happy if she puts dirty hands on everything. Would you like me to pick Isobel up at dinner time?"

"If you wouldn't mind. There's another dress for Florrie in the wardrobe and the water in the bedroom was fresh this morning."

Nell nodded. "Come along, Florrie. Let's get you cleaned up and then you can play with Leah."

Florrie wiped her hands down the front of her dress.

"Not like that. Come upstairs."

Maria had started making a batch of scones when Florrie led the way into the back room. "You were quick. I've not put the kettle on yet."

"Rebecca didn't have time to talk. A pile of soot dropped from the chimney earlier and she needs to get it cleaned up before Mr Grayson gets home."

Maria scowled. "I don't envy her that."

"That's why I've brought Florrie. Is Leah in the backyard?"

"Yes, with Alice."

Nell held open the back door. "You go and find Leah."

Maria shaped the dough on the tabletop. "If you know where this woman lives, why don't you pay her a visit?"

Nell shuddered. "I'd rather speak to Rebecca first and find out what I'm up against. I don't want to give her any more reason to cause trouble."

CHAPTER EIGHT

A cool breeze caught Nell's skirt when she stepped outside to wash the front step, but she hadn't put down her bucket when she spotted James. She hurried towards him, a grin on her face. "You're earlier than I expected. Your mam's still at the shop. Go and sit yourself down and I'll follow you in when I've washed this step."

"Is Alice in?"

"She is. And Leah. She'll put the kettle on for you."

James was settled by the fire when she joined him.

"Did you have a good trip?"

He smiled. "It was wonderful while we were in Brazil. It's so tranquil. Not to mention the weather."

Alice joined them and handed him a plate of bread and jam. "You're so fortunate. I wonder if I'll ever get to travel."

"There's no reason why not, if that's what you'd like. Look at Aunty Nell."

"Perhaps not, but it seems unlikely for someone like me."

Nell carried two cups of tea from the table. "You never

know what life will throw at you. When I was your age, I never expected to see New York, but these things happen. Just be careful what you wish for. I only became a stewardess because I lost your Uncle Jack."

"You could have gone with him, though, if you hadn't. I doubt I'll meet a sailor."

"You might." Nell took a seat but paused when the front door opened. "Change the subject."

Maria walked in with a shopping basket over one arm but stopped when she saw James.

"You're here." Her smile faltered. "At least you managed to come home first, this time."

He rolled his eyes. "It's nice to see you too, Mam."

"You know what I mean." She carried on to the kitchen. "How long are you here for?"

"Until after the wedding..."

"I should hope so. Vernon was pleased when he read your letter, although Billy could always have stood in for you."

"I needn't have bothered coming home, then. I had the chance to stay out there for longer."

Maria had disappeared into the pantry but headed for the teapot when she emerged. "It's a good job you didn't. You were away quite long enough."

"In your opinion."

Nell caught her breath at his tone. "Well, we're glad you're back. You've not missed much here. Christmas was quiet. Uncle Tom wasn't so good, so they didn't come in the evening."

James took a sip of tea. "That's a shame. How's Betty? She wasn't well last time I was here."

Alice pulled up a chair. "She's better than she was, but still not right. I'm just looking forward to when we can walk to the park again."

"If she's on the mend, it shouldn't be long."

"I hope not. Has Aunty Nell told you about Vernon? He's moved into his own house. Well, nearly."

"What do you mean, nearly?"

Nell chuckled. "He spends the evenings there but comes here for his tea."

"He's ready for the wedding, then?"

"He's quite excited, actually."

James shook his head. "There's a surprise. I didn't see him settling down so soon. This Miss Ally must be nice."

Maria sniffed. "Nice enough."

"You would say that. No girl will ever be good enough for any of your sons."

"Some of them would."

James grinned at Nell. "What are you doing this afternoon?"

"Going for a walk in the park."

His face fell. "Oh."

"With you, silly." She laughed at her own joke. "I'll get the rest of the chores done when we've had this, so we can take Elenor back to school and carry on to the park."

He returned her grin. "That sounds good to me."

The sun was shining when they arrived, and Nell lifted her face to the rays. "I know I shouldn't, but I love the feel of the sun."

"You and me both." James looked down at her. "I wish I could take you to Brazil with me. You'd love it."

"What's it like? Is it very different from New York?"

"It is. It's greener for one thing. We sail up the Amazon River to a place called Manaus. It's much wider than the Mersey, but there's thick forest on both banks. You wouldn't believe there was a city in the middle of it."

"Do passengers want to travel there?"

"Oh, yes. There's a lot of work in the rubber trade. Men are flocking there to earn their fortune. That's why I do so well for tips. Those travelling back to the coast are usually wealthy and keen to flaunt it."

"I'm sure they are." She gazed at the blossom on the trees. "Do they have flowers like this?"

"Not exactly, but those they do have are incredible, not to mention the birds. They have the brightest colours you've ever seen."

"Are you still planning on staying there, then?"

"I am. I've accepted a job, but if that doesn't work out, they're always looking for stewards to serve on the riverboats. I wouldn't struggle to find something."

"So, you won't be home anytime soon?"

He shook his head. "I'm sorry, Aunty Nell."

She sighed. "I don't blame you. I'd have done the same myself if I could. Please tell me you'll write."

"Of course I will. I hope you'll write to me, too. I'll send a forwarding address once I'm settled."

"Have you arranged it with the office?"

"Almost. I need to go in tomorrow to confirm my voyage out. I'll work one way and they've found someone to take my place on the return journey."

"You're not the only one doing this, then?"

"Oh, no. There's a real community. A group of us who all get along with each other."

"You're very fortunate... Oh gracious." The blood drained from Nell's face.

"What's the matter?"

She pulled her arm from James' and stayed where she was as a tall, thin man approached. His smile was bitter as he looked her up and down. "Mrs Riley."

"M-Mr Marsh. I-it's good to see you. It's not what you think..."

"What I think is of no consequence. You're free to be your own person."

"This is my nephew James. Mr Atkin. The one who's a steward."

James offered Mr Marsh his hand. "Good afternoon. It's nice to meet you."

"Likewise. Are you both on shore leave?"

"I am. I've been sailing to Brazil for the last year and got back this morning. Aunty Nell's on permanent leave now."

"Didn't you get my letter?" Nell garbled her words as Mr Marsh studied her.

"There were no letters when I arrived."

"I-I only posted it yesterday. I didn't expect you to be here so soon."

"I said it would be March."

"You did, but there are nearly three weeks left before we reach April. I'm sorry. I thought the letter would be waiting for you."

James scanned the footpaths. "Won't you walk with us? I'm sure my aunt won't mind."

Nell's cheeks reddened as Mr Marsh studied her. "I said in the letter I'd be happy to take a walk."

"You did?" He raised an eyebrow. "It should be there if I go and pick it up then."

"I-I imagine so."

James indicated to the footpath. "Won't you join us? We were heading to the lake for a sit-down."

"I don't want to interrupt." Mr Marsh hesitated as he held Nell's gaze, but James appeared oblivious to the tension.

"You won't be at all. We weren't talking about anything in particular." He indicated for them to carry on walking.

"Very well, then." Mr Marsh walked with his hands behind his back as Nell scurried between them. "Do you often take walks together?"

James nodded. "When I'm home. The house gets rather hectic, and Mam never seems to leave. It's the only time we get to talk."

"Forgive me for saying, but you look very similar in age to be aunt and nephew."

James laughed. "We are. I was about ten before I realised Aunty Nell wasn't my big sister."

Nell nodded. "My sister is James' mam, and she's quite a lot older than me. I was only seven when he was born."

"As old as that? I'd have thought more like three or four."

"Now you flatter me." Nell looked away and breathed a sigh of relief when James interrupted.

"Are you still working on the transatlantic ships, Mr Marsh?"

"I'm just back from Australia with White Star."

"Ah, I did that trip. I didn't find the tips to be as good as I'd hoped."

"They were enough for me. I rarely spend much money."

"Do you live on the ship?"

"Usually, although I've taken a room for this shore leave. I don't leave again until the end of the month."

"Will you go back to Australia?"

His gaze strayed to Nell. "I signed up yesterday. They'd offered me the position and there seemed to be no reason not to."

Nell closed her eyes as they approached the lake. *I've upset him again. Why didn't I write the letter weeks ago like I was going to?* A voice popped into her head. *You know very well why.* "Will that take another four months?" Her voice sounded weak when she spoke.

"I've asked for some shore leave in Melbourne and they said I could stay for a month. I thought it would be worth seeing something of the place."

James clicked his tongue. "I went ashore when I was there. It's nice enough, but I'm not sure what you'd do for a month."

"I've not accepted it yet, so I can still change my mind." He looked at his pocket watch. "It was a pleasure to meet you both, but I've taken up enough of your time. May I see you again, Mrs Riley? Once Mr Atkin has left?"

Nell smiled. "We have a wedding to attend later this week, but I'll be free after that."

"I'll be in touch, then." He raised his hat to James. "Have a safe journey. Good day to you both."

CHAPTER NINE

Nell stood in front of the living room mirror and straightened the hat she'd bought to match her Sunday dress. *How different to the one I wore for Ollie's wedding*. She adjusted the collar at her neck. *He wouldn't have looked at me in this. Which would have been a good thing*. She sighed as Maria stood beside her.

"What's up with you? You're in a world of your own."

Nell shrugged. "Weddings do that to me." She scanned the room for her bag as Rebecca joined them.

"Are you ready to go?"

Alice stood up. "We will be as soon as Dad's here. Were the girls all right when you dropped them off?"

"They were fine."

Maria bustled to the back door and shouted to George. "What are you doing out there? Vernon will think we're not coming."

He ambled into the kitchen. "Have the boys gone?"

"Ten minutes ago. Now come along. We can't be late."

Maria hurried them out, but when they arrived at the

church, Nell stopped as the familiar musty smell hit her. *Last time I was at a wedding, it was full of the scent of flowers. There isn't a single stand here. There are so few people, too. How can two weddings be so different?*

She let out another sigh as she followed Maria into the pew behind Vernon and James. *They're not even wearing matching suits.*

"What is the matter with you?" Maria glared at her.

"Nothing."

"Stop making that noise, then. Anybody would think you'd rather not be here."

"Don't be daft." She turned to Rebecca, who was on her other side. "May I have a word with you when we get to the wedding breakfast?"

"I hope you'll have more than one..."

"You know what I mean. There's something I've been hoping to ask you for weeks but not got round to. Can we find a quiet corner for five minutes?"

"That sounds interesting."

Nell smiled at Sarah and Tom as they took their places in the pew behind them. "You made it."

Sarah gave her husband a sideways glance. "Thankfully, the cough mixture's working today."

"I'm glad. Let me know if you need any more." Nell scanned the church. "Isn't Jane with you?"

"She's not coming."

Nell's mouth fell open. "But she loves a wedding."

"Betty's not well again ... *melancholy–*" she mouthed the word "–so Jane's looking after Albert."

Nell sighed. "I thought she was getting better."

"She was, but apparently she's taken to her bed again."

Nell shook her head. "Poor thing. I'll visit her myself, next week."

Their conversation was cut short as the organist struck up the opening notes of the "Bridal Chorus" and Vernon turned to get a first glimpse of his bride. Maria gave Nell a nudge.

"She looks nice."

"She does." *And happier than Lady Helen looked. How could she be disappointed marrying Ollie?*

Once Miss Ally stood with Vernon at the front of the church, Nell's attention switched to James. *I wonder if he'll meet someone in Brazil. I hope so. A merchant's daughter, perhaps. He shouldn't be planning for a life on his own. Or is that what stewards expect?*

After the opening hymn and words from the vicar, James stepped forward to hand him the wedding band and appeared relieved as he moved back to his seat. *He'll be glad that's over.* She watched Vernon slip the ring on Miss Ally's finger. *I was still hoping to see the world at his age.* Another sigh brought a glare from Maria, and she knelt with the rest of the congregation and closed her eyes. *What's done is done. I need to think of the future, not the past.*

Once the guests had thrown the confetti, and the bride and groom had left the church, Rebecca linked her arm.

"Shall we start walking?"

Nell glanced around. "I don't see why not. Maria will walk with George, and Alice is with Billy and James."

There was a skip in Rebecca's step as they set off. "It was a nice service."

"It was, although I couldn't help comparing it to the two I went to in Surrey. The church looked so drab for a start."

"It *is* Lent. They could hardly fill the place with flowers."

Nell tutted. "I'd forgotten about that. Is that why they were married now? To save a bit of money?"

"Who knows? I hope they've not scrimped on the wedding breakfast as well."

Nell chuckled. "More to the point, it better not be nicer than one of Maria's. She won't be pleased if it is."

Rebecca smirked. "What did you want to talk to me about?"

"Ah, yes." Nell gulped. "Mrs Pearse."

"What about her?"

"I get the impression she's causing trouble again. Do you know anything about it?"

Rebecca's cheeks coloured. "Not really, but I know you're not her favourite person after the way you left the girls."

"I've not been away for months..."

"She's good at holding grudges. What's she doing, anyway?"

"I'm not certain, but I think she's spreading rumours about me going away again. Elenor's getting teased at school because the girls think I'm never here."

Rebecca sighed. "It wouldn't surprise me."

"Why does everyone believe her when I'm in the playground every home time?"

Rebecca shrugged. "Would you like me to ask around?"

"If you don't mind. I'll have to speak to her if things

don't settle down with Elenor. She blames me for it, obviously."

"All right, leave it with me. I'll see if I can find out what she's up to."

Vernon and the new Mrs Atkin were waiting at the front door to her father's house when they arrived.

"Aunty Nell." Vernon beckoned her in. "You're the first here."

She grinned. "We sneaked off before everyone else. Congratulations to you both. That's a lovely dress, Lydia."

"Thank you. Mam treated me to it as a present."

Nell admired the ivory material, trimmed with layers of lace. "I hope you get your wear out of it."

She leaned forward. "The lace is only tacked on, so we can take it off after today."

"Very clever."

Rebecca agreed. "Do you have many coming to the house?"

"Not really. Only family and some neighbours. Come on in. There's some sherry on the sideboard in the front room."

Rebecca grinned as they found the glasses. "It looks like they want to keep us away from the food."

Nell studied the room, which felt small despite the chairs being pushed against the wall. "They won't be able to keep us out for long if there are many more guests. We'll be like sardines, squashed in here."

"We'd better stand near the door then, to get a quick exit."

They were by the wall next to the door when James found them.

"Here you are."

Nell smiled. "We've not been here long. Who did you walk with?"

"Billy and Alice."

Rebecca raised an eyebrow. "Were you discussing which one of you will be next to follow Vernon down the aisle?"

James grimaced. "Not at all. It certainly won't be me."

"You need to stop going away so often. When do you leave again?"

"Tomorrow."

"And when are you back?"

Nell held her breath as James' eyes flicked towards her.

"I-I'm not sure. It depends how busy we are while I'm out there."

"That's very mysterious. I don't suppose your mam likes that answer."

James lowered his voice. "She doesn't know yet, so if you could keep it to yourself."

Rebecca's face straightened. "Yes, of course. I'm not one for telling tales. When will you tell her?"

"It will have to be tonight."

"What about tonight?" Maria walked up behind him.

"Nothing. I'm saying that I leave in the morning, so I'll need to be packed."

"I want you to think on, about settling down after this trip."

James shook his head. "I'll do no such thing." He strode into the hall as the door to the living room opened, and

Nell didn't wait for the others as she followed him to the table.

"Don't let her upset you."

James snorted. "It's too late for that. It will be such a relief getting on that ship tomorrow."

Nell glanced around to check no one was with them. "Don't leave it too long before you're home again." Nell flinched as Maria arrived.

"It looks nice enough." She surveyed the food as James' forehead creased.

"Why wouldn't it?"

Maria rolled her shoulders. "We have very high standards for buffets. I wanted to see how it compared."

"I'd say it's about the same."

And this is how it should be. There's no need for seven-course meals. Or champagne. She shuddered. *If I never drink champagne again, it will be too soon.*

It was still dark the following morning when Nell swung her legs out of bed, and she crept down the stairs, hoping not to disturb the girls. James was at the table with Billy.

"Are you ready to go?"

"I am. I'll walk down with Billy."

"Has your dad gone?"

James stared at his bread. "He couldn't possibly wait. Not that I'm bothered."

"Well, you should be." Maria rejoined them from the kitchen. "All he wants is for you to stay at home and settle down."

"He's got a funny way of showing it." James stood up

and reached for his coat. "It seems strange not having Vernon here."

Nell nodded. "We're used to it now. We've only seen him in the evening for the last month."

"I'm glad I was here for his big day. He could be a dad by this time next year. Can you imagine…?"

"No, I can't." Maria shuddered. "It should be you giving me my first grandchild. I hope Miss Ally's more responsible than he is."

Nell tutted. "You can't call her Miss Ally for ever. It's Lydia."

"It's too informal."

"Not now she's family. You'll need to get used to it."

James looked at Billy as he picked up his bag. "Shall we go?"

"I'm on my way." Billy led the way to the front door, but James hung back with Nell as Billy and Maria stepped outside.

"I'll be fine, you know."

"I just want you to be happy."

He put an arm around her shoulders and gave her a squeeze. "I'll be home next year."

She wiped a tear from her eyes. "See that you are."

CHAPTER TEN

Nell held Mr Marsh's letter in her hand, her eyes fixed on the time he was calling for her. *Half past one.* She hadn't noticed when she'd first read it, but it was too late now. *What am I supposed to do with Elenor?* She looked at Alice, who was still at the dinner table with her daughters.

"Would you take Elenor to school for me? I'll pick her up this evening..." She garbled the last of her words as Elenor glared at her.

"You promised to take me..."

"Something's come up and I can't get out of it. It won't happen again."

"You always say that."

"I'm sorry." She sat down and ran a hand over Elenor's hair. "Somebody wants to talk to me, and they don't know I take you to school. I'll make sure I tell them if they want to see me another day."

Alice smiled at Elenor. "Why don't we play a game on the way? Pretend we were having a race with Mam, and we won? You can say she was so slow she missed you going into school."

Nell grimaced. "That won't make me look very good."

"It's the best I can do." Alice gave her a weak smile, but Elenor beamed.

"We can say Mam's a slowcoach."

"If it makes you happy. I'd better make sure I don't miss taking you again."

"May I race?" Leah jumped down from her chair.

"Of course." Alice grinned. "You and Elenor can run ahead if you like, so you're quicker than me."

Thank you. Nell mouthed the words as Leah giggled.

"Shall we go?"

"Not yet. Let Mam go out first and then we'll get ready. We can't be there too early. Mam wouldn't be *that* slow."

Nell rolled her eyes as she wandered to the hall. "At least you give me some credit." Her pulse was racing as she fastened her cloak, but she froze at the knock on the front door. *That will be him.* She popped her head into the living room.

"I'll see you later."

"When you pick me up from school...?"

"I'll be there."

Mr Marsh smiled as she opened the door. "Mrs Riley. You look nice." He ran his eyes over her. "Are you ready to go?"

"As ready as I'll ever be." She joined him on the footpath. "You're always so punctual."

"It's part of my training. You shouldn't catch people unawares by being early, and it's rude to be late."

"That's true. Did you have far to walk?"

"I'm in a boarding house on Windsor Street, so no."

"In that case, shall we walk to Sefton Park?"

"I'm happy to go anywhere. I was just pleased to pick up your letter. I'm sorry I doubted you."

"It's not your fault. I should have written earlier. Knowing I had so much time, I kept telling myself there was no hurry. Still, we're here now."

"We are indeed. What have you been doing with yourself since you finished being a stewardess?"

Nell sighed. "Not much, to be honest. Being a housewife is little more than a dreary routine of cleaning and taking my daughter to and from school."

"Are you no longer Miss Ellis's companion? I thought that was why you stopped going to sea first time round."

"She's married now and living in Surrey."

Mr Marsh stared at her. "That surprises me."

"It surprised a lot of people, most particularly her parents. It all happened rather quickly."

"Don't tell me she ended up marrying Mr Rodney after all the fuss she made about him."

"Gracious no, although he was the reason the marriage was arranged so urgently. She actually married Mr Cavendish. He was one of the passengers..."

"Who travelled with your friend, Mr Hewitt."

His words took her breath away. "M-my! You have a good memory."

"Have you seen him?"

"Mr Cavendish?"

"Mr Hewitt."

Her mouth was dry as she searched for the right words. "H-he was at the wedding ... but he was with his betrothed.

He's married now, too. And a father. He'll be the Earl of Ackley one day."

Mr Marsh's shoulders relaxed. "He's been busy."

Nell nodded. "Mr and Mrs Cavendish have a son, too. They all live close to each other and she enjoys being away from her mother."

"You keep in touch?"

A shiver ran down her spine. "Only by letter. I've not visited since the wedding." *He doesn't need to know which one.*

They walked in silence as the gates to the park approached, and once they were inside, Mr Marsh looked down at her. "Is that why you went back to sea? Because Miss Ellis left Liverpool?"

"Y-yes. That's right."

His face broke into a grin. "And there was me imagining you had a broken heart."

"O-oh, no. We needed the money, and once Mrs Cavendish left, I had no job."

"But you don't need the money any more?"

"My brother-in-law George has gone back to shipbuilding. He broke his leg while he was at sea and wasn't able to do any manual labour for a while, but he's fine now."

"Which means you're home and at a loose end?"

"That about sums it up. At least my sister and daughters are happy." *I think.* "What about you? What made you sign up for the Australian route?"

It was his turn to hesitate. "It's not much fun coming back to shore when no one's waiting for you."

"Yet you're staying for longer this time."

"The timing wasn't entirely of my choosing, but I wasn't sorry. If I'm being honest, I'd still hoped to see you."

"Oh."

He gave a weak smile. "For the whole of last year, our ships were never in port at the same time, so I thought the only way for us to meet up was if I stayed in Liverpool for longer. I hope you don't mind."

"Why would I mind?" The pitch of her voice rose, and she coughed to clear her throat. "It's nice to see you."

His dark eyes sparkled. "You don't know how happy that makes me."

"When do you leave?"

"Next Thursday."

"You'll miss most of the summer, then."

"Sadly, I will. After we spoke last week, I asked to cancel the shore leave I'd requested, but they've already arranged crew for the return leg of the journey, so it looks like I'll have to stay out there, whether I want to or not."

"That's a shame."

"I'm hoping something changes between now and then so I can get back sooner. If you'll see me again."

Nell paused. "As long as you realise we'll only be friends."

He searched her face as she looked up at him. "If that's what you want."

"I can't have it any other way." She turned away.

"Very well." He clasped his hands in front of him. "I told you when we met near the landing stage that I'd rather have you as a friend than not see you at all."

"Why don't you tell me more about yourself and your family, then? You hardly ever mention them..."

. . .

The walk was more enjoyable than Nell expected, but as the sun sank behind the trees, she stopped. "What time is it?"

He reached for his pocket watch. "Twenty to five."

"Oh, my goodness. I need to be at school by five o'clock to pick my daughter up."

"Let me escort you. At least part of the way..."

"Thank you. I didn't take her after dinner, because I was meeting you, but I promised I'd be there this evening." She walked at her fastest pace, unable to talk as Mr Marsh strode beside her.

"Was it because I called to collect you at half past one?"

"A little later would have been better." She gasped as they turned into Windsor Street. *Please don't let me be late.* Several women had congregated by the school gate and as soon as she spotted them, she stopped and stepped out of sight, gasping for breath as she did. "I'll say farewell here. I don't want anyone seeing us together."

"May I see you again before I leave?"

Nell froze as the school bell clanged in the distance. "I need to go. Meet me here at two o'clock tomorrow." She raced away without a backward glance and rounded the school gates as a procession of young girls filed into the playground. "Elenor. Over here." She gave an expansive wave, causing Mrs Pearse to glare at her.

"You made it." Rebecca wandered over to her with their daughters following.

"Only just. I had twenty minutes to get here from Sefton Park."

"I'm not surprised you're worn out."

Elenor studied her. "Did you race here, too?"

She nodded. "Yes. Alice and Leah must be a long way behind us. Shall we go and find them?"

Nell didn't miss Mrs Pearse staring at them as they left. "I'm glad she noticed me."

"She doesn't miss a trick. She'll be busy making up why you were out of breath."

Nell groaned. "Has she really got nothing better to do?"

CHAPTER ELEVEN

Mr Marsh was standing where Nell had left him when she walked down Windsor Street the following afternoon. She smiled as she approached.

"Have you moved since yesterday?"

His features softened. "I didn't want to miss you. Is your daughter safely at school?"

"She is, thank you."

"Perhaps we should visit Princes Park today? It's closer, if that helps."

"It does, but after nearly being late, my niece Alice has said she'll walk to school as well."

"That's very kind of her." He indicated for them to walk but kept a discreet distance between them.

"She enjoys it. She's the one who looked after them when I was at sea, but now Elenor's being teased because I've been away so much over the last few years."

"Children can be cruel."

"So can their mothers. I don't know what I've done to upset this particular one, but she seems to have it in for me."

"Envy is a common reason."

Nell shook her head. "She won't be jealous."

"You're a woman of your own means who's seen something of the world. She may have a secret desire to do the same thing."

"I doubt it. She's more determined to make me out to be a terrible mother."

"Because you went to sea?"

She nodded. "I realise it doesn't show me in a good light, but I didn't do it solely for me. I did it for them, too. Not that anyone believes me."

"I've told you before, you're not like other women. They won't understand you."

"There are times I don't understand myself."

"Now you're being hard on yourself. It's not as if you left your daughters with strangers. They had their family around them."

"Yes." A knot settled in Nell's stomach. "They love Alice, too. I think they were sorry I'd stopped going away when they found out she had to work for six days a week."

"There you are then."

Nell smiled. "Thank you for understanding."

He looked straight ahead as they walked into the park. "Do you think you'll work as a stewardess again?"

"I doubt it, but even if I do, it won't be until they're both married and I'm on my own. Assuming I'm not too old by then."

"You won't be on your own, judging by the family you have around you."

"I hope not. What about you? How long will you keep stewarding?"

"For as long as I'm able. I worked as a clerk when I first left school, so I could always go back to that if it gets too much."

"There are plenty of opportunities for that in Liverpool. It's people like George I worry about. He's well into his fifties and has a very physical job. Heaven help us when he has to stop work."

"You'll manage. Families usually do. It's when you're on your own, it's a problem. Still, I save most of the money I earn from each trip so I've something to fall back on when the time comes."

"That's very sensible."

"I don't need much if I stay on the ship and I've nobody to spend it on."

Was that aimed at me? She remained silent as they strolled to the edge of the lake but as the sun broke through the clouds, she pointed to a bench. "Shall we make the most of it?"

He waited for her to take a seat before he joined her.

"I used to sit here with Miss Ellis. I miss her now she's gone."

"Doesn't she visit her parents?"

"No, they fell out over the wedding, and she hasn't spoken to her mother since she left. They're both being equally stubborn, waiting for the other to apologise."

Mr Marsh whistled through his teeth. "They shouldn't do that. I told you my father wasn't happy when I announced I was leaving the railway company to be a steward. I didn't mention that we ended up having a huge row, which is why I didn't travel home for several years after I left. He'd passed away by the time I did and Mam said his anger had killed him. She never forgave me. My eldest sister didn't either, so after a couple of ill-tempered visits, I chose not to go back."

"I'm sorry."

He shrugged. "It was a long time ago. My mam's passed now, too, and I was never close to my sister. She should be over it, but…" He sighed. "It's easier to stay away. If you still have any influence over Mrs Cavendish, I suggest you encourage her to think again."

"I'll try, but since she found her freedom, she's rather enjoying it. I'm not sure how she'd feel coming back. I'll mention it to her, though."

"I don't suppose you're welcome down there."

"Oh, I am." Nell put a hand to her mouth as soon as the words were out. "I mean, she often asks me to visit. She has a bedroom especially for me, but it's a long way to travel on my own, and now I'm at home the girls wouldn't be happy if I left again."

"It's nice she still appreciates you…" He paused as Nell slid away from him on the bench. "Is it something I said?"

"No. Just keep talking and don't look at that woman over there."

"Which one?" He instantly stared down the path.

"Don't look." Nell turned her back on him. "She's the one spreading rumours about me at school. I'd rather she didn't see me."

"Would you like me to carry on walking until she's passed?"

"No, it will rouse her attention even more. Just pretend we're not together."

Mr Marsh shifted on the seat as Nell rummaged in her handbag, but she flinched at the sound of her name.

"Mrs Riley. This explains why you're never in the playground. A new fancy man."

"I beg your pardon?" Nell glared up at her.

Mrs Pearse tittered to her friend. "She heard me."

"I resent that remark." She moved further away from Mr Marsh. "W-we're not together."

"Then why was he waiting for you near school?"

"I ... he ... we..."

"Madam." Mr Marsh stood up and towered over the women. "Who Mrs Riley chooses to meet in her own time is of no concern to you or anyone else."

"So, you are together?"

"Not in the way you mean."

"Then why not say so?"

"Because she knows what a gossip you are. Haven't you enough to fill your days without spreading slander about an innocent woman?"

Mrs Pearse pointed at Nell. "She's not innocent. She disappeared off and left those kiddies for months at a time."

"Because a tragic accident took her husband." Mr Marsh pulled himself up to his full height. "If you ever lose your husband and have to fend for yourself, you may be able to pass judgement, but until such time, I suggest you keep your opinions to yourself. If anyone is to be accused of impropriety, then it's you."

Mrs Pearse gasped as she put a hand on her chest.

"I've never been so insulted."

"Then you've been treated far too leniently. Good day to you."

Nell's heart pounded as Mrs Pearse walked away. "That will be all round the playground by the time I get there."

"Then you need to arrive before she does. You've done nothing wrong."

"She won't see it that way..."

He smiled as he sat down beside her. "Stop worrying. Perhaps I should join you at school..."

Nell's head shot up. "Good grief, no..."

"Mrs Riley. You're a widow. Why is it so unacceptable for you to be seen with a man?"

"Because..."

"Because what?"

She sighed. "You're only a friend. It's not as if we're betrothed..."

"And that makes a difference? Nobody would propose marriage if they hadn't been walking out with the woman in question."

"But we're not walking out... They wouldn't understand."

"They needn't know."

Nell's shoulders dropped. "I'll be taking the girls to school for the next five years. Even if they don't find out now, they'll realise something doesn't add up."

"I see." He stood up and stared across the lake.

"I don't think you do. I've enjoyed spending time with you, but as you said yourself, it's not usual. I can't give them another reason to upset Elenor."

There was a long pause before he retook his seat. "Perhaps it would be better if we didn't meet. I don't want to cause you any problems."

"No." She sighed. "The truth is, if it only affected me, I wouldn't worry about it, but I have to think of Elenor."

"So, what shall we do?"

Nell shrugged. "I don't know."

He turned to face her. "Do you want this woman dictating what you do for the next five years?"

She shook her head.

"Then we need to make a stand against her. If you'll allow me to escort you to school, we can stop her gossip before it starts."

"How do we do that?"

"Let it be known that I'm the brother of your late husband. It wouldn't be unusual for me to want to see my nieces."

Nell hesitated. "I can't introduce you to the girls. What would they think?"

"I'd be Uncle Thomas. Would that be so bad?"

"I-I'm still not ready for you to meet them."

"Then I won't. I'll disappear before they come out of school."

She sighed. "Very well. I need to tell Rebecca and Alice what's going on, though. They can't be as surprised about a long-lost brother-in-law as everyone else."

After calling on Rebecca, they walked the long way round to school. She was already in the playground with Alice and Leah when they arrived, and Mr Marsh stopped by the gate.

"Stand with me for a couple of minutes."

"If you're sure." Nell shuddered as a couple of women headed towards them.

"Stop panicking." Mr Marsh waited until they were in earshot. "It's been far too long since I saw my nieces."

They smiled at him as they passed.

"See, it's as simple as that. Let a handful of them know that I'm the girls' uncle and all of this will go away."

"You won't be seeing them, though."

His gaze was gentle. "I've already told you, once you go into the playground, I'll disappear." He paused as several more women approached. "I can't believe you didn't tell them Uncle Thomas was visiting. I doubt Elenor even remembers me, given I've been at sea for so long."

Butterflies turned in Nell's stomach as the women carried on into the playground. "You're doing very well."

"I try. Ah, look who's here." He smiled as Mrs Pearse approached, but she glowered in return.

"Come to sully her daughter's minds, have you?"

"I've come to see my nieces, if you must know."

"Nieces! You've made that up. You're nothing more than her fancy man."

Mr Marsh remained calm. "Alas, my brother sought the hand of Mrs Riley while I was away. The least I can do is visit when I get the opportunity."

Mrs Pearse opened and closed her mouth several times, but nothing came out before the school bell rang.

He extended an arm towards the playground. "Aren't you going in? You don't want to keep your daughter waiting." He turned to Nell. "I'll wait for you at home. I don't want to give this woman cause for any more lies."

CHAPTER TWELVE

The blossom was fading on the trees as Nell strolled around the edge of the park with Mr Marsh by her side.

He looked down at her. "I can't believe today has come so quickly."

"Time always goes fast when you don't want it to."

"I'll write when I can, if you don't mind."

She smiled up at him. "Of course I don't. I'd like to hear about the places you visit. Especially when you get to Melbourne. Be sure to capture the details, because I'll never go myself, even if I go back to being a stewardess."

"Only if you promise to keep the letter so I can remind myself what Melbourne was like when I next see you."

She chuckled. "When I first went aboard the *Wisconsin*, I suggested to Mrs Swift we should have a painter with us to capture where we'd been, but she didn't think it was a good idea."

"I think it's a splendid idea. If I find anything with an image, I'll bring it as a souvenir."

"I'll look forward to seeing it." She sighed. "We should probably head to school."

Mr Marsh checked his pocket watch. "You're right. It's half past four. Would you like to lead the way?"

She bit her lip as they walked to the gates. "I'll miss you when you've gone."

"Really?" He looked genuinely surprised. "I'll miss you dreadfully, but I couldn't hope that you'd feel the same way. Shall we do this again next time I'm here?"

She nodded. "I'd like that ... although..." She creased her lips. "Leah starts school after Easter, but they're likely to be on holiday next time you're here. I'll have to check that Alice will be around for them in the afternoons."

"Would it matter if they came with us?"

"I should set them a good example, not let them see I'm meeting up with a strange man."

"Strange!" He raised an eyebrow.

Nell chuckled. "You know what I mean."

"Perhaps you could tell them I'm their uncle, like we suggested."

Nell hesitated as she nodded. "I suppose I could."

The playground was filling up by the time they arrived at school, and Nell stood by the gate with Mr Marsh.

"May I walk you home this evening? With it being our last time together?"

She gazed up at him. "Why not? Let me tell Rebecca and Alice what's happening."

Rebecca waved to her as she wandered towards the door. "I thought you weren't coming."

"As if I dare." She pulled her sister to one side. "I was at the gate with Mr Marsh, and he's asked if he can walk me home. He leaves tomorrow."

Rebecca's eyes sparkled. "Is this getting serious?"

Nell tutted. "No, it's not. He's going away for five months. Even if I wanted a future with him, I wouldn't. I couldn't risk losing another husband to the sea."

"What if he stayed in Liverpool?"

"He won't. It's his life. Just as it was for Jack."

"That's a shame. You obviously like him."

"He's pleasant company, that's all."

"All right, I was only saying..." The bell cut Rebecca's sentence short, and seconds later, Elenor arrived in the playground. Nell smiled as she joined them.

"Have you had a nice day?"

"No."

Her stomach churned. "Why not?"

"I don't like sums. They're too hard."

"If you practise, they'll get easier, and you'll be able to count up your money."

"I don't need to do that."

"Not now, but you will..." Nell grimaced, grateful that Isobel had joined them. "Why don't we go home with Alice and Leah? You and Isobel can run on ahead if you want to."

Elenor didn't wait for anyone and raced to the gate but stopped abruptly and turned to Nell. "There's a man waiting."

"He won't hurt you. That's Uncle Thomas. He's going to walk home with us."

"We can go on our own."

Nell smiled at Mr Marsh when she reached the gate. "I

know we can, but he's going to sea tomorrow, so we won't see him for a long time."

Elenor studied him. "Is he your fancy man?"

Nell gasped. "Who told you that?"

"Everyone knows."

Leah stared up at him. "Is he going to be our new dad?"

"No!" Nell's cheeks burned. "I told you, he's going away tomorrow."

"Good." Elenor folded her arms in front of her. "Dads are bossy. Everyone says so."

Nell's mouth fell open as Alice ushered the girls away from the gate. "Let's go home and Mam can follow us."

Nell took a deep breath as they disappeared. "I-I'm sorry about that. I'd no idea. Mrs Pearse has obviously been carrying on behind my back."

"They didn't seem unduly troubled by it."

"I'll get so many questions when I get home." She rummaged in her handbag for nothing in particular. "I don't know what to say."

"You needn't say anything." He offered her an arm. "May I?"

"Y-yes." A shiver ran through her as she slipped her arm into his. *He could be mine if I wanted him.*

Concern crossed Mr Marsh's face. "Are you all right?"

"I'm fine. They just took me by surprise."

"As far as I remember, children always say what they think without caring for the consequences."

"Don't I know it."

Mr Marsh clasped her arm as they walked down Windsor Street, but as they approached the house, Nell released her grip. "I'm not ready for Maria to see us together."

"As you wish." He unlinked their arms but kept hold of her hand. "You've made me very happy, Mrs Riley. I shall count the days until we meet again."

"Me too. You take care."

"And you."

It took several seconds for Nell to withdraw her hand, but even then, she hovered by the front door. "I'll see you soon."

"I'll arrange a voyage home as soon as I can." He waited for her to go into the house and she pushed the door to, as he watched.

"Goodbye for now." *Don't get upset. It's only the same as James going away.*

She closed the door tight as Maria's voice jolted her from her thoughts. "Is that you, Nell?"

"I won't be a minute." She took a deep breath and hung up her cloak before she headed into the living room.

"Who's Uncle Thomas?"

"Ah!" She glanced at Elenor, who was at the dining table.

"He's her fancy man."

"No, he's not. He's someone I used to work with."

"Ruth's mam says he is."

"Well, she's wrong. Now, I don't want to hear about him again."

Maria planted her hands on her hips. "I do."

Nell lowered her voice. "It's only Mr Marsh."

Maria's eyes bored into her as she fussed with the condiments on the table. "There'd better be a good reason he's calling himself Uncle Thomas when you've not said a word to me."

"Why do you always assume the worst?"

"Because it usually is." Maria marched to the dresser and produced a letter. "This came earlier."

"Clara." Nell sliced open the top of the envelope and took a seat by the fire, while Maria moved between the kitchen and dining table.

"Any news?"

"Not yet ... oh, wait. She's coming to visit her parents!" Nell bounced on the chair.

"When?"

"The week after Easter. How exciting! She's only here for two weeks, though. They're staying at the Adelphi, but she'd like us to take a few walks together."

"Is she bringing the baby with her?"

"I imagine so. She can't leave him... Don't look at me like that. He's only six months old."

"Six months ... two years. There's not much difference. Is she travelling on her own?"

"She doesn't say, but I doubt she'll come without Mr Cavendish. Not after what happened when she left home."

"At least it's put a smile on your face."

"I've missed her, and with you not wanting me to go down there..."

"Don't blame me. You shouldn't want to leave your daughters for so long. Not that it seems to worry you."

Nell clenched her jaw. *Don't start.* "Have you made the arrangements for Easter yet? I can't believe you've left it so late."

"Don't change the subject."

"I'm only asking."

"If you must know, Sarah called earlier and said Tom's feeling better, so they're coming for tea on Easter Sunday."

"All of them?"

Maria grimaced. "Her, Tom and the children who still live with them. I draw the line at Sam and Grace, when they have more money than the rest of us."

"What about Rebecca? You could say the same about her."

"She's different, and you know it."

"What about Jane? And Betty? I need to visit her before Clara arrives. I've not seen her for such a long time she'll think I've forgotten about her."

Maria lowered her voice. "I'm not sure now would be a good time."

"What do you mean?"

"When Sarah called, she told me they had to call the doctor because of the melancholy."

Nell's eyes widened. "Alice hasn't said anything."

"It was only yesterday."

She shook her head. *I've been so wrapped up with my own thoughts...* "What about Albert?"

"Jane's taking care of him."

"I'll speak to Jane, then. If she's feeling low, she may like some company."

Maria shrugged. "Suit yourself, but Jane's been there most days these last few weeks, and she's not shaken her from it."

"It's still worth a try. Poor Betty."

CHAPTER THIRTEEN

Nell stood beside Rebecca in the playground, their eyes firmly fixed on their daughters in front of them.

"Their first day at school." Rebecca reached for a handkerchief as Leah and Florrie stood together, holding hands. "I hope they don't split them up."

"They're bound to. They can't be talking in class."

"It seems unfair when they're so little."

Nell linked her sister's arm as a teacher ushered the girls into school. "They'll be fine."

"Maybe they will, but what will I do with myself now they're both out of the house?"

"You'll find something. You can make me a cup of tea for a start, save me from going home. Maria's still cleaning after Easter. She's already roped Alice into helping her. I'd rather not be next."

Rebecca tutted. "She cleaned the place from top to bottom last week."

"She said that having everyone round on Sunday made such a mess, she wanted to do it again."

"There weren't that many of us there."

"There's no point arguing with her when she's in one of her moods." Nell led the way out of the school gate. "Did you enjoy Easter?"

"I did. It's been a long time since we were all together. Tom looked better."

"He did, thank goodness." Nell chuckled. "He was complaining about being back at work, so he can't be that ill."

"I noticed that. I was pleased to see Jane, too. It sounds as if Betty's on the mend."

"I hope so. I'm seeing her later this week, so I'll let you know."

"Poor thing. I do feel for her, losing a child so late. Hopefully, she'll be able to have another one soon."

Nell grimaced. "I'm not so sure that's a good idea."

Rebecca gave her a sideways glance, but when she said no more, changed the subject. "At least you have Mrs Cavendish's visit to look forward to."

"I do. She's asked to meet me by Princes Park gates tomorrow." A smile crossed Nell's face. "I expect she'll be on the train now, although how she'll manage with a baby, I don't know."

Rebecca shuddered. "I couldn't imagine it."

Nell laughed. "You've never been on a train."

"Perhaps I will, one day."

"Where to?"

Rebecca shrugged. "There and back again. Just so I know what you're talking about."

~

The following day, Nell's stomach fluttered as she pulled the front door closed behind her and turned towards Princes Park. *What if she's changed and we've nothing to talk about? I'll ask after her parents … and why she's here. That should take one lap of the park.* She shuddered. *Why am I nervous? She's one of my best friends.*

A horse and carriage stood by the entrance to the park when she arrived, but before she reached it, the door flew open, and Clara waved to her.

"Mrs Riley. Over here." As soon as the coachman had rolled out the steps, she climbed down. "How good to see you."

"And you." Nell's grin matched that on Clara's face. "I was so surprised to get your letter. Does this mean you've made up with your mother?"

Clara rolled her eyes. "After a fashion. Let me get rid of this and we can talk." She spoke to the coachman, who promptly returned to the carriage and flicked the reins.

"Haven't you brought baby Edward with you?"

"Mother insisted on looking after him."

"That's a shame. I'd hoped to see him."

"And you will, but if I'd brought him out, I'd have needed the nanny, too, which I didn't want."

"Ah, so you've not left your mother in charge?" Nell laughed at Clara's expression.

"Good grief, no. I wouldn't leave him on his own with her. Mr Cavendish is joining me to pick him up, too. I still don't trust her."

"So what made you come to Liverpool? Was it anything to do with my letter?"

"Not exactly, although it was timely. Father hasn't been well, and my brother wrote asking me to visit."

"Nothing serious, I hope."

"He had a problem with his heart and ended up in hospital. Thankfully, it wasn't as bad as it might have been, but even though he's home, he spends most of his days in bed."

Nell put a hand to her chest. "Will he be all right?"

She sighed. "It's too early to say. Mother's beside herself with worry in case he has to give up work. She's already let one maid go."

"Send him my best wishes. We travelled to Liverpool together after your wedding and got along very well."

"He told me." Clara grinned. "You have a way with men."

"He was a considerate chaperone, that's all. How's your mother been with you?"

"Very cool when we first arrived, mainly because I'd left the baby at the hotel ... not to mention the fact we were staying at the Adelphi rather than with them."

"I don't blame you."

"There was no way Mr Cavendish was going to stay with them after the way she behaved."

Nell raised an eyebrow. "Has he been to the house with you?"

"Only to drop me off and pick me up again. He won't go in."

"It's such a shame. Is your mother showing any signs of remorse?"

"Not at all, although she's suddenly interested in how wealthy he is. She really is the limit."

They strolled along the path close to the Mansions. "Is she likely to be watching us?"

"I'm hoping Edward will distract her. She wasn't pleased I was seeing you, if I'm honest. She holds you responsible for everything that happened."

"Probably to ease her own conscience." Nell's scowl suddenly brightened. "How's Peters?"

"He's wonderful. He really fits in with the rest of the staff and will often help at Ackley Hall if there's a ball."

Ackley Hall. A tingle ran down Nell's back. "Do they have many balls?"

"Every couple of months or so. They usually have some excuse or another, although last month it was for no other reason than Lady Helen wanted one."

Don't ask about Ollie. "So, you're enjoying yourself down there?"

"Oh, yes. Mother did me a huge favour, behaving as she did. Before she started interfering, I was hoping to persuade Mr Cavendish to settle up here, but I realise now he would never have been happy. We belong in Surrey."

"That's something to be thankful for, then."

The lake came into view as they rounded the corner, and Nell gestured to a bench. "Shall we?"

Clara took a seat. "I miss sitting here and having our chats."

"So do I. Not that I blame you for leaving."

"I wish you could have moved with me."

"You know I couldn't."

Clara smiled. "Forgive me. I shouldn't keep mentioning it. What have you been doing with yourself? Your letters have been rather brief lately."

"I'm sorry. I've been busy with James being home and then Easter. And Leah started school yesterday."

"Really! Did she like it?"

Nell shook her head. "She wasn't as happy when she came out as she was when she went in. I'm hoping she'll settle more today now she knows what to expect. I need to leave here by quarter to five so I can pick her up."

"Then you'd better start telling me what you've been doing. I'm only here for two weeks, and a little bird told me you have a man friend."

Nell gasped. "Who?"

Clara grinned. "If you must know, it was Mother. She saw you from the drawing room window. More than once, too, so you need to tell me all about him."

"There isn't much to tell..."

"Nonsense. You were always adamant you didn't want to remarry and now you're walking out with someone."

"I'm not. We're just friends..."

"Friends! I don't believe you for a moment."

"It's true. He's an old acquaintance who was in Liverpool on shore leave."

"A steward!" Clara put a hand to her mouth. "Not Mr Marsh? It is, isn't it!"

Nell's cheeks burned. "He was home from a voyage and asked if we could meet..."

"And you said yes! I knew he liked you."

"Even if he does, it doesn't alter the fact he's away at sea more than he's here. He left for Australia a couple of weeks ago and won't be back until August. I can't start a relationship with someone who's never here."

"Does he know?"

Nell nodded. "At first he said that men and women can't be friends, but the next time I met him, he'd changed his mind."

"So he could see you? He must adore you."

Nell shrugged. "I've grown fond of him, but it's more like a brother–sister sort of relationship. Walking with him is like being with James."

"Will you meet him in August?"

"He said he'd write when he's back."

Clara grinned. "Give it time. You might not want to admit it, but you'll be walking out with him properly before long."

CHAPTER FOURTEEN

Maria carried the last of the dinner plates to the kitchen while Nell took a cloth to the table.

"Are you seeing Mrs Cavendish this afternoon?"

"No, not until Friday. I was going to call on Jane to check I'm still all right to visit Betty tomorrow." Nell wiped Leah's hands. "I thought I'd invite Jane for afternoon tea, too, if you don't mind. She's been looking after Albert while Betty's been ill, and it can't be easy in that room of hers."

"I suppose so, although she might be at Sarah's. I believe she calls if she knows Sarah has her granddaughter with her."

Nell's brow creased. "Grace leaves baby Ethel there, knowing Tom's as ill as he is?"

"Regularly."

"But she's not yet one."

Maria shrugged. "Sarah always said Grace was lazy, but apparently, she can't do her cleaning and look after a child at the same time. Heaven help her when she has another one."

Nell puffed out her cheeks. "That's up to them. I'll call on Jane anyway, just in case." She clapped her hands as she returned to the table. "Time for school. Get your cloaks."

"Do we have to?" Elenor's shoulders drooped. "Even Leah doesn't want to go."

"You need to learn to read and write and do your sums. Once you can do that, you won't have to go again."

"I can do that already." Elenor pouted.

"Not well enough. Now get a move on." Nell reached for her own cloak and slipped back to the kitchen. "I'll see you later. I'll invite Rebecca, too. She's often at a loose end now she doesn't have Florrie to look after."

"It's a good job I did some baking yesterday."

Once the girls were at school, Rebecca turned towards the gates.

"Would you like to go to the park?"

"I was going to call on Jane. I've not seen her for a while, and I told Maria I'd invite the two of you for afternoon tea."

"That's nice. We don't do it often enough."

"How do you keep busy on the days I see Mrs Cavendish?"

"I don't, really. It's baking and knitting, mostly."

"It won't be for long. At least Mrs Pearse has latched on to another mother, so she shouldn't trouble you."

Rebecca grunted. "I can see how she manipulates her, too. I can't believe she took me in."

"It's easy to fall for women like her, but you saw sense, eventually."

They turned into Elaine Street and Nell knocked on Jane's front door before letting them in.

"Jane. Are you there?" She walked up the stairs as Jane appeared at the top.

"What are you doing here?"

"That's a nice welcome. We've come to see how you're doing and invite you to afternoon tea."

Jane straightened her skirt. "I'm sorry, I'm not used to having visitors here. Afternoon tea would be very nice." She held open the door to her room but hurried to catch Albert as he toddled to the top of the stairs. "I can't take my eyes off him for a minute."

Rebecca took him from her. "Let me. I've not seen him for a while."

Nell stroked his hand as Rebecca bounced him up and down. "How's Betty doing? I said I'd call on her tomorrow but wanted to check she was up to it."

Jane shook her head. "It's probably not a good idea. She's not been out of bed for days, so Mr Crane called the doctor again. He wanted to admit her to the asylum."

Rebecca gasped. "Did you stop him?"

"Eventually, but Mr Crane wasn't there when the doctor first called, and he wouldn't listen to me. He said it's the preferred option for women with melancholy."

Nell scoffed. "Only because doctors like him don't know what to do with us."

"Exactly. Anyway, he needed Mr Crane's permission to admit her and when he came back last night, Mr Crane refused. Goodness knows when they'd have let her out if they'd admitted her."

"So, did he give her anything for it instead?"

"He gave her another tonic, but it's made her very drowsy. She was asleep when I called for Albert this morning."

"So, Albert was on his own?" Rebecca shook her head. "Do you know what's brought all this on? I thought she was over the baby."

Jane sighed. "I thought so too, but now I'm not so sure. She's never really talked about what happened, but I know she was upset having to deliver it. With hindsight, I suspect she put on a brave face over Christmas, but once the dark days of the new year came, it was too much for her."

Nell shuddered. "January can have that effect even if you haven't got any worries. Next time you see her, tell her I'll call, but only when she's ready. Are we ready to go?"

Jane nodded. "I am. Did you tell Maria you were inviting me?"

Nell smirked. "Don't worry."

"Oh, I'm not worried. I just like to know how much of an argument there'll be when I get there."

Albert's pram was in the backyard, and once Jane had retrieved it, Rebecca pushed him to Merlin Street. "I miss having a pram. I'm so looking forward to being a granny."

Nell groaned. "Don't wish your life away. You've a long time to wait yet."

"Nell's right. You could have another one of your own before you're ready for a grandchild. You're still young enough ... just ... and you have a husband, which helps."

"A husband who doesn't like children." Rebecca's shoulders drooped. "He'd give our two away if he could."

"Nonsense. There's only one reason to give up a child, and once you're married, it's not an issue."

Nell gave her a sideways glance. "That's not strictly true."

"Why would anyone give up a child if they had a husband?"

Nell shrugged. "I've heard of cases where it's happened. I don't know the details."

Jane tutted. "That's terrible. The poor children."

"What about the poor mothers? They wouldn't have done it if they didn't have to."

Rebecca interrupted. "Nell may be right. Hugh can't be the only man who doesn't like children, and, in some cases, it may be in the child's best interest to have them adopted."

Jane stared at her. "Did he want to give your two away?"

"No, because he knows how much they mean to me, but not all men are like that. Besides, there may be other reasons..."

"Well, it's wrong, if you ask me."

Nell took a deep breath as they reached the house, and she opened the front door. "Here we are."

Maria was by the unlit fire when they went in.

"Is Alice not back yet?"

"No. She won't be home until about four o'clock." She pushed herself up from her seat. "I'll put the kettle on."

Jane had the pram in the hall when Nell returned.

"You should have left it outside."

"Albert's asleep and I don't want him waking up, not knowing where I am."

Once she'd hung up her cloak, Nell ushered her sisters into the living room.

Rebecca took the seat next to Jane. "Do you look after Albert every day?"

"No, only twice a week."

"If you ever need any help, especially now Betty's as she it, I'll have him for you. As long as I can bring him back to you on the way to school."

"Betty wouldn't complain if you want him overnight."

Rebecca shuddered. "I couldn't even consider it while Hugh was there. He gets so grumpy if anything wakes him up."

"He may be more amenable to having a boy around the house. Most men are."

"I doubt it." Rebecca picked up a biscuit from the plate in front of her. "If it's all the same to you, looking after Albert for a couple of afternoons a week would suit me fine, and Hugh need never know."

CHAPTER FIFTEEN

The sun was warm as Nell and Clara strolled around Sefton Park with the nanny pushing the pram a discreet distance behind them.

"Are you looking forward to going home?"

"I am. It's been lovely being back, but I don't know how I ever lived with Mother."

Nell chuckled. "I don't remember you being very happy when you did."

"You're right. Still, at least we're talking again. It's reminded me, though, that if I invite them to Surrey, I mustn't extend the invitation for longer than two weeks. It's more than enough."

"How's your father doing? Will he be able to travel?"

"Thankfully, he's a lot better than he was, but he couldn't take a train at the moment. I'm hoping he'll be well enough by the end of the year."

"That must be a relief to your mother."

"It is to all of us. I don't know what we'd do with her if anything happened to him."

"Let's hope it doesn't come to that." They rounded a corner and Nell pointed to a secluded spot with a couple of empty benches. "Shall we sit here? The nanny can have the next seat along."

"Yes. It's a nice space to position the pram."

Clara wandered to the nanny but groaned as she returned to the bench Nell had settled on. "Isn't it typical? He's dozed off. I expect he'll be awake for half the night now."

"Can't you wake him?"

"It's not worth it. He's so grumpy if you do that. I'd rather Nanny sat up with him later."

Poor nanny. "At least I've seen him a couple of times this week."

Clara took a seat beside her. "I hope he sleeps on the train. He was far too restless on the way up here."

"It's something exciting, that's why. I'd have been excited to go on a train when I was a child. How's Mr Cavendish taken to being a father?"

"He takes everything in his stride. He's out a lot, so doesn't spend much time with Edward. He has plans for the future, though, especially when he inherits the house and estate from his father."

"It's a different world to living around here. I forgot to ask what he's been doing while you've been with me or your mother."

"Oh, he's had some people to see. It all fit in rather well, actually."

"Has he done what he needed to?"

"I think so. Not that he gives me any details. He said he might be early picking me up tonight, which won't please

Mother, but at least we'll be able to eat at a reasonable time and get to bed."

"What time do you need to be at your mother's?"

"About four o'clock, if you don't mind."

"Not at all. I'll have to get used to you not being around again. I don't know what I'll do with myself."

"Your sisters will keep you entertained."

"I expect so."

"We've been invited to Ackley Hall this Saturday. It's Lady Helen's birthday. Can you believe she's still only twenty-five?"

Nell shook her head. "That makes me feel old. I imagine it does the same for Ollie..." Nell put a hand to her mouth as soon as the words were out. *Why did I mention him when I'd been doing so well?*

Clara laughed. "I doubt he's noticed. It certainly doesn't trouble him."

"It's different for men..."

"Especially when your wife's younger and you're set to inherit a title and estate."

Nell said nothing as she stared at some tulips, trying to avoid Clara's gaze.

"Do you still carry a torch for him?"

"No." She shifted in her seat. "What makes you say that?"

"The look on your face."

"It reminded me of my visit to Surrey, that's all."

Clara sighed. "It's not healthy clinging on to what might have been."

"I'm not."

"So, you're over him?"

"Why wouldn't I be? I've not seen him for eighteen months."

"Does that mean you'll give Mr Marsh a chance, then? He may be what you need."

"I've told you a thousand times, I'm perfectly happy on my own."

"Except you're not!" Clara threw her hands in the air. "When will you admit it? You complain about being bored, and the way your sister treats you. The highlight of your day is walking to and from school. Are you going to put up with that for the rest of your life?"

"Having a husband wouldn't change any of that."

"Well, if you want my opinion, you've been on your own for too long."

"I've not."

Clara rolled her eyes. "I won't argue with you, but think about what I've said when I've gone. Right, it's time we were going. Mr Cavendish will wonder where I am."

The sun had disappeared behind a large cloud by the time they reached Princes Park Mansions, and Nell slowed her pace when she spotted a carriage waiting by the entrance.

"Will that be Mr Cavendish?"

"It's his carriage, but if he's not here, he'll have gone for a walk."

"I won't delay you then if you need to call on your mother and father before he gets back." She turned to wait for the nanny to catch them up. "Let me say goodbye to Edward before I go."

Clara approached the pram and lifted out her son.

"There we are. He's awake now. Are you going to wave to Mrs Riley?" She held his hand and shook it at Nell. "I hope you see him again before he starts walking."

"Will you be visiting so soon?"

"Only if Father's too ill to travel, so I hope not. No, I'd like you to come to Surrey."

Nell sighed. "You know I can't..."

"You said you were over him."

"And I am..."

"So why won't you visit?"

Nell flapped her arms by her sides. "I can't explain."

Clara shook her head. "Ollie wouldn't be around much, if that's what's worrying you."

"I'd rather he wasn't there at all."

"There's a good chance he wouldn't be. He's so busy learning about the estate that we only see him at the weekend."

"Doesn't he go to London then?"

"He did to start with, but Lady Helen prefers Ackley Hall. She's never liked London and most of her friends are in Surrey."

Is that because she knows he has someone else there? What would have happened to me if I'd moved and he didn't stay in London?

Clara sighed. "What's the matter now?"

"Nothing. I'm just not ready to visit."

"If you want my opinion, it would do you the world of good to see him again and get it out of the way."

"But I can't..."

Clara took a deep breath. "Very well. We'll arrange something when we know he won't be around. You could come from Monday to Friday, and possibly extend it if he's at a weekend house party. Not that they've been away lately with having the baby. Lady Helen's keen to resume her socialising as soon as possible. She's bored being at home waiting around for Ollie."

Why are people never happy with what they have? She turned at the sound of footsteps.

"Good afternoon, Mrs Riley."

"Mr Cavendish. It's nice to see you again."

"Likewise." He smiled at his wife. "Have you said farewell to your mother?"

"No. We've been talking." She turned to Nell. "I'd better go, but I'll see you soon."

Mr Cavendish watched his wife disappear. "You're coming to Surrey, are you? Clara's been so looking forward to you visiting now we've finished the house. Peters asked me to send his regards, too."

Nell coughed to clear her throat. "We haven't made any firm arrangements. It's such a long way to travel on my own."

He nodded. "I'll arrange a chaperone for you, if it helps."

"Oh ... there's no need for that."

"Trust me. If it makes the difference between you visiting or not, it will be money well spent."

Nell nodded. "Let me think about it, then. Good day, Mr Cavendish."

He raised his hat to her. "Oh, before you go. Ollie sends his best wishes. He was hoping to travel with us for this visit, but Lady Helen was less keen."

"H-he was?" *My goodness.* Nell's eyes widened. "I can

understand why she wouldn't want to be without him for two weeks."

Mr Cavendish grinned. "I don't think that was the reason."

"Oh!" Nell's cheeks reddened. *Does Mr Cavendish know? And Lady Helen, too?* "I-it was nice to see you, but will you excuse me? I-I have to get to school. I can't be late picking up my daughters."

CHAPTER SIXTEEN

The housekeeper showed Nell into Mrs Robertson's drawing room, and she smiled at Violet as she toddled towards her.

"There's a good girl."

The child giggled and ran to her mother as Nell took her usual seat by the fire.

"How was the voyage?"

"Very nice, thank you. It's so much easier with Violet being that bit older."

"Have you any plans to go again?"

"My husband left this morning for a month, and we'll travel with him on his next trip."

"You're so fortunate."

Mrs Robertson's smile fell. "It's fortunate we can accompany him, but it's difficult while he's away. Violet's started to miss him, too."

Nell nodded. "I remember Elenor being like that. They don't understand time at all."

"No, but he'll be home soon enough. How are you? Did you enjoy yourself with Mrs Cavendish?"

The smile fell from Nell's face. "I did."

"Then why the scowl?"

"It was disappointing she had to leave."

"She'll be back."

"Not in a hurry. She came to Liverpool because her father was ill, but he was on the mend when she left."

"So will you go down there?"

Nell puffed out her cheeks. "She wants me to, but I can't do it. I've spent the last eighteen months trying to get Mr Hewitt out of my head, but one look at him will undo all my good work."

"You don't know that. You may find your feelings have changed."

"They've not." She studied her fingers. "The thing is, Mr Marsh was on shore leave while you were away, and we spent a lot of time together."

Mrs Robertson's eyes lit up. "And how was that?"

"He's really very sweet." She sighed. "I've no idea if there's any future for us, but seeing Mr Hewitt would ruin any chance we might have."

"Why don't you tell her that?"

"I told her about Mr Marsh, but I can't admit to her that I still have feelings for Ollie. She's convinced I wouldn't see him, but I don't believe her."

"And you're sure seeing him once would be enough?"

Nell nodded. "Not only that. When I spoke to Mr Cavendish, I got the impression he knows what happened at the wedding. Even worse, he suggested Lady Helen does, too. What if she invites her for luncheon? I couldn't look her in the eye."

Mrs Robertson gasped. "I don't doubt it."

"I don't know how she knows, though. I can't believe it would be from Clara, but it must be. As far as I'm concerned, the only people who knew what happened that night were her and Ollie, and I doubt he'd say anything."

Mrs Robertson cocked her head to one side. "I wouldn't discount it being him. From what I've seen of men on the ships, they're not shy about admitting what they've been up to."

"Not to their wives."

"But he may have mentioned it to Mr Cavendish."

"That makes it worse." Nell pushed herself up and strode to the window. "If he's told Mr Cavendish, how many more of his friends know? What will they think of me?"

The housekeeper let herself in and Mrs Robertson stood up to take the tray from her. Once they were alone, Mrs Robertson guided Nell to her seat.

"Come and sit down. There's got to be a way to tell her you can't visit without upsetting her."

"I don't know what it is. Mr Cavendish said she's so excited about me visiting and he offered to arrange a chaperone to escort me on the journey."

"Oh dear."

"Quite."

They both stared at the teapot as Mrs Robertson poured out two cups and sat back in her chair. "I'd tell her what you've told me. That you're fond of Mr Marsh and don't want to jeopardise anything by becoming reacquainted with Mr Hewitt."

"She'd be giddy with excitement if I said that."

"Does that matter if it gets you out of going to visit?"

"I don't suppose it does."

"Well, then."

A smile flicked across Nell's lips. "Will you write that down? I'll have forgotten it by the time I get home."

Mrs Robertson smirked. "If I can remember myself. Hopefully, she'll understand."

"I'm just sad it's come to this."

"It will sort itself out. Give it a little more time." Mrs Robertson took a sip of tea. "How's Betty? I've not heard from her since I got home."

Nell sighed. "She's been struggling with her melancholy since Christmas."

"That's a long time. Has she seen a doctor?"

"She has. He wanted to admit her to the asylum, but thankfully, Mr Crane wouldn't let her go."

Mrs Robertson's mouth dropped. "Good grief. I'd no idea she was so bad."

Nell shook her head. "None of us did. I've not called as often as I should because of the weather."

"The poor thing. I should invite her here, too."

Nell sat up straight. "Actually, if I call to see her, could I bring her here? There are no parks nearby, but I'm sure taking a walk would do her good."

"That would be splendid. Just tell me in advance when you want to call."

. . .

Alice and Rebecca were already in the playground when Nell arrived at school, and she sensed Mrs Pearse's eyes on her as she crossed over to them.

"What have I done now?" She nodded towards the group of women in the corner.

"Nothing I'm aware of. Although that may be the problem. She has no reason to gossip about you."

Nell shrugged. "Such a strange woman."

"Take no notice of her. Did you have a pleasant afternoon?"

"Yes, very nice."

Rebecca smiled. "I've had Albert for a couple of hours. He's a sweet little thing."

"Is there no improvement with Betty?"

"Jane says this new tonic has picked her up a bit, but she still likes to have Albert. It gives her something to do, too."

Nell nodded. "There is that."

Alice waved to Leah as she came out of school and ran towards them.

"I was the first out."

"You were quick." Alice grinned at her as Elenor and Isobel joined them.

"Where's Florrie?"

Isobel tutted. "She's coming. She's always last."

"She'll be here in a minute." Rebecca walked to the door as her youngest daughter emerged. "Come along, slowcoach. We're ready to go." She took hold of Florrie's hand as Alice led the way with Leah.

"There's a letter for you at home. It looks like Mrs Cavendish's handwriting."

Nell's stomach churned. *I hope she's not still asking me to visit.*

"You don't seem very pleased."

"Oh, I am. I just miss her being in Liverpool, that's all."

"It's a shame she had to move so far away."

"Not from where I'm standing." Rebecca smiled. "It may be selfish, but I'm not sorry you don't see so much of her."

"I wouldn't have visited as often once she was married, even if she had stayed up here."

Alice chuckled. "Unless she wanted you to look after her baby."

Nell tutted. "There wouldn't be much chance of that." *I couldn't even bring my own children up.*

Maria was setting the table when they arrived home and Nell picked up the letter from the dresser.

What's she got to say?

"It came not long after you went out. Is there any news?"

"Give me a minute." Nell scanned the page as she pulled it from the envelope.

> *Nice to see you ... train journey uneventful ... Peters is keen for you to visit ... Mr Cavendish is coming to Liverpool ... Ollie will travel with him...*

What! She reread the sentence.

Mr Cavendish has some outstanding business in Liverpool and needs to visit again. I can't endure another six-hour journey, and so Ollie's offered to travel with him. He suggested they invite you to afternoon tea at the Adelphi.

He can't do that. The blood drained from her face. *I've got to stop him. What about Lady Helen? Mr Cavendish said she wouldn't let him travel. Does she know about this?*

"Nell, are you listening?" Maria called to her from the table.

She flinched as she looked up. "Oh, yes, sorry. What?"

"You were supposed to be helping. George and Billy will be home any minute."

Nell glanced once more at the letter before pushing it into the envelope. "What do you want? A pot of tea?"

"You could serve out the girls' tea before everyone arrives, too."

She stood up, but Maria caught hold of her arm.

"Are you all right? You've gone as white as a sheet. Is Mrs Cavendish all right?"

"Y-yes, she's fine. It was a tiring journey, that's all." She disappeared into the kitchen without waiting for a reply. *I need to write to her tonight. She has to speak to Ollie and tell him I can't see him ever again. Either in Surrey or in Liverpool. If she gets the letter the day after tomorrow, she'll have plenty of time to stop him.*

CHAPTER SEVENTEEN

Maria carried some plates to the dining table as Nell set them out for their afternoon tea. She smiled at Alice as she delivered the cups and saucers.

"I'm so pleased the tonic worked for Betty."

Alice sighed. "So am I, but she still looks ill. I was shocked when I saw her yesterday."

"At least she's able to leave the house..." She broke off as the letterbox clanged.

"I'll go." Alice wandered to the front door and returned with a stylish cream envelope. "It's for you. Mrs Cavendish by the looks of it."

Nell's heart raced as she stared at the envelope. *So, she got my other letter. I bet she's furious with me.*

"Aren't you going to open it?"

"Not now. The others will be here in a minute."

"You've probably got time..." Alice stopped when Nell glared at her "...although if you'd rather wait..." A knock on the door interrupted her. "They're early."

Maria carried the teapot to the table. "It was well-timed, actually."

Jane was the first to join them. "A new cake. I'm honoured."

"I didn't bake it for you..."

Nell rolled her eyes and slipped the letter into the drawer of the dresser before going into the hall. Alice crouched on the floor beside Albert while Betty hovered by the door.

"You made it." She gave Betty a warm smile. "How are you feeling?"

"I can get myself out of bed now, which is an improvement."

"So is coming here."

"I only managed it because Bert arranged a carriage for me. I've been in the house for so long, I couldn't have walked so far if I'd tried."

"We'll sort that out soon enough." She paused as Rebecca joined them. "Come on in. Maria's been baking."

Betty grimaced. "I must confess, I've not been eating very well. My dresses are hanging off me."

"I'll give you an extra big slice, then." Nell served out the cake while Maria poured the tea.

"Will you be able to visit again next week?"

"I should be able to, but after that, I'll need to ask Bert for more money."

Jane rolled her shoulders. "He should pay for more than two visits. He's only got you and Albert to look after."

"You can tell him, then. I'm not up to arguing."

"You shouldn't need to..."

Nell held up a hand. "She doesn't want to quarrel with you, either."

"I'm only trying to help..."

Betty sighed. "I know, but we're not made of money. Bert will let me have what he can."

Maria's eyes narrowed. "Did you say you're not eating properly? You won't get your strength back if you don't."

"I'm getting stronger now Mam's cooking for me."

"You!" Maria stared at Jane. "You can't cook."

"I'm perfectly capable, thank you. I just don't have the opportunity where I live."

"What have you been making?"

"All sorts."

"Good for you." Nell glared at Maria, but she wouldn't be silenced.

"You can help me with the baking next time there's a family gathering, then..."

"I'm better at dinners. I couldn't possibly do cakes as well as you."

Nell took a deep breath. "That's enough. As long as Betty's getting fed..."

She sighed. "I've not much of an appetite, to be honest."

"Once you start eating again, it will come back. I hope so, anyway, because Mrs Robertson was asking after you and said you were always welcome to visit. I'll go with you if you like."

Betty smiled. "That would be nice."

"We won't be able to go before June because she's away."

Maria scowled. "She's taken that child on a ship again?"

"It's perfectly safe, and she can't go once Violet starts

school, so they may as well make the most of it now. It's difficult living on your own while your husband's away so much."

"You don't need to tell me..."

Jane pouted. "At least she has a husband who comes home."

Nell groaned. "You have the boys and all of us here. She has no one."

"Except the staff."

"It's not the same as you well know."

"How would I? I've never had a domestic."

Nell puffed out her cheeks. "What's the matter with you this afternoon? Are you spoiling for a fight?"

"I've things on my mind, that's all." She glared at Maria as she opened her mouth. "Private things."

"All right, pardon me for trying to help." Maria collected up the dirty plates. "Does anyone want anything else? Vernon and Lydia are coming tonight, so I need to see to the tea."

Nell stared at her. "You didn't say."

"I only found out yesterday."

Jane's smile reappeared. "Are they after a free meal?"

"Not at all. We've not seen each other for a few weeks. What's wrong with that?"

"It seems unusual, that's all. For Vernon, that is. Maybe they've got something to tell you."

"Like what?"

Jane raised an eyebrow and glanced at Albert, who was sitting by the fire.

"Don't be ridiculous. It's too soon after the wedding for that."

"That doesn't mean anything."

"Wash your mouth out. My son wouldn't..." Maria's cheeks flushed as she stared at Betty.

"Don't look at her like that." Jane raised herself up in her chair. "They'd been married for nine months before they had Albert."

Maria gritted her teeth. "So I noticed."

Nell played with the watch she wore on her chain, and as half past four approached, she stood up from the table and looked at Betty.

"I need to go for the girls shortly. Have you arranged for a carriage to collect you, or will you walk up to Windsor Street with me?"

"We'll come with you. It's cheaper than arranging a pickup and I need to stretch my legs."

"There should be plenty of carriages at this time of the day."

Maria stood by the front door as they all filed out. "I don't know why it needs three of you to pick up the girls from school."

Jane groaned. "Because it gives them a chance to get out for half an hour, that's why." She let Alice and Betty walk on ahead but waited for Maria to close the door before she pulled Nell away from Rebecca. "Would you mind if I have a quick word with Nell? I won't be long."

"Oh." Rebecca glanced at Alice, then back to Nell. "Yes, I'll go."

Nell watched Rebecca hurry to catch the girls. "You could have spoken in front of her."

Jane lowered her voice. "It's about money. Do you remember the problems we had when I had to pay for Matthew's apprenticeship?"

"I'm not likely to forget."

"Well, you said I should ask if I ever needed any more."

"What do you want more for?"

"John finishes school in a couple of months, and I wondered..."

Nell studied her. "How much do you want?"

"Five pounds, ten shillings."

Nell sucked air through her teeth. "I've not worked for six months. I don't know if I've enough."

"Please, Nell. I wouldn't ask if it wasn't important. I'm trying to save, but I'll need another five pounds for Matthew next year and I can't manage both. If you help, they'll both pay you back once they're working, I promise."

"Let me think about it. I'll have to ask Billy how much I have in my account. I don't want to leave myself short."

"It would be like a saving scheme for you. You'll get the money back in a few years, when you may need it more. You'd only spend it if you had it."

Nell huffed. "I'd only spend it if I needed to."

"But you've a good heart. Please, Nell. They won't forget it."

Nell's forehead creased when they got home from school as the smell of cooked pastry permeated the house.

"Did you make that while we were out?"

"No, I did it yesterday." Maria placed the last of the cutlery on the table and turned to point at the mantlepiece.

"I found that letter in the dresser while I was looking for something. Have you forgotten about it."

"No, I put it there for safekeeping."

"It's perfectly safe on the top. Aren't you going to open it?"

"Later. There isn't time now."

"That's not like you. You usually want to read them as soon as they arrive."

"It's been a busy day..." Her shoulders relaxed as the front door slammed and Billy joined them.

"Something smells good."

"Meat and potato pie." Maria smiled at him. "When you told me Vernon was coming for tea, I thought I'd make an effort. They don't come round nearly enough, so hopefully, this will tempt them back."

Billy rubbed his hands together. "Is there mushy peas, as well?"

"They're warming through. Where's your dad?"

"He stopped to speak to the chap up the street who's having trouble with his landlord. You know the one I mean."

Maria tutted. "I do. I hope he doesn't keep him long."

Billy took a seat by the fire. "He'll get a move on if he sees Vernon." He looked up at Nell. "Where's everyone else?"

"Alice has taken the girls to wash their hands." She peered into the kitchen to check Maria was occupied. "While we're on our own, may I ask you about the money in the Friendly Society?"

"Do you want me to draw some out?"

"Possibly." She crouched down by the side of the chair.

"I'd like to know how much I've got first. Do you remember?"

He screwed up his face. "You had fifteen pounds when you stopped working, but you've drawn a bit out. You may have ten or eleven left. I'll need to check."

Nell bit her lip. "All right. As long as I've got ten pounds, would you draw five out for me?"

"Five! Why do you need so much?"

She put a finger to her lips as Maria bustled in with a fresh loaf of bread. "I'll tell you later. Not a word." She flicked her eyes towards Maria.

"I wouldn't dream of it. Is this our guests?" Billy stood up and headed for the hall as the front door closed and Vernon's voice filtered into the living room. "You remembered the way then."

"I followed my nose."

Billy laughed as Alice and the girls joined them. "I bet you did."

"Good evening, Lydia." Alice pulled out a chair. "Would you like a seat?"

"Thank you … if you're sure your mam doesn't need any help."

Alice grinned. "You're a guest. She'll call me or Aunty Nell if she does. How are you, Vernon?"

"Starving."

Maria appeared from the kitchen. "Nothing's changed, then. Did you pass your dad on the way in?"

"He said he'd follow us." The front door opened. "It sounds like he's here."

Maria sighed. "Good, now, everyone at the table."

George grunted as he took his seat. "What's all this in aid of?"

Vernon helped himself to some bread. "Can't we come to visit?"

"I daresay you can, but I know you. What are you after?"

"Nothing, other than some of Mam's cooking."

Maria passed George his plate. "Why can't they come for tea without a reason? It's only the third time they've been since they were married."

"That's not three months."

"It is ... nearly." Vernon picked up his knife and fork. "As near as makes no difference, anyway."

"It doesn't matter. I'm just pleased to see you." Maria handed a plate to Lydia. "Are you settled into the house?"

"Yes, thank you, Mrs Atkin. It feels like home now."

"Don't say that." George scooped up a forkful of mushy peas. "She'll want to know when she's going to be a granny. She's been feeling left out ever since Jane had a grandchild."

"No, I've not."

"All right, Sarah then."

Maria sighed. "Only because James hasn't settled down yet. I should have been the first..."

George snorted. "I wouldn't wait for him."

"I'll be patient, then. I'm sure Lydia won't keep me waiting for long."

Nell's eyes didn't leave Lydia as her cheeks coloured. *Something tells me we'll have less time to wait than Maria would like.*

CHAPTER EIGHTEEN

Nell bent down to pick up the familiar cream envelope and studied the unusually untidy handwriting. *She must wonder why I've not replied to the other letter.* She pushed it into her apron pocket. *As if she doesn't know.*

Maria looked up when she returned to the living room. "Anything exciting?"

"Only a letter from Clara. I'll read it this afternoon when you and Alice are out."

"Alice is visiting Betty on her own. I'm not going anywhere."

"Didn't you say you were going to see Sarah?"

Maria shook her head. "No. Although I probably should. Tom's off work again."

"I thought he was better."

Maria shrugged. "So did I, but knowing him, he'll be skiving."

Nell grinned. "You should go and give him what for then."

"As if it makes any difference." Her forehead creased as she studied Nell. "Why do you want me to go out?"

"I don't. I just thought you'd said you were."

"You could come to Sarah's if you're not seeing Rebecca."

"Actually, I'd like time to read Clara's latest letter and write back. We've had a busy few weeks, so I'm falling behind..."

"You've been no busier than usual."

"Maybe I'm a bit under the weather then."

"What's up with you?"

"Nothing I know of. Look, why don't you visit Sarah and I'll cook the tea?"

"If you put it like that, I will." She studied the clock. "It's nearly time for you to fetch the girls. Don't dawdle on the way home so we can get dinner served and tidied up before I go."

The house was eerily quiet when Nell arrived home, and she shuddered as she hung her cloak in the hall. *This is the first time I've been on my own since I got back. I need to make the most of it.* She climbed the stairs and opened the drawer in the bottom of the wardrobe. *There it is.*

She retrieved the still unopened letter and went back downstairs, taking a seat by the fire. Her hands trembled as she retrieved the more recent letter and sliced the envelopes of both of them. She studied the older of the two. *I should have opened this one sooner.* She scanned the neat cursive script.

> *... are you going to let this ruin our friendship ... all because of one night when we'd all had too much champagne ... nearly two years ago ... Ollie's happily married now ... whatever your feelings...*

Whatever my feelings. She rested her head on the chair and closed her eyes. *For someone who writes books, she's no idea.*

> *I've been excited to tell you I'm in the family way again, but you've made me so cross...*

She groaned. *What a horrible friend I've become. I need to apologise...*

> *I hope you've had second thoughts since you last wrote, because Ollie doesn't believe that you don't want to see him. He thinks he should at least speak to you and, if you must know, I agree with him. You need to get any tension out of the way so you can visit again.*
>
> *They've had to delay the trip because Lady Helen's not been well and they think she's with child, too. They're now aiming to travel in July when her condition settles. I'll write with further details nearer the time.*

Again! He's not wasted any time. The other child can't be six months old yet. He told me he wouldn't be close to his wife...

She squeezed her eyes tight before picking up the second letter. *I hope this isn't another one criticising me.* She took a deep breath. *Let's get it over with.*

...I've very disappointed that you didn't respond to my last letter. You couldn't even offer any congratulations on the baby. I had hoped I'd talked some sense into you, but Ollie will have to do that himself. He knows how much I want you to visit and he's as baffled as I am about why you won't. He's even offered to act as your chaperone, although I persuaded him against being so forward...

He and Edward will be in Liverpool for the last two weeks of July and he's insistent on taking you for afternoon tea. He's as disappointed as I am that he hasn't seen you...

Nell dropped the letter onto her lap and held the arms of the chair to stop her hands from shaking. *What sort of friend have I become?* She gasped for air as tears rolled down her cheeks. *I don't even know why she still wants to see me. Mrs Robertson was right. I need to tell her about Mr Marsh. Surely then she'll understand.*

Her reply took over an hour to write, but it was in its envelope by the time Maria arrived home. She stood up to take it to the postbox but cowered from the look on her sister's face.

"What's the matter?"

"The tea! Why can't I smell it cooking?"

Oh, goodness. "I-I was about to make it."

"If it's not in the pan already, it will be too late. You needed to start it as soon as you came in from school."

"What is it?"

"I told you. Pig's trotters. Don't you ever listen?"

"I-I'm sorry. I got distracted. Have you anything else in? We'll do them tomorrow."

"Bread and cheese. You can explain to George why that's all he has for his tea?"

A shiver ran through her. "Let me go to the shop and see if they've any boiled ham."

"At this time?"

"It's worth a try. I'll do some potatoes, too." She didn't wait for an answer before she picked up the letter and darted into the hall. "I'll go straight to school once I've got it." The door hadn't closed behind her when she hit her head with a hand. *I've not brought any money. If I get it on tick, I'll be in more trouble when she finds out. Well, I'm not going back inside.*

Nell checked her pocket watch as she stepped out of the shop. *Twenty minutes to spare. Enough time to walk to the postbox.*

She tucked the cooked meat under her arm and set off along Windsor Street. The sun was warm, and she admired the trees as she approached the park's boundary. *It's a shame Mr Marsh isn't here to see them.* She gasped before smiling to herself. *What am I thinking? Perhaps I like him after all.* She rounded the corner and pushed the letter into the postbox, but her smile disappeared. *He won't be back for another couple of months … assuming he doesn't stay in Australia. Why did he go so far away?*

"Nell?"

She flinched as Jane waved a hand in front of her face.

"Oh, I'm sorry. I was in a world of my own. And Betty. Here again?"

"I'm feeling a lot better, and Mam offered to pay for a carriage. I couldn't have come otherwise."

Nell glared at her sister. "Where've you got the money from?"

"I had a couple of shillings put by..."

Nell smiled at Betty. "Will you excuse us?" She pulled Jane to one side. "Have you dipped into the five pounds I gave you for John?"

"No!" Jane's voice was too high.

"Yes, you have. How much have you spent?"

"A couple of shillings, that's all."

"Well, if you keep on, it will be gone before John's signed his indenture. I knew I shouldn't have given it to you.

"I promise I'll put it back. I'm waiting for a payment from the guardians."

Nell's cheeks coloured. "You really are the limit. There's no more where that came from ... and I still want it returned..."

"And you'll get it."

"If John can't start his apprenticeship because you've spent the down payment, he won't have a trade to be able to afford it."

"Stop worrying. I'll have the money by next week."

"You'd better." Nell bit her lip as she took a deep breath.

"Are you all right, Aunty Nell?"

"I'll be fine." She stroked Albert's hand as he sat in the pram. "How's he doing?"

Betty smiled at him. "He's as good as gold."

"He's probably happy that he doesn't have to spend so much time with his granny." Nell glowered at her sister. "I need to go."

The road was ominously quiet as Nell approached the school, and she reached for her watch. *Good grief. How can I be late?* She lifted the front of her dress and broke into a run. *Please don't let them be waiting.*

She turned into the gate as Mrs Pearse ushered her daughter through them. "Mrs Riley. Been with your fancy man again?"

Nell's glare caused Mrs Pearse to take a step backwards. "I am not in the mood for you today. Another word, and I'll tell the whole playground what a controlling, vindictive woman you are."

"You'll do no such thing."

"Just you try me."

CHAPTER NINETEEN

The sun burned into Nell's back as she and Rebecca walked to school for the last time that summer, but as soon as the girls appeared in the playground, they raced out of the gate and disappeared.

"They're not very upset about it being the end of term."

Nell tutted. "Elenor's been counting down the days. I don't know what I'm going to do with them for four weeks. They'll be bored with playing in the street by this time next week."

"We can take them to the park to feed the ducks." Rebecca smiled. "If we go a couple of times a week, it will help to split things up."

Nell shrugged. "Why not?"

Alice met them at the top of Merlin Street. "Are you on your own?"

Nell rolled her eyes. "The girls were so keen to get away from school, we couldn't catch them. Please feel free to take them to visit Betty over the holidays."

Alice chuckled. "Of course I will. Albert needs more

company, so he'll love it."

Nell opened the front door when they arrived home, and Leah ran down the hall to meet them.

"We beat you."

Alice ruffled her hair. "You were too quick for us. Mam and Aunty Rebecca can't run that quickly."

Leah giggled. "This was through the door." She thrust an envelope at Alice.

"Who's it for? Can you read it yet?"

Leah shook her head.

"Let's see then." Alice pointed to the words. "Mrs E. Riley. That's Mam."

Nell's heart skipped a beat as Leah took the letter from Alice and handed it to her. *Mr Marsh. Is he nearly home?* Her cheeks flushed as Leah stared at her.

"Who's it from?"

"I ... erm ... I don't know yet."

"Open it!"

"Let me get in first." Nell walked to the living room and slid the letter into the drawer of the dresser. "Is your tea ready?"

"No."

"Yes, it is." Maria appeared from the kitchen. "I didn't expect them to come running in as they did. Were you late again?"

"No, I wasn't. They just wanted to get away. Let me butter them some bread."

Nell hadn't finished when the front door closed and Billy joined them.

"Evening, all. I've brought a visitor with me."

"Vernon!" Alice beamed at him. "Are you staying for

tea?"

"I won't say no if there's any going."

"It's a good job I've made a pan of scouse." Maria arranged another place at the table. "Is Lydia with you?"

"No. She's at her mam's so I'll pick her up later."

"He's having a night out ... while he can!" Billy smirked at his brother.

Maria looked between the two of them. "What's that supposed to mean?"

Vernon's ears turned red as he stared at the floor. "I'm going to be a dad."

Maria gasped as a rare smile spread across her face. "That's wonderful. When?"

Vernon bobbed his head from side to side. "We're not sure. Probably December."

"He's not wasted any time." Billy nudged him, but Vernon retaliated as the colour reached his cheeks.

"Leave him alone." Alice bounced on the spot. "If you ever need someone to look after it..."

"I'm sure Lydia will do that."

Nell added her congratulations. "How is Lydia?"

"Well enough, now she's got used to the idea. She didn't want to tell anyone to start with."

"She could have told us. We've both been through it." Maria held out a chair for him. "Take a seat. This tea's ready."

Billy's forehead creased. "Aren't we waiting for Dad?"

"Isn't he with you?" The scowl had returned to Maria's face.

"He nipped into the alehouse."

"At this time! I'm not waiting, then. He knows when

tea's ready. What made him do that?"

"He ... erm ... he wanted Vernon to tell you his news while he wasn't here."

"Why?"

Billy shrugged as he sat down. "I don't know. He just said he'd follow us and for Vernon to be quick."

"At least that means he won't be long."

As the end of the evening approached, Maria collected up the playing cards and put them away in the dresser.

"What's this?" She held up an unopened envelope.

"Oh ... it's the letter that came earlier. I forgot about it. You go to bed, and I'll follow you."

"You could be a while, it's very thick."

"That's why I waited to read it."

Alice stood up. "I'll leave you to it as well, then. I'll need all my energy over the next few weeks with the girls being at home."

Nell grinned. "You know you enjoy it."

"I do. It's certainly better than being in that tailor's shop. Goodnight."

Nell bid them both goodnight and waited for them to reach the top of the stairs before she sliced open the envelope and took a seat by the fire.

My dear Mrs Riley.

By the time this letter reaches you, I should be within a fortnight of arriving in Liverpool. I hope you are in good health and that you are still happy to see me when I return.

She nodded to herself. *More than you'd believe.*

If you'd rather I didn't trouble you, please leave a letter at the White Star office and you won't hear from me again...

Is this what I've reduced him to? Worrying every time he comes home... I'll write to him in the morning.

She returned to the letter and read of his time in Melbourne, visualising each building as she soaked up his descriptions. *He remembered to give me the details. What a marvellous place it sounds, too.* She sighed. *Maybe one day.*

She was still walking the streets of Melbourne when the front door disturbed her.

"You're up late." Billy took the seat opposite.

"I'm reading a letter. Mr Marsh has been to Melbourne in Australia, and he's detailed a wonderful picture of the city."

Billy grinned. "The steward you hated for twelve months."

"I didn't hate him, he annoyed me. There's a difference."

"But you like him now?"

"We're friends, if that's all right with you."

"I'm happy, if you're happy."

Nell studied him. "I am for now. How was Vernon tonight? Full of the joys of impending fatherhood?"

Billy laughed. "Full of ale, more like. He's done his bit."

Nell sighed. *Never a truer word.* "Is he enjoying

married life? We never seem to get a straight answer when we ask."

"He seems to be. Why?"

"No reason. Marriage can do strange things to people. Is he in the alehouse every night?"

"Not as much as you'd think."

"I'm glad. Lydia's a nice girl. She doesn't deserve to be left."

"Are you thinking of Betty?"

Nell's eyes narrowed. "What do you mean?"

"Mr Crane's in there most nights."

"On Windsor Street?"

Billy nodded.

"But he insists on living in Everton. Why don't they move back here so Betty can be closer to her friends?"

Billy shrugged. "I don't ask questions like that."

"Perhaps you should. Betty's not said anything about it. I thought he'd stopped going to the alehouse when she was ill."

"He did for a while, but now she's on the mend, he's back to his old ways."

"It won't last if he's never at home." She shook her head. "Some of these young men need a clip round the ear. They've no idea how to take care of their wives. I hope you look after yours when you have one."

"I'll make sure I do." He pushed himself out of the chair. "I'd better get to bed. I've an early start in the morning."

Nell watched the door close as he left. *What's the world coming to? A man like Mr Marsh wouldn't leave his wife every night.*

CHAPTER TWENTY

Nell pulled the brush through her newly washed hair and groaned as water continued to drip from it. She squeezed it once more with a cloth before she let it hang down her back. "I need to sit in the sun."

Maria looked up from her seat at the table. "You'll catch a chill going outside with wet hair."

"Not in this weather. There's hardly a cloud in the sky and I'm sure you'd rather me do that than put the fire on."

"I don't know why you needed to wash it. You only did it a couple of weeks ago, and you'll only tie it up when it's dry."

"It's a nice day, and Mr Marsh is due home shortly, that's why. I want to be able to style it nicely."

"I thought you said he was only a friend."

"He is."

"Then why does it matter what you look like?"

Nell picked up a dining chair. "Because it does."

The door was already open as she carried it outside and positioned it at the end of the outhouse. She brushed her hair once more and arranged it across her shoulders as she sat down. *This could take a while.*

The sun was warm on her back, and she closed her eyes, trying to remember the descriptions of Melbourne that had been so vivid the night before. *Maybe we could go together one day. The girls won't be little forever.* She sighed. *That would be nice.*

"Have you gone to sleep there?"

She flinched as Maria stood over her. "I'm resting my eyes."

"Well, you'd better open them. This has come for you." She handed Nell an embossed cream envelope. "I sliced the top."

Ollie? Her mouth fell open as she stared at the lettering.

"Aren't you going to read it?"

"I-in a minute ... is the kettle on?"

"Not yet."

"Will you put it on? I'll make the tea when it's boiled."

"If you want me to go, why don't you just say so?"

Nell stared at the letter long after Maria had flounced back into the house. *I thought I'd made it clear to Clara.* She shook her head. *He must be on his way to Liverpool...* Her pulse raced as she pulled out the single sheet of paper and scanned the familiar writing. *He's already here...*

> *Mr Cavendish and I would like to take you for afternoon tea. We'd call at the house to collect you, but I fear your sister would chase us away.*

Nell raised an eyebrow. *Maria has her uses, after all.*

Instead, we'll wait for you on the corner of Merlin Street and the road you walk down on your way to the park. Shall we say four o'clock on Tuesday?

Her breathing stopped as she held the seat of the chair. *Tuesday. That's today!* She checked her watch. *In just over an hour's time.*

She coughed as her lungs fought for air. *Calm down. If I don't show up, he'll get the message and leave me alone. I need to ignore him.*

Maria's voice carried out into the yard. "Are you making this tea? The kettle will be boiled dry."

"I'm coming." She stuffed the letter into her pocket on her way to the kitchen, taking a deep breath as she walked in. *Don't panic. It will be fine.*

She fumbled with the tea caddy, spilling tea onto the worktop as she spooned it into the pot.

"What are you doing?" Maria was by her side in seconds.

"Nothing. I banged my hand. I'll tidy up."

"See that you do. We can't afford to waste any."

The tea hadn't properly brewed when Nell poured it, and she handed Maria a cup of milky-coloured liquid.

"Did any tea go into the pot?"

"Yes, it did. I mustn't have left it standing long enough. You can top it up when you've drunk some."

"So much for you making it. Is your hair dry yet?"

Nell ran her fingers through it. "Not even close. I'd better go outside again." She picked up Mr Marsh's letter on the way to the yard. *Hopefully, another tour of Melbourne will distract me.*

Despite Mr Marsh's vivid descriptions, Nell's attention barely left her watch, but at half past four, she put down the letter and ran the brush through her hair once more. *Nearly done, and Ollie should be at the hotel again by now.*

Maria was in the kitchen when she went inside. "Do you need a hand with the tea?"

"Everything's ready. It just needs warming through. You can set the table if you like."

"Will do."

She was putting out the knives and forks when the front door opened and Leah ran in. "A man wants to see you. In the street."

"A-a man?" A lead weight settled in the pit of her stomach as Leah nodded.

"He knew my name." She beckoned Nell to the door. "Come on..."

"I-I'm coming." She ripped off her apron and dusted a patch of soot from her light grey dress. *That will have to do.* The street was full of children as she stepped out of the front door, and she glanced in both directions.

"He's up there."

She looked in the direction Leah pointed and saw Ollie leaning against the wall of the end house. *He's on his own.*

She hadn't moved when he noticed her, and he stood up straight. When she remained rooted to the spot, he started walking. *He can't come here...* She pulled the front door shut and hurried towards him, her hair catching in the breeze as she did.

"My, Mrs Riley. How different you look."

She glanced around. "We can't talk here. The neighbours will have a field day."

"We can sit in the carriage if you like? Or go to the hotel..."

"That's not what I meant. We need to be away from prying eyes." She didn't wait for him to escort her as she raced around the corner and leaned against the gable end of the row of terraced houses.

He smirked as he joined her. "It's good to see you. It's been too long. What happened to our appointment?"

Her heart pounded as she clenched her hands in front of her. "I ... erm ... I'd just washed my hair when I got your letter."

He ran a hand through the wavy brown hair that rested over her shoulder. "And I thought you'd done it for me."

"Oh, no." She grabbed her hair and twisted it down her back. "I've not had time to fix it."

"Perhaps we could take afternoon tea tomorrow instead. Will you be ready by then?"

"Yes ... no ... I mean, my hair will be dry, but I'm busy. And the next day."

He studied her as her cheeks reddened. "So, Clara wasn't lying when she said you didn't want to meet me?"

She lowered her head. "I-I'm sorry, but I can't. You know what you do to me ... you have to let me go."

"You've met someone else?"

She bit her lip as she nodded. "He can't know I've seen you."

Ollie straightened up. "He's a fortunate man. Will you marry him?"

"W-we've not spoken about it."

"Will he look after you if you do?"

Nell fidgeted with her fingers. "If I let him."

"Why wouldn't you?"

She raised her eyes to meet his. "You know why."

"I only want what's best for you."

She caught her breath. "Then we can't see each other. Please. For my own sanity, I need to forget you."

"You're serious, aren't you?"

She nodded. "You're a married man. I won't steal another woman's husband."

"You wouldn't be stealing ... just sharing."

"I can't do it, Ollie, whatever you say."

He held her gaze. "What about how you feel?"

"It doesn't matter how I feel."

"It matters a great deal." He reached for her hand and kissed the back of it. "We'd be good together."

"It would never work. Our worlds are too different."

He glanced around at the rows of terraced houses. "I could take you away from this."

"This is where I belong."

He nodded, for once the sparkle missing from his eyes. "Such a shame." He kissed her hand once more. "Farewell, Mrs Riley."

She leaned against the wall, her heart racing as he sauntered to a carriage further down the road. *Farewell, Ollie.*

She didn't stop watching until the carriage disappeared from view. *I knew I shouldn't have seen him. How will I face Mr Marsh now? It will be like starting all over again.* With a great effort, she pushed herself away from the wall. *How many of the neighbours saw us? I guess I'll soon find out.* She twisted her hair together and tied it into a knot at the base of her neck as she strolled to the house. *At least there's no one looking out for me.*

Maria was putting the cups and saucers on the dinner table when she got home. "Where've you been? You were supposed to be doing this."

"I was, but I needed to go outside."

"What for?"

"Oh ... no reason. Leah wanted me, that's all."

"You could have told me."

"Sorry. I didn't think I'd be long."

"Well, the men will be home any minute. You can make a pot of tea while I call the girls. If you can manage."

"I'll be fine." The kettle was boiling when Nell got to the kitchen, and she warmed the teapot before spooning the tea leaves into it. *That sounds like Billy now.* She poured the water into the pot but froze when Leah arrived in the living room.

"What did the man want?"

Maria's voice was stern. "What man?"

"The one who wanted to speak to Mam."

"Nell."

Her heart skipped a beat. "What?" *Who needs neighbours...?*

Maria was at the kitchen door by the time she turned round. "Leah said there was a man looking for you."

"Y-yes. It was ... erm ... it was Mr Marsh. He's arrived in Liverpool and called to ask if we could take a walk later in the week."

Maria's eyes narrowed. "Why don't I believe you?"

She shrugged. "I don't know. I told you he was due. That's why I washed my hair."

"When are you seeing him?"

"Soon."

"When?"

"We didn't set a date. He said he'd write."

Maria clicked her teeth. "You never were any good at telling lies."

CHAPTER TWENTY-ONE

Nell hummed to herself as she stood in front of the mirror over the fire and put the last of the hairgrips into her newly styled updo. Once she was happy with it, she carefully positioned her hat in the centre.

"You sound very cheerful." Maria took the seat to her right.

"What's wrong with that?"

"Nothing, but you weren't so enthusiastic when Mr Marsh called earlier in the week."

"He took me by surprise, that's all. I wasn't ready."

"Well, you've certainly made an effort today. I don't believe for a moment that you're only friends."

"You can think what you like. As far as I'm concerned, it won't be any more than that, unless he gives up going to sea."

Maria cocked her head to one side. "Is that likely?"

"I've not asked him."

"But if he did?"

"If he did, it would change things." She glanced at the

clock on the mantlepiece. "He'll be here in a minute. He's always punctual."

"So, he wouldn't turn up unannounced?"

"N- Will you stop it? Not usually, but sometimes it's different." She smiled at the knock on the front door. "That will be him. I'll see you later."

Mr Marsh raised his hat as she opened the door, revealing his recently cut dark hair that had been neatly greased back. "Mrs Riley. How lovely to see you."

"And you, too. You're as punctual as ever."

He grinned. "I wasn't going to be late. You look wonderful. Is that a new dress?"

"I wore it for Miss Ellis's wedding, but I've not worn it much since."

"You should. That shade of blue suits you." He ushered her onto the pavement and extended an arm. "May I be so bold? Or are you too close to home?"

Her eyes flicked around the neighbouring houses. *I've probably ruined my reputation already.* "Why not?"

He held his head high as they set off, but Elenor and Leah ran up to them.

"Is Uncle Thomas your fancy man now?"

Nell stared at Elenor, her mouth open. "No, he's not. We're walking to the park."

"But you're together." She pointed to their arms.

"H-he's being a gentleman. You've seen me walk like this with James and Billy."

"That's different."

Before she could answer, the two of them ran to their friends, giggling.

"I-I'm sorry about that. I forget that Elenor's growing up."

"Has it got anything to do with Mrs Pearse?"

"Not this time. Elenor must have remembered from your last visit."

"She has a good memory, then. It's been too long." They walked to the end of the street. "Do you have a preference for where we walk?"

Nell shrugged. "Not especially, but Sefton Park might be nice."

"I'm happy wherever we go. I've missed our walks."

"Being in Melbourne must have made up for it, though. Your letter was wonderful, describing all the streets and buildings. I felt I was there with you."

"I'd have enjoyed it much more if you had been." He smiled down at her. "Maybe one day ... if you're ever a stewardess again, I mean."

"Perhaps... How long were you there in the end?"

"Two weeks. Your nephew was right, a month would have been too much and there was a ship that needed a replacement steward."

"That was fortunate. What about now? Will you be in Liverpool for long?"

"I asked for extended shore leave because I cut my stay in Melbourne short, so I'm here for three weeks."

"Really?" Nell's face lit up, but she immediately looked away. *You're only supposed to be friends.* "That's nice. It never entered my head to do that while I was working."

"They don't like you doing it, but they can be accommodating if they want to be. Is your nephew still away?"

Nell sighed. "He is, and he's not coming back. Not this year, anyway. He's taken a job as a manservant at a grand house in Brazil."

Mr Marsh sucked air through his teeth. "That's a big change."

"What's worse is that he didn't tell his mam or dad before he left. I think he hoped I'd do it, but his mam will kill me if she finds out I knew and she didn't."

"Oh dear. She's bound to find out, eventually."

"I'm dreading it when she does." She fell silent as they walked past the entrance to Princes Park Mansions. "I do miss visiting Mrs Cavendish."

"If she's any sense, she'll miss you, too. Do you hear much from her?"

"I've not recently, but she came to visit her parents after Easter, so we spent time together then."

"Is she likely to stay down south?"

"Oh, yes. They're very settled, and she has her little boy now. Edward. He's growing up fast."

"They do that. Not that I've had a lot to do with children."

"You wouldn't, being a steward. I was always thankful there weren't many in first-class."

"It's one of the perks of being upstairs. Steerage was full of them."

The park loomed into view, and once they'd crossed the road and made their way through the gates, he indicated to the right-hand footpath.

"Shall we walk to the lake?"

"We can, but I doubt we'll get a seat. It's busy already."

"We can keep walking until we do. I'm not in a hurry."

. . .

The crowds were thinning out when Nell pulled her pocket watch from the front of her dress.

"It's later than I thought. We'd better be going."

Mr Marsh stared at her. "Is that a watch?"

"Haven't you seen it before?" She held it out to him. "I've had it a couple of years now. Billy found it for me in a pawn shop, so I could watch the time when I was visiting Mrs Cavendish."

He shook his head. "Most women have a man to escort them, but once again, you're different."

"Men are at work when I want to go out."

He chuckled. "I'm not criticising, just making an observation. I've never known such an independent woman. You fascinate me."

She shrugged as they headed to the entrance. "It seems perfectly reasonable to me."

"Then who am I to argue?" He offered her his arm. "Shall we?"

"What will you do while you're in Liverpool?"

"I'm hoping to see a lot more of you, for one."

"That would be nice, although not every day."

"No, I understand you still have your own life. When are you next available? Perhaps you could show me the sights of Liverpool."

"That would make a change. I'll have to decide where to go."

"It's your choice. I really don't mind."

Nell gave another wistful glance at Princes Park Mansions as they strolled past the entrance and stopped as a carriage pulled out in front of them. *Ollie! Oh, dear Lord, no.*

"Are you all right?" Mr Marsh patted her hand but stiffened himself as the door swung open.

"Mrs Riley."

Nell's mouth opened and closed several times, but no words came out.

"*You.*" Ollie glowered at Mr Marsh before he rounded on Nell. "Is this who you were telling me about the other day?"

"What do you mean?" Mr Marsh released Nell's arm as he stepped backwards, a look of disgust on his face.

Ollie ignored him as he pulled Nell towards the back of the carriage. "Tell me you're not walking out with *him*. Not after all we've been through."

"P-please, Ollie." Tears spilled from her eyes. "Don't do this to me."

"I've not done anything. How could you even consider being with *him* when I could offer you so much more? You hate everything about him."

Mr Marsh's face paled. "Is that true?"

"No ... it was a long time ago..."

"But you and him?" Mr Marsh flicked his eyes between them. "I always knew there was something going on, but I wanted to believe you when you said there wasn't..."

"I never lied to you. There was nothing to know."

"Nothing!" Ollie gasped. "Is that what you call it?"

Mr Cavendish appeared from the carriage and dragged Ollie away from her. "Stop it. It's none of your concern."

"I care a great deal about Mrs Riley." He turned to her. "I was prepared to put our relationship to one side when you told me you'd found someone else, but I won't let you be with *him*. Of all people..."

"Y-your relationship?" Mr Marsh's face was white as Ollie sneered at him.

"We've been close these last few years. *Very* close. She enjoyed it too ... with you out of the way."

"Ollie, stop it." Tears streamed down her face, but she didn't care. "We didn't have a relationship. It was the champagne..."

Mr Marsh glared at her. "So, my first impression was right all along..."

"No. We were friends..."

"Friends!" He ran a hand over his eyes. "I don't believe this. You and him...? No. I can't even think about it. I need to go. For good." He turned on his heel, but as Nell went to chase after him, Ollie grabbed her arm.

"Let him go. You can do better than that."

"Ollie, enough." Mr Cavendish pulled Nell to him. "She has the right to choose who she walks out with. Just because you don't like him..." He put an arm around her. "Will you be all right?"

"No." She buried her face in Mr Cavendish's chest. "Why can't he leave me alone?"

"Come with me." He helped her into the carriage. "Take a seat while you compose yourself. We'll wait outside." She sobbed uncontrollably as he closed the door. *How could he?*

She had no idea how long she'd been there when Mr Cavendish opened the door and peered inside.

"How are you feeling?"

"Terrible." She gasped for air as he took the seat opposite her. "I'll never be able to face Mr Marsh again."

"I'm sorry. We didn't know..."

"Ollie knew. Clara told him, but he wouldn't listen."

"She didn't tell him about Mr Marsh."

"Well, she should have done. It would have been better for him to be angry in Surrey, rather than here." She shook her head. "Mr Marsh will never trust me again."

"If he likes you, he'll be back."

"He won't..." She flinched as the door opened and Ollie popped his head inside.

"Have you forgiven me yet?"

"Forgiven?" She glared at him until the sparkle faded from his eyes. "How can I ever forgive that? I never thought I'd say this, Ollie, but I hate you."

"I was only doing what was best for you."

"You were doing nothing of the sort. You were being selfish." She scrambled towards the door, but Ollie barred her exit.

"Let me go."

"We'll give you a lift."

"I don't want to spend another second with you." She looked at Mr Cavendish. "Will you let me out?"

"Ollie. Close the door. I'll take her home."

"I'm not waiting..."

"You've done enough damage. Now move out of the way..."

After a moment's pause, he rolled up the steps and slammed the door, kicking the wheel as he did.

Mr Cavendish shook his head. "I'm sorry. We were only here because Clara asked me to call on her father."

She wiped her eyes. "How is he?"

"Much better, thank you."

"At least that's something. You will tell her what happened, won't you? She needs to understand why I can't ever visit."

"She'll be furious with him."

"That will make two of us." She stared out of the window as the carriage turned into Merlin Street. "We need to stop here. The last thing I need is for my sister to see us."

He banged on the roof to alert the coachman. "I hope you sort things out with Mr Marsh."

"If I know him, he'll already be at the White Star office asking to be on the next voyage out of Liverpool."

"Do you want to drive there now and stop him?"

She shook her head. "Do you think I'll be able to look him in the eye now Ollie's ruined my reputation?"

Mr Cavendish sighed. "I don't know what to say."

"There's nothing left to say. Just tell Ollie that I meant it when I said that I never want to see him again. Ever."

CHAPTER TWENTY-TWO

The late summer sun was sinking in the sky as Nell carried a chair into the backyard and found some shade. She settled for a corner by the outhouse and pulled a letter from her apron pocket. She groaned as she read it. *It's still not right... Not that it matters. He'll probably throw it away without reading it.*

My dear Mr Marsh

This is the hardest letter I've ever had to write, but I want you to know how very sorry I am for what happened when you were in Liverpool. My heart is broken at the way you left, but I realise how angry and upset you must have been.

I don't expect you to understand the friendship I had with Mr Hewitt, but I promise you, that's all it was. He once described me as being the sister he never had, and I can only assume that's why he was protective towards me. Not that he had any right to insult you.

My friendship with him is over and he knows I won't

ever see him again. Not that I expect that to be any consolation to you.

If you could find it in your heart to forgive me...

She took a pencil from her pocket and crossed out the last sentence. *I've done nothing wrong. Not that he'll see it that way.* She sighed. *How do I end it?* She held her pencil over a blank part of the page. *How about 'If you're able to forgive me, I'll be waiting for you.'?* She grimaced. *That's too much. What about 'I'd like to see you again.'? That's better. I'll rewrite it tonight when Maria's gone to bed.*

She flinched when the pipes in the kitchen rattled, and water ran into the kettle. *Is it that time already?*

"Nell!"

She let out a sigh as Maria repeated her name twice more. "What are you doing?"

"Sitting outside." Her voice was weak, but seconds later, Maria joined her.

"What are you skulking out here for? Isn't it time you snapped out of this mood?"

"I wanted to be by myself. Can't I do that?"

"You've been missing for half an hour. Anyway, we've got a letter. Is it from James?"

A lead weight settled in Nell's stomach as she looked at it. "It is."

"Take it off me, then. I've been waiting for this for weeks. He should be home any day now."

"Why don't you make the tea first? And bring out a chair."

"I'm not sitting out here. Just get a move on and read it before the kettle boils."

The top of the envelope had been sliced, and Nell gulped as she took out two sheets of paper.

"Well?"

"Give me a minute." She scanned the unusually careless handwriting. *Oh James. How could you do this to me?*

"What's the matter?"

She turned back to the first page. "He says they had a good journey and arrived in Manaus a week before he wrote."

"He can't be far behind it then, if they turned around and came back." Maria's face broke into a smile.

"He likes it where he is and says the weather's wonderfully warm and they're surrounded by forest..."

"I'm not interested in all that. When will he be home?"

Nell ignored the question. "There are a lot of British people living out there and ... he's been offered a job."

"He already has one."

"A different one ... working as a manservant on a plantation."

Maria's forehead creased. "A servant?"

"I-it's more like a butler. He says it pays more than he'd earn on the ship."

Maria stared at her. "Has he accepted it?"

She bit her lip as she nodded. "Yes. He says we're not to worry because he'll get one paid voyage home a year..."

"One? What about the rest of the time?"

Nell rested the letter on her lap. "There won't be any other times. He wants to settle out there and start a new life..." Nell jumped up as Maria's face paled and she ushered her to the chair. "Don't cry. He'll be happy out there."

"How can he be? It's time he found a wife and had a family. He shouldn't be moving halfway around the world."

"He may find someone over there. He said there are a lot of British..."

"Men, maybe. Not nice young ladies."

"Perhaps he doesn't want to settle down."

"But he's thirty..."

"Which means he's old enough to make his own decisions. It's his life. You can't tell him what to do."

"He's my son. Has he no consideration for me?"

"That's got nothing to do with it." Nell scanned the end of the letter. "He says he'll try to be home for Easter of next year. It doesn't sound so bad when you say it like that."

"Not bad! It's months away. Easter's late next year, too."

"He might not realise."

"Why can't he at least come home for Christmas? Everyone should be here for that."

Nell sighed. "I suspect the weather has something to do with it. The last few times he's been here, he's complained how cold it is. He won't want to come in the middle of winter."

"You know a lot about it."

She held up the letter. "Only because of what it says in here. He's sent a return address, so we can write. Why don't we do that tomorrow?"

Maria rocked on the chair. "George had such high hopes for him when he was born. Our first son. We thought the world of him. How did it go so wrong?"

"It hasn't gone wrong. He's doing a job he enjoys. You should be pleased for him."

Maria dabbed at her eyes. "George will be furious."

"Why will he? He got rid of most of his anger years ago."

"Being a steward was bad enough, but becoming a servant is even worse. We paid for him to have a trade, and look how he's repaid us..."

"It can't be that bad if he'll be earning more money than on the ships. They pay well..."

"What about us? Will we get any of this money? We rely on James' contribution."

"Perhaps it's time we didn't. If he found himself a wife and got his own home, he wouldn't be supporting us."

Maria glared up at her. "Don't you care?"

"You know I love James as much as you do, but..." She sighed. "You have to let people go. He's not a little boy any more." She stepped back across the yard. "You stay there while I make a pot of tea. It will all work out in the end."

The following afternoon, Nell straightened her hat in the mirror as Rebecca let herself in.

"Are you ready?"

"Give me a second. Have you found the girls?"

"They're outside." She looked at Maria. "Don't you want to come with us? It's the last time we'll be going to the ducks before school starts again."

"I'd love to, but these legs won't let me. Have a nice time."

Nell picked up the letter they'd written to James that morning and pushed it into her bag with the one she'd finished for Mr Marsh. "I'll make sure this gets in the post. See you later."

Rebecca called the girls as they left. "Where are we going? Sefton Park?"

Nell took a breath. "Do you mind if we don't?"

"I thought you wanted to go to the postbox. It's on the way."

"I'm not ready to walk that way yet. Can we go to Princes Park via the one on Windsor Street?"

"When will you tell me what happened with Mr Marsh?"

Never. "There's not much to tell. They were short of a steward and asked if he'd fill in."

"He'd only been here for a day or two. Didn't he want to spend more time with you?"

Nell shrugged. "Why would he? We're only friends."

"I got the impression you were looking forward to seeing him, though."

"He obviously wasn't as excited."

They rounded the corner onto Windsor Street, and Nell reached into her bag for the letters.

"Who are they for?"

Nell showed her the top one addressed to James. "We had a letter from him yesterday telling us he isn't coming home. Not for a while, anyway. He's staying in Brazil."

"Is that why Maria looked as if she'd been crying?"

Nell nodded. "George was furious too. He's given up stewarding to work as a manservant."

Rebecca tutted. "It must have been a big decision."

"It was, but Maria doesn't understand. I think he did the right thing telling her by letter, even though it wasn't pleasant having to read it to her."

"I can imagine." Rebecca glanced down at the letters. "Who's the other one for?"

"Oh ... Mr Marsh. I said I'd write to him."

"Where's he gone?"

"He didn't say."

Rebecca's eyes narrowed. "That's not like you. You're usually keen to hear where everyone goes."

"We ... we didn't have time. The company should know where he is, though, so they'll forward it to him." *I hope.*

CHAPTER TWENTY-THREE

The days were getting shorter, and the ground was wet underfoot as Nell and Rebecca walked to school.

"Winter's well and truly on its way."

Nell groaned. "I hate this time of year. There's nothing but months of dreariness to look forward to." She kicked at a pile of leaves on the corner of Windsor Street. "We had another letter from James this morning telling us about his new life. I don't blame him for not wanting to come back to this."

"How's he getting on?"

"He's happy. He's in charge of the entire household and he says the weather doesn't change from one month to the next. It's always sunny."

"How was Maria when the letter arrived?"

Nell huffed. "She wasn't interested. Not in his job, where he's living or anything."

"She probably doesn't want to admit how good a life he has."

"Either that, or she's trying not to upset herself. Thankfully, she has Vernon's baby to think about."

"I've never seen her so excited."

"Because she'll be a granny like Jane and Sarah, that's why. I hope the child doesn't grow up too quickly, because it needs time to wear all the clothes she's knitted for it."

Rebecca chuckled. "She'll slow down soon enough when she starts baking for Christmas."

"I've a feeling you and me are going to get lumbered with that. The baby's due around the middle of December, so she'll be preoccupied."

"That's more than a month off, but I don't mind. There's not much else to do when the weather's bad."

"No."

"That's a weary sigh."

Nell huffed. "I'm sorry, but I can't help envying James."

"You're not thinking of going away, are you?"

"What's the point? It would cause more trouble than it's worth, and I couldn't join James even if I wanted to. There are no jobs in Manaus for women." She gave her sister a sideways glance. "I've asked him."

"You've not?"

She shrugged. "Why not?"

"That would finish Maria off."

"Which is why I'll have to make do with the descriptions of places he gives me in his letters. It should help brighten up the winter months.

Rebecca studied her. "Won't you be seeing Mr Marsh again? He should be back from the trip they sent him on, shouldn't he?"

Nell shrugged. "I haven't had a reply to the letter I sent

him, so either they sent him on a long voyage, or he doesn't want to stay in touch with me."

"That's a shame. You seemed to be getting on well together. I don't know how they can send someone so far away at such short notice. It's a good job you're not still working if that's how they treat the crew nowadays."

Nell feigned a smile. "Maria would have been up to the office in a flash and given them what for."

"And quite right too. They shouldn't treat stewardesses like that."

"They may not, but I don't suppose I'll ever find out."

"You'll have to ask Mr Marsh next time you see him."

If I see him again. Not that I'm holding out much hope.

The school playground was filling up when they arrived, and Alice hurried over to them.

"Here you are. Mam's had to go to Vernon's house. Lydia's had her baby. A little girl."

Nell and Rebecca stared at each other, their mouths open, before Nell looked at Alice.

"It wasn't due..."

"Don't think Mam didn't notice, but she says she must have been early. It can happen sometimes."

"If she's over a month early..." The colour drained from Rebecca's face. "She might not survive."

"Don't say that."

Alice tutted. "Stop worrying. The midwife called with the news shortly after you'd gone out and she said they were both fine."

Nell gave a sigh of relief. "Thank goodness for that."

Although it suggests the baby wasn't early at all. "Hopefully, your mam won't be late home so we can get the details. Imagine. Vernon a dad."

"No." Alice giggled as Leah and Florrie ran to them.

"Here you are." Leah hugged Nell's skirt.

"I'm always here."

"You're usually nearer the door. I couldn't find you."

"I'm sorry. Shall we go and wait for Elenor? I don't want her thinking I'm not here."

"She's with Ruth." Leah pointed towards a group of girls near Mrs Pearse.

What on earth...? Nell stared at Rebecca. "What's going on?"

"Don't ask me. Isobel's with them, too."

She turned to Alice. "Have you any ideas?"

"Don't look so worried. You should be pleased they're friends rather than falling out with each other."

"But what's brought it on?"

Alice shrugged. "Children can be fickle. Would you like me to get them for you?"

"Please. The less I have to do with that woman, the better."

The house was empty when they got home, and Nell shivered as the last embers of the fire struggled to stay alight.

"It's a good job we weren't much longer. The place would be freezing." She put a scoop of coal onto the cinders. "Is there any tea made, or do we need to do it?"

Alice checked the pantry. "We'll have to make some."

"We'd better get a move on, then. Your dad will be home shortly, and he'll want his tea on the table." She stood up from the fire but gasped when she noticed a letter propped up behind the clock. *Mr Marsh!* She put her hands over her mouth. *Did he get my letter?*

Alice called to her. "Are you coming, Aunty Nell? These kidneys need frying up while I peel the potatoes."

"One minute." She took a deep breath. *Calm down. I can read it later. What if he wants to see me? What if he doesn't? Which would I prefer? You know perfectly well...*

She staggered to the kitchen and threw a large knob of butter into a pan, quickly followed by the kidneys.

Alice peered into the pan. "Aren't you cutting them?"

"I'm sorry, I forgot. I'll get them out."

"Are you all right? You've gone very pale, all of a sudden."

"I'll be fine." The kidneys flicked around the pan as she tried to lift them out.

"Here, let me do it." Alice took the spoon from her. "You do the potatoes. And cut them small so they cook quicker."

The water hadn't come to the boil when George and Billy joined them.

"What's going on here?" George's voice was rough. "Where's Maria?"

"She's at Vernon's. Lydia's had her baby."

"Already?" George turned to Billy. "Did you know about this?"

"No, although I wondered why we didn't meet him on the way home."

"She arrived sometime this morning, so maybe he knew something was happening before he left for work."

George scowled. "There's no tea then?"

"It's just cooking..."

He looked at Billy and gestured to the front door with his thumb. "We may as well have a drink to celebrate the baby while we're waiting. We'll be back in half an hour."

Nell puffed out her cheeks as they left. "At least he wasn't angry about us being late. Let's set this table before your mam gets home."

"I'm hungry." Elenor climbed up onto a chair.

"I'll get the bread in a minute."

"Mrs Pearse always has Ruth's tea ready."

Nell's stomach squirmed. "How do you know?"

"She told me. She's my friend now."

Nell forced a smile. "That's good. When did that happen?"

"Today. She said her mam told her to be nice to me."

Why would she do that? "Has she realised I'm not going away again?"

"It's because she thinks you'll get me a new dad. She doesn't like girls with no dads."

What a horrible thing to judge people on... She was about to answer when the front door opened, and Maria walked straight into the living room.

Nell grinned at her. "Congratulations. How is everything?"

"Very well, thank goodness. The baby was early, but she's still a good weight and looks healthy enough."

"Have they chosen a name yet?"

"Maud, after Lydia's mam."

"Was Mrs Ally at the house with you?"

"Oh, yes." Maria unclipped her cloak. "I'm going to have trouble with her interfering all the time."

"She might think the same about you."

"I only want to help..."

Nell tutted. "I'm sure that's what she wants, too, and Lydia is her daughter."

"And Maud is as much my granddaughter as hers." The smile had returned to Maria's face once she'd hung up her cloak. "I can't wait for you to see her. She's beautiful."

"All in good time. This tea's nearly ready. George and Billy have nipped to the alehouse to drink a toast to the baby, but they shouldn't be long."

"That's a relief."

"Was Vernon there while you were with Lydia?"

"He came in from work shortly before I left. He seemed rather flustered by it all."

"He'll get used to it soon enough."

Once the cards were put away later that evening, and the table laid for breakfast, Nell walked Maria and Alice to the foot of the stairs. *Will you go!*

"Goodnight. See you in the morning."

"You're keen to be rid of us."

"It's getting late, and you've had a busy day."

Maria squinted at her. "If you say so."

As soon as they were upstairs, Nell closed the living room door and reached for the letter behind the clock. *Will he forgive me or hate me?* She shuddered as she sat down. *There's only one way to find out.*

Dear Mrs Riley

I'm sorry for the delay in writing, but I've been travelling between Liverpool and South Africa for the last four months and have only recently had a chance to read your letter.

I must admit, it made interesting reading. I only wish I could believe you.

Unfortunately, I saw the look on your face when you realised it was Mr Hewitt in the carriage. It was in the second before you remembered I was with you. You've never looked at me like that. You never call me Thomas, either, despite my offers, yet you didn't use Mr Hewitt's full title once. It was always 'Ollie'.

The familiarity between you was obvious and I wonder, if you've lied about this, what else you've hidden.

I thought I should tell you I've accepted a position to go to Australia again, but I'll be joining another ship when I get there. I'll be travelling between Australia and New Zealand for the foreseeable future and don't expect to be in Liverpool for at least a year. If ever.

Yours sincerely

Thomas Marsh

She leaned back in the chair, her arms resting limply by her sides. *That's it. He's gone.* She stared at the wall opposite. *What did he mean, the look on my face...? I didn't have a look. Did I?* She closed her eyes. *I knew I shouldn't have seen Ollie again.* Her chest was tight as she reread the letter. *Did I lie?* She ran through some of their conversations. *I don't think so, although I've not always told him the whole truth. Perhaps that's what he means. It was only because I didn't want to upset him.* She sighed as she pushed the letter into the envelope. *I'm clearly not good enough for him. It just took him a while to realise it.*

CHAPTER TWENTY-FOUR

Fourteen months later

Nell let herself into the house and shook the rain from her cloak.

"It's horrible out there. I've decided the girls can walk themselves to school from now on. The beginning of a New Year is a good time to start a new routine."

Maria looked up from her knitting. "I don't know why you've gone with them for as long as you have."

Nell shrugged. "It's something to do. Is Maud still here?"

"She is, but she was groggy and felt very warm, so I put her to bed. I hope she's not sickening for anything."

"There's a lot of illness going round at the moment. You've not taken her to Tom's lately, have you?"

"We called last Tuesday, but Tom was in bed, so we didn't see him."

Nell shook her head. "He's such a fool. If he'd let me get a doctor for him years ago when I had some money, he'd be as right as rain by now."

"They called the doctor last week, but he said he can't do much for him other than give him laudanum to make him comfortable."

"I still say he's a fool. Why wait until you're bedridden before you ask for help?"

Maria stood up and went to the kitchen. "It's not that bad. He's been ill for years but always recovers enough to make it to the alehouse."

"He didn't use to take himself off to bed."

"He's not as young as he used to be."

"He's a year younger than you."

Maria put the kettle on the range. "And I feel my age most days. It was turning fifty that did it."

Nell laughed. "You were moaning about your feet and legs long before that."

"They've got worse. Not to mention my back. You wait."

Nell rolled her eyes as she lifted the cups and saucers from the dresser. "Something else to look forward to. Are we expecting Alice soon or did she walk up to Betty's?"

"She shouldn't be long. She only popped to see Miss Hopkins from church. The rain was too much, even for her."

"At least Betty's baby isn't due for another couple of months. The weather should be better by then."

"And my next grandchild won't be long after that. What a year to look forward to." Maria smiled as she put a pot of tea on the table, and Alice joined them.

"That was good timing. I'm frozen. It's trying to snow out there." She moved to the fire to warm her hands. "I bumped into Aunty Sarah while I was out. She said Uncle Tom's having a bad day, and she was on her way to fetch the doctor."

Nell raised an eyebrow. "Again? She wouldn't do that twice in two weeks unless it was urgent."

Maria sighed. "I'll pop round tomorrow and check on him."

"You won't have Maud then, will you?"

"No. Mrs Ally has her on Wednesdays."

"Lydia must be thankful she has you with the morning sickness she's having with this latest baby."

"Thankfully, she's over the worst of it, but it's been lovely having Maud." Maria offered Alice a chair as she turned away from the fire. "I took her to bed about an hour ago. You can bring her down when we've finished this, if you like."

Alice grinned. "Of course I like. What time's Lydia picking her up?"

"Not until four, so there's no rush."

Maria was washing up and Nell wiping the table when Alice came downstairs.

"There's something wrong with Maud. I've woken her, but she wants to go back to sleep."

Maria wiped her hands on a towel as she joined them. "Is she still warm?"

"Very, although it may be because she was snuggled under the blankets."

"That won't have helped, but she shouldn't be that hot." Maria draped the towel over the back of a chair and followed Alice up the stairs.

"There, there." Maria lifted her granddaughter out of bed as Nell arrived. "Come to Granny."

Maud wheezed as Maria rested her over her shoulder.

"I don't like the sound of that." Nell passed Maria a wet cloth. "Let me wipe her face. It might cool her down."

"I've some brandy downstairs. We can give her some of that, too. We want you better by the time Mam arrives, don't we?" She kissed the top of the child's head before offering her to Nell. "Will you carry her? She's getting too big for me."

Maud was hot to the touch, and Nell carried her straight to the front room. "She'll be better in here. It's cold with no fire on."

"We can't leave her on her own."

"She'll be fine. You find the brandy, and we'll put her in her pram. She'll be quite safe."

Maud snuggled into Nell's chest while they waited, but Nell sat her up straight when Maria reappeared.

"Here we are. What's Granny got for you?" Maria offered her a teaspoon of brandy, but Maud gagged and coughed it onto Nell's lap.

Nell nodded to the bottle. "Mix it with some milk. It's too strong on its own."

Alice disappeared into the other room and returned with a cup of milk, but Maud choked on every mouthful.

"Let me put her in her pram. She's getting upset."

Alice rocked the pram gently, but she stopped when Lydia let herself in.

"What are you doing in here? It's freezing."

Maria put a hand on Maud's forehead. "She has a temperature, so we thought it may help to cool her down."

Lines appeared on Lydia's face. "She was warm this morning when I woke her."

Maria raised an eyebrow. "You had to wake her?"

"Vernon was up and out earlier than usual, so I put it down to that."

"It may be more than that. I'd say she's picked something up. If she's not better by tomorrow, fetch the doctor."

Lydia stared down at her baby. "I hope it's nothing serious."

"I'm sure it won't be, but we need to keep an eye on her." Maria stroked the child's cheek. "We don't like you being poorly, do we?"

"No, we don't." Lydia pulled the pram into the hall. "Thanks for having her, but I'd better get her home. The sleet went off while I was walking here, so it would be nice to get back before it starts again."

Nell held open the front door. "Let us know how she is tomorrow." Once Lydia had left, she closed the door and followed Alice into the living room. "At least she doesn't have far to walk. It's a shame Betty isn't as close. Your Aunty Jane's so excited about having another grandchild she'd be visiting every day if Betty was closer."

Alice sniggered. "Don't tell her I said this, but I suspect that's one of the reasons Betty's staying where she is. Now she's over her melancholy a couple of visits a week is quite enough."

~

Nell arrived at the table with the girls the following morning and poured herself a cup of tea, while Maria hovered over Billy. George looked up at his wife.

"What's got into you?"

"I want this table cleared so I can go and see how Maud is."

"Lydia won't want you there at this hour. Just sit down and let us eat in peace. We'll be gone in five minutes."

Maria huffed as she sat down but sprang up again when Vernon barged into the house.

"I can't stop because I'm late for work, but Lydia asked if Mam could call and fetch the doctor for Maud on the way round. I didn't have time to go for him and come here, too."

"How is she...?" Maria's question remained unanswered as Vernon disappeared without another word. "I told you." Maria grabbed for the plates.

"Calm down." Nell took the crockery from her. "Me and Alice can do this. You go."

"Won't you come with me? I can't walk as fast as you and if I have to go for the doctor as well..."

Alice pushed Nell towards the door. "You go. I can manage here."

Nell nodded. "Very well, I'll call for Doctor Flynn then follow you to the house."

Maria had gone before Nell fastened her cloak and Billy held open the door for her.

"Hopefully, Doctor Flynn will have Maud sorted out by the time we get home."

George grunted as he stepped out behind them. "He'll

need to sort your mam out if he doesn't. See you later."

Nell turned right and headed towards Princes Park. *I hope nobody's beaten me to the doctor's this morning.*

The surgery was locked when she arrived, and she rattled the doorknob until a bleary-eyed housekeeper answered.

"Do you know what time it is? Doctor Flynn's been up half the night..."

"I'm sorry, but it's my little niece. She's very poorly..."

The doctor appeared in the hallway. "What's the matter with her?"

"She was hot and listless yesterday, but she's worsened overnight."

"How's her breathing?"

"I-I've not seen her, but she was wheezing yesterday."

Dr Flynn reached for his bag. "I've seen several cases of diphtheria this last week. I hope this isn't another one."

Diphtheria! A cold sweat broke out over Nell's brow as the doctor brushed past her. "It's Greta Street."

Maria was waiting at the window when they arrived, and she opened the door as soon as she saw them.

"Thank goodness you're here. The poor little mite's struggling to breathe."

Nell followed the doctor into the single downstairs room, where Lydia sat by the fire with Maud on her knee.

"Let me see." Doctor Flynn put down his bag and lifted Maud onto the floor. Her neck was swollen, and she cried as the doctor forced open her mouth to check her throat.

Maria twisted her fingers together. "Will she be all

right, doctor?"

"I'll prepare some vapours for her. They should ease her breathing." He pulled several bottles from his bag. "We need to move her to the bedroom. Will one of you take her for me?"

Nell hovered by the door as Lydia wiped her eyes and picked up her daughter. "Has anyone told your mam? Would you like me to fetch her?"

"Please." Lydia sobbed as she made her way up the stairs. "I didn't see her yesterday. She doesn't even know she's ill."

Nell hovered outside Mrs Ally's house, stamping her feet to keep out the cold. *Where on earth is she?* She arrived twenty minutes later.

"Mrs Riley. What are you doing here?"

"Looking for you. Maud isn't well and Lydia would like to see you."

"Oh dear. Let me put my shopping away..."

"Actually, could we go now...?"

The woman stared at her. "You go if you're in a hurry. I'll follow when I've done this. You look frozen."

Nell didn't wait to be told twice. "Don't be too long. The doctor's with her now." The footpaths were icy, and she made her way back to Vernon's more slowly than she would have liked, but Dr Flynn was leaving as she turned the corner. *Have I been gone that long? Hopefully, it means he's made her comfortable.*

She increased her pace, but as she approached the house, Maria appeared at the bedroom window and pulled the drapes across. *Oh, my goodness, no. Please don't let that mean...* A wave of nausea washed over her as she raced to the front door, stopping when the sound of sobbing hit her. *Upstairs.* She dashed to the bottom of the stairs but stopped when Maria met her coming down.

"I need to close the drapes."

"No! Has she gone?"

Maria nodded but said nothing as she went through the motions of stopping the clock and covering the mirror.

Nell clung to the handrail as she followed Maria into the back bedroom, and she coughed as the vapours caught her throat. "Lydia. I'm so sorry."

Lydia stood like stone over Maud's cot as Maria stared at her through her tears.

"She couldn't breathe... Why weren't you here?"

"Mrs Ally wasn't at home..."

Lydia suddenly looked up. "Is Mam here?"

"She's following me. She won't be long." Nell stared into the cot. "Poor little thing. At least she'll be in heaven now."

"The doctor said there was nothing he could do. Her throat was all infected, and just closed up."

Nell wiped away her own tears. "Why didn't we call for him yesterday?"

Maria blew into her handkerchief. "My little angel..."

Nell ushered Maria to the door, but Lydia refused to move.

"Someone has to stay with her."

Nell's heart pounded and her head spun as she put an arm around Maria. "Let's get you downstairs. I don't know about you, but a tot of brandy wouldn't go amiss."

CHAPTER TWENTY-FIVE

There was a hint of warmth in the sun as Nell walked towards her brother's house, and she was thankful her short period of mourning for Maud was over. Sarah was coming down the stairs when she let herself in.

"Is Tom in bed?"

She nodded. "He's just dozed off."

Nell followed her into the back room. "Has the doctor seen him lately?"

"He called yesterday and gave him some more laudanum." Sarah's eyes filled up as she looked at Nell. "He says he won't get better this time."

"What do you mean?"

"He's got consumption. Apparently, he's had it for years, but it's getting worse. That's why he's wasting away."

"Can't you feed him up?"

Sarah wiped a hand across her eyes. "It doesn't work like that. The doctor thinks Tom was right all along, and he probably caught it in the warehouse."

"So, he wasn't skiving."

Sarah shook her head. "Unfortunately, he cried wolf once too often and none of us believed him."

"I'm sorry. Does Tom know?"

"No, and I don't want you telling him. He'll give up if he finds out."

"Would you like me to tell Maria?"

"She's not over Maud's passing yet. Do you think she could deal with it?"

"It might be better to warn her."

"The doctor reckons he's got a few months yet, so we could wait a little longer."

"At least that's something." Nell sighed. "After having such high hopes for this year, it's turning out to be terrible. I hope bad news doesn't come in threes. Betty's baby's due anytime now and she's had enough misfortune as it is."

"Don't think Jane hasn't thought of that. She's worried sick."

"Does she know about Tom?"

"Not yesterday's news, but after what happened to Maud, she's not been her usual self."

"Perhaps we shouldn't tell anyone until after the baby's born. There's no point worrying them."

Nell's shoulders slumped as she left Sarah's, but she straightened her back when she spotted Alice walking towards her.

"Are you on your way home?"

"I am."

"How's Betty doing?"

"She's ready for this baby to be born. She says it's a lot harder when you already have a toddler."

"It is, although I was fortunate that I had your mam to help me. I kept telling Betty to move closer so she could have more visitors."

Alice laughed. "She'll manage. Albert's old enough to play with the other kids in the street, and there are a couple of older girls who look after him for her."

Nell pushed open the front door. "What would we do without young girls to help?"

Maria was setting the table when they walked in. "How is everyone?"

"Betty's fine."

Nell sighed. "Tom's not so good, but the doctor's keeping an eye on him."

"Did you see him?"

"No. He'd had some laudanum not long before I got there, so he was asleep."

"I'll call tomorrow."

"I ... erm ... I wouldn't do that. He's rather poorly at the moment. You'd be better waiting a few days."

"You're probably right. I shouldn't go round there all miserable." She blew her nose on her handkerchief. "I've not been like this since Fred..."

"That was a long time ago; you can't bring it all up again."

"I'm trying not to, but I called to see Lydia earlier, and it was as if the years had rolled back. To have a child who can walk and play..."

"I know, but at least she's expecting another one soon..."

Maria turned on her. "Because having another child helps, does it?"

Nell's mouth fell open as she glared at her sister. "There was no need for that."

Alice glanced between the two of them. "What's going on?"

Nell blinked several times. "Take no notice of your mam. She's obviously had a difficult afternoon."

"That's right, blame me." Maria stormed into the kitchen as Nell took a seat by the fire.

"The memory of Fred has clearly upset her."

Alice slowly nodded her head. "You must have been upset, too."

"I was. More than she'll ever know." She breathed a sigh of relief when the front door opened and Billy walked in.

"Evening, all."

"Is your dad not with you?"

"We walked with Vernon, and it got on to babies, so I left them to it."

Alice scowled at him. "You'll have some of your own one day."

"And when I do, I'll take some notice."

Nell rolled her eyes. "How is Vernon?"

"He's all right..."

"Don't tell me your dad's giving him advice?" Maria carried the bread to the table. "I don't remember seeing much of him when I was in a similar situation."

Nell groaned. "He went through it, too. He just dealt with it differently."

"Knowing him, he'll tell Vernon to get himself down to the alehouse and let Mrs Ally deal with Lydia."

Billy grinned. "Sounds like a good idea to me."

"Billy Atkin, have you no shame?" Maria clipped the back of his head. "We've lost your niece and you're making fun of it."

"I'm not making fun. I'm very sorry about Maud, but the alehouse is a man's place of refuge. Dad could give him worse advice."

"Vernon should be at home with Lydia."

"How can he do that if she's living at her mam's?"

"Maybe she wouldn't be there if Vernon was more sympathetic." Maria flopped onto a chair and buried her face in her hands. "Don't any of you care?"

Nell put a finger to her lips to silence Billy. "You know we do, but we can't bring her back. We can only hope Lydia has a healthy baby in May."

The fire was burning low, and Nell was struggling to keep her eyes open when the front door closed and Billy joined her.

"You're still here."

"I was about to go upstairs." She put the magazine she'd been reading on the side table. "How was tonight?"

"The same as most other nights."

"Did Vernon join you?"

"He popped in for a quick one but then left to see Lydia. He wants her home."

"She's not left him, has she?"

Billy's face creased as he sat down. "Not officially, but she's been at her mam's since the funeral."

"Who's doing Vernon's cooking and washing?"

"He's been going to Mrs Ally's."

"So, they're still talking to each other?"

"After a fashion, but he never sees her on her own."

Nell leaned back in the chair. "Losing a child brings so much heartache. Lydia will never forget, but the pain will pass."

He studied her. "It sounds like you're speaking from experience."

"It was a long time ago."

"I don't remember it."

"It was shortly after I married your Uncle Jack, and we didn't live with you."

He clicked his teeth. "At least you have Elenor and Leah now. Dad was telling Vernon that the best thing she can do is focus on the next baby... Take her mind off Maud..."

A warm sensation rose up through her body until her cheeks burned. "It's not always as simple as that."

"I'm not trying to pry, but what do you mean?"

"Oh. Nothing really." She stood up and stepped away from the fire. "I should be going to bed. Goodnight."

"Night, Aunty Nell."

She felt his eyes following her as she left the room and, once she was in the bedroom, she leaned against the door, her heart pounding. *That was careless.* She gazed at Elenor and Leah as they lay side by side in the double bed. *It's been buried for so long; I need to make sure it never gets brought up again.*

CHAPTER TWENTY-SIX

Nell picked up the letter lying on the doormat as she let herself in, and held it in her teeth while she took off her cloak. Maria was in the kitchen when she found her.

"I didn't hear the postman. Did you meet him in the street?"

"No, you must have been beating that mixture too vigorously." Nell peered into the bowl of butter and sugar. "You're late doing that."

"Sarah called, so it set me back an hour. Tom's been out of bed today, so she left him by the fire while she nipped out."

"Did he have someone with him?"

"Ada's always there, but it was a treat for Sarah to leave the house. She's not been out for weeks."

"Let's hope he's on the mend, then. Perhaps I'll call tomorrow. I don't remember when I last saw him."

"Me neither." Maria nodded at the letter. "Who's writing to you?"

"Clara. She must have some news because I've not heard from her for a while."

"Did you fall out?"

Nell huffed as she sat down. "We had a difference of opinion about me going to Surrey, and when I wouldn't visit, things cooled somewhat."

"Why didn't you want to go?"

"Well … you wouldn't have been very pleased for one thing…"

"That didn't stop you going to sea for the best part of two years."

"Maybe I've become more considerate." She pulled three sheets of paper from the envelope. "What did I tell you? She's in the family way again. It's due in August."

"The other two can't be very old."

"No." Nell stopped to think. "Edward must be three, three and a half, and George will be coming up for eighteen months." *The same age as Maud.*

She continued reading to herself.

Lady Helen's rather envious of me having another child.

Nell tutted. *She's already got two boys. Isn't that enough?*

The thing is Ollie's spending more and more time in London, and she hardly sees him…

He'll be visiting his mistress in her fully furnished apartment, I shouldn't wonder. Nell clenched her teeth.

She's welcome to him. At least I can hold my head up high. Even if he did ruin my life.

Now he's never at home, perhaps you can visit...

She groaned. *Don't start that again. I'm not risking being within a hundred miles of him.*

Maria joined her in the living room. "What's all the muttering about?"

"What? I'm sorry, I didn't realise I was. I must have been engrossed."

"Have you fallen out with Mrs Robertson as well? You've not seen her for months."

"Not at all. Can you believe Violet's due to start school in September? So she's making the most of being able to travel with Captain Robertson."

"So won't you see her until the autumn?"

"I might. She said she wasn't going on all the voyages, but I'll have to wait for her to let me know when she's home."

"It will be a change for her when Violet's at school."

"She's not looking forward to it, but short of taking a governess with them, there's nothing she can do about it."

"Is she likely to do that?"

Nell shrugged. "She hasn't mentioned it, and I don't want to give her any ideas. I'd like to have someone to visit again."

~

There was a light drizzle in the air as Nell hurried to Sarah and Tom's the following afternoon, and she let herself in as soon as she arrived.

"It's only me. May I come in?"

Sarah met her at the living room door. "Are you on your own?"

"Yes, why?"

"Tom's downstairs for the second day running. Come on in."

The smile fell from Nell's face when Tom's gaunt face gazed up at her, his moustache too big for his face.

"Nell."

"T-Tom. What a change to see you out of bed. How are you feeling?"

"I can breathe without a pain in my chest and I'm not coughing so much, so things are looking up."

"That's good." She pulled up a chair from the table. "Maria sends her regards."

He nodded. "How is she? I heard about young Maud."

She's not so good, but she'll get over it. She's a tough nut."

"She is that." He wheezed as he took a breath. "And how are you?"

She tried to smile. "My social life is non-existent, but other than that, I'm fine."

"You never did like sitting around doing nothing. A word of advice, don't ever get consumption." He paused for breath. "You can't do much when you're like this."

"Are you able to go outside? Even into the yard? Some fresh air might do you good."

"I went out this morning until the rain came."

"Well, that's something." She fidgeted with her fingers. "Have you seen anything of Jane?"

He shook his head, but Sarah spoke for him. "She visits when she can, but Tom's been in bed the last few times she's called."

"You won't see much of her over the next few weeks with Betty's baby due anytime."

"She'll call when she has news."

Nell glanced at the clock. *I've not been here ten minutes.* "If you need anything, you know you've only to ask."

"We're fine for now." A guttural noise came from Tom's throat. "I'm hoping to be back at work soon. We can't rely on Ada and Len to keep us going indefinitely."

"You won't go back to the warehouse, will you? I thought that was what caused the problem in the first place."

"What choice do I have? I'm not up to making barrels."

"But even being in the warehouse must be hard work."

He looked at her with watery eyes. "That's why I'm here and not there. Give me time."

Nell waited for the front door to close behind her before she leaned against the wall of the house and squeezed her eyes tight. *How's it come to this? A strong, fit man like Tom...* She wiped her eyes with the back of a hand. *Maria can't see him like that. Or Rebecca. I shouldn't even speak to Jane about him. Not before the baby's born.* She took a deep breath and pushed herself off the wall. *I'll tell her he was out of bed.*

Maria looked up from her knitting as she went into the living room.

"You're early."

"Tom's still not well. He doesn't have the energy to talk for long."

"You saw him?"

"Yes." She managed a smile. "He was in the living room."

"That's a good sign. I'll call myself tomorrow."

"Actually, I wouldn't." Nell hesitated. "He says he feels better, but he looks dreadful. Give him a week or two to start eating again."

"Why can you see him and not me?"

Nell ran a hand over her face. "To be honest, I wish I hadn't. It's upsetting seeing him as he is, and with everything else that's going on, it may be too much for you. I sent him your regards."

"Has Jane been?"

"Only when he's been in bed; she's not seen him."

"What about Rebecca?"

"No."

Maria carried on with her knitting. "That's something. I don't want him cutting me out."

"He wouldn't do that. As long as you don't go for an argument."

"If only. It would be nice if he was well enough to argue with. This has been such a terrible year and we're still only in March."

"Things will get better. We have to believe that."

"I suppose so. I just can't find any joy in life since we lost Maud."

Nell took the seat opposite. "I know it's not easy, but you dealt with Fred's passing all those years ago. How did you get through that?"

"I didn't have time to grieve. George went away shortly after and left me with the rest of you. Thankfully, James and Billy were at school, but Vernon was only a baby, and I had you and Rebecca, too."

"Perhaps you've got too much time on your hands now."

"Was that your problem, too?"

Nell gasped. "Why've you brought that up?"

"Because you've been through it."

"And you know perfectly well the problems I had were nothing to do with being on my own." She stood up. "I'm going to put the kettle on. I don't want to talk about it.

CHAPTER TWENTY-SEVEN

Nell leaned over the crib as young Betsy Crane caught hold of her finger and gurgled.

"She's beautiful, Betty. You must be so relieved."

Betty sat with Albert on her knee. "I'm glad it's over and she's perfect. I can't tell you how worried me and Mam were after what happened to Maud."

"We all were, although we kept it to ourselves." Nell pulled her finger away and sat down. "Is she feeding all right?"

"Like a dream. I can't believe how different I feel compared to when I had him." She squeezed her son. "I must admit, I'm not looking forward to seeing Lydia or Vernon again. Alice told me Lydia's been living at her mam's and has only recently gone back to Vernon."

"She's been terribly upset, and Vernon hasn't known what to do."

"I'm not surprised. Bert never does either. At least her new baby will be here in a couple of months. Once she's had that, it should make things easier."

I hope so.

Betty sat back in her chair. "I remember how sorry for myself I felt when I lost the other babies, but they hadn't turned into real-life children. I couldn't imagine losing Albert."

"And you mustn't worry about it. You've two of them to look after now. They need you to be cheerful."

"I'm doing my best." She put Albert on the floor next to a pile of wooden blocks. "I'll put the kettle on."

"Is your mam calling today?"

"No, she's been every day for the last few weeks, so she was visiting Uncle Tom today. I believe he's not well."

Nell puffed out her cheeks. "That's an understatement. I saw him last week, and even though he said he felt better, he looked terrible. He can't get out of bed now, so goodness knows how bad he is."

"Mam's worried about Aunty Sarah. She knows what it's like to lose a husband."

"So do I."

Betty put a hand to her mouth. "I'm sorry, I forgot. It was before I knew you..."

"You don't need to apologise. It's been over six years now. These things fade."

"You do very well, though. I'm not sure Aunty Sarah will manage as well as you."

"I had a lot of help from Aunty Maria. She may come over as domineering, but I couldn't have managed without her."

"It won't be easy for her when Uncle Tom ... you know..."

Nell sighed. "That's the next thing I'm worrying about.

She's been so down after losing Maud, we've not told her how ill he is."

"I don't blame you, although I'm not sure I'd trust Mam not to say anything."

"She'll have to find out sooner or later. She'll just be mad if she finds out I knew but didn't tell her. Perhaps I'll tell her myself, later."

Betty put a tray of cups, saucers, milk and sugar on the table. "Oh, I was going to tell you. Mam had a letter the other day from one of our old neighbours in Ireland. His wife's recently died, and he's moving to England. He wondered if we could recommend anywhere to stay."

"If he wants to be in Toxteth, there are plenty of boarding houses on Windsor Street. What does he do for a living?"

"He's a tailor."

"That's handy. If he needs any contacts, Alice may be able to help."

Betty smiled. "I'd forgotten about that. It seems an age ago that she was working."

"She'd rather forget about it altogether. Do you know him well?"

"Not really. His name's Harry Wood, but he's older than me, so I didn't have anything to do with him."

"Still, he'll know your mam. When's he coming over?"

Betty screwed up her forehead. "I can't remember. I've not been thinking straight lately."

"With good reason. You've more important things to think about." Nell peered into the crib. "She's fast asleep. Shall I pour the tea? You've got enough to do without waiting on me."

. . .

Maria was on her own when Nell got home.

"Where's Alice?"

"She was at a loose end, so she walked up to school to get the girls."

"They'll like that. Or at least Leah will. I'm not sure Elenor appreciates being picked up any more. She thinks she's too old."

"It happens to them all." Maria stood up and wandered to the dresser. "This came earlier. From James." She passed Nell an envelope that had already been opened.

"Has Alice read it to you?"

"She has. He says that by the time we get the letter, he should be ready for home."

A smile crept across Nell's face. "That's good news. Let's see what else he has to say."

Sorry to hear about Maud. Send my condolences to everyone...

Enjoying my time here, but I'm preparing for my trip home ... the British community out here continues to grow ... small animals called monkeys are getting used to us and often come out of the forest. They have four legs and long tails and like to steal our food ... they use their tails to move from tree to tree ... I'll describe them better when I get home ...

I'll be leaving Manaus at the end of April so should be with you in early June... Don't bother writing back because I'll be on my way before your letter arrives... Looking forward to seeing you...

"He seems to be enjoying himself."

"Too much, if you ask me. He hardly said a word about Maud."

"She was the first thing he mentioned. What would you have him do, write a eulogy to her?"

"He could have written a bit more."

"He's probably busy."

"Not too busy to tell us about these creatures with long tails who live in the trees. It's more important to remember Maud."

Nell groaned. "It's because he knows I like to read about where he is. Why are you always so hard on him?"

"Because he should have given me a couple of grandchildren by now. If he had, I wouldn't be missing Maud so much."

Nell shook her head. *I think I'll tell her about Tom tomorrow.* "There's no talking to you when you're in one of these moods. You should be pleased he's on his way home."

"And I am, but did you notice he didn't tell us how long he's staying? He'd better be here for longer than he was last year. Ten days at home when he's not here for the rest of the year isn't enough."

"Which you made perfectly clear, but he can only take the time his employer gives him. Don't forget, he's away from Brazil for two months more than he stays with us."

"It's still not right."

Nell stood up and peered into the kitchen. "Is the tea ready, or do you want me to do anything?"

"It's all done."

"So, you didn't go out while I was at Betty's?"

"I nipped over to Rebecca's, but she was out."

"Perhaps she called at Tom's. She said she might."

"Good luck to her. Sarah's keeping everyone away at the moment."

For our own good. It's not pleasant seeing him as he is. "She'll let us see him when she can."

CHAPTER TWENTY-EIGHT

Despite it being close to midsummer, the room was dark as Nell followed Maria, Jane and Rebecca into Tom and Sarah's front bedroom. The elder of their children stood behind them as they lined up at the foot of the bed. The only light was from a solitary candle to Tom's left and Sarah positioned it so the glow fell onto the Book of Common Prayer in the vicar's hands.

He opened his arms to welcome them. "Who will separate us from the love of Christ? Whether we live or whether we die, we are the Lord's."

Nell gazed down at the brother who had been ever-present throughout her life. *This is it.* Her eyes flicked to Sarah, who stared resolutely at the vicar as he continued reading.

"This is indeed the will of my Father..."

Fifty-one. I suppose it's a good age. Although it's no age when you reach it...

Tom's face looked nothing more than skin and bone, his

raised eye sockets highlighting his sunken cheeks and thin lips. His eyes flickered open as the vicar laid his hands on his chest and Nell fancied she saw a look of recognition on Tom's face as his gaze met hers. The moment was lost as the vicar continued.

"Into your hands, O merciful Saviour, we commend your servant Thomas Parry..."

Sarah reached for Tom's hand as Nell fumbled for her handkerchief. *Rest in Peace, Tom.*

The rattle in Tom's chest was noticeable as the vicar recited the final prayer before making the sign of the cross and striding to the door.

"I'll leave you now."

Nell glanced around at her sisters as they bowed their heads over the bed. Maria looked stern, undoubtedly hiding the emotions she was feeling, while Jane and Rebecca sniffled into their handkerchiefs. *Jane will miss him the most. After Sarah, obviously.* She bit her lip as Sarah sobbed, gasping for breath. *It can't be long now.*

At eleven minutes past three, Sarah stood up from the chair by the bed and stopped the clock on the dressing table. Sam, her eldest son, took her cue and pulled the sheet over his father's face.

That's it. Nell pinched the bridge of her nose. *Another life gone.* There was a momentary pause before Maria walked to the bedroom door.

"I'll close the downstairs curtains."

Jane followed her, but Nell caught Rebecca's arm.

"He's at peace now."

"I know." Her voice squeaked. "This will be all of us soon though, won't it?"

Nell ushered her to the door. "Not necessarily. We're a good bit younger and Maria is fit enough, except for her legs."

"It still brings it home..."

"Come on. Where's your stiff upper lip?" She led the way down the stairs and into the living room, where Ada was pouring glasses of sherry. Nell accepted one. "He's in a better place."

"I'm not sure how we're going to manage without him." Ada pursed her lips, but her eyes were dry as she offered each of them a glass. "This might help."

Sam joined them before Nell could take a sip. "Mam's staying upstairs for now and I'll join her shortly." He picked up a glass and raised a toast. "To Dad. May he be forever in our thoughts."

Nell raised her glass. "To Tom."

Rebecca linked Nell's arm as they followed Maria and Jane from the house.

"We need to get our mourning dresses out again. I'd hoped I'd seen the back of them for a while."

Nell groaned. "It should be for the whole of summer too, although I don't plan on staying indoors until October."

Rebecca nodded. "Tom would understand. He wouldn't lock himself away."

"Not if there was an alehouse open."

"Perhaps we could start walking to school with the girls again. We're allowed to do that."

"Elenor won't be pleased. Not that's she's happy about anything at the moment."

"Be thankful she's another year to go. It's not been easy keeping Isobel occupied since she finished, and Hugh won't hear of her working."

"At least you have help with the housework."

Jane turned to wait for them at the turn-off to Merlin Street. "I'll see you soon."

Nell nodded. "Will you be all right walking home on your own?"

"It's only another hundred yards, and the boys will be back soon enough." She waved as she crossed the road, but they watched her walk to her front door before heading home.

Maria's shoulders sagged as she stood with them. "It's a good job I bought that boiled ham this morning. We won't have a lot of time to make tea before George and Billy are home."

Nell sighed. "We have a good reason. George will be upset when he hears, too. He wasn't expecting it today."

"If he is, he won't let on."

"Not to us, but he may in the alehouse." Nell released Rebecca's arm as they separated in the street. "See you tomorrow." She pushed open their front door but stared at the coat hanging in the hall before she barged into the living room. "What are you doing here?"

James smirked as Maria joined them. "We were early docking, so I thought I'd come straight here. Not that I expected to find an empty house. Even Alice was out when I arrived. I've never known it before. Congratulations on being a granny again. Baby Henry, I believe."

Maria removed her hat. "Thank you. Not that I feel much like celebrating today."

His face straightened. "Alice told me you were at Uncle Tom's..." He paused as he looked between them. "Has he gone?"

Maria nodded. "Eleven minutes past three."

"I'm sorry."

"I don't know what Sarah's going to do without him. I couldn't imagine losing your dad."

"Dad's made of sterner stuff. Uncle Tom's been ill on and off for years."

"But your dad's a lot older." She took a deep breath. "It's just too close for comfort."

Alice was by the back door. "You take a seat and I'll see to the tea. Shall I put the kettle on?"

Nell joined her in the kitchen. "I'll do it. I'd rather have something to do than sit around."

"How's Aunty Sarah?"

"Numb. Even though she knew he wouldn't get better. I don't think it's sunk in."

"What do you mean? She knew."

Nell counted to three before turning to Maria. "The doctor had said he couldn't do any more for him."

"How long have you known that?"

"A few weeks ... we didn't want to tell you so soon after Maud... And then with the new baby. You were so happy..."

"I still had a right to know... Had she told everyone else?"

"Not Rebecca."

"But she'd obviously spoken to Jane."

Nell sighed as she pulled up a chair. "We were only thinking of you. You were already in mourning..."

Maria leaned back and closed her eyes. "What a terrible year. Please, Lord, don't take anyone else. Not yet."

"We're all fit and healthy, so we should be fine. Now, let me make that tea."

Elenor squirmed at the table as Nell stared at her.

"Eat that all up. I don't want any left."

"I don't like cheese..."

Nell spoke through gritted teeth. "You can still eat it. Now don't make me cross. Not tonight."

"Not any night." Maria glared at her before turning to Billy. "I hope you're not going to the alehouse tonight."

Billy looked at George, who pushed himself up from the table.

"Why shouldn't we? Tom would expect no less."

"We're supposed to be in mourning."

"And if you think sitting here in silence will help, you're wrong. We've all got our armbands."

"Can't you even wait until after the funeral?"

"We need to tell everyone. There'll be a lot want to pay their respects."

Billy stood up as George passed him his cap. "I thought I'd call on Vernon first. He was close to Uncle Tom."

"For all the wrong reasons." Maria stared at James. "What about you? Are you going too?"

"I wasn't planning on it, but if you're going to be like that."

Nell patted him on the hand. "Your mam's upset, that's all."

George stared at his son. "You'll be paying Tom more respect if you come with us. It's the least you can do seeing you're never here. Will you still be at home for the funeral?"

"Assuming it's within the next week, then yes."

"A week?" Maria stared at him. "Are you only here for seven days?"

James stood up and reached for his jacket. "It's actually nine, but perhaps Dad's right. I should pay my respects at the alehouse." He smiled at Nell and Alice. "I'll see you later."

Nell waited for the front door to close before she picked up the teapot. "I'll top this up."

"It's not right when we're in full mourning."

"It's different for them. They still have to go to work."

"I'm not complaining about that. It's the socialising. I don't care what they say, they're not paying their respects."

"They are in their own way." Nell returned with the teapot. "Besides, would you rather they were here every night for the next four months?"

"I wish James was."

"Then why chase him away?" Nell shook her head. "One of these days, you'll learn to bite your tongue. You may find you're happier for it."

CHAPTER TWENTY-NINE

The sun was beating down on the flags in the backyard, and with no hint of a breeze, Nell wafted her face with a fan. She smiled at James as he joined her.

"Was Liverpool busy?"

"Busy enough for someone who's used to being in the middle of the jungle. Are you all right out here?"

She grimaced. "Not really. It's way too warm even holding this umbrella."

"You'd be better inside."

"It's so dark in there. I'll be glad when the funeral's over and I can take a walk. It's always cooler at the park than it is here."

James glanced around. "It's the high walls that do it. It's about this temperature in Brazil, but it feels different."

"Have you met anyone special out there?"

He tutted. "Did Mam get you to ask me?"

"No, she didn't, but I don't like to think of you being on your own."

"I'm not. There are a lot of ex-stewards with me now

and the town is very welcoming. We even have our own equivalent of an alehouse."

"So, you've no plans to come back?"

"I'm afraid not." He stared down at his feet. "What about your steward friend, Mr Marsh? Is he still in Australia?"

"I presume so. He said he wasn't coming back."

"I thought he may have changed his mind. It must have been quite an argument."

Nell grimaced. "It was nothing of the sort. We just realised there was no future for us."

"And you worry about me being on my own?"

"I'm hoping Elenor and Leah will look after me in my old age. Or at least their husbands."

James grinned. "Maybe they'll take in a lodger if I ever decide to come back."

"I'm sure they would for you." She peered through the living room window. "I take it your mam isn't home."

"I've not heard her."

"She'll be panicking at Sarah's because they've run out of time. I don't know what she'll do after tomorrow, because preparing the food has kept her going these last few days."

"She'll find something. Didn't you want to go with her?"

"Not really. Besides, there's not enough room for all of us. I promised to make the tea for tonight instead. What time is it?" She pulled out her pocket watch. "Gracious. Four o'clock. I'd better make a start."

Despite the clear sky the following afternoon, Nell shivered as she stood at the side of the grave with a piece of earth in her hand. Once Sarah's soil had landed on the coffin, she threw in her own and turned to leave, grateful for the veil on her hat.

She wandered to the footpath and dabbed her eyes as she waited for James and Billy.

"Are you all right, Aunty Nell?" James rested a hand on her shoulder.

"I will be. It was a nice service."

"Under the circumstances. I don't like to see you out here, though."

"I couldn't let your Aunty Sarah be the only woman here." She looked up at George as he joined them. "Are we ready to go?"

George nodded. "There's no point staying here."

Maria was at the house when they arrived, and she took Nell's arm and ushered her into the front room. "Come and sit by the fire. You shouldn't have gone to the grave."

Nell folded back her veil. "Sarah was there, and I've as much right to say farewell to Tom as anyone else."

Maria tutted. "Why are you always different? Just sit there and warm up."

"I'm not cold. Have you seen the weather? And I've just walked from the cemetery."

James interrupted as he handed Nell a glass of sherry. "One of these will do you more good than a lecture." He gave Maria a sideways glance.

"I'm only trying to look after her."

"She's not a child."

Nell winced as her sister disappeared. "You shouldn't have said that. Not today."

"I'm sorry, but she needs telling. She'll still be mothering you when you're sixty."

Nell patted the chair beside her. "Sit down and take a deep breath."

He did as he was told. "You deal with her far better than me."

"There's not a lot of choice."

He glanced around the room. "Has anyone said how Aunty Sarah's going to manage now she's a widow?"

"What do you mean?"

"With the house. Will she be able to afford to stay here?"

"I don't know. I'd assumed so, with Len and Ada working. They've been supporting the family while Uncle Tom was ill, and that's quite a few months."

"I suppose so. It's to be hoped neither of them wants to marry in a hurry."

"I've not heard that either of them is walking out with anyone, so they should be fine for another year or two." Nell looked towards the door. "Are people eating yet? I'm ready for something."

"Let's find out." James led her into the living room, where Betty and Alice were near the table.

"Here you are." Betty smiled at her. "I didn't realise you'd gone to the grave."

"I wanted to pay my respects." She studied the faces around her. "Did Lydia not come in the end?"

Alice shook her head. "She couldn't bring herself to, not that she could have left the new baby with anyone."

Nell nodded. "That's true. Uncle Tom wasn't directly family for her, either. Are your two with Mr Crane's mam, Betty?"

"They are. I know this is supposed to be a sombre affair, but it's rather nice having some time to myself."

"Then make the most of it." Nell emptied her sherry glass. "I need something to eat now I've had that. Will you excuse me?"

Jane was already at the table when she went to collect a plate. "Good afternoon, Nell."

"Good afternoon. The spread looks nice. Did you help with any of the baking?"

"Gracious, no. When do I bake?" She leaned in with a furtive glance. "I gave Maria moral support, though."

Nell rolled her eyes at her before she reached for a piece of pork pie. "I'm not sure if that was a joke, but I noticed the two of you getting along better this week. Has Tom's death brought you both to your senses?"

Jane shrugged. "I've been no different."

"It must be Maria, then. She's been rather subdued since he passed. It hit her hard with her being the eldest, and George being older again."

"Neither are close to their three score years and ten, though. Tom obviously had a delicate constitution."

"I hope you're right. And what about you? How will you manage without him? He's been very good to you since you moved back from Ireland."

"He has, but I've still got George." She chuckled as Nell's mouth fell open. "I'm teasing. I won't do anything I shouldn't. You should know me by now. I like to tease." She leaned in closer and lowered her voice. "Being serious for a minute, I've an idea for Sarah that may help me as well."

Nell raised an eyebrow. "Have you told Sarah?"

"Not yet. The timing's not been right."

"Are you going to tell me?"

She glanced towards the kitchen where Sarah was putting out more cakes and ushered Nell into a corner of the room. "I had a letter several months ago from the son of one of my old neighbours in Ireland."

"Betty mentioned him. He's coming to Liverpool, isn't he?"

"He's already here, living in a boarding house on the dock road. Anyway, he's not happy. He writes to me occasionally, which is what made me think. Sarah's going to need an extra income, and he'd like to live with a family, so why not introduce them?"

"That seems reasonable." Nell's eyes narrowed. "What's in it for you?"

"Well, if I'm introducing them, I could ask for a commission ... or take a small weekly fee ... or both..."

Nell tutted. "You really are the limit. Sarah needs the money, and I doubt this young man will earn enough to keep both of you."

"I need to live, too. Tom used to slip me a bob or two when he was working, so I've not had anything for a while."

"You've managed, though. You should be taking in more mending now both boys are out all day every day."

Jane sighed. "You are a spoilsport."

"I'm not, but I know what you're like. As for the other part of your idea, I think it's a good one."

"You do? I'll mention it to her, then. Not today, obviously."

"I should hope not today. Have you said anything to the young man?"

"Not yet, but I'll write to him this week. We should have a family gathering to meet him."

"I'm sure that won't be necessary, but if you want to bring him round for a cup of tea, you're more than welcome."

CHAPTER THIRTY

James wrapped an arm around Maria's shoulders and gave her a squeeze before he did the same to Alice and finally Nell.

"I'll see you all next year."

Maria wiped her eyes. "Next time, I expect you to stay for good."

His face tensed. "I've a job to do, Mam, and I'll be back to stay when I'm ready." He raised an arm in a wave and headed off towards Windsor Street.

"Time passes so quickly when he's here."

Nell nodded. "It does. Still, he's happy and that's the main thing."

Elenor and Leah were at the table when they went back inside, and Nell checked the clock.

"We've time for another cup of tea before we tidy up this lot. Do you have any plans for today?"

"I'm bleaching the flags in the yard. With one thing and another, they've not been done this year."

"Oh." *There goes my afternoon of sitting outside.*

"Perhaps I'll walk to the park, then. Rebecca would like that."

"You can't go out. Tom's not been dead a fortnight."

"Me staying in won't bring him back, and two sisters in mourning is hardly socialising."

Maria tutted. "I don't know what this world's coming to."

Nell glanced at Alice. "Are you seeing Betty today, too?"

"I was going to. I don't need to be in mourning for as long as you."

"Well, I hope Aunty Sarah doesn't see you."

Nell tutted. "Well, if she does, it's because she's out as well. We can't all stay locked up for the rest of the year."

Alice nodded "I'm not going to Everton, either. Betty's coming here and I'm meeting her at Aunty Jane's. I'm hoping we can walk to the park ourselves this afternoon."

Maria stood up. "Well, you can do the fires and sweep the floors while I do the windows, then. Nell, you turn the beds. I don't want the place neglected while you both go swanning off."

Nell straightened up and stretched her back when the last of the beds were made. *Was that the postman? It's a good time to stop if it was.* She ventured downstairs and found Maria in the front room. "Are you ready for a cup of tea?"

"Give me another five minutes."

Nell looked at the doormat. "Didn't I hear the postman?"

"It's on the dresser."

She wandered into the living room and smiled at the handwriting. *Mrs Robertson. I hope this means she's home.* She sliced open the top of the envelope and sat down.

> *...we arrived in Liverpool last week, but I'm not sailing again until next month. If you'd like to visit, any day will do. I'll look forward to it...*

Splendid. I'll go after dinner. She flinched as Maria joined her. "I thought you were putting the kettle on."

"Sorry. The letter was from Mrs Robertson, and I got distracted."

"Is she home?"

"She is, and she's here for the next few weeks. I'll pay her a visit this afternoon."

"You said you were going out with Rebecca."

"I haven't mentioned it to her, so we can go tomorrow. If I see Mrs Robertson today, I should be able to fit in another couple of visits before she leaves again."

Maria sighed. "Do I have to keep reminding you you're in mourning? Visiting Mrs Robertson counts as socialising."

Nell groaned. "I don't care. I've not seen her for months and it may be September before she's home again. If anyone asks why I'm out in mourning clothes, I'll tell them I'm on an errand."

Once dinner was over, Nell and Alice walked down Elaine Street together and Nell waved to her as they reached Jane's house. "Enjoy the park if you go."

Alice looked up at the sky. "We will. You have a nice

afternoon."

"I will. We've so much to catch up on."

The walk to Everton was pleasant and Mrs Robertson's face lit up as the housekeeper showed her into the drawing room. "You didn't waste any time ... but the dress..."

Nell ran her hands over her black skirt. "My brother. The one who was always skiving off work. It seems he was more ill than we thought."

"I'm sorry. He leaves a family, doesn't he?"

"A wife and eight children, although, thankfully, most of them are grown up. Only the youngest is still at school and she'll leave next year."

"You should have written to let me know. I wouldn't have expected you to call."

"Not at all. I've been stuck at home for long enough already. That's why I came today."

"Well, I'm very glad you did."

Nell studied the room. "What have you done with Violet?"

"She'll be here later, but with her due to start school in September, I wanted to try out a couple of governesses."

"To take on the ship?"

"That's the plan. It will be expensive, but hopefully worth it if it means we can continue going to sea. Besides, we plan on saving money by not paying rent for this." She glanced round the overfilled room.

"So, you'd give it up ... and not come back?" Nell's eyes widened.

"Our home port would still be Liverpool, but I'd stay on the ship while we're docked. Like I used to. Don't look so worried. I'd invite you on board while we were here."

"Or you could take a carriage to Toxteth, and we could walk around the parks. Give your legs a stretch."

Mrs Robertson smiled. "I'd like that, if it all goes to plan. I just need to see these governesses first."

"I'm sorry. I must be interrupting. Should you be watching over them?"

"Not yet. Today is to see if Violet takes to this one."

"Oh, good." Nell sighed. "Is that why you're staying in Liverpool for so long?"

"It is. My husband leaves in the morning. Only to Boston." She paused while the housekeeper delivered the tea tray. "I'll miss this voyage, but I should have decided on someone by the time he comes back."

"So, how was the latest trip? I presume Violet's happy on board?"

"She is and the matron and the stewardesses dote on her, which helps when I want to go to dinner."

"It sounds wonderful..."

"I'm very fortunate. We had one of your old colleagues from the *Bohemian* on the most recent voyage. Mr Cooper. Do you remember him?"

Nell's forehead creased before she caught her breath. "Yes! He was the one who thought women shouldn't work on board. He tried to keep us in the ladies-only section."

"I don't remember that."

"It was before I met you, but he caused havoc when he was made head steward."

Mrs Robertson's eyebrows drew together. "Head steward?"

"It didn't last long. He created so many problems, he was sent to steerage."

"Ah. That explains it. He's in first-class now, but only as a regular steward. I didn't recognise him to start with, but he remembered me. I think he was trying to get out of doing something, so we ended up having quite a chat."

Nell pursed her lips. *I'm surprised he knows how to speak to women. Maybe the captain's wife is different.* "I heard he'd gone to Australia."

"He did, for several years, but realised he was missing home and came back."

"He doesn't strike me as the type to miss anyone. I had him down as a bit of a loner."

"Perhaps he's mellowed. He told me he's seen some of the other stewards too. Do you remember Mr Cunningham...?"

"Do I ever. He was responsible for spreading cholera around the ship and he didn't even get a formal warning from what I understand."

"Ah. Well, he's working the Australia route now."

"Causing so much trouble hasn't inconvenienced him, then."

"Did you expect it to?"

"Not really."

"Mr Cooper said he'd bumped into Mr Ramsbottom in South Africa, too."

"Really!" Nell shook her head. "He caused me no end of problems. I hope they're keeping him away from the female passengers and stewardesses."

"It's not easy now there are so few male-only ships. He must have improved though, because he's met someone and was planning to get married when Mr Cooper spoke to him."

Nell smiled. "I'm glad for him. I think that was all he ever wanted. He just picked the wrong person when he came after me. Oh, well, tell Mr Cooper that if he sees him again, to send my regards."

Mrs Robertson stood up to pour the tea. "There is one other steward he's in touch with."

Nell stared at her, unable to take the cup and saucer being offered. "You're going to say Mr Marsh, aren't you?"

"Apparently, they correspond with each other, although I don't know how." Mrs Robertson put the tea on the tray and sat down.

"I-is he still in Australia?"

"I believe so."

"That's the best part of two years he's been away."

Mrs Robertson raised an eyebrow. "You have a good memory for dates."

"I had nightmares about the way he left, for months after. Do you know…?" She took a breath. "Did he say if he has any plans to come back?"

"I don't. But I could find out…"

"No. Don't go to any trouble. I-I just wondered if I was likely to bump into him."

"Do you want to see him again?"

"There wouldn't be any point. I wrote to him shortly after he left to explain that I was only a friend to Ollie, but he basically said he didn't believe me."

"You still like him, don't you?"

"I wish he wasn't so uptight and quick to judge…"

"You never know. Maybe time's mellowed him, too."

Nell huffed. "I doubt I'll ever find out."

CHAPTER THIRTY-ONE

Maria was on her own when Nell arrived home, and she bustled to the table with a fresh loaf of bread.

"I'm glad someone's bothered to come back."

"Isn't Alice here?"

"I've not seen anyone since the girls took themselves off to school."

"That's strange. Perhaps Alice walked to meet them."

"I wish she hadn't. A little help wouldn't go amiss."

Nell sighed. "What do you want me to do?"

"Nothing now, it's done."

"I'm sorry, but it's a two-hour walk to Everton and back, not to mention the time I spend with Mrs Robertson."

"I know that. It's Alice I'm cross with. She only went around the corner."

"Leave her. It's not often Betty comes over." Nell paused as the front door sounded. "This will be her. Try putting a smile on your face."

Alice stopped in the doorway as they both looked at her. "What's the matter?"

Nell smiled. "Nothing. I expected you home before me, that's all. Have you had a nice afternoon?"

"It was different."

"Didn't you go to the park?"

"We did, but when we got to Aunty Jane's, she had a visitor. A man."

Maria's brow creased. "What do you mean? Has she found herself a gentleman friend?"

"Not at all. His name's Mr Wood and he used to be her neighbour in Ireland."

Maria sniffed. "Don't tell me he's a Catholic."

"I ... erm ... I didn't ask."

"It doesn't matter whether he is or not." Nell rolled her eyes, but Maria ignored her.

"I hope she wasn't on her own with him in that room."

"They were in the shared living room downstairs. Aunty Jane wanted us to meet him before she took him to Aunty Sarah's."

Maria stopped what she was doing. "Why would she do that?"

Alice glanced at Nell, and Maria immediately followed her gaze.

"What do you know about this?"

"Not much. Only that Mr Wood is the son of her old neighbour and he's looking for somewhere to live in Liverpool. Now Sarah's on her own, Jane suggested she could take him in as a lodger."

"How long have you known this?"

"Only since the funeral..."

"That's nearly a week ago."

Nell sighed. "People might tell you more if you didn't

judge everything they say." She turned to Alice. "Did he go to Aunty Sarah's?"

Her niece's cheeks coloured. "There wasn't time. He sat with us while we had a cup of tea and when we looked at the clock, it was too late."

Maria's eyes narrowed. "What does that mean?"

"We were talking..."

Nell interrupted. "Betty told me he's a tailor's assistant, so I expect you had a lot in common."

Alice's face brightened. "That's right. He has a job in Liverpool, but he's not happy with it, so I was telling him about other places he might try."

"He must be living somewhere, if he's working. Why would he want to move in with Sarah?"

Nell tutted. "She needs the money, and he'd prefer something more homely. He's in a boarding house on the dock road at the moment."

"It sounds as if they've got it all worked out. What's he like?"

Alice gulped. "He ... erm ... he's very nice."

"I told Jane she could bring him here for a cup of tea if she wanted to introduce him."

"Why would she do that for a lodger?"

Nell shrugged. "She seemed keen for us to meet him ... to help him settle in."

The following afternoon, Nell knocked on Rebecca's front door and let herself in.

"Are you ready to go?"

"I am." Rebecca picked up a parasol. "Is this too bright, given we're in mourning? I don't have a black one."

Nell stared at the cream flowered material. "It doesn't exactly match, but if it keeps the sun off you. Could you put some crepe over it?"

"Not in a hurry. I should have thought of that earlier." She placed it in the umbrella stand. "I'd better go without it. At least this hat has a wide rim."

Nell touched her own summer bonnet. "It's wider than this one. We'd better stay under the trees."

"After you, then."

Rebecca studied her as they walked. "How long will you stay in mourning?"

Nell huffed. "I don't know. I expect Maria will do the full four months, but I only managed three for Jack when it should have been two years."

"You had good reason, though."

Nell nodded. "We'd have starved if I hadn't been allowed to work for so long. The people who come up with these rules have no idea..."

"Thankfully, neither of us is desperate."

"But we could be. How about we aim for a month? That should keep Maria happy."

Rebecca smirked. "I will if you do."

The park was busy and Nell stood beside the lake with her hands on her hips. "Not a spare seat in sight. We should have gone to Sefton Park instead."

"It doesn't look as if anyone's about to leave, either."

"I don't blame them." Nell huffed. "Maybe it's God's

way of telling us we shouldn't be out. Shall we go home for a cup of tea?"

"We don't have a lot of choice unless we want to keep walking." They turned to head for home. "What sort of mood was Maria in when you left?"

"She was all right. Alice was in her bad books yesterday because she was with Betty for hours, so she stayed in with her today."

"You can't blame her for being out so long. It's a good walk up to Everton..."

"The problem was that Betty was at Jane's, so she hadn't gone far. She was late because Jane had a visitor. The son of one of her old neighbours from Ireland. Have you heard about him?"

"You know me. I'm always the last to find out anything. What's he doing over here?"

"He's come to settle, and Jane thought he'd be a good lodger for Sarah."

"Does Sarah know?"

Nell laughed. "She does now. They're going to meet her later."

"Have you met him?"

"Not yet. It might be a bit intimidating if he met us all at once."

"He can manage if he's come over here on his own. Besides, it's only Maria he need worry about."

"Don't we all."

Nell pushed open the front door when they reached the house, but she turned to Rebecca before she stepped inside. "We have visitors."

"Who?"

Nell paused to listen. "Jane ... and a man. Mr Wood?"

Rebecca squealed. "How exciting." She followed Nell into the living room. "Good afternoon."

Maria looked up at them. "I wasn't expecting you so soon."

Nell felt the side of the teapot. "The park was so busy we couldn't find a seat, so we decided to come back. I'm glad we did. You must be Mr Wood." She smiled at a young man with neatly combed light brown hair and a pencil moustache.

He towered over her as he stood up. "I am, but I'm afraid you have me at a disadvantage."

"Give me a minute." Jane tutted. "These are my sisters, Mrs Riley and Mrs Grayson."

"Then I'm very pleased to meet you. I'm still confused, though. Alice was telling me yesterday of an Aunty Nell, who lives here. Do either of you respond to that title."

Nell grinned at the twinkle in his green eyes. "That would be me. And for completeness, this is Aunty Rebecca."

"Ah. That makes more sense. I believe you live over the road."

"I do indeed." Rebecca took a seat as Nell disappeared into the kitchen with the teapot. "Where's Alice? We thought she was staying in this afternoon."

"She had to go to the shop. I'd forgotten the butter." Maria's voice was less than convincing, and Nell peered into the pantry. *We have butter*.

Maria continued with an edge to her voice. "Is there anything Alice didn't tell you yesterday? You seem to know a lot about us."

"We had quite a chat. She's a lovely girl."

"She is indeed. She's also only twenty-one."

Nell grimaced at the image of Maria glaring at the young man and headed into the living room. "It doesn't matter whether she's eleven, twenty-one, or thirty-one, she'll always be a lovely girl." She shot Maria a look, but Mr Wood appeared unfazed.

"I hear she's been very good to Betty."

"She's good to us all." Nell put the teapot on the table and collected some cups and saucers from the dresser. "My daughters love her."

"I heard about them, too."

Nell glanced across at Maria. "This will explain why Alice was late home yesterday. Did she get your family history, too?"

He laughed. "We'd still be there if I tried. Mam was one of eight, Dad one of ten, and I've a brother and two sisters."

Maria glowered at Nell. "He was about to tell us why he's left them all to come here."

"We were in good time, then." Nell gave the teapot a stir. "Would everyone like a top-up before he starts?"

"There's not much to tell, really. Belfast isn't a safe place at the moment. It's being overrun with Catholics, and with the tensions rising, I decided I'd rather stay out of trouble."

Maria's face softened. "So, you're not one of them? A Catholic, I mean."

"I am not. I'm a proud Belfast Protestant." His rough Irish accent was suddenly accentuated. "After last year's riots, many of us are choosing to leave, and Liverpool or

Glasgow are the closest cities to Belfast. Given I knew Mrs Read, it made sense to come here."

Nell's forehead creased. "Surely, if all Protestants leave, you'll be handing the city to the Catholics."

He sighed. "You may be right, but I'm a man of peace, as most of us are, but there are plenty who are ready for the fight."

Jane patted his hand. "He's a good lad. You looked after your mam while she needed you, didn't you?"

"I'm hardly that. I'm thirty this year and already a widow."

"A widow?" Maria's eyes widened.

"Sadly, my wife was taken from me last year, along with our child. A son. He would have been our first."

"I'm sorry."

"It made it easier to leave. I've no memories over here."

"What about the rest of your family?"

"They're all settled. My elder sister married shortly after Mam left us, and the younger one lives with my brother."

Maria relaxed into the chair. "That's something."

He nodded. "Do I pass?"

Nell put a hand over her mouth to cover her smile as Maria fumbled with her teaspoon.

"I-it wasn't a test. I just like to know what's what. It's a big thing, having someone move in with my sister-in-law when my brother hasn't long been gone..."

Nell gave him a grin as she stood up to offer him a biscuit. "I'd say you did."

CHAPTER THIRTY-TWO

Nell swivelled in her seat as a young woman in uniform brought Violet into the Robertsons' drawing room before leaving them again.

"She's the governess you've chosen, is she?"

"She is." Mrs Robertson looked down at Violet. "You like her, don't you?"

"Yes."

"Then I hope it works out for you." She stood up and reached for her bag. "I'm afraid it's time I was leaving."

Mrs Robertson joined her by the fire. "I'll be in touch. We'll be in Liverpool this time next month, if you'd like to call."

"Will you still be here?"

"We will. I want to make sure we can all manage on board before we pack up our personal possessions."

Nell bent down to Violet. "I'll see you next month, then."

Mrs Robertson walked her to the front door, and with a final wave to Violet, Nell left the house and turned onto the main road to head for home. *Why aren't there more parks in this part of town? Mrs Robertson would enjoy a walk if she had the chance.* She glanced up at the clear blue sky. *Especially in weather like this.*

She cut through to St George's Hall and passed the Adelphi as she headed towards the rows of Georgian houses beyond. She was almost at the junction with Upper Parliament Street when her pace slowed and she edged towards the houses. *Is that Alice? And Mr Wood?* She waited while they crossed the road, before following them at a safe distance along Windsor Street. *He's not been here a month and they're linking arms.* They stopped on the corner of Elaine Street and stood gazing at each other before Alice gave Mr Wood a discreet wave and continued on her way. *Goodness!* Mr Wood watched her until she disappeared down Merlin Street, before he turned for home.

He'd vanished by the time Nell reached the spot where they'd stood and she followed Alice, slowing her pace so as not to arrive too soon after her.

Maria was laying the table when she arrived, and Nell smiled as she joined her.

"Are you on your own?"

"No, Alice is in the kitchen. She's not long been in."

Nell peered through the door. "I didn't see you there. Have you had a nice afternoon?"

"Yes. I walked up to Betty's."

"How is she?"

"Fine. Betsy's getting stronger. She can hold her head up without support now."

"That's good. I'll call up there myself this week."

"Oh. Tell me when you're going, so we're not there together."

"It wouldn't matter if we were."

"No, but ... I'm sure she'd prefer separate visits rather than two people in one day."

"Is Aunty Jane usually there?"

"I've not seen her recently, but–" Alice pursed her lips "–she leaves before I get there."

"I told her she needs to spend more time doing the sewing she takes in, so maybe she listened."

Alice's shoulders relaxed. "That must be it."

"Sarah called earlier." Maria lifted the cups and saucers from the dresser and set them on the table. "She seems happy having Mr Wood as a lodger. She says he's polite and it's a relief having the extra money."

"I'm sure it is." Nell studied Alice as she stirred a pot on the top of the range. "Did he find a new job?"

"Erm ... I think so. Betty mentioned something. I'm not sure where, though."

"I'm surprised he hasn't let you know."

"Why would he? I-I've not seen him."

"But you were the one who told him where the best tailors are. He seems the sort who'd call to thank you."

Alice's cheeks coloured. "He's probably not had time."

Or perhaps you're not being honest with me. Why would that be?

~

The walk to Betty's was even further than to Mrs Robertson's, and Nell was relieved to sit down as Betty brewed a pot of tea.

"I can't believe how Betsy's growing." She sat the child on her knee and bounced her up and down as she laughed at the movement. "She's such a love. I didn't appreciate my two when they were this age. I was too busy doing everything else."

Betty shouted through from the small kitchen. "You had Aunty Maria to help you."

"I still did most of the washing and feeding myself. Once I'd had Leah, it felt as if I didn't have a minute."

Betty laughed. "Aunty Maria could hardly feed them for you."

"I know. It didn't help that Elenor was so slow, either. I'd sit with her for hours."

"At least she's grown up fit and healthy."

"She has. You seem to manage better than I ever did. Do you have many visitors?"

"There's someone here most afternoons. Mam mainly, but Bert's mam's here a couple of times a week and Alice, obviously."

"I hear she comes most days."

"Not that often, usually three times a week."

Nell studied Betty as she set down two cups of tea and handed Albert a biscuit. "Does she confide in you?"

"Sometimes... Why?" Betty's smile disappeared.

"What do you know about her and Mr Wood?"

"Mr Wood?" Betty's voice squeaked. "What is there to know?"

"That's what I'm wondering."

"They get on well together, but there's no more to it than that."

Nell raised an eyebrow. "Really?"

"All right, she told me she likes him."

"And he likes her?"

"Yes."

"Has she told you they're walking out together?"

Betty fell silent as she added two teaspoons of sugar to her tea.

"Don't worry, I won't tell her we've spoken, but I saw them the other day, yet she claimed not to have seen him."

Betty sighed. "She's frightened of what Aunty Maria will say."

"That doesn't surprise me, but I can't help worrying about her. Mr Wood's a lot older, and a widower. Men like that have needs ... as you well know."

Betty's cheeks flushed. "I've warned her about that, but she says he's a perfect gentleman."

Nell rubbed a hand over her face. "Can you imagine Aunty Maria if Alice had to have the same conversation with her that you had with your mam?"

Betty shuddered. "It doesn't bear thinking about."

"You will keep an eye on her, won't you? Don't let her do anything foolish."

"I'll try my best."

Nell turned her attention back to Betsy, who'd become bored. "It will be practice for when she grows up."

Betty took her daughter from Nell and held her close. "It's such a worry having girls."

Nell grimaced as she picked up her tea. "And I have two of them."

. . .

There was no sign of Alice when Nell arrived home, even though Elenor and Leah were at the dining table. She took a seat beside Leah.

"Did you have a nice day at school?"

"We've finished now. We don't go again for weeeeeeks."

Nell laughed. "Are you glad about that?"

"I am." Elenor interrupted. "When can I stop going? Isobel hasn't been for ages."

"When you're the same age as she was. She's older than you."

Leah grinned. "We did painting this afternoon."

"What did you paint?"

"A picture of you!" Leah pointed at her. "I had to leave it at school, though. It was wet."

"Did you paint, too?" She looked at Elenor, who sat with a pout on her face.

"We had to do darning." She held out her hands. "Look. They're all sore."

"You'll get better at it, and at least you don't need to do it for a few weeks."

Maria appeared from the kitchen. "I was going to give her some of George and Billy's socks to darn, so she doesn't forget."

Elenor banged her elbows on the table. "I don't want to."

"You'll do as you're told, young lady. You won't find a husband if you don't know how to look after him."

"I don't want a husband."

"You'll go hungry then."

Nell held up a hand. "There's no need to make a fuss. She's only nine."

"She has to learn..." Maria disappeared into the kitchen.

"Is Alice not home yet?"

"No. She was going to the park with Miss Hopkins."

Really? Nell pursed her lips. *That might be what she told you.*

CHAPTER THIRTY-THREE

Church was over for another Sunday, and Nell followed Alice out of the pew. "Are you ready to walk home?"

Alice glanced around, her eyes lingering for longer than necessary on Mr Wood. "I ... erm ..."

Nell nodded towards him as he stood with Sarah and her son. "Are you hoping to speak to him?"

"I-I was wondering how his job was going ... but I can't approach him on my own."

"We could go together to see Aunty Sarah."

"I couldn't..." She paused as Mr Wood spotted them and walked over, the usual grin on his face.

"Good morning, ladies. How are you today?"

Nell smiled. "Very well, thank you."

"Y-yes." Alice's cheeks were pink. "A-are you enjoying your job?"

"Yes. Thanks to you. It's much better than the last one." His eyes didn't leave her face and Nell shuffled her feet as she glanced around.

"Where are you working now?"

Mr Wood flinched as she spoke. "The menswear department of Lewis's, the store opposite the Adelphi. Do you know it?"

Oh yes. "It's a smart place."

"It is. I'm amazed at how many men want suits making. You can tell there are more clerks in Liverpool than there were in Belfast."

"It should keep you busy, then."

"I hope so." He studied Alice. "Are you about to leave? Perhaps I could walk you and your aunty home."

She hesitated and turned to Nell. "Are you happy for Mr Wood to join us?"

"That would be nice." Nell looked around. "Let me check the girls are with your mam and I'll be right with you."

Nell shielded her eyes from the sun as they left church and sauntered through the churchyard.

"It's going to be warm this afternoon. It would be lovely in the park, if I had anyone to go with. One downside of Sundays is that the men are at home."

Mr Wood grinned at her. "We are allowed one day a week off. Won't you be taking the girls to Sunday school?"

"They take themselves, nowadays, although there isn't any today. The teacher's gone to visit her family."

Alice's face brightened. "We could take them to feed the ducks. They'll like that."

Mr Wood smiled at Alice. "I might meet you there, then. I thought I'd do some exploring myself this afternoon."

"Why not come with us and we'll show you round...?"

Her cheeks turned crimson. "If you don't mind, Aunty Nell."

Nell studied the two of them. "Not at all." *It will be an opportunity to get to know Mr Wood better.*

Nell and Alice were the first home, and Nell went to the range to check the meat.

"Your dad and Billy must have gone to the alehouse, but I don't know what's keeping your mam."

"She wanted a word with Aunty Sarah, so they're probably talking."

Nell slid a pan of cabbage onto the heat. "Mr Wood's a nice man."

"He is."

"He seems to like you, too."

Alice carried some plates to the table. "He's only being friendly."

"Are you sure that's all it is?" Nell took a deep breath. "I saw you walking together and it looked like more than friendship."

Alice gasped as she spun round.

"Why are you keeping it a secret?"

"I ... because ..." Alice's shoulders sagged. "You know what Mam's like."

Nell tried to keep her voice steady. "Is it serious then?"

"No. Not at all. I've not known him long."

"That needn't matter if you find the right man..."

"We enjoy being together..."

Nell studied her. "You won't do anything silly, will you? Like Betty did."

Alice turned her back to her. "I wouldn't dream of it. And neither would he. He's a gentleman."

"He's also a lot older than you ... and he's been married before."

Alice's cheeks were crimson. "That's why Mam can't find out. You won't tell her, will you? Not yet. She'll only spoil things."

"You can't keep pretending to walk to Betty's every day."

"I don't pretend, but he walks me there in his dinner hour, and I walk past Lewis's on the way home and we walk home together."

"That's why you've been late of an evening?"

"Is it obvious?"

"I guessed something was going on, but possibly only noticed because I'd seen you. I don't think your mam suspects anything, but you need to be careful."

"We will be."

"I'm not talking about him. It's you I'm worried about. It's easy to have your head turned and then..." She stopped as the front door opened and Maria bustled in.

"Here you are. I was waiting for you at church." She looked at Elenor and Leah. "Go and wash your hands before Uncle George comes home."

"I'm sorry. I didn't see you when I left, so I thought you'd already gone."

"I was talking to Sarah. I wanted to ask what she thinks of her new lodger and make sure she's managing. It still doesn't seem right, her having a strange man in the house."

"He's not strange..." Alice stopped abruptly. "He's a friend of Aunty Jane's. That's got to count for something."

Maria pointed a finger at her daughter. "Don't think I haven't seen the way you look at him. I don't want you having anything to do with him. He's far too old."

Alice stared at the floor. "I can't be rude if he speaks to me."

"I'm not asking you to be rude. I'm telling you not to be overfamiliar. Men like him don't need any encouragement..."

"Mam!"

"Mam, nothing. I've not forgotten what it's like to be twenty-one."

Nell interrupted. "You were married with a baby before then."

"That makes no difference. I've still seen women's lives ruined, and I don't intend to sit by and watch you make the same mistakes."

Nell put an arm around Maria's shoulders and ushered her to the kitchen. "That's enough. She's a grown woman..."

"That's the problem."

"All right, I'll keep an eye on her. Now, not another word. George and Billy are here."

The sun was warm on Nell's back as she stood by the lake in Princes Park. Elenor and Leah broke up their bread and threw it to the ducks, but Nell was more interested in Alice and Mr Wood as they sat at opposite ends of a bench further along the footpath. *Should I offer to be her unofficial chaperone? What would Maria say if she found out?* She shook her head. *Alice is old enough. If she wants to meet with Mr Wood, it should be her choice.* She huffed. *When has that ever made any difference to Maria? I'll be forty next year and she still interferes.*

"Mam, I've run out of bread." She looked down to see Leah holding out her empty hands.

"Does Elenor have any left?"

Elenor put her hands behind her back. "It's mine."

Nell sighed. "I'm not saying it isn't, but it's time to go when it's gone."

"Well, it's not."

Nell stroked Leah's head. "You'll have to watch the ducks eat everyone else's bread."

Leah's dark curls fell down her back as she looked up. "I don't want to. May I go to Alice? She looks lonely over there." Her forehead creased. "Why isn't she standing with us like she usually does?"

"Her ... erm ... her leg was hurting, so she wanted to sit down. Wait until Elenor has finished and then we'll all go."

Leah ran to Elenor and pushed her shoulder. "Hurry up. Alice is waiting for you."

Nell closed her eyes. "No, she's not. She's watching you. Wave to her."

Alice waved back.

"There, see."

Elenor threw her last piece of bread and wiped her hands on her dress. "Why's that man talking to her?"

"He's the one who moved in with Aunty Sarah."

"Why did he move in?"

"Because Uncle Tom's not with us any more and she needed the money."

Elenor cocked her head to one side and studied them. "They don't look like friends."

Thank goodness for that. "They don't know each other very well, that's all. Alice is being polite."

"Good. I don't like him."

Nell grimaced. "Why not?"

"He's too big ... and scary."

Nell stared across the lake. "No, he's not. He's nice."

"Do you know him?"

"I met him at Aunty Sarah's. She likes him, too."

"He shouldn't be with Alice. She's my friend, not his."

Before Nell could stop her, Elenor ran along the path edging the lake, with Leah following close behind. Nell cringed as she caught up with them.

"I don't like you sitting with him."

"Elenor...!"

Alice smiled. "It's all right, Aunty Nell. I understand." She pointed to the gap between her and Mr Wood. "We're not really sitting together. We just happen to be on the same bench. Do you want to sit between us?"

"Only next to you." Elenor sat right beside Alice, glaring at Mr Wood as she did. "You can go now."

Nell smacked her across the top of her arm. "Don't be so rude."

Mr Wood stood up. "Don't worry about it. I was about to go, anyway. Good day, Mrs Riley." He gazed down at Alice. "It was nice talking to you."

CHAPTER THIRTY-FOUR

Leaves littered the footpath as Nell hurried towards the carriage waiting at the entrance to Princes Park, and she waved to Mrs Robertson and Violet, who were staring out of the window.

"You made it."

Mrs Robertson accepted the coachman's help as she climbed down the steps. "We did, although it's a shame it's nearly winter. I can see we've missed the leaves changing colour."

Nell glanced around. "Only by a few weeks, but yes, once they're ready to fall, it happens quickly."

"I wish we'd come earlier. It isn't as far as I expected."

Nell laughed. "It won't be in a carriage."

"You have a point."

"I can't believe I didn't think to invite you here before. I've been moaning to myself all summer that there are no parks near you."

"Well, we're here now."

Nell bent down to Violet. "Would you like to see some ducks?"

The child looked at her mother.

"I'm afraid she hasn't come across ducks before, so she doesn't know what you mean."

"We need to change that, then. It's a good job I brought some bread for you. Shall we go and find them?"

Mrs Robertson held onto her daughter's hand as they entered the park. "I'd no idea there was so much open space around here."

"This is the smaller of two parks and there are several others slightly further out. How was the voyage?"

"Very good. The governess has worked out a system and they do schoolwork for four hours a day."

"And does she stay with Violet while you go for dinner?"

"She does. Much to the disappointment of the stewardesses."

"I'm sure they still dote on her. Is Violet happy?"

"She seems to be."

Nell sighed. "I wish I could have done that with Elenor." She paused as Princes Park Mansions appeared through the trees to their left. "That's where Clara, Mrs Cavendish, used to live."

"Goodness, they're big houses. Mr Ellis must be important."

"I couldn't say. I heard he ran the Port of Liverpool, although I suspect he only said that for the benefit of Mr Cavendish's father at the wedding."

"What about Mrs Cavendish? Has she written lately?"

"I had a letter a couple of weeks ago, but she doesn't

write as often as she did. I expect she's too busy now, despite all the staff."

"Did she have her baby?"

"Oh, yes. I'd forgotten I've not seen you recently. She wrote shortly after you left in September. She had a little girl in August, so she'll be nearly three months old."

"What did she call her?"

Nell smiled. "Clara, after her mother."

"That's nice. Did she have anything else to say?"

"Not really. She was telling me about the parties and dinners she's been going to."

"Nothing more about Mr Hewitt?"

"She knows better than to mention him. The last I heard, he was spending most of his time in London without his wife, but that was earlier in the year. I've no idea what he's up to now. I don't care either."

"I'm glad. It means you're ready to move on."

Nell gave her a sideways glance. "I'm ready to stay as I am, more like."

Mrs Robertson ignored her. "Is that the only letter you've had?"

"Other than you and her, nobody writes to me any more." She pointed into the distance. "There's the lake coming into view. It looks as if there are some spare seats, too." She looked down at Violet. "Shall we find the ducks?"

The wind was chill as they sat, and Nell pulled her cloak more tightly around her. "You really should come in the summer."

"I will. I've enjoyed it. Violet seems to have got the hang of feeding the ducks, too."

"It's to be hoped she doesn't feed the seabirds now." Nell smiled. "Shall we make our way to the gate before we get too cold?"

Mrs Robertson laughed. "Have you forgotten how cold it gets at sea? I'm sure we'll survive."

"You don't want Violet catching a chill before you go. When do you sail again?"

Mrs Robertson took Violet's hand as they headed back along the path. "We've another few days yet, and then it's the last voyage of the year."

Nell shook her head. "That's gone quickly. What will you do over Christmas? Stay on the ship?"

"I'm not sure. We've spoken of hiring a house for a month, but we'll see."

The coachman was waiting for them when they got to the carriage and Nell watched as Mrs Robertson helped Violet up the steps.

"I was in my thirties before I went in one of those, yet she takes it all in her stride."

"She's been very fortunate. May I offer you a lift?"

"I'm happy to walk, thank you. I'm only five minutes away and the rain should keep off."

"As you wish." Mrs Robertson climbed into the seat next to her daughter. "I'll see you before Christmas, then."

Nell waited for the carriage to pull away before she looked up at the heavy grey clouds. *I'd better hurry. It will be raining again, soon.*

The clock hadn't struck four when she arrived home and Maria was helping herself to a cup of tea.

"Ooh. Is there another one in there?" Nell rubbed her hands together.

"It's a fresh pot. I wasn't expecting you yet."

"It's gone chilly, so there was no point sitting on a bench, freezing."

"Is Mrs Robertson all right?"

"She is. She goes on another trip later this week."

Maria handed her a cup. "Does it bother you seeing her leading the sort of life you would have liked?"

"I don't begrudge it her, but occasionally I can't deny I wonder how different things could have been. Still, there's no point dwelling on it." Nell put her cup on the side table near the fire and was about to sit down when the letterbox rattled. "I'm not expecting anything." Her brow furrowed. "Perhaps Clara has some news..."

She strolled to the hall but took a step backwards when she saw the envelope. *Mr Marsh. What on earth's he writing for?* She glanced down the hall. *What do I tell Maria? I don't want her to know.* After a moment's hesitation, she popped her head into the living room. "It's for next door. I'll nip and post it through."

Maria muttered something she didn't catch as she grabbed her cloak and stepped onto the footpath. *Now what? I've not even got a pocket to hide it in.* Her hands shook as she stared at the letter. *I know.* With a quick look round, she hurried down the alleyway to the backyard and locked herself in the privy, leaning against the door as she did.

She studied the handwriting once more. *Why write now? It's been over two years.*

She slipped a finger under the flap on the envelope and

tore it open, annoyed she'd ripped the edges, and pulled out the single sheet of paper. *Is that it?*

Dear Mrs Riley

I hope this letter finds you well.

I recently received some correspondence from our old colleague Mr Cooper, in which he suggested I write to you.

Why he would do such a thing, I can't imagine. I thought long and hard before I put pen to paper, but finally decided he wouldn't have suggested it without reason.

If I'm mistaken, please forgive my intrusion.

If you'd like to write back, you can send any correspondence via White Star.

Yours sincerely

Thomas Marsh

Nell's hands rested on her thighs as she took a deep breath. *Mrs Robertson. What's she thinking? That must be why she asked if I'd had any more letters.*

She rolled it up and pushed it into the front of her dress. *The question is, do I reply?*

Maria turned round as Nell returned to the house through the back door. "Where on earth have you been? This tea will be cold."

"I'm sorry. She wanted to talk and then I thought I'd nip to the privy while I was outside." She took a sip of her tea. "It's fine."

"The tea in the pot will be warmer if you want to top it up."

"I will. Let me get rid of this." Nell disappeared to hang up her cloak.

"Why did you put that on to go next door?"

"I told you, it's chilly."

"It only takes a second to post something through."

Nell took another gulp of tea. "I must have had a hunch that she'd want to talk."

"On the doorstep?"

Nell gritted her teeth. "What is this? You usually complain if I go out without it, so why ask so many questions when I do?"

"Because you never take any notice of a thing I say, and I find it hard to believe you have now."

CHAPTER THIRTY-FIVE

Lydia wheeled the pram into the hall as Nell closed the door after her.

"Snow already. I can't believe it."

"Me neither, but it's only a light covering, and it is nearly Christmas."

"I hope it doesn't get any worse between now and then. I don't like being forced to stay in."

"You'll manage if it does." Lydia lifted her son Henry from under the cover. "Shall we go and see Granny?"

The child patted her face as she carried him in and she handed him to Maria.

"Come and sit by the fire."

Lydia took the seat opposite as Nell poured her a cup of tea.

"How's Vernon? We haven't seen him for a few days."

"He's not happy at the moment."

Maria stopped bouncing Henry on her knee and studied her daughter-in-law. "What's up with him?"

"Don't look so worried. It's only something at work."

"He's not got himself into trouble, has he?"

"Not that I know. He was hoping for a pay rise but didn't get it."

"Well, I hope he doesn't do anything stupid."

"Like what?"

Nell pulled up a chair to join them. "A lot of men struck down their tools a few years ago, hoping to get more money, but they ended up losing their jobs. Vernon included."

The colour faded from Lydia's cheeks. "He's never mentioned it."

"I'm not surprised." Maria sniffed. "It took him months to get a regular job again, so don't go encouraging him."

"I won't. Not that he was planning anything like that. It's because a foreman at work left last week, and he wanted his job."

"I'm pleased to hear it." Maria resumed jiggling Henry on her knee. "Not that the extra money wouldn't have been handy, but there's time."

"That's what the boss said. He gave it to a man who's been there a lot longer than Vernon, so he needs to wait his turn. The problem is, he's impatient and thinks it could be years before he's got enough experience."

"Losing his job didn't help, but he wouldn't be told..."

Lydia creased her cheek. "I was already planning what to do with a few extra shillings, especially now Christmas is upon us. Have you started your mince pies yet?"

Maria shook her head. "That's next week's job. We've still time before we need them."

"I'm the same, but I can't decide how many to make."

Maria's forehead creased. "The same as last year, surely. Henry won't eat many."

Lydia chuckled. "It's not that. I can't decide if we'll need more. I'm thinking about having Christmas Day at home this year. It doesn't seem right celebrating after losing Maud."

"Nonsense. Christmas is a time for family, and you should be here so we can celebrate having Henry."

Lydia smiled at her. "As long as you don't mind."

"I'd be more upset if you didn't come! We'll be without Tom this year as it is."

Nell sighed. "It'll be different, for sure. Have you spoken to Sarah about what she wants to do?"

"She's coming here with the rest of them. She said she can't bear the thought of being at home without him."

Nell snorted. "She never saw him when he was here! He spent most of his evenings in the alehouse."

"It's different now, and you know it. At least she'll have Sam, Grace and baby Ethel to distract her during the day." Maria snuggled her face into Henry's midriff. "And we have to see you, don't we?" She sat him on the floor by her feet and looked at Lydia. "Have you visited Betty recently?"

"Not for a couple of weeks. She's never short of visitors, so I don't go too often."

Nell nodded. "I've not been going as much as I used to, either. Thankfully, Alice and Aunty Jane still go." She stood up to put some more coal on the fire, but the postman distracted her, and she wandered to the hall. *Splendid.*

Maria looked up as she ambled back into the living room. "Is it for you?"

She nodded. "Mrs Robertson. Hopefully, she's in Liverpool and this will tell me where to find her."

Lydia's brow creased. "Isn't she the lady you visit in Everton who lives near Betty?"

"She is, but she's also the wife of the captain I used to work for. After being onshore for five years, they've left their house, and they're living on the ship again."

Lydia shuddered. "I wouldn't like that."

"You would if you saw their quarters. She's taken a governess for her daughter, too."

"That can't be right. She should let her go to school so she can make some friends. She'll be lonely when she grows up, otherwise."

"I hadn't thought of that. Violet seems happy enough."

"Only because she knows no different. I wouldn't do that, even if we had the money."

Maria nodded at the letter. "Aren't you going to open it?"

"I was leaving it until Lydia left."

"Don't mind me. I know how excited I'd be if anyone ever wrote to me."

"All right, then." Nell moved to the table and sat down.

We arrived in Liverpool on Tuesday, and we've arranged to move to Rodney Street for a month. Do you know it?

Nell squealed, causing Maria to stare at her.

"What's the matter?"

"The Robertsons have rented a house on Rodney Street for the next month."

"You'll be visiting one of those?" Maria's voice was breathless. "You can ask if I can visit with you."

"I suspect she doesn't realise how grand the houses are around there. She asked if I knew it."

"She'll have a nice surprise then."

"I'm relieved it's so much closer than Everton. It will only take about quarter of an hour to get there." She continued reading.

...we're getting the keys tomorrow and will spend the rest of the week settling in. If you'd like to visit one day next week, we should be ready...

"She said I can visit, so I'll go on Monday after we've done the laundry."

"What's the rush? I presume she'll be here until the New Year."

"I'd like to see her more than once. Besides, I want a word with her about something."

Maria's eyes narrowed. "It had better not be about going to sea again."

"It's not." Nell paused as the front door opened and Alice joined them. "You're early."

She crouched down by Henry and stroked his hand. "I couldn't miss you, could I?"

The child giggled as Alice stacked some blocks and knocked them over.

"Oh dear."

Maria stared at her. "Where've you been?"

"I called on Miss Hopkins."

"You've been seeing a lot of her lately. I thought you were going to Betty's?"

"I was, but have you seen the weather? I didn't want to

venture too far."

"You were out for a long time then, if you've only been to the next street."

"Oh ... I went for a walk while I was out."

"In this weather?" Maria raised an eyebrow, but Alice kept her head down.

"It's different having a wander around the park compared to walking up to Everton."

"So, you walked there on your own?"

Nell stood up. "That's enough. Why do you ask so many questions? If she wanted to go to the park, what's wrong with that?"

"Exactly." Alice jumped up and reached for the teapot. "Now, let me top this up."

"And I'll get the cake out." Nell followed her into the kitchen and lowered her voice once she was sure Maria and Lydia were distracted with Henry. "Is everything all right?"

"Why wouldn't it be?"

"It doesn't look like it."

Alice sighed as she turned on the tap. "It's fine. I took my usual walk with ... you know, but didn't want to go to Betty's, so came back."

"That's not like you. Did you argue?"

"Not really, but..." She disappeared into the pantry and waited for Nell to follow. "He wants to tell everyone we're walking out together and doesn't understand why we need to keep it a secret."

"But you're not ready for your mam to find out?"

Alice shook her head. "She'll do everything she can to keep us apart."

"He's right, though. She'll find out eventually, and you can't leave it until you're walking down the aisle."

Alice studied the floor. "It might not come to that."

"But it might..."

"What are you two whispering about?" Maria's voice preceded her into the kitchen.

"Nothing. We were deciding which cake to use."

Maria pointed to the box closest to them. "The one that's been cut into. Why does that take both of you?"

"Ah, right. I wondered if you wanted a fresh one ... with Lydia being here."

"Don't be daft." Maria pulled on Alice's arm as she stared at the floor. "What's up with you?"

"N-nothing. I came in for the milk, but I can't get out with you standing there."

"You haven't even picked it up."

"Ah..." She reached onto the shelf behind her as Maria backed into the kitchen. "Why are you looking at me like that?"

"You don't seem your usual self."

"I-I'm fine. I just need a cup of tea. If you'll give me a minute, I'll bring it in."

CHAPTER THIRTY-SIX

The thick morning fog hadn't cleared as Nell walked towards Upper Parliament Street after dinner. She strained for the sound of horses' hooves before she crossed. *Thank goodness I'm not going far. It's not been this bad for a while.* She studied the houses on her right-hand side but could see little more than the lamps shining in the windows. *What a pity Mrs Robertson isn't in one of these, although I wouldn't like to live opposite a cemetery.* She shuddered as she glanced to the other side of the street. *Perhaps that's why they have their own front gardens.*

She turned twice through the streets of Georgian houses until she looked up at the four-storey buildings on Rodney Street. *I hope she's not at the far end.* She slowed her pace and found the house about ten doors down. *This should be it. I hope so, anyway.*

A housekeeper answered the door and opened it fully when Nell announced who she was.

"Madam's expecting you. Follow me." She showed Nell into a room to the right of the hall, with two large windows to the front, both dressed from floor to ceiling with red velvet drapes.

"Gracious. They're impressive."

"Aren't they?" Mrs Robertson grinned as she offered Nell a seat on one of the two settees straddling the fireplace. "This is such a lovely room. I could get used to living here."

"I'd say we all could." Nell gazed up at a glass chandelier hanging from the high ceiling.

"How do you light that?"

Mrs Robertson chuckled. "I don't think you do. I've decided it's only for show, so we use the gaslights on the wall."

"Quite sensible. How did you find this place?"

"It was when we travelled back to the ship after we'd seen you at the park. The coachman brought us home along this street and I found out where we were. My husband then asked the office if they could find a house around here for us. Sadly, even if we wanted to, we couldn't stay indefinitely. The owner has gone abroad for three months, and he needed someone to look after it."

"How marvellous." Nell admired the country scenes in the paintings on the walls while the housekeeper arrived with a tea tray. "Did you have a good voyage?"

Mrs Robertson grimaced. "I've had better. About nine days in, the weather turned, and we had some of the worst seasickness I've seen. Even some of the crew were ill."

"Goodness. I'm glad I wasn't with you. Did you have enough brandy and ginger biscuits on board?"

"Only just. We had to restock in Boston."

"There's a reason people don't travel at this time of the year."

"And they're very sensible."

Nell took the cup of tea Mrs Robertson offered. "Was Mr Cooper on the ship with you again?"

"He was, but he was in charge of steerage, so I didn't see much of him. Why?"

Nell raised an eyebrow. "I wondered if you'd asked him to write any more letters."

Mrs Robertson's face brightened, and she dropped the lump of sugar that had been destined for her cup. "You've had a letter from Mr Marsh? What did he say?"

"Not a lot." She took the envelope from her handbag. "It was very curt and said Mr Cooper had written to suggest he contact me. Why were you talking about us to Mr Cooper?"

Mrs Robertson returned her attention to her tea. "Because the two of you need your heads banging together. It's obvious you like Mr Marsh, and Mr Cooper said Mr Marsh had gone to Australia to get away from some troubles. That must mean you, after what happened. Can't you see, you should be together, not on opposite sides of the world."

Nell unfolded the paper. "He ended by saying *he'd done his best to forget me since our last meeting...*"

"That's only because he cares about you and it's his way of coping. Have you replied to him?"

Nell shook her head. "Not yet. I wanted to know what Mr Cooper might have told him. Mr Marsh wasn't very forthcoming."

Mrs Robertson sighed. "When Mr Cooper mentioned they were still in touch with each other, he knew you were the reason he'd gone to Australia."

"He did?"

"So he said. That was when I told him how upset you were that Mr Marsh had left."

"You must have said more than that because Mr Cooper suggested he write to me. Did you ask him to do that?"

Mrs Robertson cocked her head to one side. "Would you be angry if I did?"

Nell sighed. "I don't know. You're right that I like him, but I won't ever be the upstanding woman he expects me to be. Whenever we get close, I say something that upsets him and he sulks off. We can't have a relationship if he's going to do that all the time."

"He may have changed. He must hold out some hope if he wrote to you."

"I don't know." Nell continued to stare at the letter. "He said he'd thought long and hard before writing."

"What are you frightened of?"

"Being hurt again. It was horrible when he found out I was on such good terms with Ollie."

"I told Mr Cooper you hadn't remarried."

"That wasn't the problem. He knew I'd never marry Ollie, but–" she shrugged "–I don't know, it was as if he guessed there'd been something between us. He probably still thinks there is."

"Then tell him there isn't."

"I tried that, but he didn't believe me."

"So, tell him again."

She shook her head. "There's no point. He's in Australia. Even if I wrote today, he wouldn't get it until about March of next year and then I wouldn't get his reply, assuming there is one, until at least May."

"Well, I suggest you stop wasting time and get a letter in the post. He plucked up the courage to write to you..."

"What do I say?"

"You'll think of something. Just promise me you'll write. I'm a firm believer in fate and I'm convinced I met Mr Cooper for a reason."

Nell bit her lip. "Very well. I promise I will before Christmas."

The light was already fading when Nell left Rodney Street, and with the fog still thick, she kept close to the railings at the front of the houses. The street felt deserted except for the horses trotting past with their carriages. *Would it be worth a shilling so I don't have to walk in this?* She pulled her cloak tightly around her as she peered behind her. *I doubt they'd see me even if I wanted to hail one. Keep going.*

She was out of breath by the time she approached Upper Parliament Street but stayed away from the railings that surrounded the cemetery. *How did I end up on this side of the road? Don't stop now.*

She sensed that the fog was thinning as she neared the junction, but stopped abruptly when a man with long, greasy hair and no hat stepped out in front of her.

"A pretty lady all on her own?"

A shiver ran down her spine. "No ... I-I'm meeting my nephew. He's waiting for me on the corner."

He grinned as he came closer. "I've just come that way and there was nobody there."

"He'll be there any minute..." Nell backed into the

railings, but he reached round each side of her, trapping her between his arms.

"You looking for a bit of business?"

"No..." Her voice screeched. "I'm not that sort of woman."

"A likely story and if this *nephew* lets you down..." He leaned into her, his breath warm on her lips as his steely blue eyes searched her face. "Very nice."

"Get off me..." She raised her hands to push him away, but he grabbed them.

"There's no need to pretend. Nobody can see us."

"Somebody..." Her mouth was dry as she tried to shout.

"Ain't nobody going to hear that. You know you don't mean it..."

She struggled to push him backwards, but he kept hold of her wrists, pulling her with him.

"Like it rough, do you? I can do that..."

"Stop it." Nell kicked out at him as he pressed her to the railings, but they both stopped as footsteps approached. "Over here..."

He clamped a hand across her mouth. "Keep that shut."

Nell jerked her head backwards. "Help..."

"I said, shut it..." He raised a hand to strike her, but someone grabbed it as Alice's voice pierced the fog.

"Aunty Nell?"

Nell gasped. "Get away. Don't go near him..."

"I've got him." Mr Wood wrested the man from her. "You scum of the earth..." He aimed a single blow at the man's jaw, sending him spinning backwards. He landed in a heap on the footpath and Mr Wood stepped forwards to kick him in the ribs. "If you haven't cleared off in ten seconds, the next one won't be so feeble..."

The man scrambled to his feet and ran towards Upper Parliament Street.

"Are you all right, Mrs Riley?"

Nell's heart raced as Alice put an arm around her. "I will be. Thanks to you."

Mr Wood peered down at her. "What on earth are you doing out on your own on a day like this?"

"I-I thought I'd be home before it went dark. I'm sorry."

"You shouldn't have been out in this fog even in the daylight."

"I-I wasn't thinking..." She couldn't stop the tears rolling down her cheeks as Alice squeezed her shoulders.

"Come on, let's get you home."

"Give me a minute." She gasped for breath as her heart pounded. "Not a word to your mam. She'll be beside herself."

"She won't hear about it from me." Alice gazed at Mr Wood as Nell steadied herself on the railings.

"I hadn't thought of that." She suddenly stared at Mr Wood. "What time is it? Why aren't you at work?"

Mr Wood checked his pocket watch. "It's five to four, but I finish early on a Wednesday, so we took a stroll around town before walking home."

Nell nodded. "Well, thank you. I don't know what I'd have done if you hadn't been here."

"Please, Aunty Nell. You won't tell Mam, will you?"

Nell finally caught her breath. "I'd say we both want to keep this to ourselves."

CHAPTER THIRTY-SEVEN

Nell added a tablespoon more brandy to the mincemeat mixture and squeezed the ingredients firmly through her fingers as Maria arrived at the table with a cloth.

"Haven't you finished that yet? It should be in the jars by now."

"I'm about to do it. Pass me that spoon."

Maria pushed it to her. "I'd be quicker doing it myself. I don't know what's been up with you this last week."

"Nothing."

Maria shook her head. "Why do you keep everything to yourself?"

"I don't. I'm thinking, that's all."

"What have you got to think about other than Christmas?"

Nell shrugged. "I'm wondering when to visit Mrs Robertson again."

"You can't go this side of Christmas."

"Why not?" She pushed some mincemeat firmly into

the first jar. "We won't be making the mince pies for another week."

"There are plenty of other things to do, and I thought she was here until mid-January."

"Only until the start of the second week, and I can't leave it that late. They'll need to pack all their personal property once the festivities are over."

"I don't want you disappearing before Christmas." Maria added lids to the jars already filled. "I'll get these in the pantry."

Nell finished the last jar as Alice joined them. "How was ... erm ... Miss Hopkins?"

Alice smiled. "Fine, thank you. Where's Mam?"

"In the kitchen. Will you be going again tomorrow?"

Alice's eyes flicked to the kitchen. "I can go whenever you like."

Nell nodded. "I'm about done here, so you can put the kettle on if she hasn't already."

"It's on." Maria rejoined them and fastened the final lid. "You can wipe the table if it's not too much trouble."

Nell took a deep breath. "I can manage that."

The fire was burning low when Maria stood up and looked at Alice.

"Time for bed."

"I'll follow you up."

"What's wrong with coming now?"

"I ... erm ..."

Nell smiled at her. "You go up. I'll see you tomorrow."

Maria stared at her. "What are you doing?"

"I've a letter to write ... to Mrs Cavendish..."

"At this time of night?"

Nell shrugged. "We were busy, and I couldn't do it while we were playing cards."

"Well, don't be long. We need to start the cleaning in the morning."

Alice hung back as Maria went up the stairs. "Do you still want an escort next time you visit Mrs Robertson?"

"If you don't mind. I'm still unsettled by what happened."

"I'm not surprised. When would you like to go?"

It depends how I get on with this letter. She sighed. "Wednesday might be best; we'll be late coming home if we go another day."

Alice nodded. "I'll make the arrangements with Mr Wood." She closed the door as Nell lifted out the writing set.

I could do with Billy and George staying at the alehouse a little longer. She set the pen and ink bottle on the table and straightened the paper in front of her. *What on earth do I say?* She tapped the end of the pen on her teeth. *"Dear Mr Marsh" is a good start.* The nib scratched on the paper as she wrote. *Should I tell him about Mrs Robertson and Mr Cooper meeting up?* She nodded. *That way, he'll know I wasn't the reason for the letter.* She bit her lip as she finished the last sentence. *What about Ollie? Do I even mention him?* She sighed. *I should say that I've not seen or heard anything from him for over two years. Whether he believes me is another matter.* She reached the bottom of the third page and blotted the ink before turning over. *Now what?* She stared at the living room door. *How do I ask him to write back? What about...?*

I understand you may still be angry, but if you'd like to reply, I'd be happy to hear from you. I've often thought of you over these last two years and wondered how you are and what you've been doing. I can only hope you're happy.

With warm regards
Elenor Riley (Mrs)

She reread the whole letter. *Does it sound too forward? Maybe. Is that wrong? Probably.* She flinched and quickly folded the paper as the front door closed and Billy joined her.

"You're still up?"

"I had a letter to write, and your mam's kept me busy all day. Is your dad with you?"

"He'll be here in a minute. He walked home with Mr Grayson, and they were finishing an argument."

Nell's mouth fell open. "Not about anything serious, I hope."

"Nothing major, they're disagreeing on how the government should deal with these Irish nationalists..." He laughed as the front door opened again. "That will be him."

"Ah. I'm glad they keep that sort of debate for the alehouse." She stood up and pushed the letter into her pocket. "Let me put this away, then I'll go up."

George stopped in the doorway as she slipped the writing set into the dresser.

"I didn't expect to see you still here."

Nell's cheeks coloured. "And if you'd been a minute later, you wouldn't have. Goodnight."

The girls had already disappeared downstairs by the time Nell sat on the edge of the bed and read the letter she'd rewritten more than once every day for the last three days. *It will have to do. I need to get it in the post.*

Maria shouted up to her. "Are you coming down, Nell?"

"In a minute." She folded the paper neatly and put it in the envelope. *We can walk past the letterbox on the way to Mrs Robertson's.*

Maria looked up as she arrived in the living room. "About time, too. I want this table tidied away so we can make a start on the pastry."

Nell's eyes widened. "You're making the mince pies today?"

"I told you."

That's all I need.

"Don't tell me you're going out."

"I've arranged to visit Mrs Robertson. I thought we were doing the baking tomorrow."

"When will you listen to a word I say? I remember telling you we were doing it today. Not that it should matter, because I asked you not to call on her before Christmas."

"I must have misheard you."

Alice collected up the girls' plates. "It will all be fine. We can get the pastry made and the mince pies rolled this morning, so all you have to do is put them in the range this afternoon."

Maria glared at her. "Are you going out as well?"

"Not for long..."

Maria snatched the dishes from her and stomped to the kitchen. "Why I ever expect any help, I don't know."

"Thank you." Nell mouthed the words to Alice. "I'll just have a cup of tea and you can clear everything else away."

"You need some bread, too." She handed Nell a plate. "Butter a slice now and sit by the fire while I tidy up."

The first batch of mince pies was cooking when Nell pulled the door closed behind her and Alice, and they turned left towards Windsor Street.

"Thank you for walking with me. I need to post this on the way. It shouldn't make you late."

"Whether it does or not, after what happened, I wouldn't be happy letting you walk on your own. Neither would Mr Wood."

"I know. At least I hope it was a lesson to you about how easy it is for a man to overpower you."

Alice nodded. "I've been more careful myself since, and Mr Wood won't let me out on my own after dark."

"Is it serious between you?"

"I'm not sure what serious is, but we like each other. A lot. Do you think Mam will ever be happy for us to walk out together?"

Nell sighed. "If it's what you want, she'll have to get

used to it. You'll be twenty-two next week. That's old enough to look after yourself. Even if she doesn't like it."

Alice squeezed her arm. "Betty told me how good you were with her when she had her problems. I don't know what we'd do without you."

Nell smiled. "That's what aunties are for. Whether it will make me a good mam when Elenor and Leah get to your age is another matter."

"I'm sure you will be."

They turned into Rodney Street and Alice waved to Mr Wood as he walked towards them from the opposite direction.

"There he is. Miss Hopkins."

Alice giggled. "Don't ever tell him or he'll be mad with me."

"As if I would."

Mr Wood's gaze lingered on Alice. "That was well-timed. Were there any problems getting here?"

"No, it was all fine. It feels safer travelling together."

Nell stopped by Mrs Robertson's house. "Here we are. Shall we say three o'clock so we're home before it goes dark?"

Alice glanced at Mr Wood. "Is that all right with you?"

"Perfect." He knocked on the door for Nell and they waited until the housekeeper opened it. "We'll see you later."

Mrs Robertson stood up as Nell was shown in. "Well?" The grin on her face widened. "Did you send it?"

"I did. Just. I posted it on the way here."

Mrs Robertson gasped. "What kept you so long?"

Nell scratched her forehead. "I must have rewritten it

half a dozen times. I wanted to sound pleased to hear from him, but not too forward. It's not easy."

"But it's in the post now?"

"It is, although whether he'll reply is anyone's guess. I'll probably have forgotten I wrote by the time I get an answer."

"No you won't." Mrs Robertson sat down. "Once May arrives, you'll be looking out for a letter every day. Why do you keep denying you like him?"

Nell shrugged. "The only men I've ever loved have both broken my heart, in different ways, of course. Perhaps I don't want to tempt the gods for a third time."

"But you've not given Mr Marsh a chance."

Nell gave a wry smile. "I disliked him for so long it would be strange to admit I was wrong."

Mrs Robertson raised an eyebrow. "Would it be so hard?"

"I don't know. Maybe one day I'll get used to the idea."

CHAPTER THIRTY-EIGHT

Nell stared at the magazine on her lap, but the words were nothing more than a blur. She looked up as Maria handed her a cup of tea.

"You're quiet this afternoon."

"I'm reading. I can't do that and talk at the same time."

"It's not only today. Ever since Christmas, you've been in a world of your own."

Nell flicked her eyes to the window. "It's these dull days. It barely gets light before it's dark again."

"You always used to visit your acquaintances or walk to the park, but you've not been out."

"I don't have many options. Mrs Robertson's gone again, Betty's too far away..."

"That hasn't stopped Alice visiting her."

"I may walk up there with her next week."

"I thought you preferred going on your own."

Nell bit her lip as the image of two steely blue eyes appeared, and she flinched as his face enveloped hers. "I-I've decided I prefer company."

"What was that for?"

"What?"

"You looked like you had a fright."

She bent over to rub her leg. "A bit of cramp. That's all."

"That's because you're not getting out enough. Even I nip out to the shop each morning. Why don't you visit Betty and see what she's up to? We've not seen her since Christmas."

"Jane's not going up there as much as she used to, either. The weather's dragging everyone down this year. Except James."

"James? Have you heard from him?"

"Not since his Christmas letter, but one reason he wanted to stay in Brazil was because of the weather. It's always as warm as a summer's day. I must admit, I envy him."

"Well, you shouldn't. You'd hate being stuck out there, thousands of miles from home."

I'd be happy to try. She was about to pick up her cup of tea when the letterbox rattled.

"I'll go. I'm on my feet. Goodness..." Maria came back a moment later. "Someone's died."

Nell's stomach churned as she handed her the black-edged envelope. "It's Clara's handwriting." A wave of nausea washed over her as Maria gave her the letter opener. Within seconds, she read the brief note.

It's with great sadness that I have to tell you Father passed away...

The funeral is next week ... the only positive is that Mr Cavendish and I will arrive in Liverpool on

Thursday. Just the two of us. If you're free one day the following week, we'd love to see you...

Nell let out a deep sigh. "It's Mr Ellis. His heart never fully recovered after his last illness... He was such a nice man, too."

"I'm sorry. Will Mrs Cavendish come to Liverpool for the funeral?"

Nell nodded. "They're arriving tomorrow."

"With the children?"

"Children?" *I hadn't even considered them.* "No. Just her and Mr Cavendish." *No Ollie.* "She wants to meet up one day next week. She doesn't say when, though."

"She shouldn't be socialising at a time like this."

Nell wiped her eyes. "It may be her only chance. I expect she'll want to go home at the earliest opportunity once she's seen her mother."

"What will happen to her? Mrs Ellis, that is. She can't stay in that big house on her own."

Nell shrugged. "They'll need to sort that out. Clara won't want her in Surrey after what happened, so she'll have to hope her brother will have her." She pushed herself up. "I'll write to her now to tell her I'm free any day and leave her to choose when and where."

The corner of Princes Road and North Hill Street was quieter than usual, and Nell shuffled on the spot as she surveyed the large red-brick houses lining both sides of a central boulevard. *Where is she?* She pulled out her pocket watch for the third time. *Ten past. She was supposed to be here at three.*

She clasped the watch in her hand and smiled at a man and his wife as they walked by, willing them to slow down. *Don't leave me.* They turned into a nearby driveway and Nell resumed her study of the road, her shoulders slumping further as each approaching carriage failed to stop. *How long do I wait?* The fingers on her clock face took an age to move to quarter past. *Another five minutes?*

As it turned twenty past three, she pushed the watch back inside her dress. *I can't stay here any longer.* She started to walk but stopped when one last carriage headed towards her.

"Mrs Riley." Mr Cavendish waved to her from the window but opened the door as the coachman rolled down the steps.

"I'm sorry we're late. It was Mrs Ellis." He rolled his eyes as he helped her into the carriage.

"I suspected it might be."

Clara's face was pale against her black mourning dress. "This is a bad enough time for all of us, but as you can imagine, Mother's making it ten times worse."

"Hasn't your brother been dealing with her?"

"After a fashion, but he lets her walk all over him."

"He'll be the head of the family now, though."

Clara snorted. "You wouldn't know it. Edward's done more in two days than he has in a week."

Nell looked at Mr Cavendish. "She's finally accepted you?"

"Not at all."

Clara wiped her eyes. "She'd try the patience of a saint. Why did Father have to leave us first?"

The carriage pulled up outside the Adelphi ten minutes later, and they waited for the coachman to open the door.

"We're not going to the tea room, are we?"

"No. We've a suite of rooms, so we'll take tea up there. Edward has to visit the bank, so he'll leave us once we're settled."

The climb to the third floor was slow, but Nell gasped as Mr Cavendish showed her into a room with a large fireplace that had several armchairs around it.

"I thought the room we used the night you left for Surrey was impressive."

Mr Cavendish smirked. "It's a benefit of using the hotel as often as we have. They give us the best rooms. I ordered tea while you were walking up the stairs, and as soon as it arrives, I'll leave you in peace."

Nell let Mr Cavendish take her cloak and perched on the edge of a chair. "What have you done with the children?"

Clara attempted to smile. "The nanny has them, and Edward's mother is there if there are any problems. I couldn't bring them up here on top of everything else. Not that Mother could grasp that."

"She'll be upset they're not here, I imagine. She won't have seen baby Clara yet."

"The way she's carrying on, she never will." She wiped her eyes. "Why does she make everything so difficult?"

Mr Cavendish opened the door to a waitress, who put a

large tray on the table in front of the fire before disappearing again. "That looks enough for four. I'll have something when I come back, assuming you don't eat it all."

Clara's eyes glistened as she looked up at him. "There'll be plenty left."

He raised his hand to wave. "I'll arrange a carriage to take Mrs Riley home once I'm back, too. See you later."

"Thank you. I'd rather not be out on my own after dark."

Clara sighed as the door closed. "I'm sorry you had to see me like that. Promise we won't talk about Mother again."

Nell nodded. "I promise. Tell me about the children. How do you like being a mam?"

A smile finally lit her face. "I'm Mama at the moment, and I love every minute, especially as the nanny does most of the work. It's such a disappointment that Lady Helen didn't have a girl though..." She put a hand to her mouth. "I wasn't going to mention her."

Nell shrugged. "I don't mind hearing about her."

"That's a relief. I'm not sure who was more disappointed when she had her third boy, her or me..."

"She's had another one?"

"Ah, yes. I didn't say anything in my letters. Not wanting to upset you."

Nell sat up straight. "Ollie returned from London then?"

"Not that you'd notice. He's down there more than he's in Ackley, although he tries to be home on a Sunday."

To keep his wife happy... "So, you see a lot of Lady Helen during the week?"

"I do. Several others in our circle have children too, but most of them are boys. Poor Clara will struggle for friends when she's older."

"There's still time."

"I keep saying that to Lady Helen. She's still young."

"A lot younger than me." *And Ollie.* "It's unfortunate she has to rely on him..."

Clara clapped her hands. "That's enough of them. And of me. How are you? You don't seem your usual self."

Nell shrugged. "I was upset to hear about your father."

"You've not got any better at lying. What's troubling you?"

Nell stared at the platter of sandwiches that neither of them had touched. "I was nervous about standing on the street corner for so long."

Clara cocked her head to one side. "Why? You've done it dozens of times."

"I visited Mrs Robertson about a month ago, and on the way home, a man thought I was a lady of the night and accosted me. I've not wanted to go out since."

Clara's eyes widened. "What happened?"

"He pinned me against some railings and tried to overcome me, but thankfully, Alice and her new beau were close by and heard me scream."

Clara shook her head. "Thank goodness for that. You need to be careful. It's becoming a habit."

Nell gasped. "I ... I didn't encourage him. I didn't even know him..."

"I'm not suggesting you did, but there must have been a look ... or something."

"No! It was thick fog. I didn't see him until he was right in front of me."

Clara's face was calm as she held Nell's gaze. "I know you won't thank me for saying this, but you shouldn't be walking out on your own. Haven't you met anyone yet?"

"Even if I had, I should be able to go out without a chaperone."

"Whether you should or not, the truth is, you can't. My life's been transformed since I've had Edward to take care of me."

"You're very fortunate."

"Don't look like that. I'm only trying to help. You were there for me when I was stuck at home with Mother, so I feel as if it's my turn to look after you now. How are your girls? Growing up, I expect."

"They are. Elenor leaves school in the summer. I can't say I'm looking forward to it."

"And how's your sister? The one you live with?"

"The same as ever and still treating me like a child. The thing is, since the *incident*, I've not been going out much, so we've been stuck in the house together. Like you were with your mother."

"We need to change that, then. It's a shame Ollie scared Mr Marsh away. He'd have looked after you."

A shame. Nell took a deep breath. *Don't rise to the bait.* "He's in Australia now. He has been for nearly three years."

"How do you know?"

"Erm ... Mrs Robertson told me. A steward who worked with us on the *Bohemian* is working on Captain Robertson's latest ship. He bumped into Mr Marsh while he was in Australia and mentioned it to Mrs Robertson."

"Has he any plans to come back?"

"Not that I'm aware."

"We need to find you someone else, then. Surely your nephews could introduce you to men your age."

Nell stood up and wandered to a picture window that looked out over St George's Plateau. "I've told you, I'm not interested."

"All right, I won't go on about it. Come and sit down and have a sandwich ... or a cake. It would be a shame to waste them."

"I won't want my tea later."

"One cake won't hurt. Now, what's Mrs Robertson up to?"

The afternoon had gone slowly, and Nell rested her head on the side of the carriage as Mr Cavendish closed the door and the coachman climbed onto his seat.

What an ordeal. How can two people who were so close drift so far apart? She gazed out of the window. *I shouldn't have expected things to stay the same. She's her own woman now. I should be pleased.*

She sat up straight as they turned into Rodney Street, then headed towards Upper Parliament Street. *Would I recognise him again if I saw him? Without a doubt.* She shuddered as she studied those making their way home. *No women on their own. I was obviously asking for trouble.*

Alice was walking up Merlin Street as they rounded the corner, and Nell banged on the side of the carriage to stop the coachman.

"I'll walk from here, thank you."

"On your own?"

"With my niece." She pointed to Alice, who was approaching. "We can manage the last hundred yards together."

"As you wish. Not that she should be out on her own, either. I can take both of you if you like. The gent paid me enough."

Alice grinned. "May we? I've never been in a carriage."

The coachman scowled at her. "You should always use one when you're alone. Would you like to go around the block?"

"Yes, please." Alice's smile widened as she climbed inside. "What are you doing in a carriage? Is it because of what happened?"

"Not really. I've been to see Mrs Cavendish at the Adelphi, so they arranged this to bring me home."

"How nice. I wish I had friends like that."

"But then you wouldn't get to walk out with Mr Wood."

Alice sighed. "Why's there always a snag to everything?"

CHAPTER THIRTY-NINE

Even though they were only approaching Easter, the sun was warmer than Nell expected, and she took her seat while Rebecca handed the girls bread for the ducks.

"What a lovely day for March."

Rebecca sat beside her. "The blossom on the trees is especially nice."

"It's nice every year. We just forget so easily."

"Is Maria ready for Easter?"

Nell rolled her eyes. "You know what she's like. She won't be happy until everyone arrives, and the food's been eaten."

"She must enjoy it."

"She does really, even though she moans. She'd have nothing to do otherwise."

"Who's joining us this year?"

Nell puffed out her cheeks. "That's a good question. The house isn't big enough for us all."

Rebecca laughed. "Or the dining table."

"She's putting on a spread, so we won't be sitting down.

She's invited Betty and her family, plus Jane and the boys, but Sarah's lot are the problem. Sam and Grace won't come, but the others are all still at home, so it's difficult not to include them."

"What about Mr Wood? Sarah treats him like part of the family."

"I doubt she'll ask him, even if we had the space."

"Why not?" Rebecca's eyes narrowed. "What have I missed?"

"Not a lot, but Maria doesn't want to encourage him. She's terrified he has his eye on Alice."

"Oh dear. It wouldn't surprise me if Sarah wants him to be invited, though. She can't leave him on his own, with nothing to eat but leftovers."

Nell held up her hands. "I'm keeping out of it. If Sarah or Jane want a word with Maria, that's up to them."

Rebecca pointed down the footpath. "Talk of the devil."

Jane and Betty were heading towards them, and Albert ran to Nell.

"Good afternoon, young man. Have you come to feed the ducks?"

"Yes."

Before he could say any more, Isobel and Elenor ran to him, grabbed a hand each and escorted him to the lake where Leah and Florrie waited.

Jane smirked. "He's very popular with the ladies. A bit like his dad."

"Mam!" Betty's cheeks coloured as she parked the pram by the side of the bench.

"What? It's true." Jane squeezed onto the seat next to Nell. "You'll need to budge up so we can all sit down."

Nell and Rebecca moved to one end, while Jane made herself comfortable.

"Have you been here long?"

"Long enough for the girls to have given away all their bread."

"It's lovely, isn't it?" Jane sniffed the air. "We really should come out more often."

Rebecca leaned forward. "It's nice to see you, Betty. It's a good walk for you to get here, especially with the two of them."

Betty smiled. "I'm getting used to it."

"Thank goodness." Jane huffed. "I've never walked as far as I have these last couple of years." She lifted the front of her dress to reveal her boots. "These need resoling. I'm just praying it doesn't rain."

"If walking up to Betty's means you get out more, it's a good thing."

Jane lifted her face to the sun. "We called on Maria on the way here to find out why she hasn't invited Mr Wood on Sunday."

"You didn't..." Nell's mouth opened and closed several times, but nothing more came out.

"Why shouldn't we?"

"D-did Betty go in?"

"Of course she did. And the children."

A weight settled in Nell's stomach as Betty stared at her.

"Did Alice tell her she was visiting me?" Betty ran her hands over her face as Nell nodded. "I told you not to go."

Rebecca leaned forward. "Is this something else I've missed? Where is Alice?"

Jane clicked her teeth. "She's been walking out with Mr Wood for the last few months. Honestly, it's about time they told Maria. They're old enough to make their own decisions, and he's a very respectable man."

Nell groaned. "Maybe they should, but at a time that suits them rather than having Maria pounce on Alice when she least expects it."

Jane cocked her head to one side. "She didn't seem surprised to see Betty. If she was expecting her to be at home with Alice, she wouldn't have kept it to herself."

Betty nodded. "You're right, she acted perfectly normally. Perhaps she forgot. Or did Alice say she was going to visit Miss Hopkins?"

"I thought she said you, but perhaps I misheard. I hope I did. What did she say when you asked about Mr Wood joining us?"

Jane looked at Betty. "She went very quiet, now I think about it, and said she'd rather he didn't because there wasn't enough room."

"And that was it?"

"I told her she was being unreasonable, but she wouldn't change her mind."

Rebecca looked across Nell to Jane. "The best thing might be for him to just turn up. Once George sees him, he'll make him welcome."

"That's a good point." Nell beamed at Rebecca. "Mr Wood's part of the group in the alehouse. If George invites him..."

"Maria won't cross him." Jane nudged Nell. "Shall I have a word with him?"

"No, you won't. Leave it to me. You've caused enough trouble."

The afternoon was still bright as they strolled through the park and Nell retrieved her watch as they reached the entrance. *Half past four.*

"Will Mr Crane pick you up, Betty?"

"No, I'll walk. There's time before it goes dark."

"Make sure you go straight home. I hope Albert has the energy to walk all that way after the running around he's done this afternoon."

"He'll be fine. I sit Betsy up and he goes in the other end of the pram."

"I might walk up to Upper Parliament Street with you and hope I can speak to Alice before she gets home. I need to warn her."

Jane studied her. "Do you know where she'll be?"

"I know the route they usually take."

"You'll be early, won't you? What time is it?"

Nell tutted. "You're right. It's just turned half past four and they won't reach Upper Parliament Street until twenty past five at the earliest."

"You can't hang around the street corner."

"I'm aware of that." *Certainly not that one.*

"Do they meet each other every day?" Rebecca's voice was light. "It's late for her to be getting home if they do. I'm surprised Maria's not said anything."

Nell banged a hand to her head. "What am I thinking? It's Wednesday. She'll be home early because it's Mr Wood's half day. She could be there already."

Rebecca grimaced. "You'd better get a move on."

Jane linked Nell's arm. "I'll come with you and put in a good word for Mr Wood."

Nell shuddered. "That will make things worse."

"Why will it? She needs telling." She smirked at Nell. "Let's find out what's going on."

The house was quiet when Nell opened the front door, and she led Jane into the living room.

"Look who we met at the park..."

Maria glared at them as they walked in. "Did you know about this?" She swung an arm towards Alice.

Nell's heart skipped a beat. "What's the matter?"

"She is." Alice buried her face in her hands.

"She's only been walking out with Mr Wood behind my back..."

Jane pushed past Nell. "Mr Wood's a lovely man."

"He's a widower who's nine years older than her."

"That doesn't mean he'll mistreat her. Perhaps if you weren't so unreasonable, she'd have told you."

"But she's been lying."

"Because you're a bully. She's a grown woman, able to make her own decisions. She doesn't need you telling her what she can and can't do."

Maria squared up to her sister. "I don't need you coming in here telling me how to look after my daughter. You hardly did a good job with your own..."

Jane's face reddened. "What's that supposed to mean?"

"It means that I won't have my daughter in the family way before she gets married."

"Betty was not in the family way…"

"But she had been, hadn't she…? That's why you sent her away to *work*…"

"And you really think Vernon's first baby was *early*? Stop being so sanctimonious."

"I knew it!" Maria pushed Jane on the shoulder.

"Knew what?"

"That she'd been with child. Did she get it *seen to*, to spare your blushes?"

Jane gasped and stared at Nell as the room fell silent. After several seconds, Maria retreated.

"I-I'm sorry. I went too far."

"Yes, you did." Nell found her voice. "How could you even think such a thing?"

"Exactly." Alice stood up and towered over Maria as she squirmed in her chair. "I can't believe you think that about Betty. Or me, either. Don't you trust me? For your information, I won't stop walking out with Mr Wood. He's a good man, and we get on well together, but don't bother inviting him for Easter, because I won't be here, either."

CHAPTER FORTY

Maria wandered into the living room, a newly arrived letter in her hand.

"For you, I imagine."

Nell glanced at the handwriting. "It's from James."

"I don't suppose he's coming home anytime soon."

"Let's see." Nell scanned the neatly written text that covered three sides of paper. "He says he'll be here in the summer."

"That's good of him. Did you tell him about Alice?"

"I did, but that letter won't have reached him yet. It will be at least another month before we get a reply."

Maria played with a teaspoon on the saucer of a dirty cup. "Have you any plans to visit her?"

"I was thinking of walking up there this afternoon. It's a bright enough day."

Maria's watery eyes stared at her. "Will you ask her to come home?"

Nell folded the letter onto her lap and studied her

sister. "Why should she? It suits her living there, and Betty's happy too."

"Her dad misses her. He won't say anything, but I can tell."

"It's a shame you don't miss her, too."

Maria's tears started again. "I didn't mean for this to happen. I was trying to protect her..."

"We've been over this a thousand times. If you want her back, you can come with me and ask her yourself."

"I can't walk that far."

"Oh yes you can. You do as much running around the house as you would on a walk to Everton."

"Can't you ask her?"

"No, I can't." Nell glared at her. "I'm not making apologies for you when I don't believe you mean them. She needs to know you're happy she's found a man she likes and only you can tell her that. If not, you'll have to accept that she'll never come home because she prefers to be with him than with us."

Maria wiped her eyes with a handkerchief. "I don't not like him."

"You've a funny way of showing it."

"I worry about her."

"You've spent your whole life worrying about us all, and what good has it done? It caused me to resent you for years. You've chased James away. You fell out with Jane for far too long, and now Alice wants nothing to do with you... You need to stop this. If we make mistakes, we have to deal with them. Just stop trying to force people into doing things they don't want. Or more to the point, let people do what they want instead of stopping them." Nell didn't wait for a reply before she went to the kitchen and put the kettle on. *In times of crisis, have a cup of tea.*

Maria had composed herself by the time she walked back to the table to change the cups.

"Would you like a biscuit?"

"No. Thank you."

"Suit yourself. Don't mind me if I have one." She returned to the kitchen but flinched when Maria appeared in the doorway.

"Could you check the housekeeping tin and see if there's enough money for a carriage? One-way at least."

Nell paused then nodded. "Put it on the table and I'll look while this is brewing..."

Maria was puffing before they were halfway to Betty's, and once they reached her front door, she leaned against the wall to catch her breath.

"My feet will be bad for weeks after this."

"You'll be fine. I'll get you a bowl of water when we get home, and you can sit with them soaking."

"You'll be seeing to the tea, as well."

"If you persuade Alice to come back, I'll do it every day for the next week. Shall I knock?"

Maria took a final breath and nodded. "You may as well."

Betty was sitting by the fire when Nell let herself in, and she jumped up with a smile.

"I've brought a visitor."

Betty's smile faded as Nell stepped to one side and Maria joined them.

"Aunty Maria."

"Good afternoon, Betty. I thought it was time I paid you a visit. I've heard a lot about where you are."

"Well ... come in. Alice is in the yard..."

Nell pulled Maria to the window to show her Alice playing ball with Albert. "See how happy she looks?"

When Maria didn't answer, Nell offered her a chair. "Have a seat and I'll tell her you're here."

Alice smiled as Nell slipped out into the yard. "I wasn't expecting you today."

"It was a last-minute decision. Your mam wants to speak to you."

The colour drained from Alice's face. "Mam's here?"

"She wanted me to pass you a message, but I said she had to speak to you herself."

"I've got nothing to say to her."

"Please. Will you just listen?"

Albert distracted her. "Aunty Alice!" He bounced the ball, hitting her on the legs and she grinned as she bent down to pick it up.

"You got me! Shall we go in for some milk?"

"May we come outside later?"

"If you're a good boy."

He ran on ahead but waited for Nell to open the door.

"He's taken to you."

"I've taken to him, too." Alice sighed. "I'm looking forward to the day I have some of my own and don't need to hand them back."

Nell grimaced. "Don't wish your life away. It will come soon enough."

Maria stood up as Alice joined her. "I'm sorry about everything." The words tumbled from her mouth. "I didn't mean to upset you. Please come home. I promise there won't be another cross word about Mr Wood. He'll be welcome for tea whenever you like..."

"But you don't like him."

"I do, really, but I was worried about you. I know he's a gentleman with a respectable job ... and that you're a young lady. If you want to be together, I won't stop you."

Alice nodded. "We do. We're very fond of each other."

"Then I'm happy for you. Please, come and sit with me."

Nell didn't miss the look that passed between Alice and Betty before Betty took Albert into the kitchen.

"That's it." Maria pulled her chair close to Alice's. "How've you been?"

"Fine. Betty and Mr Crane have been very kind."

"I'm glad. Have you seen Mr Wood?"

"I walk into Liverpool to meet him from work and he walks me home. The only downside is that he has to go back to Elaine Street."

"So, you'd be better living on Merlin Street?" Maria's face brightened. "You could spend more time with each other..."

Alice studied her. "Even on a Sunday?"

"Yes." Maria's voice was shrill. "Isn't that when couples usually walk out together?"

"And you wouldn't complain?"

"No." Maria's shoulders rose and fell. "I've learned my lesson. I want you home."

Alice looked over at Nell. "All right. Not today, though. I need to pack my personal possessions, and I'll be seeing Mr Wood later. I should thank Mr Crane for having me, too."

Tears ran down Maria's cheeks as she took Alice's hand. "Thank you. You won't regret it."

The carriage pulled up outside the house on Merlin Street shortly before five o'clock and Nell paid the coachman once he'd helped them down the steps. Maria straightened her skirt while she waited.

"I don't remember the last time I rode in one of those. It feels very indulgent, but my feet wouldn't have brought me home again."

"As long as you think the visit was worthwhile, that's all that matters."

"I do. Thank you." She opened the front door but stopped to pick up a letter from the doormat. "Is it from James?"

Nell stared at the writing. "Erm ... no."

"Who's it from then? You've gone very pale."

Tell her. It's the best time. She took a deep breath. "Do you remember Mr Marsh? It looks like his writing."

Maria carried on down the hall. "Why would he write after so long? I thought he was on the other side of the world."

"He was, last I heard."

"It can't be urgent, then. Would you mind opening it

later once the tea's made? George and Billy will be home shortly."

Gladly. She pushed the letter into a drawer in the dresser. "Another couple of hours won't make any difference. Now, what do you want me to do?"

Nell cleared the last of the plates from the table as George and Billy waved farewell and disappeared into the hall.

"These won't take long to wash, and then we can get the cards out."

Maria sank into a chair by the fire. "Do you mind if we don't tonight? I'm exhausted after that walk. I'll see the girls into bed and then turn in for the night myself."

"As you like. I've a magazine to read." *And a letter.*

Ten minutes later, when Nell finished putting the plates away, Maria was snoring softly, and she shook her shoulder to rouse her.

"You'd be better doing that in bed."

Maria huffed. "I need to get there first."

"You go on ahead and I'll send the girls up."

Leah was the first into the house, and Elenor stomped up the stairs behind her. "She should go to bed before me. I'm older."

"You've both got school tomorrow, so you need to be in bed as early as each other. And behave. Aunty Maria's tired and doesn't want any nonsense from you."

Maria was waiting on the landing, and once they'd disappeared into the bedroom, Nell slipped into the living room, closing the door behind her. *All evening on my own.* Her heart raced as she shovelled more coal onto the fire and retrieved the letter from the dresser. *What if he doesn't want to keep in touch?* She tutted as she sat down. Stop it. *Read the thing first.*

Dear Mrs Riley

May I say what a pleasant surprise it was to receive your correspondence after I'd convinced myself that you wouldn't respond? Who'd have thought Mrs Robertson and Mr Cooper would have spoken about us.

What to make of your letter, however, I am yet to decide.

As is your wont, you've left me with a feeling of hope mixed with trepidation. I would dearly love to believe your words, and even continue our correspondence, but we've been here before. Should our friendship come under strain, as it has before, I fear my heart would be unable to endure further disappointment.

As it is, I've settled into a stable routine in the Tasman Sea and I'm content with my lot. Do I wish to put that all at risk because of the glimmer of hope you offer?

I'm afraid I can't answer that at the moment.

I'm currently in Melbourne, so picked up your letter as soon as it arrived. I regularly travel to New Zealand, however, and letters are not forwarded to us there.

I need to think about our relationship and if I have any further thoughts, I'll write again when I'm able.

My very best wishes

Thomas Marsh

Nell sighed as she sat back in her chair. *I can hardly*

blame him, but what now? Should I write again and suggest we walk out together? She pushed herself up and studied herself in the mirror over the fireplace. *If I don't say something soon, I'll be too old. There's already too much grey in this hair.*

CHAPTER FORTY-ONE

Nell puffed out her cheeks and pushed the letter she was holding back into its envelope as Maria looked up from her knitting.

"What's the matter?"

"Mrs Robertson. She arrived in Liverpool yesterday, but she's written to say they're only in port for three days and there are things she needs to do."

"That's a shame. You've not seen her for months."

"I know. The shipping company's reduced the number of days they're in port, so she's no time. It's a good job she can travel with Captain Robertson, because if she didn't, she'd never see him. They don't care about crews suffering as long as they make money."

"It was always the same. I'm glad you're not travelling any more."

"It's a job for single women, or widows with no children, that's for sure."

"At least you got it out of your system."

When Nell didn't answer, Maria studied her. "You have, haven't you?"

"If that means, would I go away again, then yes, I have."

"You're still restless, though. What is it with you?"

Nell shrugged. "I wish I knew." She stood up and peered through the window. "I'll have a cup of tea and then walk to the park. It's annoying now Isobel's finished school. I can't go out with Rebecca like we used to."

"You'll have Elenor to deal with soon."

Nell sighed. "Don't remind me. She's still too wilful for my liking."

"I've a feeling it's school that makes her that way. Being at home with us may help."

"I doubt it. She won't thank us for making her do the housework."

"She'll have to get used to it. I managed with you and Rebecca when you were growing up."

"That was different. You had a lot more to do, looking after everyone. Now look at us. We have nothing to do but sit here."

Maria shook her head. "You need some fresh air to get yourself out of this mood."

"I'm sorry, I'm just disappointed about Mrs Robertson. I've arranged to visit Betty tomorrow, so that will cheer me up."

Betty clasped her hands together as Nell let herself in.

"You're here." She gave her a broad smile.

"That's a nice welcome." She took off her cloak and

hung it by the door. "What are you looking so pleased about?"

Betty placed a hand on her belly. "I'm going to be a mam again."

"Oh, Betty, that's wonderful. When?"

"I saw the doctor last week, and he thinks it will be in October."

Nell stared at the ceiling as she totted up the dates in her head. "So, you must be about halfway through, if there are four or five months left."

"He thinks so. I'm just relieved. Betsy's fourteen months old already, and I was beginning to think I wouldn't have another one."

"You've still plenty of time for more." She bent down to Betsy, who had toddled up to her and grabbed her skirt. "There's a good girl."

Betsy giggled as Nell tickled her tummy.

"She's a love. How's she been since Albert started school? Does she miss him?"

"She follows me round everywhere, unless Mam's here, then she stays with her."

"She'll have to make do with me today."

"She'll be happy with that."

Nell grinned. "You'll need a bigger house at this rate."

"Don't say that. We're hoping to stay here another few years yet."

"You'll be fine while the children are little. Before I was married, me and Aunty Rebecca lived on Newton Street with Aunty Maria and Uncle George and all four children, but we managed."

"It must have been a squeeze."

"It was, but they knew me and Rebecca would move out."

Betty smiled at her daughter. "Wouldn't it be lovely if they could stay like that and not grow up? It's when they get bigger the problems start."

It shouldn't start when they're ten years old. Heaven help me when Elenor reaches sixteen. I can only hope she's settled down by then.

It was almost half past four when Nell left the house, and she walked a short distance with Betty as she made her way to school.

"It's quite a walk you've got."

"It is, but it gets me out and Mam likes me walking part of the way home with her. When will you call again?"

"Next week, if that's all right. I'll check with your mam and find out when she's coming. It's nice having someone to walk with."

"Well, whenever it is, I'll be glad to see you." Betty stopped when they reached a junction. "This is where I turn off. See you next week."

Nell kept to the main road, avoiding going anywhere near the cemetery, and smiled when the sun broke out from the clouds as she approached Upper Parliament Street. *Why can't it be like Brazil and stay out all the time?*

The girls were home when she arrived, and Elenor slid from her chair.

"We're going."

"Where to?"

Maria glared after Elenor as she disappeared. "I told

them to wash their hands five minutes ago, but she took no notice. You need to have a word with her."

"I will. How's this afternoon been?"

"Quiet." She reached to the dresser and handed Nell a letter. "This came earlier."

Mr Marsh. It's less than a month since his last one. Does that mean he's made a decision?

"Is it for you?"

"Erm, yes. I'll open it later."

"Who's it from?"

Nell tried to calm her voice. "It looks like Mr Marsh's writing."

Maria's brow creased. "I thought it was all over between you."

"It is, but..." Her sentence was cut short as Elenor bounded into the room and retook her seat.

"Why do I have to wash my hands? You never do."

Nell put a hand on Maria's arm as she went to speak. "Elenor Riley, we'll have less of this answering back. If Aunty Maria tells you to do something, you do it."

"You don't."

"Because I'm a lot older than you. When you're a mam and run your own house, you can make the rules, but while you live here, you do as you're told. Is that clear?"

Leah crept into the room and took her seat at the table, keeping her head down as she did. "I do as I'm told."

"I know you do. Just don't start copying Elenor, because she'll get you into trouble."

. . .

Nell waited for Maria to go up to bed before she retrieved Mr Marsh's letter, and her heart raced as she scanned it.

> *...with the winter months approaching, I had more time to think than I expected...*
>
> *When I first read your letter, I feared my heart wouldn't stand any more disappointment, but there's little I can do about it now... You've already roused my sense of hope and I'm unable to fight it.*
>
> *I'm not yet ready for us to meet again, but I'd like to write to you on a more regular basis ... if you're happy with that.*
>
> *To that end, I'll be returning to England after this next voyage, but to save us from accidentally bumping into each other, I'll endeavour to stay on the ship and not come ashore.*
>
> *Don't reply to this letter as the office may have trouble locating me now I've moved. I'll let you know when I arrive.*

Nell reread the letter. *So, he's coming back, but doesn't want to meet up.* She put a hand to her mouth. *He won't have received my last letter yet.* The blood drained from her face. *Why was I so forward? He'll think I have no morals.* She closed her eyes and tilted her head to the ceiling. *Please Lord. Stop it from reaching him. Let it be on its way to Australia, never to be seen again.* A wave of sickness washed over her. *What a stupid thing to do without waiting to hear from him. It's bound to frighten him off. He'll think there's only one sort of woman who would write a letter like that. And it will confirm everything he already thinks about me.*

CHAPTER FORTY-TWO

Alice opened the front door to Mr Wood as Nell joined them in the hall.

"You're sure you don't mind me coming with you?"

"Of course not. Do we?" Alice nudged Mr Wood.

"What's that?"

"We don't mind Aunty Nell walking to the park with us."

"Not at all."

Alice smiled. "It's such a lovely day, and I didn't want her going on her own."

"I probably wouldn't have gone out, other than to walk to Sunday school to meet Leah."

Alice pulled the door closed behind her as they stepped onto the footpath. "I thought Elenor was with her."

"She is, but Leah's still pleased to see me." Nell paused. "Does Elenor ever talk to you?"

"Not about anything important. Why?"

Nell shrugged. "She seems distant at the moment. I don't remember you being like that at her age."

Alice grimaced. "I didn't have a choice. You're much less strict with them than Mam was with me."

"I didn't think I'd need to do much, living with your mam."

Alice studied her. "Haven't you noticed how Elenor only seems to listen to you?"

"I can't say I have. She never listens unless I shout."

"That's the thing. You don't shout very often, so when you do, she pays attention. Unfortunately for Mam, her shouting is like water off a duck's back."

"I can understand that, but I don't want to be too harsh."

"You needn't be. Just let her know her limits. I suspect that's why she preferred being with me rather than Mam while you were away. I wouldn't take any nonsense, but I wasn't telling her off all the time."

Nell smiled at her niece. "For someone so young, you've a very sensible head on your shoulders. You'll make a lovely mam, one day." She didn't miss the look Mr Wood gave Alice, but kept her eyes fixed on the gates to Princes Park. "Are we going here?"

"We were going to Sefton Park, if that's all right."

"Yes, fine with me."

Nell walked in silence as they approached Princes Park Mansions but stopped when they reached the driveway. "It seems strange that the Ellises have all left now."

Mr Wood looked at her. "You know someone who lived there?"

Alice giggled. "Not only that, she used to be a regular visitor until Miss Ellis was married and moved to Surrey."

He studied Nell with renewed interest. "Were you a domestic here?"

"No, I wasn't!" Nell straightened her back. "Although I should forgive you for thinking that. It's a long story."

"We've plenty of time while we walk around the park, so I'll look forward to hearing about it."

The crowds were thinning out by the time they left the lake, and Nell checked her watch.

"Sunday school will have finished. We might as well head for home. It's nice that you're staying for tea, Mr Wood."

"I hope we think the same when it's over. I never did thank you properly for helping us be together, especially after what happened with Mrs Atkin."

Nell sighed. "It should never have been necessary, but she's learned her lesson about trying to come between you."

He gazed down at Alice. "You were very brave doing what you did."

"Only because I knew Betty would be happy for me to stay with her. The most frightening part was when Mam came to visit. I thought I was for it then."

Nell shook her head. "Not with me there. Still, it's done now, and she's calmed down. I'm sure it makes it easier for you with Alice being in the next street."

"It certainly helps us see more of each other. And I don't go through nearly so much shoe leather."

A tingle ran down Nell's spine as Alice and Mr Wood laughed together. *To be her age again ... and have Jack with me.*

"Do you visit the alehouse much, Mr Wood?"

"I'm in there most evenings. It's the best way to find out what's happening. And it gets me out of the house."

"Aren't you happy with Mrs Parry?"

"Oh, yes, it's a lot better than where I was, but I only have the capacity for so many women at a time. If I went straight home after I left Alice, I'd be sitting with three of them who do nothing but chatter while they do their sewing."

Nell laughed. "They can talk. So, you get on well enough with George and Billy?"

"Aye, and Vernon."

Nell cocked her head to one side. "I didn't think he was in so often nowadays?"

"Not as much as the rest of us, and he's usually not in until later, but he's friendly enough when I see him. The only brother I've not met yet is James. Is there any word on when he'll be back from Brazil?"

Nell's shoulders slumped. "No, and we've not heard from him for about a month. He said he'd be home once a year, but it's been about fifteen months since we last saw him."

"He must like it out there."

"Oh, he does. To be honest, I suspect the only reason he comes back at all is because of his mam."

Alice's bottom lip stuck out. "I should hope he wants to see us, too."

"I'm sure he does, but while he's out there, there won't be any urgency for him to leave."

"Can't he see that the longer he puts it off, the more

upset Mam will be when she does see him, and that it will put him off coming even more?"

Nell nodded. "I had hoped he'd be here before the end of summer, because I know he hates the winter, but he's cutting it fine for that now."

Mr Wood's eyes flicked between the two of them. "It sounds like he'd rather stay where he is."

"The problem is, his mam and dad have moaned at him for years and it's taken its toll."

"All right." Mr Wood took a deep breath. "You've made my mind up for me. Excuse us, Mrs Riley." He put an arm around Alice's shoulders and led her to a nearby bench. Nell stayed where she was as he took Alice's hand and kissed the back of it. A moment later, Alice shrieked as her face lit up.

"You've spoken to Dad?"

Mr Wood nodded, and she turned to Nell. "Did you hear?"

"Not what Mr Wood said."

"He proposed marriage to me. And Dad's agreed to it!"

Nell grinned as she walked towards them. "Congratulations."

Mr Wood gazed at Alice. "I'd been wondering when to ask and hoped James would be home when I did, but if there's a chance he might not come this year..." He took her hand. "I didn't want to wait any longer."

Alice leaned into Mr Wood's arm. "This is so exciting. Am I allowed to tell everyone at tea?"

"I don't see why not. Although–" his forehead creased "–perhaps not before we've eaten. I'm still nervous about how your mam will react."

Nell tutted. "As long as you tell her when George is there, she'll be fine. What about a date? Should you announce that as well?"

Alice sighed. "Do we have to?"

"Not if you're not ready, but your mam's bound to ask."

Alice huffed. "She'll have to wait."

Nell helped to clear the plates as Maria carried a fresh pot of tea to the table. She'd no sooner retaken her seat when Mr Wood stood up.

"Before everyone leaves the table, I've an announcement to make."

Maria's mouth opened, but she stayed silent.

"While we were out, I asked Alice if she'd be my wife, and I'm delighted that she said yes."

George stood up and shook Mr Wood's hand as Billy patted him on the shoulder.

"Congratulations. To think, my little sister getting married..."

Mr Wood grinned and reached into his pocket. "As a token of our commitment, I have this for you." He produced a box and, with a well-practised twist of his hand, opened it to reveal a gold ring with three small diamonds across the top.

Alice gasped. "It's gorgeous."

He took it from the casing and slipped it onto her finger. "Nearly as lovely as you."

Leah clapped, swiftly followed by Elenor, but Maria remained silent. Alice stared at her.

"Can't you be happy for us?"

"I am, but–" she reached for a handkerchief and dabbed her eyes "–you're my little girl. How can you be getting married already?"

George took his wife's hand. "You'll be as proud as punch when I walk her down that aisle."

"I don't doubt it. I hope you'll be happy."

Alice gazed at Mr Wood. "We will be."

Maria sniffed as she put her handkerchief away. "What about a date?"

"Mr Wood only asked me as we were leaving the park, so we've not thought about it. I'd like to know when James will be home, before we choose. We want him to be here."

Maria's face hardened. "Don't we all."

CHAPTER FORTY-THREE

Nell hummed to herself as she turned the beds, unable to keep the smile from her face. *At least he's got good weather.*

Maria shouted to her up the stairs. "Are you nearly done up there?"

"I'm just straightening the bedspreads. You can put the kettle on."

"It's boiled. James will be here any minute."

"I'm coming." Nell gave the last cover a quick flick and raced down the stairs. "I can't believe he only gave us a couple of days' notice."

"He'll have to take us as he finds us."

Nell rolled her eyes. "He used to live here, remember? He won't be bothered."

"He will now he lives in one of those fancy houses in Brazil."

Nell suppressed a grin. "So, you do listen when I read his letters?"

"Of course, I do. I'll give him what for, for being so late..."

Nell held up a hand. "You won't do anything of the sort. Whatever you were going to say, leave it. He should be here any minute and he'll be more likely to come again if he gets a friendly welcome. You shouting will only drive him away for longer."

Alice arranged the cups on the table. "Aunty Nell's right. The more you complain, the less likely you are to get your own way. Be nice to him for a change."

"I'm always nice..."

Nell raised an eyebrow at her sister. "Really? Anyway. Let's not argue. Just put a smile on your face."

The tea was brewing, and a selection of bread and scones was on the table when the front door opened and James let himself in.

Nell burst into the hall to greet him. "You're here!"

"I am." He put an arm around her shoulders and squeezed before he did the same to Alice. "Mam." He stared at Maria as she waited by the living room door.

"Welcome home." A smile spread across her face and James momentarily stared at Nell before he gave his Mam a peck on the cheek.

"It's good to see you all."

Nell grinned. "We've been looking forward to seeing you for five months. What kept you?"

"Ah, that's a tale. May I come in first?"

They all escorted him to the table and Maria poured a cup of tea and pushed it to him. "Help yourself."

Nell's brow creased. "Do you work on the ship when you travel, or are you a passenger?"

"I'm a passenger. And very nice it is too, being waited on." He reached for a piece of bread but stopped when he noticed Alice's hand. "What have I missed? Are you engaged to be married?"

Her cheeks flushed as she fidgeted with her ring. "I am. To Mr Harry Wood. He wanted to wait until you were here before he proposed marriage, but we didn't know when you were arriving, so he asked me last month."

"Well, congratulations. I look forward to meeting him."

"I expect you'll see him in the alehouse tonight. He usually calls in after he brings me home."

"I'll make a point of looking out for him then." He grinned at Maria. "Does he meet your approval?"

Maria took a deep breath. "He does."

James' forehead creased. "Wait a minute. Was this man the reason you left home? It's coming back to me now."

Nell pushed the butter towards him. "It was a misunderstanding, that's all. Now, are you going to tell us why we've not seen you for so long? The summer's nearly over."

"It was Mr Smith's fault."

"Who's Mr Smith?"

"The man I work for. He knew I'd arranged to travel in April, but he had some house guests visit at the last minute and wanted me to stay until they left."

Maria breathed in deeply. "Did it have to be you who looked after them?"

"Normally, it wouldn't be, but these guests were special. The owner of the plantation and his companions, so they needed the best attention. He couldn't leave them to the general servants."

"I thought you worked for the owner."

"No, he's the manager. The owner doesn't get his hands dirty with the day-to-day goings-on."

"Oh." Maria's forehead creased. "How long did they stay?"

"Two months. It was hard work, but they all left happy."

"So, why didn't you come home in June?"

James rolled his eyes. "There was so much to do once they'd gone and then I had to speak to Mr Smith again about leaving. He wasn't pleased, I can tell you."

"But you're entitled to it."

James tutted. "This is Brazil, Mam. Things are different over there. Anyway, I'm here now. Have I missed anything besides Alice's engagement?"

"Probably a lot, but it's so long to remember what you know and what you don't."

"All right. I'm sorry. How's Aunty Sarah managing? It was Uncle Tom's funeral last time I was here."

Nell smiled. "She's fine. Mr Wood is the one who moved in with them as a lodger and he's fitted in very well."

"I'd say." He grinned at Alice, then turned to Nell.

"What about you? Is there anything you're not telling me?"

Nell shook her head. "No."

He looked at her from the corner of his eye. "That was a little too definite."

"Because there's nothing to tell." She stood up and picked up the teapot. "Let me top this up before it stews."

. . .

Once dinner was over, James sat by the fire while Nell and Maria tidied up.

"Does Alice always go out at this time?"

Nell straightened up. "Several times a week. She goes to visit Betty when she can, but on Wednesdays she meets Mr Wood. He finishes early, so she walks up to meet him, and they have the afternoon together."

"I can't believe she's getting married." He watched Maria disappear into the kitchen. "Do you like him?"

"I do, and he'll look after her."

"I thought he was only a couple of years younger than me."

"He is, but he's good for her. Trust me."

"Very well. Are you nearly finished here? We could take a walk."

"I'd like that. Give me a minute and I'll be with you."

Once the table was clean, she reached for her hat and stood in front of the mirror. "I won't be wearing this for much longer. In another few weeks, summer will be over." She paused as the letterbox clanged.

"I'll get that." James was on his feet before she could turn round. He returned waving a letter. "It's for you."

"It will be from Mrs Cavendish."

"That's not a woman's handwriting."

Nell took it from him. "Yes, it is." Her heart raced when she saw the envelope. "Would you give me a minute? L-let me check it's nothing urgent."

She slipped into the front room, closing the door behind her, and perched on a chair by the unlit fire.

Mr Marsh. Her stomach somersaulted. *Does this mean he's in Liverpool?*

My dear Mrs Riley, or may I call you Elenor?

I trust you won't mind the informality if we're to walk out together.

She gasped. *He got the letter I sent to Australia.*

Not in my wildest dreams could I have imagined receiving a letter like that. There was a time it would have made me think harshly of you, but after the last two years, it was just what I needed.

Before I received it, I feared that moving back to England had been a grave mistake. I'd hoped it would make me feel closer to you, but in reality, I may as well have stayed on the other side of the world. What point is there being so close when we don't see each other?

Reading your letter has encouraged me to put the past, and my fear, behind me so we may take our first official walk together.

I'm leaving for New York tomorrow and don't have time to visit now, but I'll be in touch as soon as I return so we can meet up again.

I pray you are agreeable to this, but if it isn't possible, you know how to contact me.

I'm very much looking forward to seeing you.

My fondest wishes

Thomas

Nell flinched at the knock on the door. "Aunty Nell. Are you nearly ready?"

"Oh, yes, one minute." She wiped her eyes with the

back of her hands and pushed the letter into its envelope. *I didn't frighten him off.*

James was by the fireplace when she rejoined him. "Sorry about that. It wasn't anything important."

He raised an eyebrow but said nothing as Maria joined them.

"You'd better go if you're going. It will be teatime soon."

Nell put the letter in her handbag. "I'm ready now. Shall we?"

The clouds had thickened by the time they reached the park, but the air was still warm, and Nell took a deep breath. "It feels like old times."

"I don't suppose much has changed since I was last here."

"Not that I recall. Oh, I didn't tell you, Mrs Cavendish's father died at the start of the year and so her mother had to move out of the mansions."

"Did she go to Surrey?"

"No, but it was quite a battle. In the end, Mrs Cavendish persuaded her brother to have her. She said it would be cruel to take her away from all her friends."

James' forehead creased. "I didn't think she had any."

"She didn't, but she has more acquaintances here than she would in Surrey. Anyway, he's the heir to his father's wealth, so Mrs Cavendish said it was only right that he inherited his mother, too."

James laughed. "I like her style. Although–" his face turned serious "–does that mean I'll inherit Mam if anything happens to Dad?"

"Not if you're in Brazil."

James grinned. "Another reason not to come back then."

Nell studied him. "Were you being honest about the owner visiting the plantation?"

"Sort of. He did visit, but they didn't stay with us. They just called in occasionally."

"So why were you late coming home?"

James sighed. "To tell you the truth, I lost track of time. It's so different over there. There are no seasons as such, the length of the days hardly changes, they harvest the rubber all year round, and, if you want to know the *real* truth, I was enjoying myself. I work hard when I'm on duty, but I get time to myself, and it's nice to relax. Is that wrong?"

"It sounds wonderful. Are you sure you don't have a secret wife or sweetheart out there?"

He snorted. "No, I don't. Even if I wanted one, there isn't the opportunity. It really is us and them. Those with money and those who serve them. All the women belong to those with money, so even if I had designs on anyone, I wouldn't be able to do anything about it."

I know what that feels like. "That's a shame."

He grinned at her. "I don't mind. I'd have to find somewhere else to live if I had a wife, so it suits me to stay as I am. And what about you? I get the impression you're hiding something."

Nell bit her lip as she stared straight ahead. "Like what?"

"Like who sent that letter? I don't care what you say, that wasn't a woman's handwriting."

Her shoulders slumped. "All right, but promise you won't tell anyone?"

"Have I ever?"

"Mr Marsh has been writing to me again."

"From Australia?"

She nodded. "That was how it started, but he's back in England."

"In Liverpool?"

She nodded. "Sort of, but he stayed on the ship, and he leaves for New York later today."

James' eyes narrowed as he stared at her. "Why would he do that?"

"I don't know."

"I think you do."

Nell sighed. "I'm not going into details, but when he left, there were issues between us, and if we're to have a future together, we need to sort them out. He thought that staying on board would give us space."

"Are your differences solvable?"

She shrugged. "I don't know."

James looked straight ahead as they approached the lake. "Would you like them to be?"

When she didn't answer, he stopped and stared at her. "You would, wouldn't you?"

"I'll be forty next month, and I've realised I don't want to be on my own any more. It's different for men. You'll always have your independence, but I'm more likely to end up like your mam, stuck in the house, not able to walk out unless someone takes pity on me."

"I doubt that."

"I don't."

"And is Mr Marsh the one you'd like to spend the rest of your life taking walks with?"

"He's a good man. I could do a lot worse." *And he'll be company for my old age.*

CHAPTER FORTY-FOUR

The dock road was busier than it had been the previous week when Nell had walked with James to his ship. *It is later in the day.* Her stomach churned when she looked up at the black funnels of the SS *Alaska*, Captain Robertson's current charge. *It's so much bigger than the Bohemian.*

Her heart pounded as she stepped onto the gangplank, but as instructed by Mrs Robertson, she gave her name to the steward on the door. She breathed a sigh of relief when it was on a sheet of paper, and he showed her on board.

"Mrs Robertson is at the front of the ship, near the captain's deck."

"I imagined she would be."

He gave her a sideways glance. "You're familiar with the vessel?"

"Not this one, but I met Mrs Robertson when I was a stewardess on a previous ship under Captain Robertson's command."

"Ah." He looked her up and down and hesitated before they continued. "Have you come about a job?"

"No. Mrs Robertson and I are friends."

"Oh." Lines creased his forehead. "This way."

Mrs Robertson was on the first-class deck when they arrived, and she walked towards Nell with a smile. "How lovely to see you."

"And you. It's been too long."

The steward waited for their attention. "Would you care for tea?"

"Please, while it's warm enough to stay outside."

Nell leaned against the railings, staring down at the people rushing around beneath her. "I used to love this view. Especially when we were about to dock."

"It is amazing. I come out here whenever I can when we're in port. The weather's been so nice this summer I decided I should make the most of it."

"Don't you miss being onshore?"

Mrs Robertson sighed. "In some ways, I do, but we couldn't have a house and a governess, and the governess won."

Nell chuckled. "How long are you docked for this time?"

"Four days. We've only had two for the last few months, and we've had passengers disembarking one day and arriving the next, so I haven't had a moment."

"I wouldn't have survived."

"It has been hard on the stewardesses, especially those with families. Still, things should improve now we're heading towards winter." Mrs Robertson indicated to a couple of chairs behind them. "Shall we?"

Nell strolled to the seat. "How's Violet getting on with the governess?"

"Very well, thankfully. We've been rather cramped with all the staterooms full, but we'll have more space on the next voyage. And what about you? Do you have any news?"

Nell gave her a weak smile. "Mr Marsh is back from Australia."

Mrs Robertson gasped. "In Liverpool?"

"He's been to Liverpool, but immediately did a trip to New York. He's due back any day now."

Mrs Robertson clasped her hands. "How exciting! Did you see him before he left?"

"He wasn't ready..."

"But he is now?"

"So he says. I had a letter from him a couple of days ago that he'd posted in New York. I'm trying not to get carried away, given everything that's gone before, but there's a chance we'll be walking out together by the time he leaves."

"And you don't mind that he'll still be working?"

Nell shrugged. "There's nothing I can do about it at the moment. I can't ask him to give up his job before we've sorted out our problems."

Mrs Robertson studied her. "Are the differences that great?"

"Not as far as I'm concerned, but we need to get over the encounter with Ollie. He has to believe my friendship with him is over."

"There's a good chance he will if he wants to see you."

"That's what I'm hoping. And at least we won't bump into Ollie now Mr Ellis has died and Mrs Ellis has moved away."

Mrs Robertson gasped. "I didn't know that."

Nell shook her head. "It's such a long time since we spoke..." She paused as the steward returned with the tea and a plate of cakes. "Mr Ellis died earlier in the year and obviously Mrs Ellis couldn't stay in the house on her own. She's living with her son now."

"Does that mean you're unlikely to see Mrs Cavendish again?"

Nell sighed. "She might come up here to visit her mother, but whether we meet up is another matter. She came to Liverpool after her father died and I joined her for afternoon tea at the Adelphi. Unfortunately, it didn't go terribly well..."

The evening sun was sinking behind the warehouses by the time the steward escorted Nell from the ship and she clung to the rails of the gangplank as she made her way to the landing stage. *Such a simple, uncomplicated afternoon. Why can't all visits be like that?* She gave the ship a final glance before she turned right and headed towards Parliament Street.

Maria was in the street talking to a neighbour when she arrived home. "Here she is."

"I told you I'd be here about now. What's up?"

The neighbour leaned forward with a knowing look. "There was a gentleman looking for you."

"A gentleman? Who?"

Maria's face straightened. "Mr Marsh."

"But..." Nell's mouth fell open as Maria bid farewell to the neighbour and ushered her into the house.

"But you weren't expecting him until tomorrow? Is that what you were going to say? Why is this the first I've heard of it?"

Nell shrugged. "I was going to tell you..."

"When? I'd no idea what he was talking about when he turned up. How do you think that made him feel? Embarrassed. That's how..."

That's all I need. "Why was he here today?"

"His ship docked early, and he wanted to surprise you ... now you're walking out together."

"Ah."

"I'll give you 'Ah'. What's going on?"

Nell pulled out a chair and sat at the table. "It's not definite that we're walking out."

"He seems to think you are."

Nell fidgeted with her fingers. "It's complicated. Last time I saw him, we had a row, which is why he left for Australia. He wrote earlier this year asking after me, and then, after some correspondence, he decided to return to England."

"So, it wasn't only one letter. This must have been going on for months."

"It takes a long time for letters to get to and from Australia. Four or five months for the round trip, so there haven't been many."

"Well, he certainly seems keen."

Nell clasped her hands together. "Did he say anything? I-is he coming back?"

"Thankfully, I knew where you were, so he said he'd call at five o'clock."

"Today!" She jumped up and looked in the mirror. "I'd better get smartened up."

"You're already wearing your Sunday best."

"I'd better do something with this hair; my hat's pulled some clips out. Heavens, look at the time. It's five to, already."

"Calm down. He'll wait for you."

"It will be dark by six."

"You can invite him in if you like and give me a chance to meet him."

She shook her head. "Perhaps another day ... when we've ironed out our differences. Let me sort this hair out..."

Nell was on her way down the stairs when there was a knock on the door. *He's here.* She took a deep breath. *Calm down. There's no need to panic.*

She put on her best smile as she answered it and gazed at the tall, slim man in front of her. He appeared different as he raised his hat. *Is it the touches of grey at his temples, or the absence of grease holding his hair in place? Whatever it is, he's less stern than he used to be.*

"Mr Marsh. What a surprise..."

"Thomas, please. Good afternoon, Elenor."

Nell's cheeks coloured. "That will take some getting used to. Let me get my cloak and we can take a walk." She popped her head into the living room. "I'm going. I won't be long."

Mr Marsh gazed at her as she pulled the door closed. "You're even more lovely than I remember."

"A few years older, I'm afraid."

"Aren't we all?" He offered her his arm. "I'm sorry I missed you earlier. I'd hoped to surprise you."

"You've done that, anyway."

"Your sister said you'd been to visit Mrs Robertson. Does she live locally?"

"Not any more. She travels with Captain Robertson, and they stay on the ship when they're in port."

"You've been on board?"

"Yes. It's the SS *Alaska* if you're passing. They're docked for four days. Didn't Mr Cooper tell you?"

"He may have done. I picked up a letter from him when I arrived, but in my haste, I didn't open it. Did you see him?"

"No. We were on the first-class deck and then in Mrs Robertson's quarters. I only saw the steward who showed me on and off the ship."

Mr Marsh nodded. "I'll ask if he saw you."

Nell's eyes narrowed. "Don't you believe me?"

"Oh, yes, of course." Mr Marsh's eyes were wide. "I didn't mean anything... I'm sorry..."

Nell's shoulders relaxed. "After what happened, it sounded like you were checking up on me."

Mr Marsh remained silent as they turned out of Merlin Street and Nell studied him.

"I'm sorry, I didn't mean anything by that. I just worry you'll think I'm not good enough and leave again at a moment's notice."

Mr Marsh's shoulders slumped. "I'm sorry, I've spoiled things again. I knew this would happen."

"But it needn't."

He pinched the bridge of his nose. "I desperately want to believe what you say, but I can still see Mr Hewitt sneering at me, telling me how close the two of you were ... how you enjoyed it. And you didn't deny it."

Nell closed her eyes as a shiver ran through her. "He exaggerated. We were no more than friends."

"Men and women are never *just* friends. Look at you and me..."

Nell stared at the park gates. "Nobody was more horrified than me by what Mr Hewitt said that day, but if you'll trust me, I'll tell you about the friendship we had."

"I couldn't bear it."

"We need to clear the air between us. I doubt it will be worse than anything you've imagined." She glanced round as they arrived in Princes Park. "Why don't we sit down, and I'll hopefully put your mind to rest."

Mr Marsh's steps felt reluctant as Nell led him to the nearest bench, and he stared into space as she turned to face him, resting her hands on her lap.

"Please believe me when I say that we were never more than friends." When he kept his focus on the distance, she continued. "I don't remember how much of this I've told you already, but once we left him in New York, I doubt I would have seen him again if it hadn't been for Miss Ellis. He and Mr Cavendish called on her several times while I was away at sea, but there was one occasion when my shore leave coincided with them being in Liverpool. They took us to the Adelphi for afternoon tea."

"You told me that, but he implied there was more to it."

"There was. Once I left the *Bohemian*, they travelled to Liverpool several more times. They always took us for tea, and it was during that time that Mr Cavendish and Miss Ellis fell in love. Once they made their relationship known, they visited more often, but I was only ever there as Miss Ellis's chaperone."

"*He* needn't have come."

Nell shifted in her seat. "It's a long journey from Surrey, and Mr Cavendish appreciated the company."

"And you would know."

"Well, yes." Nell coughed to keep the squeak from her voice. "I think I told you I'd been to Mrs Cavendish's marriage service."

"And that's where Mr Hewitt plied you with champagne and..."

"No. Please don't say that. It was only a small wedding. He was the best man, and I was matron of honour, so we did see each other, but he was betrothed himself by then and his fiancée was present."

Nell's heart raced as Mr Marsh sat in silence.

"If I'm honest, I can't deny that when we first met, I was flattered he even noticed me, but there was no more to it than that."

"So, where did the champagne come in?" His eyes were moist as he turned to her.

"Mrs Cavendish, as she was by then, was always inviting me to stay with them in Surrey, and when I received an invitation to Mr Hewitt's marriage, I couldn't make any more excuses."

Mr Marsh's brow furrowed. "You went to his wedding?"

She nodded. "At Ackley Hall, the family seat he'll eventually inherit. It was incredible. Three hundred people, fabulous food, dancing, champagne..."

The confusion remained as he searched her face. "Go on."

"Towards the end of the evening, he asked me to dance and then..." She stared over Mr Marsh's shoulder and took a deep breath. "He suggested I move to London to be with him."

Mr Marsh's torso stiffened. "And did you?"

"No." She met his gaze. "I turned him down and left Surrey the following morning. Except for that unfortunate afternoon, I've not laid eyes on him since."

"He must have had a reason to ask..."

"Because I'm a woman without virtue? Is that what you're thinking?" Her face grew stern. "I don't know what he thought, but if that was it, it goes to show he doesn't know me very well."

"But you must have seen him when you visited Mrs Cavendish?"

"I've not been since, despite many requests for me to go."

"But the dance..."

"A waltz. In a room of over two hundred people..."

"So, there was no relationship?"

"No."

Mr Marsh paused. "But he said you enjoyed it."

"I enjoyed dancing at the wedding until I danced with him. He spoilt everything."

"And that's why you went to sea again?"

Nell nodded. "I couldn't risk seeing him again, and it made it easier to turn down Mrs Cavendish's invitations."

"You sound disappointed."

"Only because I lost Mrs Cavendish as a friend. When I didn't visit, she surrounded herself with new friends. I don't blame her, but we have little in common nowadays."

Nell's voice quivered. "You'll never understand how much I hate Mr Hewitt after what he said to you. It was pure spite."

"You mean, if he couldn't have you, he didn't want anyone else to?"

"It was more than that. You were the last man in the world he wanted me to walk out with."

"You know that?" He raised an eyebrow.

"He never forgave you for the way you tried to keep us apart on the ship."

Mr Marsh shook his head. "There's so much to take in."

"There is, but please believe that it's the truth. If we're to walk out together, there shouldn't be any secrets between us."

Their eyes met as he looked down at her. "And you're sure that's it? There's nothing else?"

"No, I promise."

He ran a finger down her cheek. "We need to get to know each other better. Can we start again?"

"I'd like that."

He gazed up at the darkening sky. "I'd better get you home, but we've so much more to say. May we spend tomorrow afternoon together?"

"I'd be disappointed if we didn't."

CHAPTER FORTY-FIVE

A leaf from a nearby tree fluttered in the breeze and landed on Mr Marsh's lap as he settled onto a seat overlooking the lake. He held it up and studied it.

"I've had two winters this year, but no summer. Not very good planning." His eyes sparkled as he handed it to Nell. "Not that I'm complaining. I felt as if I'd had a weight taken from me yesterday after we talked."

She smoothed the leaf between her fingers. "I'm glad. Things are rarely as bad as our imaginations make them out to be."

"I should have learned by now, but I let it run riot every time." He gazed at her. "It's only because I like you so much."

"Thank you for giving me another chance. I missed you when you went away."

"Really?"

She grinned. "Really."

"Are we officially walking out together, then?"

"On one condition."

His face fell. "Is it my job?"

"That wasn't what I was going to say, not yet, anyway. It won't be ideal, you being away all the time, though."

"Don't think I've not thought about it. I'd give the company notice of my intention to leave immediately, if it meant we could be together, but–" he shook his head "–when I asked about moving routes, they insisted I signed a long-term contract. I'll be away for most of this year and some of next. Does that change anything?"

She bit her lip. "We'll make sure it doesn't. I knew you couldn't give up your job before we sorted things out between us."

"I'll finish as soon as I can." He studied her. "So, what was your condition?"

A smirk crossed her face. "I'd like you to call me Nell, rather than Elenor. It's what everyone else calls me."

He cocked his head to one side. "Elenor's such a pretty name; it suits you. I was never one for abbreviations."

Nell laughed. "That doesn't surprise me."

"Would you be upset if I called you Elenor?"

She paused to study him. "Only if my daughter isn't around. It could get confusing. And as long as you don't sound like Maria when I was a naughty child."

He smirked at her. "Very well. I'll reserve it for when it's just the two of us, and never in anger. Not that I ever want to be angry with you."

"I should hope not." Her face became serious. "How are you feeling about meeting Maria properly later?"

"I've not really thought about it. Should I be worried?"

"As long as you don't mind being interrogated. She'll have your family background out of you before we get to the cake. Oh, and George will probably want to take you to the alehouse once tea's over. If you're happy to sup a few pints of ale with him, he'll like you."

"Ah."

"Is that a problem?"

"Ale isn't really my thing."

Nell's cheek creased. "Could you try?"

"I could, although it doesn't agree with me. Especially not if I have more than one."

"What would you normally drink?"

"Perhaps a sherry."

Nell grimaced. "Don't have that at the alehouse."

"I doubt they'll sell it. What about a brandy?"

"That should be all right. The thing about George is he's very much a man's man and hates to see men doing anything that a woman would do. It took him a long time to accept that my nephew James wanted to be a steward."

"That's not women's work."

"It's fetching and carrying after *toffs*, as he calls them, which is one problem. The other is that he sees waiting on tables and cleaning as women's work."

"So, being a steward and drinking sherry won't go down well?"

"Er ... no. Just be careful what you say, and you'll be fine." *I hope.*

Maria and Alice were setting the table when Nell led Mr Marsh into the living room.

"You're here." Maria smoothed her hands over her skirt. "It's nice to meet you officially, Mr Marsh."

"And you, Mrs Atkin." He gave a slight bow. "This must be your daughter."

"It is."

Alice's cheeks coloured. "Pleased to meet you. Did you have a pleasant afternoon?"

"We did, thank you. You're fortunate to live in such a nice place."

Nell ushered him to the fireplace. "Take a seat. The girls will be home shortly, and then the men arrive not long after half past five."

"You don't walk to school to meet them any more?"

"No. Elenor finished earlier this year, but she still walks up to meet Leah. Despite what she might say, I think she misses it."

"And she couldn't possibly admit to that."

Maria pulled a dining chair to the fire. "Are your family local, Mr Marsh?"

"I'm afraid not. I've three brothers and two sisters who are in Carlisle, near the Scottish border. One brother and both sisters are married and have about ten children between them."

"About?" Maria's forehead creased.

"I'm sorry, I didn't mean to sound flippant, but I rarely see them, and we only exchange cards at Christmas."

"What a terrible state of affairs. I couldn't imagine not seeing my family."

"It's not ideal, but when you work on the ships, you don't get more than a couple of days off between voyages. My father wasn't happy about me leaving, and the easiest way to deal with it was to stay away."

Maria shifted uncomfortably in her chair and stood up. "If you'll excuse me, I need to see to the tea."

Mr Marsh's brow furrowed as Nell leaned towards him.

"I'll tell you later." She swivelled in her chair as the front door closed and Elenor and Leah joined them.

"Uncle Thomas?"

"You remembered." Nell ushered them back to the door, but Leah stared at him.

"Is he the one who's your fancy man?"

Nell's cheeks burned. "No! I told you, we're friends."

Elenor's eyes narrowed. "I don't have boys who are friends."

"Because you're too young, that's why."

"I've finished school."

"That still isn't old enough. Now, Mr Marsh, Uncle Thomas, is staying in Liverpool for a few days. I've invited him for tea so go and wash your hands."

The girls hadn't returned when George and Billy joined them, and Mr Marsh stood up and offered George his hand.

"Mr Atkin, I presume."

George looked at Nell. "Who've we got here?"

"This is Mr Marsh, the gentleman I was telling you about. We met when I was working on the ship, and we recently ran into each other again."

George nodded but ignored his hand. "Are you courting her?"

"I am."

"Only since yesterday." Nell's voice was breathless. "I wanted him to meet everyone before he goes back to sea."

"You're a steward?"

"Yes, sir."

"Don't go all hoity-toity on me." George turned away and took his seat. "Mr Atkin will do."

"I-I'm sorry."

"Shall we sit down?" Nell pointed to the right-hand side of the table. "Mr Marsh, you sit between me and Billy. We should be able to squeeze in."

Billy pushed out the chair. "Nice to see you again. We met once when I escorted Aunty Nell to the ship."

Mr Marsh studied him. "I remember now. I met your brother too, on a separate occasion. The one with the ginger hair."

"That will be James. He takes after Dad."

"He does not." George's face was red. "He's never done a proper day's work in his life..."

Maria put a hand on George's arm, and he glared at her before helping himself to a slice of bread. "Where's this tea?"

"It's coming."

Nell jumped up. "Let me help."

George was staring at Mr Marsh when she returned. "Have you been married before?"

"No, no, I've not. I've been on the ships for the last sixteen years and never got around to it."

"You don't know what you're taking on, then."

"Excuse me." Nell glared at him as she handed the girls' plates to Alice.

"He knows what I mean. Will you carry on going to sea?"

"For the time being..."

"Not committed, then?"

"George, please." Tears welled in Nell's eyes. "Can we

have a civilised tea?"

"I'm being civilised."

Maria joined them and smiled at Mr Marsh. "I hope you like cottage pie. I made it especially."

"It looks lovely. Thank you. It's nice to sit round a family table."

"You've obviously been away too long. We miss James and our other son, Vernon. He's married now, but we've a lot to be thankful for. Haven't we, George?"

George grunted without looking up. "If you say so."

Billy scooped up a forkful of minced beef. "Are you staying in one of the boarding houses?"

"I've stayed on the ship this week. It didn't seem worth booking anywhere for three nights." He checked his pocket watch. "In fact, I'd better not stay much longer. There are still chores to do while we're docked."

"More cleaning?" George emptied his plate and pushed it away.

"No, not tonight. I'd offered to help the barman restock the bar ... before Mrs Atkin's generous offer."

"Familiar with working a bar, are you? I used to do that myself when my leg was bad. What ale do you carry?"

"No draught, I'm afraid. Only bottles."

"Pfft. Another good reason not to go on one of those things." George finished his cup of tea and pushed himself up. "Are you ready, Billy?"

His son's plate wasn't empty. "You go and I'll follow. I like the look of that cake."

"Suit yourself." He raised an arm to wave. "Good to meet you, Mr Marsh."

Nell closed her eyes and took a deep breath as the front door slammed. *Thanks for nothing, George.*

"Don't mind Dad, Mr Marsh." Billy cleared his plate. "He hated it when James became a steward and clearly hasn't got any better."

Mr Marsh laid his knife and fork on the plate. "I quite understand. I expect he'd prefer his sons to follow in his footsteps."

Maria gave a feeble smile. "My husband thinks work should involve something with tools. He won't hold it against you. Not once he gets to know you."

The clock hadn't struck seven when Nell pulled the living room door closed behind her and showed Mr Marsh to the front door. His smile was weak as he collected his hat.

"Don't look so sad."

"I'm sorry. Things didn't go as well as I'd hoped."

"It's not your fault. Mr Atkin's attitude reminded me of my father."

"You didn't go home for years after you left."

He put a finger under her chin and lifted her face to his. "If you think I'd let something like that keep me away, then you don't know me well enough. It's taken us six years to get this far. I won't walk away for something as trivial as that."

A tingle ran down her spine. "I'm glad. Will I see you tomorrow?"

"Most certainly, although perhaps I won't stay for tea."

She chuckled. "I won't be inviting you. On the bright side, George's behaviour made Maria stand up for you. I'd say she likes you."

"Then it was worth it. May I pick you up at half past one?"

She nodded. "I'll be ready."

Mr Marsh released Nell's arm as they arrived at the house the following afternoon after a visit to the park.

"This is where we must part. For now, at least."

Nell forced a smile. "I've enjoyed these last two days. Thank you."

"It's me who should be thanking you. I feel complete again."

"When are you due back in Liverpool?"

"The end of October. I'll have one more trip after that and then that will be it until next year."

"I'll look forward to it."

He gazed down at her, studying every inch of her face. "How I wish I could carry your picture with me."

"Photographs aren't for the likes of us. You'll be back soon enough, and I won't have changed in that time."

"I'll be counting the days." He checked his watch. "I'd better go before your brother-in-law arrives. I'd rather not see him again so soon."

"Have a safe trip."

He raised his hat and set off towards Windsor Street. She waited for him to wave from the street corner as he turned off, but before she went back into the house, Rebecca came out to meet her.

"Is that it for now?"

Nell nodded, unable to speak.

"Did you have a nice afternoon?"

"Y-yes." She coughed to clear her throat. "I don't know how I misjudged him for so many years."

"You were working then. It must have been different."

"It was."

"Come on, cheer up. It gets easier."

Nell's eyes narrowed. "Mr Grayson's never left you."

"I'm talking about you, and how we all felt when you left us."

"It can't have been the same."

Rebecca raised an eyebrow. "Tell that to Maria, or the girls. Or Alice." She nodded towards her niece as she approached them.

Alice waved as she approached them. "What are you doing out here?"

"Mr Marsh has just left."

"Is that it for this visit?"

Nell sighed. "It is. How's Betty?"

Alice grimaced. "She was quite uncomfortable today. She thinks the baby might be ready to join us."

"Did you call the midwife?"

"Not yet. She said it's not that close. I called to tell Aunty Jane on the way home and she said she'd be there tomorrow."

"At least Mr Crane will be with her soon and I'll call later in the week, if nothing's happened by then."

CHAPTER FORTY-SIX

Jane kept a steady pace alongside Nell as they strode down the Everton road on their way to Betty's.

"She's desperate for this baby to be born." Jane looked both ways as she led them across the road. "We've had the midwife out a couple of times already, but they've been false alarms."

"At least Albert's at school."

"She's still been walking up there to drop him off and pick him up when she's on her own."

Nell's eyes widened. "Doesn't she have a neighbour who can help?"

"She won't ask. I'll go for him today and speak to some of the mams."

"Let's hope the baby isn't ready to arrive, then."

Jane didn't knock on Betty's front door before she pushed it open and held it for Nell. "It's only us."

"Up here." Betty's voice was tense, and they raced up the stairs to the only bedroom where Betty was perched on the edge of a large bed. Betsy sat behind her.

"It's coming."

Jane edged to the door. "Nell, you see to Betsy, I'll fetch the midwife."

Nell scooped Betsy into her arms but stopped as Betty squirmed. "Are you comfortable there?"

"I'm not comfortable anywhere. I just want to squeeze the baby out."

"Shall I help you onto the bed?"

She shook her head. "Just stay with me."

"Of course." Nell put Betsy in her cot and sat on the chair beside it. "It's a mercy you were able to wait."

"I hope this isn't another false alarm." Betty's face contorted as she fought a shriek.

"It doesn't look like one to me."

Betty panted as the pain gripped her but relaxed again as her breathing settled. "It may come while you're here."

Nell grimaced. "As long as it's not before the midwife arrives..."

Betty shifted on the bed. "Are third babies born quicker than the first or second?"

Nell hesitated. "I-I don't know..."

"I hope they are..." Betty's smile disappeared as another wave of pain swept over her. "Argh..."

Betsy began to cry and Nell picked her out of the cot. "She shouldn't be in here. Let me take her downstairs and I'll be back."

"She ... she's not likely to stay where you leave her."

"Is there a bottle I can give her?"

Betty grunted. "In the kitchen..."

Betsy was almost settled when Jane returned.

"Thank goodness you're here. I think she's ready."

The midwife headed straight to the stairs. "Leave it to me. Have you taken any water up?"

"N-no. Not yet."

"Towels?"

"I'm sorry. I'm not used to this."

Jane tutted as she hung up her cloak. "You stay here, I'll get them."

Nell handed Betsy her blocks, but as Betty's cries grew louder, she closed her eyes and shuddered. *It doesn't get any easier.*

Jane joined her while she waited for the kettle to boil. "What's up with you?"

Nell stared at her. "Betty. Doesn't it bother you?"

"The baby has to come out."

"It's still horrible..."

"But look what you get at the end." She bent down to pick up her granddaughter. "We wouldn't have you if we didn't go through that, would we?" She looked back at Nell. "It will be your turn to be a granny next."

"Not for a good few years. Elenor's only ten."

"I didn't mean soon, but you and Rebecca still have it to look forward to. You shouldn't have left it so long before you had Elenor."

Nell's cheeks flushed. "I-it wasn't as straightforward as that."

"Have I remembered correctly that you preferred to go to sea instead?"

"Who told you that? You were in Ireland."

"Sarah."

Nell rolled her eyes. "Obviously. You knew all about us, while we didn't even know where you were."

"It wasn't my choice to go..."

Nell held up a hand. "All right. Let's not argue. Will you take the water up while I put the kettle on again?"

Jane put Betsy on the floor. "If I must."

The child had dozed off by the time the kettle had reboiled and Nell made the tea while Jane laid Betsy on a rug by the fire.

"Poor little mite can't even go in her cot. Hopefully, it's only for the day." She paused. "Do you hear that?"

Jane straightened up. "What?"

"It's gone quiet. Does that mean the baby's arrived?" A moment later, Nell gasped as a cry filtered down to them. "Yes! How exciting! That didn't take long."

Jane bustled up the stairs and knocked on the bedroom door. "Is everything all right?"

Nell peered over her shoulder as the midwife cracked open the door.

"It's all over. You have a little boy. I'll get Betty tidied up, then you can come in."

Jane bounced on the spot. "Another boy. How wonderful! Mr Crane will be pleased."

Half an hour passed before the midwife called and Jane led Nell to the bedroom where Betty sat cradling her son.

"Look at him!" Jane stroked the child's face with a finger. "So tiny, too. Have you chosen a name?"

"Not yet." Betty smiled at the bundle in her arms. "We will tonight."

Nell put a cup of tea on the table by the bed. "You've earned this."

"Thank you." She smiled as she passed her baby to Jane. "Would you like a cuddle?"

"What a silly question." She lifted the child effortlessly from Betty's arms. "I'm not surprised he didn't take long to arrive. He looks so content, too."

"Let's hope he stays like that."

Nell pulled a chair over to the bed. "How are you? Did it go well?"

"I'm glad it's over. Bert will have a shock tonight when he comes home. We'd no idea when he went to work."

"It's a lovely surprise. It's as well we both came over."

Betty took a sip of her tea. "I wasn't expecting the two of you. Was it planned?"

"Only at the last minute." Nell's cheeks coloured. "I had a letter from Mr Marsh this morning telling me he'd be arriving in Liverpool later this week, so I thought I'd better call today."

"Are you excited about seeing him?"

"I'm looking forward to it, if that's what you mean."

"Is that all?" Betty raised an eyebrow.

"Yes!" Nell smirked. "If you think you're getting me to say any more than that, you're mistaken."

Nell was weary by the time she walked towards Windsor Street, but she beamed at Alice, who was with Mr Wood waiting to cross Upper Parliament Street.

"You'll never guess what?" Nell didn't wait for a response. "Betty's had her baby. A little boy!"

Alice squealed. "When?"

"This afternoon while I was there with your Aunty Jane. It was all rather quick in the end."

"Are they all right?"

Nell nodded. "They're fine. Betty sat and chatted to us once the midwife left."

"How lovely. I'll visit her tomorrow. I can't resist holding a baby. Did she mention a name?"

"No, she's waiting for Mr Crane to come home."

Alice's mouth fell open. "You've not left her on her own?"

"No, Aunty Jane stayed with her."

"That's a relief. My guess is that they'll call him Patrick after her dad."

"It would make sense. And what have you two been up to? You're late home for a Wednesday."

Mr Wood raised his hat to her, a grin on his face. "Good afternoon, Mrs Riley."

She laughed. "I'm sorry. I didn't mean to ignore you, but it's such exciting news."

"It is, indeed. We've been making the most of the dry weather before winter sets in."

"I don't blame you. It will be here before we know it. Have you thought any more about a date for the wedding?"

Alice glanced up at Mr Wood. "We want to wait for James to come home, and we can't fix the date until we know when that will be. Hopefully, he'll speak to his boss when he gets to Brazil and let us know."

"I can't see it being before this time next year."

Alice's shoulders slumped. "Don't say that. I was hoping he'd be home for Easter, like last year."

"I doubt it. He only did that once, and now he's staying

away longer each time. I can't see that changing. You saw what your dad was like with Mr Marsh when he found out he was a steward. He's treated James like that for far too long, and when you combine that with your mam telling him to stay in Liverpool and settle down, you wonder why he comes home at all."

"But it's our wedding."

"If you want my opinion, I'd write to him and ask when he'll be here. Tell him you need to know so you can book the church. I suspect he needs reminding that he has arrangements to make."

CHAPTER FORTY-SEVEN

Nell's heart fluttered as she stood in the front window and watched Mr Marsh approaching the house.

"He's here!"

Maria appeared by the living room door. "Are you going to invite him in?"

"I wasn't..." She took a deep breath when he knocked. "Just give us a minute." She waited for Maria to disappear before she opened it.

"Welcome back."

There was a twinkle in his eye as he grinned at her. "What a sight for sore eyes. You're looking even more lovely than I remember."

She chuckled. "You say that every time."

"I must mean it, then."

Nell hesitated as Maria called something to her. "You'd better step in while I fasten my cloak." She lowered her voice. "Maria would like a word."

"Then who am I to refuse?" He stepped in and

wandered into the living room. "Good afternoon, Mrs Atkin."

"Mr Marsh. It's nice to see you again. Did you have a pleasant voyage?"

"Yes, thank you. Are you keeping well?"

"I can't complain. Not much has changed since you were last here."

Nell joined them. "We have a new baby in the family."

Mr Marsh turned to Nell. "Does it belong to anyone I've met?"

"Our niece Betty had a little boy earlier this week. I'll take you to visit her when you're here for longer."

"Is she local?"

"She's in Everton." Nell rolled her eyes. "It's not ideal for anyone who wants to visit, but she's happy there. Her mam, our sister, lives round the corner from here." She looked at Maria. "Should we invite her for afternoon tea when Mr Marsh is next here?"

Maria raised an eyebrow. "Are you sure he's ready for her?"

She grimaced. "Maybe not." She turned to leave. "Shall we go?"

The wind was cold as they set off, and Nell pulled her cloak tightly around her. "I've not been out much in the bad weather. I'm getting less tolerant as I get older."

"It won't improve for a good few months, either. Perhaps we can find somewhere else to go when it gets colder."

"Like where?"

"I've noticed several tea rooms in Liverpool while I've been wandering around. We could visit each one in turn."

"I'd like that. It would certainly be better than sitting in the park in the rain."

He chuckled. "May I treat you tomorrow? I only have two days onshore this month."

"Is that all?" Nell's shoulders slumped. "Mrs Robertson told me they were reducing the time in port, but she said it was mainly over the summer."

"And it is, but for some reason, they want to get on their way for this last voyage. On the bright side, it means I'll be back sooner in November."

"That's good. Will you book into a boarding house over Christmas?"

He grinned at her. "I've already arranged one on Windsor Street. There's no point being further away from you than I need to be."

"So, we can get to know each other properly."

"That's what I'm hoping." He smiled as she leaned into his arm.

"How was your voyage? Do you have any interesting stories to tell me…?"

The girls were already at the table when Nell arrived home and Maria tutted at her.

"What time do you call this?"

"I'm sorry, we were talking and didn't realise how late it was."

"It's dark!"

"Only because we were in Sefton Park."

"Will it be like this every time he's in Liverpool?"

Nell scowled at her. "He's only here for two days."

Elenor stared at her. "Are you talking about Uncle Thomas?"

"Yes, he's here for a couple of days."

"Why are you even seeing him if he keeps going away?"

"Because ... because he doesn't know anyone else around here, so he'd be on his own if I wasn't his friend."

"Doesn't he have friends on the ship?"

"He sees them every day and wants a change. Now, will you stop the questions? I've known Uncle Thomas a long time, and it's nice to see him when I get the chance."

She bustled into the kitchen, and leaned against the sink, her hands covering her face. *Am I going to have this every month? Perhaps I should tell them we're walking out together and be done with it. No. That would give Mrs Pearse no end of gossip.*

Maria shouted to her. "Bring those potatoes through. George will be here any minute."

"Will do."

As soon as George and Billy were at the table, she served out some mashed potatoes while Maria sliced into a liver and kidney pudding.

"This should warm you up." She spooned a portion of meat over the potato. "Don't let it go cold."

George didn't speak while he ate, but once he was finished, he pushed his plate away and looked across at Nell. "I bumped into that friend of yours while I was walking down Windsor Street."

"Mr Marsh?" She coughed as she choked on a piece of potato. "Did he see you?"

"I spoke to him."

Nell held her breath as she stared at him. *And?*

"He's fond of you."

"He's a nice man once you get to know him. Did he say much?"

George shrugged. "Not really. He showed me where he'll be staying when he's next here."

"Oh, he's not shown me yet. We usually walk the other way to the park."

"He told me he's taking you to a tea room tomorrow to keep out of the cold."

Maria looked up from her plate. "You didn't tell me."

Nell put down her knife and fork, conscious of the girls' eyes on her. "I've not had chance. We only arranged it earlier."

George grunted. "He's not the type of man I'd ever mix with, but he'll take care of you."

Nell's voice cracked. "I think so."

"As long as you're happy."

"I am. Thank you." Her eyes flicked to his empty cup. "Would you like a top-up?"

George glanced around the table. "Why not? I'll only have to wait for Billy, anyway."

The tea room was tucked away in a side road off the main shopping street and Nell waited for Mr Marsh to open the door before she stepped inside. It was bigger than she expected, with a dozen tables dotted around the room, each covered with a starched white tablecloth. Potted palms partially shielded each table, and Mr Marsh held out a chair for her as they chose a spot in the window.

Nell studied their surroundings. "It's nice in here."

"Probably not as smart as the Adelphi, but comfortable, I hope."

She sighed. "I hadn't even thought to compare it, and you shouldn't either."

"I'm sorry. It was the one thing making me anxious. I can never compete with..."

"You don't have to. Who am I sat with now? And who do I want to see again? It isn't a competition, but if it were, you'd be winning."

He found a smile. "Thank you for reminding me. My inferiority complex comes from years of serving people who are better than me."

"You don't know they're better. Everyone you serve could be horrible. The only advantage they have over you is they have more money."

He nodded. "I need to tell myself that more often. Especially when they look down their noses at us."

"Only the horrible ones do that. The decent ones wouldn't dream of it."

"True again."

Nell studied him as he reached for a menu. "I'm surprised you think that way about yourself. You always come across as confident."

He grimaced. "It's all part of the act. I don't want the passengers assuming they can get the upper hand."

"Well, you surprise me."

"Unfortunately, there are times I overdo it. That was my downfall when you were around. I wanted to impress you but ended up having the opposite effect."

A tingle ran down her back. "It doesn't matter now."

"I should be thankful I caught cholera. You'd never have seen the real me, otherwise."

Nell tutted. "I'd have preferred it if you weren't so ill."

"It served its purpose." His gaze lingered on her. "As you say, it doesn't matter. We're here and that's all that counts. Now, what would you like? Sandwiches, cake or both?"

Full from their afternoon tea of cold meat sandwiches, scones and Victoria sandwich cake, Nell held Mr Marsh's arm as they left town.

"Which way would you suggest?"

Nell bit on her lip. "I usually stay on the main roads."

"Quite sensible, especially when you're on your own." He paused as they reached a junction. "Down here?"

"Yes." Nell's heart was pounding as the roads grew quieter. "I don't usually come this way when it's going dark."

"I should hope not." He looked down at her. "Are you all right? You've gone very pale."

"I'm fine." *Or I would be if I could be rid of the image of that confounded man.* "I-it must be that when you drop me off, that will be it for another month. I won't know what to do with myself."

"I'm hoping the time will pass quickly. I'll write to you on the outbound voyage and post the letter as soon as we get to New York."

"I'll watch out for it." She tried to smile but a wave of sadness took her by surprise. *I'm actually going to miss him.*

"I'll look forward to exploring more of those tea rooms when you're back. I enjoyed this afternoon."

"I did too." He ran a finger down her cheek. "I've a feeling we'll be good together, Elenor."

"I hope so."

CHAPTER FORTY-EIGHT

Nell stared at the letter in her hands, tears blurring her vision, as Maria scrubbed the floor around her.

"Would it be too much to ask for you to lift your feet up?"

"I'll go..." She jumped up and hurried to the front room, closing the door behind her. *Why do things like this always happen?* She read the last few sentences again.

We'll be in New York for at least a week while they mend the engine. I'll write as soon as we know a departure date. I'm already counting the days until I see you.

It will be December before he's back. Her mind drifted to the time Jack was sailing. *I can't go through all that again.*

She wandered to the window and gazed at the pounding rain. *What a miserable day.* She flinched as Maria followed her into the room.

"What's the matter?"

"An engine was damaged on Mr Marsh's ship, so they

were late arriving in New York, and they have to stay there until it's mended."

"Is he all right?"

"He's fine, but I was expecting him in the next few days. It's going to be another couple of weeks now."

"It will pass soon enough."

Nell pointed to the window. "Have you seen the weather?"

"Mr Marsh being here won't change that."

"At least he'd take me for afternoon tea."

"Come on, cheer up. There'll be plenty of time for that when he's back. Didn't you say Mrs Robertson's in Liverpool?"

She nodded. "They docked earlier this week, but they're moving into a house near the docks, on Upper Pitt Street, so I can't visit until Monday."

"She's doing all right for herself. There are some nice houses down there."

Nell sighed. *That should have been me.*

"It won't be such a walk, either. If you go there next week, and walk up to Betty's once or twice, we'll fill the rest of the time getting ready for Christmas. You can make a start on the mincemeat for the pies, and it's nearly stir-up Sunday. The time will pass."

"I know. I just thought I was past all this waiting around."

"You'll never be over it if you fall for a man of the sea."

"We don't know each other well enough yet for me to ask him to change job, and at this rate, we never will."

"Don't be silly, there's no rush. Would he look for something else if you wanted to settle down?"

Nell nodded. "I would say so." *He'd probably do anything I ask.*

Maria hadn't started the tea when Alice came home, her cloak soaked through. She shook it in the hall before hanging it over a chair in front of the fire.

"What a day, on a Wednesday, too."

Nell passed her a cloth to wipe her face. "I thought you were going to the tea room I told you about."

"We did. I got this wet on the way back." She held up a soggy envelope. "Even this is wet."

"Where did you get that from?"

"The postman saw me outside. It's from James. I hope the ink hasn't smudged."

Nell took it from her. "It's not too bad. Let's see if I can open it in one piece."

The letter inside was only damp, and Alice took the seat opposite Nell as she unfolded it. "What does he say?"

Nell checked Maria was listening. "He's in Manaus, and everyone was pleased to see him, especially Mr Smith."

Maria groaned. "I hope that doesn't mean he'll stay over there as long as he did this year."

"He wants him to wait a year between visits, so he'll be here for the first two weeks of November."

Alice huffed. "That's so frustrating."

Maria stood with her arms folded. "You needn't wait for him. It's his fault if he misses out."

"I'd like him to be there, though, and I'm sure you and Dad would appreciate the extra time to prepare, too."

"Well, yes, it would certainly help."

"I'll speak to Mr Wood later and see what he has to say."

Nell folded up the letter. "The time will go quickly enough if you want to wait."

Maria laughed. "Says you, who's impatient about waiting two weeks for Mr Marsh."

"That's different. At least Alice and Mr Wood see each other most days."

Alice looked between them. "What's happened?"

Nell sighed. "Nothing major, but Mr Marsh is stuck in America and won't be back until December."

"There are worse places to be. What a shame you're not with him."

"Don't say that!" Nell rolled her eyes. "I'm already wondering what I'll do for the next couple of weeks. I'll visit Mrs Robertson on Monday, but when are you going to see Betty?"

"Tomorrow. Would you like to walk up there with me?"

"That would be nice. I've not seen little Patrick since he was born."

"Then a visit's long overdue."

The following afternoon, Alice and Nell bid Betty farewell before Alice pulled the front door closed behind them.

"She looks so happy."

Nell sighed. "I'm not surprised. Betsy's as lovely as ever and Patrick's a good baby."

"I can't wait for that to be me."

"It will come soon enough."

"That's what everyone says, but it's the one downside of waiting for James to come home."

"You've definitely decided on a November wedding?"

"We have. We spoke about it last night and decided it wouldn't seem right without him. We just need to confirm the date."

"He'd better not change his mind, then."

Alice's eyes widened. "He wouldn't, would he?"

"Not if you let him know your plans and tell him he's the reason you're waiting. He won't want to disappoint you."

"I hope not." Alice cocked her head to one side. "Do you realise I've already known Harry for a year and a half? It's gone so fast it was another reason we chose to wait."

"There are things to do, too. You'll have to sort out your dress, not to mention planning the food with your mam. She'll want to give you a good spread."

Alice laughed. "She's already started. I'm just glad she's accepted that we'll be married."

"Not only that, she does actually like Mr Wood. Not that she'd admit it."

"I'm sure it wouldn't hurt her." Alice shivered as they turned the corner and a gust of wind caught beneath her cloak. "I don't like the look of those clouds."

Nell followed her gaze. "Hopefully, the rain will hold off until we get home."

"It had better. This cloak's only just dried out from yesterday."

"You must have been cold when you were out last night."

Alice grinned at her. "Harry always raises my temperature."

Nell stared at her.

"What?"

Nell scrambled for words. "You're not ... he doesn't..."

"No!" Alice gasped. "I've enough sense about that. I mean, my heart beats faster when I see him."

"Thank goodness for that." Nell's cheeks flushed as she took a breath. "Your mam will go off him very quickly if you end up in the family way."

"There's no chance of that." Alice shuddered. "Harry knows it's not an option, but if he ever had any ideas, I'd only need to imagine the reaction if I had to tell Mam, and I'd be away from him like a shot."

Nell laughed. "That's a good ploy. I hope she has the same effect on Elenor and Leah when they're your age."

"*I'll* be like that with them, never mind her."

Nell gasped as a maid showed her into the living room of Mrs Robertson's latest residence.

"Good grief. These houses are getting bigger."

Mrs Robertson glanced around. "They are. I feel quite spoiled, but we were fortunate with this one. It's owned by someone my husband knows and he's letting us stay here for nothing while he's away."

"How wonderful." She studied the stone fireplace. "It's bigger than me."

"And me. Unfortunately, it takes a lot of coal, and we have to buy our own."

Nell sat in the middle of the settee opposite Mrs Robertson. "How long are you here for?"

"Until the fifth of January. I'll be busy, though. The governess we had has chosen not to travel next year, and so I need to find another one while I'm here. Life at sea clearly isn't for everyone."

"It's one of those things people either love or hate. How was your last trip?"

"Uneventful, thankfully. And we weren't full, which always makes it easier. I even had time to talk to Mr Cooper and hear about you and Mr Marsh."

"Me...? What did he say?"

Mrs Robertson grinned. "Don't look so worried. He'd had a letter from Mr Marsh thanking him for suggesting he come back to England. I heard you're walking out together."

Nell's cheeks coloured. "We are."

"Are you as taken with him as he is with you?"

Nell smiled. "Not quite so much, but now we're over the incident with Ollie, I'm very fond of him."

"Was he still upset?"

"He tried not to be, but he couldn't hide it."

"What did you say to him? You didn't tell him about the wedding?"

"Not in detail. I said I'd been to the ceremony and that at the end of the night, when we'd had far too much champagne, we danced together, and he asked me to move to London."

Mrs Robertson's eyes widened. "You told him that?"

"I only said he asked me while we were dancing, and that I was so horrified, I left immediately, and hadn't seen him since."

"Did he believe you?"

"Why wouldn't he? Most of it's true." She paused. "I almost believe it myself now."

Mrs Robertson raised an eyebrow. "It's to be hoped he doesn't meet Mr Hewitt again."

Nell shuddered. "I don't even want to think about it."

"I'm glad. You make a lovely couple. When's he due in Liverpool?"

Nell huffed. "I presume you didn't hear he's been stranded in New York."

"No, he must have written before he left. What's the problem?"

Mrs Robertson listened as Nell explained. "Were you disappointed when you got the letter?"

"More than I expected. I'm beginning to think there might be a future for us."

Mrs Robertson laughed. "I look forward to getting an invitation to the wedding."

"Slow down a bit!" Nell gasped before breaking into a smile. "I don't know about Mr Marsh thanking Mr Cooper. It's me who should thank you. None of this would have happened otherwise."

"I'm glad it's worked out then, not that I had any doubts."

"The only person who did was me, although I still don't think I'm ready to get married again."

Mrs Robertson chuckled. "If you ask me, you'll be Mrs Marsh by this time next year and you'll wonder why you resisted for so long."

Nell shuddered. *Mrs Marsh. That would take away my last link to Jack. Will I ever be ready for that?*

CHAPTER FORTY-NINE

Maria rubbed a stale lump of bread over a grater and cupped the crumbs into a bowl.

"How's that cranberry sauce doing?"

Nell stirred the ruby red liquid. "It's done." She lifted it from the heat and carried it to a dish on the table. "Have you much left to do?"

"No. These breadcrumbs will do for the stuffing, then I'll do some for the bread sauce. Everything else will have to wait."

"Aren't you stuffing the bird tonight?"

Maria groaned. "I'm not. I've had enough for one day. I'll be up early in the morning, so I'll do it then."

"On Christmas Day?"

"If I don't stop now, it will be Christmas Day anyway, and I'd rather get some sleep first. I could do with a cup of tea before I go to bed, though."

"I'll do it." Alice stacked the last of the crockery on the dresser and bounced into the kitchen. "I hope the table's big enough. I've had to squeeze everyone in."

"It should be. There are only nine of us."

Nell returned with the pan. "The children are bigger now. They can't share seats like they used to. It's as well Vernon and Jane are going to Mrs Ally's for dinner."

"And that James isn't here." There was a tinge of sadness in Alice's voice.

"I'm never pleased when anyone's missing, but at least we have replacements for them both. I take it Mr Marsh and Mr Wood are still joining us?"

Alice answered. "Mr Wood was honoured to be invited. He's looking forward to it."

"I'm not sure Mr Marsh is. He's rather nervous after the way George behaved last time he came."

Maria tutted. "He'll be fine. George has promised to be on his best behaviour and it's Christmas, so I expect everyone to be in a good mood."

"And we will be." Alice's voice squeaked. "I'm so excited."

Nell's stomach churned. *That's not the word I'd use.*

Nell was down early the following morning, but Maria, Alice and the girls were already in the living room.

"Merry Christmas! What time did you all get up?"

"Merry Christmas!" The girls bounced up and down, but Maria darted to the kitchen.

"I don't know, but it was still dark."

"It's still dark now and will be for another couple of hours."

"It doesn't matter. The goose is stuffed, the potatoes are

peeled, the punch is mixed and the eggs are ready to cook for breakfast..."

"My, you've been busy."

"I want everything done for when George and Billy come down. They don't get many days off."

"Has the kettle boiled?"

Maria banged a hand on her head. "I knew there was something else. Come on, out of the way, I can't move in here. Is the table ready? We only need cups, saucers and side plates. Everyone can butter their own bread before I bring the eggs in."

Nell smiled as she joined Alice at the table. "Is Mr Wood joining us in church?"

"He is. What about Mr Marsh?"

"He'll walk up and meet us after the service."

Alice's forehead creased. "Doesn't he go to church?"

"It's not easy when you're on a ship."

"But he must go at Christmas."

"I didn't think to ask. Maybe he'll turn up and surprise me."

"I'm so glad the two of them will be new together. It should make it easier for both of them."

"That's what Mr Marsh is hoping."

The service was over when Mr Marsh strolled up the church path and watched Nell as she greeted the vicar. He raised his hat when she joined him.

"Merry Christmas, my dear."

"And to you. Have you been waiting long?"

"Only a few minutes. Are you ready to go?"

"I'd better let Maria know what we're doing. I don't want her panicking any more than she is already."

"Not on my account, I hope."

Nell shook her head. "No, she's been preparing for today for weeks and won't be happy until all the food's been eaten and enjoyed."

"I'll make sure I do both, then." He raised himself up onto his toes before settling again. "I presume that's Mr Wood with Miss Atkin?"

Nell turned to see them walking towards them. "It is. Let me introduce you before we get to the house."

"Good morning." Alice smiled as they joined them. "I thought now would be a good time to make some introductions."

Mr Marsh offered Mr Wood a hand. "Pleased to meet you."

"And you. Have you been to Christmas dinner before?"

"No, it's my first time. I'm usually on a ship or in a boarding house at this time of the year. What about you? Do you have family in Liverpool?"

"No, they're all in Ireland. I'll go and see them one day."

"You can talk more when we get home." Nell looked at Alice as she took Mr Marsh's arm. "Have you seen your mam?"

"She left about five minutes ago."

"Blimey, we'd better not keep her waiting."

Elenor and Leah ran on ahead, but Leah waited by the front door. "It smells funny in there."

"What sort of funny?" Nell stepped inside and took a deep breath. "That's the punch. It smells delicious."

Leah held her nose. "I don't like it."

"I'm very glad. It's not for you. Now, in you get."

Maria was fussing over the table when they went in. "Mr Wood, Mr Marsh. Merry Christmas! Come on in. I'd normally offer you a seat by the fire, but George will be here shortly." She turned to Nell. "Have you seen him?"

"He was following us."

"Good." Maria rubbed her hands together. "I always imagine I've forgotten something, but I don't think I have."

Mr Wood smirked at her. "There is one thing I've not spotted."

"What?" Maria's eyes widened.

"Where's the mistletoe? You can't have a Christmas party without that."

Alice's cheeks turned crimson, and she stared at the floor as Maria took a playful swipe at Mr Wood's arm. "You'll have to wait until later when everyone else is here. I expect you to be on your best behaviour over dinner ... and this evening, come to mention it."

He gave her a mischievous grin. "Aren't I always?"

"I can see I need to keep you busy. Why don't you pull the chairs away from the table so we can sit down for a glass of punch? We'll stay in here until dinner, then go in the front room to open the presents." Maria gave a sigh of relief as the front door closed and George and Billy joined them. "You're here. Billy, will you fetch the yule log? It's time it was on the fire."

"What about the front room?"

"You can do that while we're washing up. There's no point letting it burn down too soon."

Billy nodded. "I'll have an ale, if you're asking."

Maria rolled her eyes at him. "George, you take a seat

and I'll get you a drink. The punch is nice, or would you prefer ale?"

George sniffed the air. "I'll try the punch. It smells like there's plenty of brandy in it."

"Right you are. Mr Wood, Mr Marsh, what about you?"

When they asked for punch, Maria disappeared to the kitchen while Nell waited at the table to serve it out.

"I hope you're hungry. James was very generous when he was here, so we've cooked a goose and a piece of beef this year."

Mr Wood's eyes lit up. "Are we allowed a bit of both?"

"I don't see why not. As long as there's enough to go round."

"There'll be plenty." Maria placed the pan of punch on the table. "Don't fill yourselves up too much, though. There's a spread later, too."

Nell spooned the punch into the glass cups and passed them to Alice to hand around. Once everyone had a drink, George rose to his feet.

"Before we eat, I'd like to propose a toast. To everyone present and those who can't be with us. Merry Christmas."

"Merry Christmas." Nell sighed as everyone raised their glasses. *He still can't bring himself to mention James by name.*

Once he'd taken a mouthful of punch, Mr Wood beckoned Alice to him. "May I also propose a toast to my lovely wife-to-be, Alice."

"Alice!"

"We wanted to let you know that we've set a date for the wedding." He paused as cheers rang around the room. "James will be home for the first two weeks of November, so we've gone for a date in the middle, which is Monday the eleventh."

Everyone raised their glasses again. "Monday the eleventh!"

"Splendid." George looked at Mr Marsh. "Will you make a toast?"

"I'd actually like to propose two. First, shall we raise a glass to Mrs Atkin and thank her for preparing such a marvellous meal? May we not leave a morsel."

"Mrs Atkin! May we not leave a morsel!"

"Second, I'd like to toast the most wonderful woman in my life. She's known by many names: Mam, Nell, Mrs Riley ... and Elenor." He held her gaze as he spoke. "May she never leave us."

Nell's cheeks flushed as a confusion of names rang out. "I'm not going anywhere." Her eyes flicked around everyone's glasses. "Let me top you all up before we sit down to eat."

CHAPTER FIFTY

The dinner had been eaten; the dishes washed and presents opened before Maria finally settled into a chair by the window in the front room.

"I hope you're all happy."

There was a murmur of agreement amongst those who were still awake.

"Would anyone like a cup of tea?"

Nell gasped. "Can't you sit down for five minutes? You'll be wanting to put out the food for tonight, soon."

Mr Marsh shifted in his seat. "How many are we expecting?"

Nell's forehead creased, and she looked at Maria. "I've not totted it up. Do you know?"

"Fourteen adults and assorted children."

Mr Marsh grimaced. "Goodness. Is that besides those here already?"

"It is. It's a bit of a squeeze, but Alice and Betty normally take the little ones upstairs."

"Alice does?" Mr Wood's face dropped as he stared at her. "Won't you be around for the mistletoe?"

Alice's cheeks coloured as Maria glowered at him.

"I'd say being upstairs is the best place for her. You seem a little too keen on this part of the proceedings."

"It wouldn't be Christmas otherwise..." He stopped as the front door opened and a moment later, Vernon popped his head into the front room.

"Afternoon, all. Merry Christmas."

Maria was on her feet. "You're early. How lovely."

He glanced over his shoulder and lowered his voice. "Mrs Ally's dinner wasn't a patch on yours. No punch or ale, either. All I've had is a small glass of sherry." He rubbed his hands together. "Is there anything left of that punch I can smell?"

Maria grinned. "I think I can find some. What have you done with Lydia and Henry?"

"They're here." He opened the door wider to show his wife taking their son from the pram.

Maria beamed as she went to see her grandson. "Vernon, take this pram to the backyard while I sort out your drink. You can't leave it here."

"Give me a minute."

"No, now. Nell, you come with me and make some more punch. Alice, it's probably time to set the table. Everyone will be here before we know it."

Nell followed her to the kitchen. "Do we have everyone's contributions for the spread?"

Maria rolled her eyes. "What do you think? Jane couldn't possibly make anything, so she was waiting for

Betty to do it. As if the poor girl hasn't enough to do with those kiddies."

The front door slammed, and alarm settled on Maria's face as Jane's voice travelled to the kitchen.

"I wasn't expecting her yet. Did you warn Mr Marsh about her?"

Nell grimaced. "I did, but I'd better introduce them properly. I'm not sure he's ready for her, the mood she seems to be in."

Nell smiled at Betty as she arrived with a large trifle.

"Mam promised you this, I believe."

"She did, although we didn't realise you'd be making it."

"I don't mind ... and she did help."

Nell scowled at the noise coming from the front room. "Will you excuse me?"

She stepped through the door as Jane pulled a bunch of mistletoe from a bag. "In case you men thought you were missing out. George, help me put this up, will you?"

"Merry Christmas, Jane."

"Oh, Nell. Merry Christmas. You've been released from the stove, have you?"

"Don't be like that. Someone has to do it. Maria already has mistletoe for the other room."

"Really?" Jane beamed at her. "That's even better. Who wouldn't want to get caught under it on a day like today?" She held it over her head as George stood beside her. "Shall we break the ice?"

Nell glanced at Mr Marsh, who sat mesmerised. *I knew I should have introduced them sooner.* She took a step towards him but stopped when the front door opened again, and Rebecca joined them.

"Merry Christmas, everyone."

Nell smiled as she stepped back to her sister. "I'm not sure whether you've come at a good time or bad. I was about to join Mr Marsh."

Rebecca chuckled. "It looks like you'd better go."

Mr Marsh stood up as Nell approached. "Are you finished out there?"

"Not quite, but I thought you could do with some company..." Nell glanced at the mistletoe hanging from the ceiling light. "My sister Jane always likes a party."

"Did you mention me?" Jane paused beside them. "Now then, who do we have here? Is this the gentleman you've been walking out with for months without introducing me?"

"Erm ... yes. This is Mr Marsh."

"I can see why you've kept him to yourself. He's rather handsome." She offered Mr Marsh her hand. "I'm Nell's sister, Mrs Read, or Jane, to my friends."

Mr Marsh hesitated as he took her hand. "It's nice to meet you. Have you had a pleasant day?"

"We've been to my daughter Betty's. I'm only in a boarding house, so can't do my own entertaining. I would if I could, obviously." She leaned forward with a conspiratorial tone. "Have you got your feet under the table here?"

Nell tutted. "He joined us for dinner, if that's what you mean."

"Congratulations. Don't upset Maria though, she tends not to forget."

Nell put her hands on her hips. "Shouldn't you wish her Merry Christmas before you start? She's been busy for weeks with all this."

"I will. I'll hurry her up with the drinks, too."

Nell shook her head as Jane disappeared. "I'm sorry about that."

"Is she always so outgoing?"

"Only at party time. She is one for the men, though. And don't look at me like that. Despite what you might think, we're not alike."

"I didn't say a word."

"No. Well." She stopped as Mr Grayson strolled into the room. "Ah, Mr Grayson, may I introduce you to my companion, Mr Marsh?"

Mr Grayson offered him a hand. "Pleased to meet you. You look as worried about this whole thing as I usually do."

Nell sighed. "If it's that bad, perhaps I can leave him in your capable hands while I help Maria."

By nine o'clock, a single white berry remained on the mistletoe in the centre of the room, and Jane's shoulders slumped as Mr Crane crept up behind Betty and planted a kiss on her cheek.

"I did it!" He pulled the berry from the twig. "The last one."

"That's not fair! You're married." Jane scowled at him. "We may as well go home now."

Betty reached for her cloak. "It's time we were leaving, anyway. The carriages will stop running shortly, and the children should have been in bed hours ago."

Jane tutted. "Pass me my cloak, then. Are you coming, Sarah?"

"I am."

Maria appeared at the living room door as the guests congregated in the hall.

"Is everyone leaving? Rebecca and I were going to have a cup of tea."

"Sadly, some of us have a longer walk than she does." Jane helped Betty with the children. "We'll see you tomorrow."

The house felt empty once they'd gone, and Nell took a seat in the back room while Maria handed round the cups.

"Does anyone need anything else to eat?"

Alice put her hands on her stomach. "I won't need anything for a week. It was lovely."

Rebecca accepted her tea. "It was, thank you."

"As long as you all enjoyed it, that's all that matters."

The conversation was muted and once the clock struck ten, Rebecca stood up and put her cup and saucer on the table.

"We'd better leave you to get cleared up. The girls are overtired, which is never a good thing where Hugh's concerned."

Nell looked up at her. "He's enjoyed himself tonight. He and Mr Marsh seem to get on well."

"I thought that. It makes a change to see him with a smile on his face, although Jane always intimidates him. Not that he'd ever admit it."

Maria snorted. "He wouldn't be the only one."

Nell followed Rebecca to the hall and waited while she spoke to her husband. "Is he ready?"

"He is."

A moment later, Mr Marsh followed Mr Grayson from the front room, pulling the door closed as he did.

"It was nice to meet you."

"And you." Mr Grayson picked up his hat. "I'm in the alehouse on Windsor Street most evenings after nine o'clock, if you ever want to join me. I'd welcome the company."

"That's very kind. I may well take you up on the offer." He stepped to one side as the family left but hesitated when Nell closed the door after them.

"I should go too. Except for Mr Wood, I'm the last one here. Thank you for a lovely day."

"I'm glad you enjoyed it. It's often chaotic, but everyone means well."

"I ... erm ..." He glanced down the hall to the closed living room door. "I ... well ... you may have wondered why I didn't steal a kiss under the mistletoe."

Nell lowered her eyes. "I guessed you weren't ready."

"Then you'd be wrong." He tilted her face towards his. "I've been ready for years but didn't want our first kiss to be part of a flippant party game."

Her heart pounded as he leaned towards her.

"May I?"

"Yes." *I think so.* She caught her breath as his lips touched hers and a tingling sensation spread through her body.

"I wanted it to be special." His eyes searched her face. "I love you, Elenor." He didn't wait for a response before kissing her again. "You've made me a very happy man."

CHAPTER FIFTY-ONE

Eleven months later

Rebecca fastened the buttons down the back of Alice's bridal dress while Maria straightened out the pleats at the front of the skirt. With a final flick of the fabric, Maria stood up.

"There. It looks lovely."

"I can't wait to see it." Alice bit her lip as Rebecca closed the hook and eye at the neck.

"Your dad will be so proud of you." Nell smiled as Alice stepped towards the mirror.

"I hope so. And Harry, too. Thank you, Aunty Rebecca, it's gorgeous." Alice looked around. "Are the girls ready?"

Nell nodded. "They are. They're in the front room with your dad and Mr Grayson under strict instructions to do nothing but sit and behave."

Alice grimaced. "They won't dare move, then. I'm just

sad that Betty isn't here. I can't believe that all three children have measles."

Nell sighed. "She's as upset as you, but it's one of those things. I spoke to Aunty Jane yesterday, and she said the rash is fading on Albert and Betsy, but Patrick's still poorly."

"I know, and I feel mean complaining, but to lose my matron of honour after waiting so long..." She huffed. "I hope they all get over it soon."

"We can't worry about that now." Maria reached for the veil. "Let's get this on you and then we can go."

Nell left them to it and went downstairs to the front room. "Are you all ready? Alice will be down in a minute."

George stood up. "Thank goodness for that. The carriages will be here anytime, and I don't want them standing idle."

"They won't be." Nell stepped over to the girls. "Stand up and let me straighten your dresses. I want you to do Alice proud."

"We will." Leah grinned at her cousins. "Even Elenor."

Nell pointed a finger at her. "Stop it. I know Elenor will."

"Yes, Leah..." Elenor scowled at her, but Nell clapped her hands.

"I don't want any arguing. Now, stand by the fire and wait for Alice."

George stood to the side of the door as his daughter arrived at the foot of the stairs.

"My word." He turned to Mr Grayson, who was by the window. "Your wife's done us proud with the dress."

Rebecca smiled. "I won't know what to do with myself now."

"You'll find something." Mr Grayson appraised Alice as she stepped into the room. "Very nice."

"Two carriages have arrived outside, we'd better go." Maria checked her hat was securely attached. "I don't want the wind dislodging it. Why you couldn't get married in the summer, I don't know."

Nell tutted. "Yes you do. Now stop complaining and let's be going."

James and Billy were waiting by the church doors, and Billy escorted them to their seats on the bride's side of the aisle. Nell let Rebecca and Mr Grayson lead the way before she followed, with Maria behind her.

She smiled at Mr Wood in the opposite aisle as Maria sat down. "He's looking very dapper. Did you bring a spare handkerchief?"

"Two."

"At least she's not going anywhere once they're married."

"I hope it's the right decision. It will be strange having another man in the house."

"I doubt we'll see much of him between going to work, being in the alehouse, and spending time with Alice."

"You're right."

They hadn't been sitting for five minutes before the organ struck up and Nell twisted round to see Alice walking towards them on George's arm. A veil covered her face, but once the bridesmaids had taken their seats, she turned to George, who revealed her broad smile.

"She looks so happy." Nell watched Alice acknowledge

Mr Wood before she thumbed through the hymn book for the right page.

"I should hope she does."

The vicar's voice was soothing as he read through the service, but Mr Wood's thick Irish accent echoed around the church as he repeated his vows.

Alice's gaze didn't leave him as she said her oath, and she beamed as they were pronounced man and wife.

Rebecca leaned towards Nell. "Who'd have thought she'd have married an Irishman after all the trouble we had with Jane?"

"There's one big difference, don't forget."

"As if I could."

"She's waited a long time for this, too." Nell wiped a tear from her eye as the congregation knelt in prayer. *And I'm here on my own.*

Rebecca nudged her. "Cheer up. He'll be back soon."

Nell nodded, unable to speak. *But then he'll leave again.*

Once the marriage register was signed, Nell watched the girls follow the bride and groom to the back of the church.

"Their dresses turned out well." Rebecca smiled at her handiwork.

"They look very smart. I'm pleased Leah and Florrie will grow into the bigger ones."

"Always a bonus. Shall we follow them?"

Nell walked behind Rebecca and Mr Grayson, but paused when she reached James, who was ushering guests from the pews.

"You didn't have too many people to deal with."

"Enough." He smiled as the last of them departed. "I'm glad Alice waited for me to come home. It was very thoughtful of her."

Billy joined them as they reached the door. "Are you going to throw your confetti, Aunty Nell? They're almost ready."

"Only if you wait for me. I'm feeling out of sorts seeing everyone with a partner."

James grinned. "I wouldn't say everyone. Look at me and Billy for a start, then there's Aunty Jane and Aunty Sarah."

"I suppose so, but I've got used to having Mr Marsh around. Hopefully, he'll be here later in the week."

"Do I need to plan next year's visit around your wedding?"

"No, you don't. He's not even proposed marriage."

"You've been walking out for over a year, so it can't be long before he does."

Nell shook her head. "In all the time I've known him, we've probably spent less than a month together. It's no way to get acquainted with each other."

Billy's forehead creased. "I thought he was going to finish as a steward."

Nell reached into her handbag for the confetti. "How can he? I don't want him to give up his job unless we're sure we have a future, but we won't know how well we get on while we spend so little time together."

Billy raised an eyebrow. "You seem to get along pretty well to me."

"Maybe, but it's different when you're married."

"If you say so." He winked at James, who smirked.

"In case you're wondering, I'm hoping to be home in October next year."

Nell shared out the confetti with Elenor and Leah and rubbed her hands together as the last pieces fell to the floor. Alice giggled as she dusted it from her hair, and gave a final wave before Mr Wood escorted her to a waiting carriage.

As they disappeared round the corner, James offered Nell an arm.

"Given that the other carriage is for Mam, Dad and the bridesmaids, shall we start walking?"

"We better had. Not that it will take long. Where's Billy gone?"

"He's keeping Len company. Being Mr Wood's best man means he's on his own now."

Nell glanced round to see the two of them talking to Vernon. "We may as well go, then."

Alice and Mr Wood were by the open front door when they arrived at the house.

"Congratulations!" James shook Mr Wood's hand. "To think my little sister's a married woman. I can't quite believe it."

"Don't worry, I'll take good care of her. Besides, your Aunty Nell will keep an eye on us, now we're living here."

Nell laughed. "It's not me you need to worry about. I'll give you six months before you decide it's time to find your own house."

There was a twinkle in Mr Wood's green eyes. "I'm already looking, to be honest with you. I expect it to be a bit of a squeeze here."

"We'll manage. It will help Maria feel better about Alice being married. She won't be losing her daughter immediately."

"Even if we move out, we won't go far, so she needn't worry."

"I'm pleased to hear it."

Maria was in the kitchen when Nell joined her. "What do you want me to do?"

"You can make sure everyone has a drink. I'm not putting the food out too soon."

"Will do."

Sarah and Jane were in the living room when she turned around. "How are you both doing?"

Sarah sighed. "It's times like this I miss Tom the most. Not having someone's arm to walk on."

"We're all in the same boat."

Jane took a step back. "You have that nice Mr Marsh."

"Not today, I don't. It's funny. Being on my own never bothered me until I started walking out with him." She stared at Jane. "What about you? You've been on your own a long time."

"I miss having a house of my own, but other than that, I'm happy enough. Or I will be once I know Patrick's all right."

"How is he?"

She sighed. "He was in a bad way when I left last night. The doctor said he'd developed something called pneumonia and was struggling to breathe."

Nell grimaced. "That sounds nasty. Will he be all right?"

"He couldn't say. That's why I can't stay. I only wanted a quick bite to eat…"

"Wait there. I'll see what I can find." She returned a minute later with a slice of pie and piece of cake. "How's that for you?"

"It's probably more than enough. I've had butterflies in my stomach all morning, worrying about Patrick and Betty."

"Has the doctor given him anything?"

Jane shook her head. "Other than some vapours to open his airway, there's nothing he can do." After a couple of mouthfuls, she put down her plate. "I'm sorry, it's very nice, but I can't eat it. I don't have a good feeling about things…"

"It would probably be easier if you were at Betty's, so you know what's going on."

"I'm going."

Nell followed her to the hall. "Send Betty my love and tell her I'll call as soon as I can."

CHAPTER FIFTY-TWO

It was the second time in a week that the family had been to church, and Nell pulled her cloak more tightly around her as she focussed on the tiny coffin by the altar. *Goodbye, Patrick.* She glanced at Betty and Mr Crane, who sat two rows in front of her. *Poor Betty. As if she hasn't had enough to deal with.* Tears ran down her face as the vicar gave the blessing. *If He loves us all so much, why does He do this?* Nell leaned into Mr Marsh as the vicar strode purposefully to the side entrance.

"I'm so glad you're here."

"So am I." He placed an arm around her shoulders. "Not that it's the sort of homecoming I was expecting." He gave her a squeeze before leading her and Rebecca from the pew. "Let's get you home."

"Not yet." She pointed to Betty, who was by the door, wrapped in Mr Crane's arms. "Someone needs to stay with her. She shouldn't be on her own while the men go to the grave." She flinched as Alice came up behind her.

"That was horrible."

"It was. Would you like to ask Betty if she wants to walk with us?"

"Aunty Jane's with her and they want to wait for Mr Crane and her brothers."

"Will they be able to stay in church? They'll freeze if they have to stand outside."

"I think so. She doesn't want to go home without Mr Crane."

"She won't go to the grave?"

"No. She promised me. We can go to the house if you like. Mam will be wondering where we are."

Rebecca picked up her bag. "I need to get home and give the girls their dinner. Thankfully, Hugh gave me this." She held up a shilling coin and looked at Mr Marsh. "Would you mind finding me a carriage?"

"Not at all. Wait by the door and I'll be as quick as I can."

Nell watched him go. "Thank you for having the girls. It's not often we're all out."

"It's the least I can do. I'll call over to see you when you're home."

The walk to Betty's was short, but with the icy wind and little conversation, it seemed to take an age. Maria was soothing Betsy when they arrived at the house.

"How was it?"

"Terrible. I feel so sorry for Betty." Nell kept her cloak on as she rubbed her hands in front of the fire. "Losing a child is one of the worst things in the world, and after all her other problems..."

"He was such a sweet little boy, too." Alice bent down and took Betsy from Maria's knee. "How's she been?"

"Missing her mam. Is Betty following you?"

"She's waiting for Mr Crane."

Maria sighed as she disappeared into the kitchen but came back a moment later with a bottle of brandy. "I brought this with me. Let me pour you a drink before the others arrive. Would you care for one, Mr Marsh?"

"Only a small one. The wind's enough to cut through you today, so those who've been to the grave will have more need of it than me."

"I'll put the kettle on, too. I noticed a few pies and cakes in the pantry, presumably for anyone who joins us. They'll want something to wash them down with."

He gave her a grateful smile as she handed him a glass. "What would everyone do without you?"

"I'm only doing what I can to help."

Nell accepted her glass and sat by the fire. "I hope we can offer Betty some comfort before we leave."

Alice coughed as she took a gulp of the brandy. "I promised to pick Albert up from school so she doesn't have to think about it." She took another sip of her drink. "Look at the time. I'd better go. I'll finish that when I get back."

Once the front door closed, Nell sat Betsy on her knee while Maria busied herself in the kitchen. Mr Marsh took the empty seat opposite her.

"I get the impression this isn't the only child's funeral you've been to."

She shook her head. "It seems to be a rite of passage in this family."

"And in too many others. I'm sorry."

Nell sighed. "It was nearly three years ago when Vernon's daughter, Maud, passed. She was Maria's first grandchild."

He swirled the brandy around his glass. "I hope you don't mind me asking, but how long ago was it when you lost a child?"

Nell's head shot up. "What do you mean?"

"You said losing a child is one of the worst things in the world ... as if you spoke from experience."

"Yes." Nell's voice fell. "I had a son when I was first married. We called him Jack after his dad, but he was taken from us when he was seven months old. My husband was away at the time..." She sighed. "Days like this bring it back."

"I'm sorry."

"He'd be seventeen in January..." Nell stopped as Maria joined them.

"What are you talking about things like that for? You need to put a smile on your face for when Betty arrives, not wallow in self-pity."

"I'm sorry. It was my fault." Mr Marsh stood up. "May I help with anything?"

"No, thank you. I don't want to do too much until they're here. You sit down."

Nell gave Betsy her dolly while they waited, but as soon as the front door opened, the child wriggled from her grasp.

"Mama."

"I'm here." Betty swept her into her arms. "Have you been a good girl?"

"My missed you."

"I missed you, too."

Mr Marsh offered her his seat. "Come and warm yourself."

Betty looked at Maria as she moved to the chair. "Was she all right?"

"As good as gold. You sit down, and I'll get you something to drink. Would you prefer tea or brandy? I brought some with me."

"That's very thoughtful, but just tea for me."

"Mr Crane?"

"I'll take a brandy, a large one." He sat at the table. "And something to eat... I need to get to work."

"What about the other men? Will they be joining us, or have they gone already?"

"No, it's just me."

Maria nodded. "Leave it to me."

Jane followed Maria to the kitchen. "I'll have a brandy, if you're asking. There's no point carrying it home."

"You can come and help. You know where everything is."

Nell watched Betty as she settled in the chair. "How are you doing?"

She shrugged. "I'm managing. You have to, don't you?" Her eyes flicked to Mr Marsh, as he spoke to Mr Crane, and she lowered her voice. "Don't tell anyone, but I'm in the family way again." Tears welled in her eyes. "How can I be happy for this new one after what happened?"

"Oh, Betty..." An icy shiver ran down Nell's spine.

"It may be a distraction, but I don't know that I'm ready."

Nell's hand shook as she reached for her glass. "A-are you sure? Have you seen a doctor?"

"Not yet, but it's started to show beneath my clothes."

"Who knows?"

"Only Mam."

"You've not told Alice?"

"No, I was going to tell her." Betty paused as she gazed around the room. "Where is she?"

"She went for Albert..."

Betty gasped and put a hand to her mouth. "I'd completely forgotten about him. How could I?"

"Stop worrying. She said she'd promised to collect him..."

"Oh ... I remember now." She clung more tightly to her daughter. "I should be grateful I only lost one. It could have been all three of them."

Nell shook her head. "I doubt God would be that cruel."

Mr Marsh stood by the carriage and helped Nell, Maria and Alice down the steps before slipping a coin to the coachman.

Maria smiled at him. "Thank you, Mr Marsh. I doubt we could have walked home after a day like that."

"I'm glad I could help." He turned to Nell. "May I see you tomorrow?"

"Aren't you coming in?"

"Only if I'm not in the way..."

Maria pushed open the door. "You won't be. You're welcome to stay for tea, if you like."

He followed them into the house. "I'll have a cup of tea,

then, thank you. I told my landlady I'd be back. She likes to know in advance if I'm eating with them."

Nell smiled. "We'll have to invite you the day before, then. You take a seat by the fire and..." She stopped as Rebecca burst into the room, her eyes red. "What's the matter?"

"It's Hugh. He's got a new job."

"That's good, isn't it? I presume he'll earn more money."

"It's in Aigburth Vale!" She wiped her eyes with the back of a hand.

"Why on earth would he want to work there?"

'It's not only working. He says we have to move house."

Nell's mouth fell open. "That's miles away."

"I know." She sobbed into her handkerchief. "What am I going to do?"

Maria took her arm. "Sit down and take a deep breath for a start. Has he definitely decided?"

Rebecca nodded. "He said he's seen a place over there and he'll speak to our landlord tomorrow so we can move next week."

"Next week!" Nell gasped. "What's he thinking?"

She shook her head. "He isn't. I've told him it's Christmas and I've the food to prepare, but he won't listen..."

"And what about Florrie? She can't walk so far to school."

"He thinks she can until the Christmas break and then move to a new one in January."

Alice joined them at the table. "It will be dark."

"That's what I told him, but he said it's a good

opportunity, and he doesn't want to be walking an extra two hours a day."

"But he'd let his daughter...?"

Mr Marsh stood up. "I was hoping to see Mr Grayson in the alehouse this evening. Would you like me to have a word with him?"

"Would you?" Rebecca's doelike eyes stared up at him. "He won't change his mind about moving, but if he could at least put it off until the New Year it would be a huge help."

Mr Marsh nodded. "I'll try my best. I must admit, I enjoyed his company in the alehouse last time I was home, so I'll be disappointed if you leave, too."

Nell smiled at him. "And hopefully, if he knows you're here until January, it will be a reason for him to stay."

CHAPTER FIFTY-THREE

Mr Marsh held open the door of Rathbone's tea room and ushered Nell inside. She stopped to study the red-and-gold flock wallpaper and thick carpet.

"Goodness, it's nice in here. I'm surprised it's on the main street. You'd think they'd hide it away to keep the rabble out."

Mr Marsh laughed. "The idea is to bring people in."

"Then everyone should take their shoes off so they don't spoil the carpet."

Mr Marsh shook his head as Nell accepted a seat at a corner table, partially screened by a large palm.

"People on the ship didn't do that."

"They were first-class passengers. This is quite different." She sat up straight as a waitress handed her a menu. "This looks very nice."

"I wanted the best for you today. I feel as if we've hardly seen each other with everything that's been going on."

"At least you sorted things out for Rebecca with Mr Grayson. She was so relieved."

"He hadn't thought it through, that's all."

Nell raised an eyebrow. "Are you sure, or was he trying to get away from us before Christmas?"

Mr Marsh smiled. "There may have been an element of that, but I told him he'd be expected to visit anyway and moving would only give him a longer walk home."

Nell chuckled. "That's true. Did you tell him you'd be here until January, too?"

"I did. That seemed to sway it."

"You must have a way with you. You're the first person in the family who's ever got on with him. Even George gives him a wide berth."

"Which is why he's keen to move."

Nell put a hand to her mouth as the waitress returned for their order. "We've not looked yet."

Mr Marsh folded up his menu and handed it to the young woman. "I took the liberty of calling this morning and ordering two full afternoon teas. I wanted to check you were happy before they brought it out."

"It sounds wonderful, thank you." Once they were alone, she gazed around the half-empty room. "At least they'll make their money. I don't suppose a wet afternoon in December is a good time for business. Especially when the men are at work."

Mr Marsh twisted in his seat. "There are several tables occupied by women."

"They must have rich husbands, then. Or they're widows who were well-provided- for. I couldn't come here with Rebecca."

He smiled at her. "Perhaps one day."

Nell sat back in her chair. "My brother always said I

should have received compensation when Jack's ship went down, but nothing ever came of it. The inquest found the captain was at fault, not the company, so they got away with it scot-free."

"I'm sorry."

She shrugged. "These things happen for a reason, and if I'd had any money, I wouldn't have taken a job on the *Wisconsin*."

"And we wouldn't be sitting here now."

"Exactly." She stopped as the waitress delivered a large pot of tea. "Will you bring some boiling water for that? I don't like it stewing."

"Certainly, madam."

Mr Marsh grinned as he studied her.

"What's the matter? Is my hat lopsided?"

"I enjoy looking at you. Is there anything wrong with that?"

Her cheeks coloured. "You make me blush, that's what."

"You've nothing to be embarrassed about." He watched the waitress place a tiered cake stand laden with sandwiches and cakes in the middle of the table. "I hope you're hungry."

Her eyes widened. "I won't eat half of that."

"Let's see, shall we?"

The pot of hot water had been poured into the teapot and the empty cake stand cleared away before Nell sat back and rested her hands on her stomach.

"That was delicious. Thank you."

"It's my pleasure. We could come here more often if you like."

Nell puffed out her cheeks. "Once a week is enough if I'm to fit in my dresses."

"Can you believe we'll be running out of places to visit soon? We'll have to start again ... or return to your favourites."

"I've enjoyed them all."

"And there was me thinking I had no preference because of the company I was keeping." There was a twinkle in his eyes and Nell leaned forward, resting her arms on the table.

"Maybe I thought that, too."

"I'd be delighted if you did."

A tingle ran through her as he stroked the back of her left hand.

"So delicate."

Her eyes darted around the room, but when she realised they were alone, she inched it closer to him, only stopping when she became aware of the wedding ring on her third finger. "I-I've never thought to take my ring off before."

"You had no need."

"Suddenly it feels wrong to be wearing it while I'm with you."

"Would you take it off for me?"

She stared down at her finger before raising her eyes to meet his. "If you want me to."

"May I?"

When she nodded, he reached for the thin gold band and with a gentle tug, pulled it over her knuckle and let it fall to the table. They both stared at her hand before their eyes met again.

"I hope you don't mind."

"It was time." Her heart pounded as he raised her hand to his lips.

"I don't like to see you without, though." He reached into his jacket pocket. "I'd like you to wear this instead." He opened a small box to reveal a gold band set with a row of diamonds.

Nell's eyes widened. "That's for me?"

"I want to spend the rest of my life with you. Will you do me the honour of being my wife?"

She searched his face, taking in the shape of his narrow nose, his brown eyes and the slight parting of his lips, before she nodded. "Yes."

"Oh, my dear Elenor, I promise you won't regret it." He slipped the ring onto her finger. "It's perfect. You're perfect..."

Her heart skipped a beat as he kissed her hand, this time more slowly.

"You don't know how happy you've made me."

She smiled. "I didn't realise I could be so happy myself."

His face straightened. "You know I'll give up going to sea?"

"I hoped you would. When?"

"Before the wedding, certainly, but sooner if I can find a job. I don't want to leave you for a second longer than I have to."

Nell stroked her new ring. "We need to set a date."

"That will be your choice, but we needn't decide now."

"No. James said he hoped to be home in October next year, so we could aim for then."

His smile faltered. "So long?"

"We can make it sooner if you want, but it's Christmas next week, and you'll need to find a job, which won't be easy once you go away again. We'll need somewhere to live, too."

He took her other hand. "I can see we have some planning to do. Let's be thankful we have a couple of weeks together before I leave again."

"We better make the most of it."

It was dark by the time they reached Merlin Street, and Nell giggled as she gripped the doorknob.

"I'm quite nervous about telling everyone."

"Would you like me to do it?"

She shook her head. "You'd better leave it to me. I need to watch what I say to the girls."

"They're bound to notice the ring."

She spun it around to hide the diamonds in the crease of her hand. "Is that better? It's only a little thicker than my other one."

"It helps."

She paused to collect her thoughts. "We won't be eating after everything we've had, so I could make a general announcement once everyone's home."

"Shouldn't you tell Mrs Atkin first?"

"You're right. Let's see what mood she's in."

Maria was setting the table when they walked in, and she looked at the clock. "What time do you call this?"

"I'm sorry. Mr Marsh took me for a lovely afternoon tea..."

"Oh, good afternoon, Mr Marsh. I didn't see you there. I presume you won't need anything to eat."

Nell gulped. "No, thank you. Just a cup of tea. I ... erm ... we've something to tell you."

She took a deep breath but stopped when Alice joined them.

"We were wondering where you were."

"Oh ... we went for afternoon tea, and..." she gazed at Mr Marsh "...Thomas has asked me to marry him. Look."

Alice squealed and her hands flew to her mouth as Nell showed them her ring. "That's wonderful. Isn't it, Mam?"

"It is. I'm so happy for you." She grinned at Mr Marsh. "I hope you can rid her of this restless streak she has."

"I don't want to change her at all." His eyes sparkled as he gazed at her. "She's perfect as she is."

"You wouldn't want her going to sea, though?"

"I hadn't thought of that, although I wouldn't object if she wanted to come with me."

Maria's face paled. "Please don't encourage her..."

Nell rolled her eyes. "Stop panicking. It hadn't even crossed my mind. Thomas has promised to get a job in Liverpool, and we'll live locally."

"I'm sorry." Maria put a hand on her chest. "Have you chosen a date?"

"Not yet, but it will be October at the latest. That's when James will be home."

"How do you know?"

"He ... erm ... he mentioned it last time he was here. I'd like a date when Captain and Mrs Robertson can join us, too. If it wasn't for Mrs Robertson, we wouldn't be here now."

Maria's forehead creased. "Why?"

"Oh ... it's a long story. I'll tell you later."

"Well, if she's travelling as much next year as she has been this, you'll have a job finding a date she and James can make. Even if they know in advance when they'll be in Liverpool."

Nell paused. "I hadn't thought of that." She looked at Mr Marsh. "Perhaps we should choose a date that suits us."

CHAPTER FIFTY-FOUR

Rebecca put her hands to her head as she stared at the food Maria had put in the pantry. "What do I do with all this?"

Maria tutted. "First of all, Happy New Year!"

"Sorry. Happy New Year to you, but what do I do?" Rebecca's eyes were wide.

"You don't need to do anything. It only needs plating up, but if you leave it here for now, we can get the eggnogs mixed. Did you buy some rum?"

"Yes, it's here." Rebecca reached in the cupboard. "I can't believe that in all these years, this is the first time we've hosted a gathering here."

Nell chuckled. "I'm more amazed Mr Grayson agreed to it."

"He wouldn't have done if we weren't moving tomorrow. I'm just grateful we don't have many personal possessions. One carriage should do it."

"What's the new house like?"

"I've not seen it, but he told me it's similar to this." Rebecca sighed. "I'll miss you all."

"We'll still see you, and perhaps with the extra money he's earning, he can give you a couple of shillings for a carriage."

Rebecca snorted. "There's not much chance of that. I'll have to save up myself if I want one."

"You can get there easily enough through Sefton Park. On a nice day, you'll be able to meet in the middle."

Nell stared at Maria. "How do you know? You've not been up there for years."

"George and I used to do our courting around there, away from prying eyes."

Nell's gasp turned to a chuckle as Rebecca laughed. "Who'd have thought?"

"I was young once, you know. Now, can we get these eggnogs mixed?"

Nell pulled out the watch around her neck. "What time are we expecting the men from the alehouse?"

"About four o'clock. Was Mr Marsh joining them?"

"He was. It will be his last visit before he leaves. Next time he's here, he'll miss Mr Grayson as much as I miss you. He's really helped him settle in."

"He's good for something then."

Maria looked up from the bowl where she was beating a dozen eggs. "Are you two going to do anything other than talk? Those spirits won't measure themselves."

Rebecca sniggered. "I'm sorry. You can tell what a poor hostess I am. Let me get some glasses to pour them into."

. . .

It was quarter past four before the men arrived and Mr Marsh grinned at Nell as she ushered them in.

"Are you ready for us?"

"Just about. Have you had a good afternoon?"

"Very pleasant. Mr Grayson's invited me to visit him next time I'm home."

"That's nice. Perhaps we can walk there together." She grimaced as Maria shouted her. "I'd better go." She wandered to the kitchen as Maria lifted some sausage rolls from the range.

"Are you serving this eggnog?"

"Give me a minute." She poured out eight glasses and offered one to George. "Don't drink it too quickly, it's rather strong."

"That's the best sort." He waited for her to hand out the rest before he stood up. "Has everybody got one?"

Maria joined them and took a glass. "We're not all here yet."

"Well, we're not waiting." He raised his glass. "Happy New Year to those present, and commiserations to those who haven't joined us. They don't know what they're missing."

They all raised their glasses and repeated the toast, before Mr Grayson called for quiet. "May I propose a toast to Mr Marsh and wish him safe travels?"

Mr Marsh beamed as his name rang out. "Thank you all for welcoming me to the family. By this time next year, I'll be a fully signed-up member."

They all laughed before he raised his glass once more. "I'd like to raise a toast to Mr and Mrs Grayson. May they be happy in their new home."

"Mr and Mrs Grayson."

Nell sipped her drink, the brandy and rum overpowering the custard mix. "I'd better slow down with this. We probably shouldn't have finished the bottle."

Rebecca giggled. "I don't mind. It's one less thing for me to pack tomorrow."

Billy emptied his glass. "Do you have any games planned?"

Maria shrugged. "Only the usual. What would you like to play?"

He stared at the ceiling. "We could start with charades before the children arrive. Where are they, by the way?"

"With Alice and Mr Wood. They wanted some time to themselves while everyone was out."

Vernon nudged his brother. "I wouldn't say having four children to look after was having time to themselves."

"It will be good practice for them." Billy sniggered but straightened his face as Maria scowled at him.

"That's enough. This is a respectable family."

"They're married, aren't they?"

"That's beside the point. Now, are we having men against women for charades...?"

As the evening came to an end, Nell clung to Mr Marsh's arm as he escorted her home.

"Are you all right?"

She giggled. "I think the eggnog's gone to my head. I need a sleep."

"It's a good job it's bedtime then."

She held his gaze as they reached the other side of the road. "I hope you enjoyed yourself."

"I did, thanks to you. I'm just sorry it had to end."

"So am I. I've got used to having you around, but we'll be back to stealing a few days here and there from now on."

"It won't be for long. I promise." He gazed down at her, his lips parted, but she stepped back.

"There are too many people out tonight."

"Down here, then?" He nodded to the narrow entry leading to the backyard.

She hesitated as he took her hand and led her into the darkness. "I can hardly see you in here."

"Your eyes will adjust." He pressed her against the wall and cupped her face with his hands. "I want to remember tonight; it will be too long before I see you again." His lips found hers and her whole body tingled as she relaxed into his arms.

Oh, Ollie... No! She went rigid and fought for breath as Mr Marsh pulled away.

"What's the matter?"

"N-nothing. I'm sorry. I-it must be the eggnog..."

He wrapped his arms around her. "You're not used to being intimate, that's all. Not that I am."

"Y-yes. That must be it. I'm sorry."

He kissed her once more. "There's no need to apologise. I'd rather that than it be a common occurrence."

"I-I've always told you it's not..."

"And I believe you. Come here."

Nell stared into the darkness as he held her. *Where did Ollie come from? I should have forgotten about him by now.*

"I'm counting the days until you're my wife."

"Yes..." She shuddered as a gust of wind blew over them, and he wrapped her in his arms.

"You're cold. Would you like to go inside?"

"I'd better. Maria will be wondering where we are."

He held her close. "I won't come in. It's late and I need to be up early in the morning." His lips found hers. "This must be where we say farewell. Until next month, my love."

Nell carried the last package from Rebecca's front room and handed it to the coachman before returning to the house.

"Is that it?"

"I think so." Rebecca threw her arms around Nell's neck. "I'm going to miss you."

"I'll miss you, too. And Mr Marsh. Did you have to go on the same day?"

Rebecca rested her head against Nell's. "Knowing Hugh, he probably planned it. He has no thought for anyone else."

"At least it will give Florrie time to settle in before school starts."

Maria joined them, clutching a meat and potato pie. "To save you cooking when you get to where you're going."

"Thank you." Tears welled in Rebecca's eyes as she took it from her. "I tell you, I'll insist we move back if I don't have neighbours like you."

"Then you won't be gone long." Maria wiped her eyes. "We'll be over to see you next week."

"You'd better be."

Once Mr Grayson had made a final check of the house,

he helped Rebecca and his daughters into a second carriage. "That should do it." He nodded to Nell. "Mr Marsh has our address for when he wants to visit."

"He said." Nell choked back a tear. "Look after them all."

"Naturally." He climbed into the carriage seconds before it moved away.

Maria sighed. "It's the end of an era."

"It is." Nell walked across the street as they disappeared towards Windsor Street. "You do wonder why Mr Grayson had to move. Will he be earning that much more money?"

"I don't know. I doubt Rebecca does either."

"I'll have to see if he told Mr Marsh ... if I remember by the time I see him again."

Maria smiled at her. "Come on. Cheer up. At least you have your wedding to think about. Did you settle on a date before Mr Marsh left?"

"No. We'll decide when he's back."

"Will you wait for James to come home?"

"I don't think so. Mr Marsh doesn't want to wait that long."

"Well, you need to give Rebecca enough time to make your dress."

"I will." *But I already have a dress that's far nicer than anything we could make. It's a shame it comes with too many memories.*

CHAPTER FIFTY-FIVE

Maria pulled down the last of the holly from over the fireplace and stacked it in a pile on the floor.

"There we are. Christmas and New Year over for another year."

Nell stared at the berryless mistletoe mingled with the other evergreens and smiled. *It was fun when Mr Marsh stole a few kisses. I won't throw the berries away yet.*

"What are you thinking?"

"I was only dwelling on what a nice time we had. Thank you."

"You're welcome. Now, once we get this lot into the yard, we're finished."

"Let me." The holly scratched Nell's hands as she picked up an armful, but she hurried outside, dumping it in a corner before rushing back indoors. "My, it's cold out there."

"Put the kettle on if you like. We're ready for a drink and it will warm us up."

Maria swept the bits from the floor while Nell arranged the tea tray.

"What are you doing now?"

Nell shrugged. "Nothing much. Rebecca gave me a few old magazines, so I may sit and read them."

"I've some knitting to do for Betty's new baby."

Nell's forehead creased. "Doesn't she have enough?"

"One little jacket won't hurt, and it will give me something to do before the others get home."

"It's such a blessing her having this baby after what happened to Patrick."

Maria raised an eyebrow. "You think so?"

"It is for her. She was nervous at first, but she's looking forward to it now."

"Then I'm glad." Maria picked up the remnants of the foliage. "You can make that tea. I'm about ready."

Nell carried the tray to the table but stopped when the letterbox clanged. "Who's writing to us?"

"I'll get it." Maria disappeared into the hall. "Oh..."

"What's the matter?"

She passed Nell the black-edged envelope. "Who's it for?"

"Me!" Nell's voice cracked. "I don't recognise the handwriting either. Who's died?"

"Open it."

Nell's heart pounded as she sliced the envelope and pulled out the single sheet of paper. The blood drained from her face as she read, and she flopped into a chair by the fire.

"Who is it? Not Mr Marsh?"

Nell shook her head but couldn't pull her gaze from the letter.

"You have to tell me." Maria nudged her shoulder. "Nell, who is it?"

Tears rolled down her cheeks as she stared at her sister. "Mary."

Maria's mouth opened and closed several times. "Jack's sister-in-law, Mary?"

She nodded.

"Dead?"

"Yes."

"Who wrote the letter?"

"His brother."

Maria's chest heaved. "That's all right then ... isn't it?" She perched on the seat opposite as Nell sobbed.

"He says he can't cope with her now he's on his own."

"Edith?"

Nell nodded.

"But he can't get rid of her!" Maria's eyes were wide. "I-I mean, not after what happened."

"He wants her to come here."

"To visit?"

"To live." She stared at Maria as she struggled to breathe. "W-what am I going to do?"

"Do you want to see her?"

"No... I don't know..." Nell ran a hand over her face. "It will ruin everything... For pity's sake, why did it have to happen now?"

"All right, calm down." Maria took several deep breaths. "We'll think of something."

"Like what?" Nell thought her heart would burst through her chest. "He asked when he can send her."

"But he can't... Not just like that. How will we afford another mouth to feed?"

"I don't know." Nell's head swam. "Should I ignore him?"

"Do you have any choice?"

Nell put a hand to her mouth as an acrid taste rose to her throat. "What if he sends her, anyway?"

"Could we pretend we've moved house and say we're the new people? She won't know what we look like."

Nell squeezed her eyes tight as she rested her head on the chair. "I couldn't do that if she turned up on the doorstep."

"I don't know what to suggest, then. I always said this would come back to haunt you."

Nell jumped to her feet. "I don't need your judgement. If you can't say anything useful, don't say anything at all."

"I'm trying to help."

"Well, you're not."

"I'm sorry. Come and sit down again."

Nell flounced onto the chair. "If Mr Marsh finds out..."

"He won't. He's on his way to America and it will be sorted out before he's back."

Nell wiped her eyes. "What if it isn't?"

"We'll make sure it is."

Billy looked across the table as they finished their evening meal.

"You're quiet tonight, Aunty Nell."

She shrugged. "Twelfth Night always does this to me. It doesn't help that Mr Marsh isn't here."

"He won't be going away for much longer."

Nell looked up. "What's he said?"

"Nothing he hasn't told you. Just that once you're married, he doesn't want to be going away." Billy snorted. "Not that the others in the alehouse took him seriously. They said that once he'd been married for a year or two, he'd be keen to get away again."

If we make it that far. "What did he say to that?"

"He laughed."

Her stomach cramped. *He won't be laughing when he comes home.*

"Come on. Cheer up. He must be over halfway to America already."

She nodded. "He will be. They'll see land in the next day or two."

"There we are, then. He'll be on his way home in no time."

He needn't rush.

Alice caught Nell's eye as she reached for her cup. "Betty was looking well today."

"That's good. How are the children?"

"The same as ever. I said I'd call on Friday if you want to come with me."

"I might. Thank you."

"When do you think you'll visit Aunty Rebecca?"

"I ... erm ... I've arranged to go on Wednesday. She said she'd be settled in by then."

"Oh, that's a shame." Alice's shoulders slumped. "I was going to walk with you, but it's Harry's half day."

"I'm sorry, I clean forgot. Maybe we can go together next week. I'll arrange another day with her."

Maria topped up Nell's cup. "I was planning on walking there with Aunty Nell, so you'd be as well waiting."

"You were?" Alice looked as shocked as Nell felt.

"Don't look so surprised. I want to see where she is ... and keep your Aunty Nell company."

Nell smiled. "I'd like that. Thank you."

The walk through Sefton Park was pleasant, even though the clouds were dark.

"It's so different in the winter."

"The snowdrops will be out soon enough."

Nell sighed. "I hope Rebecca's in."

"I thought you'd arranged to visit."

"I didn't have time. I only chose today to stop Alice coming with me. I want to speak to Rebecca about the letter."

"You're going to tell her?"

"I need some advice, and besides you, she's the only one who knows the truth. I've not slept for two nights worrying about what to do."

"Isobel may be with her."

Nell closed her eyes. "I'd completely forgotten. We'll have to send her to the shop if she's in."

They left the park through the gate at the far end, and once they found the right road, Nell studied the numbers. "We need number thirty-four." They walked about a hundred yards. "There it is." *Please let her be in ... and be on her own.*

She knocked on the door, and pushed on the doorknob, but stumbled backwards when it was locked. "That's not a good sign."

"No, it's not."

Nell moved to the window and peered in. "She's not in there." She rapped the knocker again and breathed a sigh of relief when the key turned and Rebecca opened the door, a smile lighting up her face as she did.

"What a lovely surprise. Come in."

"Why's it locked?"

Rebecca rolled her eyes. "Hugh told me to lock it until I know more people. I'm not sure what he thinks will happen, but it's easier to do as I'm told when it doesn't really matter."

They walked into the living room at the back of the house.

"This is nice furniture." Maria pressed down on the seat of the settee. "It's almost new."

"It's comfortable too. Take a seat and I'll put the kettle on."

Nell followed her to the kitchen. "Are you on your own?"

"Yes, Isobel's gone to the park with some friends. She won't be home until dark."

"That's good."

Rebecca rested the kettle on the range. "Why?"

"Put that on the heat and come and sit down. I need some advice."

By the time Rebecca joined them, Nell had pulled the

letter from her handbag, and she passed it to her sister as she took her seat. Rebecca's face paled as she read it.

"When did you get this?"

"Monday."

"Have you replied?"

"Maria thinks we should ignore it."

"I wouldn't, if I were you. It reads as if he'll send her, anyway."

"That's my fear, but I doubt he'll take any notice whatever I say."

"So, one way or another, she's likely to turn up sometime soon."

Nell's heart pounded as Rebecca passed the letter back to her. "I don't know how I'll face her after all this time. What do I say?"

"More to the point, what do we tell everyone else?" Maria stared between them. "George doesn't even know what happened. He was away at the time, but now he'll have to provide for her."

Rebecca pursed her lips. "Will she know who you are?"

Nell shrugged. "I doubt it. It's not the sort of thing they'd talk about."

"Why don't you tell her you're her aunt? It's not a lie."

"Not a lie..." Nell's eyes were wide.

"Her dad and your husband were brothers."

"Yes." Slowly Nell nodded. "How do we explain why she's never heard of me before?"

"She may have, but they live miles away, so it would explain why she's not seen you."

"It's not that far. I visited several times with Jack before ... you know."

"It's a long way if you can't afford a carriage."

"That's true, but what if she hasn't heard of us? How do I explain that?"

"You don't have to. It would have been up to her mam to mention you."

Maria nodded. "She has a point."

"So, we tell everyone she's my niece? We can do that, can't we?"

"As long as her dad hasn't told her the truth."

Nell shuddered. "I doubt he will have done, but I'll have to write and tell him what we're doing."

Rebecca puffed out her cheeks. "Let's hope it works."

CHAPTER FIFTY-SIX

Alice and Nell put their heads down as they walked along the road towards Everton. Nell held onto her cloak as the wind got beneath it.

"I hope Betty's got the kettle on. Did you check whether Aunty Jane would be here today?"

"I did, and she won't be. The weather's getting to her, so she only calls about twice a week."

Nell sighed. "What do we need to do to persuade Betty to move closer?"

"She's not the problem, it's Mr Crane. Living where they do means he can walk to work in ten minutes."

"He should look for a new job then." Nell looked up as they reached the corner of Betty's road. "We're here now."

Alice knocked on the door before pushing it open, but they stopped when they saw Jane, her eyes red.

"Aunty Jane. What's the matter? I thought you weren't coming today."

Jane sobbed. "She's lost the baby ... again."

"No!" Alice gasped.

"The doctor's with her now, but–" she wiped her eyes "–it was fully formed. Another boy... He would have fit in the palm of my hand."

"Oh, Jane." Nell crouched down by her sister's lap. "I'm so sorry."

"Is this all punishment for what they did...?"

Betsy stood up from the rug and hugged her granny's legs. "Don't cry."

Jane wrapped an arm around her. "Why is it so difficult?"

"I don't know." Nell wiped her own tears as Alice stepped into the kitchen.

"How long's the doctor been here?"

"Since dinner time. He had to help her deliver it."

The colour had drained from Alice's face when she rejoined them. "How awful. How did you know to come?"

"Mr Crane came for me in a carriage. He'd come home for dinner and found her in such distress, he went straight for the doctor but needed someone to see to the children."

Alice grimaced. "We were complaining about the walk on our way here, but it's as well he works so close to home."

Nell clung to the chair to stop herself swaying. "I can't even imagine it. Not after everything else she's been through."

"I don't want to. Thank goodness for the two we have."

"Is Betty all right?"

"I don't know. She was hysterical when I arrived..." She stood up as the doctor made his way down the stairs. "How is she?"

"Very distressed. I've given her a sedative and I suggest

you keep her asleep for a few days while she heals. I've left a bottle by the side of the bed."

"What about the kiddies?"

"I'm afraid someone else will need to take care of them. Mrs Crane is in no fit state."

Nell gulped. "May we see her?"

"You can go to the bedroom, but she won't know you're there. You'd be better spending time with the children. Now, if you'll excuse me, I've patients waiting."

Nell flopped into the chair as Alice finished making the tea. "What a dreadful start to the year."

Jane lifted Betsy onto her knee. "That's not all of it either. Have you seen Sarah lately?"

"No, but Maria was expecting her this afternoon. Why?"

"She's struggling with the rent. I've told her she spends too much on food, but she won't listen."

"What will she do? Take in another lodger?"

Jane sighed. "She said the boys are growing up so fast, she's no room, so she's moving to a cheaper house."

"Not something smaller?"

"As if she could. No, she's seen one on Pickwick Street that's empty. For good reason, if you ask me, but it's two shilling a week less than she pays where she is."

Nell grimaced. "What's it like?"

"A mess, but it will be fine once she's cleaned it from top to bottom."

Nell huffed. "Why are we so dependent on men?"

"It's nice to be looked after."

"Not if there's no one to look after you."

Alice carried the tray to the table. "Come on, now's not

the time for this. Let's leave this to brew and go and see Betty."

The walk home was slow, and Nell sighed as she reached the front door.

"We'll have to go through all that again for your mam's benefit. As if once wasn't enough."

"She'll be wanting to tell us about Aunty Sarah, too."

Nell shook her head. "What an afternoon."

They both hung their cloaks in the hall and Nell followed Alice into the living room but grabbed for the door frame as she stared at the strange but familiar face by the fire. Maria pushed herself out of the chair opposite.

"Nell, Alice. I'd like to introduce you to Edith."

Nell's chest tightened, and she gasped for air as Alice smiled at the young girl.

"Good afternoon."

"Are you Alice?"

"I am, and this is my Aunty Nell."

Nell fought for breath as Edith studied her.

"Mrs Atkin says she's my Aunty Nell, too."

"Really?" Alice stared at her mam.

"Yes." Maria's voice squeaked as she struggled to find her words. "Pull up a chair and I'll explain."

Nell didn't move as black dots danced before her eyes.

"Edith's your cousin. We've just not seen much of her over the years."

Alice's forehead creased. "Who does she belong to?"

"You remember Uncle Jack? He has a brother, who's

Edith's dad. Unfortunately, her mam passed away a couple of weeks ago and he asked if we could take care of her."

"Don't you have any other aunties?"

"I do, but Dad wanted me to come here."

Alice nodded. "She looks very like Leah."

A bitter taste rose to Nell's throat as Edith glanced between the three of them. "Who's Leah?"

"Aunty Nell's daughter. Her youngest. She has two. You can tell you're related." Alice's smile disappeared as she turned to Nell. "Are you all right?"

"I-I..." She pulled on the neck of her dress as it stuck to her. *Calm down. She doesn't suspect a thing. But she will. It's only a matter of time.* "I need air..." She stumbled to the table but didn't make it before everything went black.

Her eyes flickered open as Maria slapped her face. "Nell. Wake up. Can you hear me?"

Her heart pounded in her ears. "W-what happened?" She attempted to sit up, but Maria pushed her back to the floor.

"Stay where you are. You fainted. Alice has told us you had a difficult afternoon with Betty."

She closed her eyes again. "The poor girl. She doesn't deserve it..."

"What's up with Aunty Nell?" Edith stood over her as Nell's eyes sprang open.

"I'm sorry ... it's so hot ... I need some air..."

"Nonsense. It's freezing outside."

"Just for a minute..." She tried to sit up, grateful when Maria helped her.

"I'll leave a cup of tea here for you then." Alice placed it near the fire. "Aunty Jane told us about Aunty Sarah, too. Did she come to visit you this afternoon?"

"She did, but she didn't stay long. She has packing and cleaning to do."

Nell gasped as she reached the back door. "Did she see Edith?"

"No, she'd gone before she arrived."

Thank heavens for small mercies.

"Are Aunty Jane and Aunty Sarah my aunties, too?"

Alice joined Edith at the table. "You can call them aunty, but I'm not sure they really are. I'll explain the family to you later. There are quite a lot of us." Alice cocked her head to one side. "If we're looking after Edith, where will she live?"

Maria left Nell by a crack in the back door and wandered to the girls. "Here."

"Do we have enough room?"

"We'll make room."

Alice's voice was gentle. "Where did you live while your mam was alive?"

"West Derby."

"That's miles away."

"Dad doesn't want me any more."

Alice gasped. "Doesn't want you... How could he? You can't abandon your own flesh and blood."

"I don't mind. I've never liked him. It was only Mam who cared..."

Except she didn't. Tears spilled from Nell's eyes as she rested her head on the door. *You have the worst mam in the whole world. And you can never know.*

. . .

The tightening in her chest had faded by the time Elenor and Leah came home and they both stopped to stare at Edith before Elenor spoke.

"Who's she?"

Nell stared at the ceiling, remaining silent as Maria told them.

"Will she be sharing our bed?"

"I'm hoping so. There's enough room."

"No there's not." Leah raised her voice. "Elenor wriggles and keeps me awake. Mam, tell her..." She stopped and stared at her. "Are you poorly?"

Nell nodded. "M-my head hurts, that's all. You sit at the table."

"It must hurt a lot."

Not as much as my heart. She flinched when the front door slammed and George joined them.

"What's going on here?"

Nell closed her eyes as Maria retold the tale, but she opened them when Billy spoke. "How come we knew nothing of them, Aunty Nell? You never mention Uncle Jack's family."

Nell ran her hands over her face. "After he was taken, it was too painful. Too many memories..."

"I've never heard of him." Edith's voice was quiet, but Billy continued.

"You must have done. How old are you?"

"Fifteen, but it's my birthday next month."

Billy looked across at Nell. "How long ago was it when Uncle Jack passed? Nine years or ten?"

Nell's heart skipped a beat. "Nine." *In two weeks' time.*

"So, you'd have been seven. You must have known about him. You probably even met him."

Nell's breathing stopped, and she twisted her head to see Edith shrug. "I don't remember."

Maria carried a couple of plates to the table and put the first in front of George. "Stop all the questions. Edith's had a hard enough time coming here without you all quizzing her. Are you joining us, Nell?"

"I couldn't eat anything."

Billy laughed. "You've not had another admirer taking you out for afternoon tea, have you?"

"No, she's not."

Nell imagined the look Alice must have given him.

"We've not had a good afternoon and don't need any jokes."

"I was only asking. I'll be glad when Mr Marsh gets a new job. We may get back to some normality."

Nell closed her eyes. *I very much doubt it.*

CHAPTER FIFTY-SEVEN

Edith stood up and wandered to the window overlooking the backyard.

"Is this all you do all day? Clean and knit?"

Maria sighed. "It's enough when the weather's like this."

"Not for me."

Nell managed a smile. "I often visit friends or go for a walk if it's dry. There are some nice parks around here."

"You've not been out since I got here, and that's over a week ago."

"The weather's not been good enough. I will soon."

"So, what will I do?"

Maria put down her knitting. "How did you busy yourself when you lived with your mam and dad?"

"I had a job. It wasn't much, but we needed the money."

"What did you do?"

"Sewing for a tailor."

Nell shifted in her chair. "Alice used to do that, not that she enjoyed it. She missed being at home with the girls."

"I liked it because it got me out of the house and away from my brothers. They always teased me for being different."

"There's nothing wrong with that."

"They thought there was."

Maria studied her. "Would you like to get a job in Liverpool? Alice or Mr Wood may be able to help. He's a tailor too, but he works in one of the big shops. I'm not sure they take women."

"I don't mind where it is as long as I can walk there. It would be better than sitting and doing nothing. I'd have some money, too."

"It's Wednesday, so they'll be home early tonight. Why don't you ask Mr Wood?"

"I will." She pushed her nose against the window. "It's stopped raining. May I go out and have a look around? It's only three o'clock."

Nell looked at Maria and shrugged. "I don't see why not as long as you remember your way back ... and you're home before dark."

A rare smile brightened her face as she skipped to the door. "I won't go far. See you later."

Nell let out a deep sigh as the front door closed. "Thank goodness for that. I've not relaxed for a week."

"Why haven't you taken yourself for a walk, or gone to visit Rebecca?"

"I was frightened she'd want to come with me. I'm not ready to be alone with her. She asks too many questions."

"Because everything's new to her. You can't blame her."

"I don't, but she makes me uncomfortable. I don't know how I'll cope when Mr Marsh gets back."

"Tell him what we've told everyone else. Nobody's batted an eyelid."

"I will, but he'll be here next week, and I can't help worrying." She stared at Maria. "Have you seen how like Leah she is."

"You can hardly miss it, but if they're cousins, it wouldn't be unusual."

"What about the fact she looks like her aunty, too? We're not even supposed to be directly related."

"Nobody's said anything."

"But you've noticed?"

Maria sighed. "Only because I know. Men never pay attention, and the girls are too young."

"Jane and Sarah will notice. And Mr Marsh definitely will." She groaned. "He's bound to say something."

"Just stick to the story and you'll be fine."

"I'm not so sure. Do you think we could find a job for her before he arrives? It would save me having to introduce them?"

"It would be a bit of a stretch, even if Mr Wood knows of any positions."

"I hope he does. I need to get her out of the way, or I'll be on tenterhooks the whole time he's here."

"He'll have to meet her sooner or later."

"I'd rather it be later. Preferably, once we're married."

Billy offered Nell his arm as they set out for church, but she pulled him back as Maria walked ahead with George and the girls.

"What's the matter?"

She reached into her handbag. "I couldn't remember if I'd picked up my handkerchief. Ah, yes. There it is."

"Shall we go, then?"

"We're not in a rush."

He looked down at her. "You've been in a strange mood lately."

She shrugged. "There's been so much going on. How are things at work?"

"Same as ever. Why?"

"Are you not interested in a promotion, now Vernon has one? I'd have thought you could do with the extra money."

"He wanted to feel more important. I'm not interested in that. I'm happy to get in, make my barrels and come home again." He raised an eyebrow. "Are you happy?"

"Me? Why wouldn't I be?"

"Do you miss Mr Marsh when he's away?"

"Of course, but it doesn't mean I'm unhappy."

"What about having Edith around? She seems to have unsettled you."

"Not at all." She coughed to clear the squeak in her throat. "It's a change of routine, that's all."

"You used to love trying different things."

"I must be getting old. It will happen to you soon enough."

They were almost behind Maria by the time they reached church, and Nell slowed her pace. "I'm not in a hurry to go in. It will probably be colder in there than it is outside."

"I doubt it with this wind. It will be quieter too." He

glanced up at the church tower, where a peal of bells rang out.

"All right, come on." She kept her head down as she walked in and waited for Billy to follow Edith into the pew.

He frowned at her. "I should be on the end."

"I-I want a word with your Aunty Jane if she's here ... to ask after Betty."

Billy nodded towards the opposite aisle. "She's over there already."

Nell shuddered. *I can't be seen too close to Edith.* "Never mind. If I'm on the end, I can get out quickly."

She paid little attention to the service, and once the vicar had retired to the back of the church, she jumped up. "Wait for me outside."

Jane was still in her seat when she arrived. "I was hoping to see you."

Nell's heart skipped a beat. "Why?"

"I wondered if you'd be able to visit Betty this week."

"Oh, yes." She exhaled slowly. "That's what I came to ask about. How is she?"

"Not very well, but Mr Crane can't afford to have the doctor calling every day."

"I'll call tomorrow if you like."

"That would be a relief. Will Alice go one day, too?"

"I'm sure she will."

"Good morning, Nell."

She flinched as Sarah joined them. "Good morning. How did the move go?"

"We're almost straight. I've had Ada and Mabel helping me clean the place and it's nearly as good as new."

"Are you open to visitors yet?"

"Just about." She nodded towards Edith. "Who's the young girl with you?"

"Oh, that's Edith. She's Jack's niece, but his sister-in-law died a few weeks ago and so she's come to stay with us."

"I can see the family resemblance."

Nell ran a hand around the back of her neck. "Yes, it's quite uncanny."

"Are you going to introduce us?"

"What, now? S-she's rather shy..."

"You could bring her to the house if you prefer."

Nell hesitated. "I could, but I don't know when. She'll be working soon."

"Working? Are you making her pay her keep?"

"Not intentionally, but she's not one for sitting around doing nothing, so she asked if she could take a job."

Sarah's eyes narrowed. "That doesn't sound normal."

"Oh, it is. She worked in a tailor's shop before she came to us."

Jane studied her. "Why's she with you?"

"I'm one of her closest relatives, apparently."

Sarah's forehead creased. "Who did you say her mam was? Jack's sister-in-law?"

"You probably won't remember her from the wedding, and they lived in West Derby so we never saw them."

"Has Jack's brother passed too, then?"

"Erm ... no, but ... he couldn't cope with her at home."

"How old is she?"

"Nearly sixteen." Nell's hands were clammy as Sarah stared at Edith.

"You'd have thought he'd have wanted her to keep house for him."

Nell shrugged. "They ... erm ... they didn't get on."

"That doesn't usually matter."

"No. Actually, I need to be on my way." She turned to Jane. "Tell Betty I'll call tomorrow."

Sarah caught her arm. "Will you tell Maria I'll pay her a visit tomorrow? I've hardly seen her since we moved house."

"Oh, she ... erm ... she'd like to call on you. I know she's keen to see where you are."

"And leave your new lodger on her own?"

"She won't be. She likes to go out. To the park ... or into town."

"How strange that the two of you can't sit still."

The heat rose in Nell's cheeks. "I-I've been telling you for years, it's not unusual for women to want to do things other than knit and sew."

"You may have told us, but until now I've met no one who agrees with you."

"Well, there are a lot of us. You obviously don't meet the same people as me."

CHAPTER FIFTY-EIGHT

Nell pushed away her half-eaten dinner and stood up as Edith stared at her.

"Don't you want that?"

"I'm not feeling my best. You can finish it if you like."

"Are you always like this? You've been ill for as long as I've been here."

"I-it's the time of year. I don't like winter."

"I don't either." Edith stabbed a piece of sausage. "I'm so happy Mr Wood found me a job."

Alice smiled. "We told you he would. I hope you like it more than I did."

"I will. I hate being stuck in the house."

"You can walk to school with me." Leah smiled at her. "I've told all my friends I have a new cousin and they want to meet you."

Edith shrugged. "I may as well. I've nothing better to do." She looked at Nell. "What are you doing this afternoon?"

"I ... erm... Someone's calling to take me out."

"You're not well."

"I'm hoping the fresh air will help."

Edith sat back in her chair. "My mam would never let me go out if I said I was ill."

"I've not been able to tell him not to call."

"Him!"

The girls giggled as Edith's eyes widened.

Elenor lowered her voice. "He's her fancy man. They're getting married soon."

A scowl crossed Edith's face. "How can you marry someone you never see?"

"He works on a ship, so he goes away. He should have arrived in Liverpool this morning."

"Ah." Edith finished the last of the sausage. "I wish my dad had worked on a ship."

Leah's eyes were wide. "Our *mam* worked on a ship. We didn't like her going away, though."

Edith looked at her with renewed interest. "What did you do?"

"I was a stewardess. I served the passengers when they travelled to America."

"You've been to America! Gosh! I'd like a job like that. Will you tell me about it?"

Nell glanced at the clock. "I will later. Mr Marsh will be here in a minute, and I need to get my hat and cloak."

The churning in her stomach hadn't stopped, and the nausea was overwhelming by the time the familiar knock sounded on the front door. She poked her head into the living room.

"I'll see you later."

Mr Marsh raised his hat as she opened the door. "Good afternoon, my dear. What a wonderful sight you are."

She forced a smile. "Welcome home. Did you have a pleasant trip?" She stepped outside before he answered.

"There were no problems if that's what you mean. Are you keen to leave? I was going to have a word with Mrs Atkin before we left."

"S-she's busy at the moment. Perhaps later."

"Very well." He offered her an arm. "Where would you like to go?"

She looked at the sky. "How about Sefton Park? The rain should hold off and I've brought my umbrella, in case it doesn't."

"That's fine with me." He smiled as they set off. "I've been looking forward to this moment since the day I left. I didn't realise I could be so restless."

"Did you speak to anyone about handing in your notice of intent to leave?"

"I did." He beamed at her. "I spoke to the captain, and he only needs to know a month in advance."

"So, you've handed it in?" Nell's stomach flipped.

"No, but I intend to when I return to the ship. I'm in Liverpool for five days, so I want to confirm the date for the wedding and make some enquiries about a job in the office. Have you had any thoughts?"

"Erm ... no, not exactly, we've had a lot going on while you were away."

He lowered his eyebrows. "What have I missed?"

Nell sighed. *Where to start?* "We had Rebecca's house move on the day you left."

"I'd forgotten. Did it go smoothly?"

"Well enough. I've visited a few times since, and she seems to have settled in. It's actually a pleasant walk through Sefton Park and out the other side."

"That's good. I'm hoping to see Mr Grayson while I'm here. Was that it?"

"No. Unfortunately, Betty's been ill, so I've been to see her a few times."

"Nothing serious?"

"Women's problems."

"Ah. I'm sorry. Is she all right?"

Nell shook her head. "Not really. Jane's been with her every day, but she needs a break. I'll start calling again once you've gone."

"Anything else?" He raised an eyebrow at her.

She took a deep breath. *Stay calm and tell him what you practised.* "We have a new house guest."

The smile disappeared from his face. "A lodger?"

"Not exactly. My niece, Edith. Her mam passed away last month, and her dad can't take care of her by himself."

His mouth fell open. "It wasn't one of your sisters?"

"Oh, no. It was my husband's brother's wife... You didn't know her."

"It's still unfortunate. How old is she?"

"She'll be sixteen next month. A month today, in fact."

He stared into the distance. "So, if she belongs to your husband's brother, it means she's not Mrs Atkins' niece."

Nell held onto his arm as her knees buckled. "No ... she's not. Why?"

"I was just thinking, if she's *your* niece, but not your sister's, you'll want her to live with us once we're married."

"Oh, yes." Nell's mouth opened and closed several times. "I-I'm sure Maria would let her stay with them if it's a problem."

"It shouldn't be, given you already have two daughters."

"Oh. Thank you. Not that she'll be around much. She's found herself a job in a tailor's shop. She starts tomorrow."

He grinned. "She sounds like her aunty."

"Oh, no, really she's not." Nell fought to keep the contents of her stomach down. "We're not directly related. It's just a coincidence."

"Maybe there are more independent women than I imagined."

"Yes. That must be it."

"How long's she been with you?"

Nell's heart pounded as she paused to think. "This will be her third week."

"I look forward to meeting her."

Nell fumbled with the catch of her umbrella as large spots of rain splashed onto the lake.

"This wasn't supposed to happen. There's nowhere to shelter at this time of year, either." She pushed the clip up the shaft and held it over her head.

Mr Marsh put an arm around her shoulders as he bent under it. "I'd better get you home. I don't want you going down with anything."

"It can't be three o'clock yet. I'm sure it will go off."

"Really?" He gazed up at the clouds. "I'd say it's set in for the afternoon. Come on. I needn't stay long if Mrs Atkins is busy."

"But..."

"No buts... We'll be wringing wet if we stay here, even with an umbrella. We need to hurry."

Nell's stomach cramped as they turned the corner into Merlin Street, and she paused for breath.

"Are you all right?"

"I-I've not been feeling myself these last few days. It must be with everything that's been going on."

"All the more reason to take you home. Why didn't you say?"

"I'd hoped some fresh air would do me good."

He shook his head. "You should be tucked up in bed, not walking in the rain. The sooner we're married, the better."

She nodded. "I'll go for a lie-down as soon as we get to the house, so you can get away."

"If I didn't know better, I'd think you were trying to get rid of me."

"Why would I do that?" She slowed down as they neared the house. "Will I see you tomorrow?"

"I hope so, even if we have to sit in."

"There'll be no need for that. I'll be fine by then."

"How can you be so sure?"

"Just a feeling..." She rested her hand on the doorknob but stayed where she was. "If you go now, you'll probably have time to get into Liverpool and find out about a job..."

"Only once I know you're on your way to bed..." He stopped as Maria opened the door, causing Nell to fall against the frame.

"I thought I could hear something."

"Well, I wish you wouldn't open the door like that. I nearly did myself a mischief."

"Then what are you doing out here in this weather? Come in."

Mr Marsh hesitated. "As long as you're not too busy."

"Not at all. There's only so much cleaning I can do."

Nell's heart skipped a beat as she stepped inside, and Mr Marsh handed his hat to Maria.

"It's turned out nasty. I'm glad I'm only round the corner."

"Are you in the same place as usual?"

"I'm even closer. It's nicer too."

Maria hung up his coat and beckoned him in. "Come and sit by the fire and I'll put the kettle on."

Edith was at the table with Elenor when they went in and she stared at Mr Marsh. He hesitated before nodding to her.

"Good afternoon. You must be Edith."

Her eyes flicked to Nell. "Have you been talking about me?"

"Only to tell Mr Marsh you'd moved in."

He gave a slight bow. "May I offer my condolences?"

"You don't have to. It's nicer here than it was with them."

"Oh ... well, I'm sure you've been made welcome."

"We've tried our best." Maria threw more coal on the fire. "Mr Marsh, you sit here. Where've you been?"

"Sefton Park. We were over by the lake when the rain started." Mr Marsh gave Nell an affectionate glance. "It was only when we were nearly back that she told me she's not been well."

Maria paused as she placed a plate of biscuits on the table. "You've not had another turn, have you?"

"It wasn't too bad." She fought to keep her face straight as her stomach cramped again.

"I've told her she should be in bed."

"She's been like that ever since I arrived." Edith helped herself to a biscuit. "It must be me, because Elenor said she's never normally ill."

"Don't be silly." Nell's voice squeaked. "It's nothing but a coincidence."

Mr Marsh's smile was fixed. "They seem quite common at the moment."

CHAPTER FIFTY-NINE

A smile flicked across Nell's lips as a cluster of snowdrops greeted her and Mr Marsh as they walked into Princes Park.

"How wonderful. Can it really mean that spring is on its way?"

He patted her hand. "I hope so. I can't believe how wet it's been this week. Still, I've enjoyed our afternoon teas."

"And at least the weather's been kind enough to let us take one last walk today. I can't believe you leave again tomorrow. Time goes so quickly when you're here."

"It won't matter for much longer." There was a twinkle in his eye. "I called at the office this morning, and they have a job for me next month."

Nell gasped. "Really! So, this is your last trip? That's wonderful."

"It became more urgent when we set the date for the wedding. I know May seems like a long time off, but if I need to live in the parish for at least four weeks before we can have the banns read, I won't have time to go away again.

I'll hand in my notice of intent tomorrow when I get back to the ship."

Nell smiled. "How exciting. It will be such a change for you."

"I'm ready for it. I'd marry you tomorrow if we didn't have to go through all the formalities."

"Perhaps it's as well we do, then. We need somewhere to live before we tie the knot."

"That won't take long."

"We need a family house, remember? We can't just take a room in a boarding house. I'd like to stay close to Maria, too. I know she can be overbearing, but I don't know what I'd do without her."

"We can do all that. I've been able to save a lot of money over the years, so once I'm back in Liverpool, we can start looking."

"I'm so looking forward to having my own house again."

"So you haven't always lived with Mrs Atkin?"

She smiled. "No, although it feels like it sometimes. Jack rented Merlin Street shortly after we were married, but then he went to sea and I ... *struggled* ... being on my own. George worked on the ships too, so after a while, Maria and the family moved in with me. She found it difficult to make ends meet when George was on a long voyage, and so it made sense."

"So, your husband lived in your current house?"

Her smile dropped. "Yes, why?"

"No reason." He pointed to a bench as they reached the lake. "Shall we?"

Nell rested her head on his shoulder as they sat in solitude overlooking the water. "I like this time of year when it's bright and doesn't rain. There are a lot fewer folks around and you can always get a seat."

"You can do this too." He leaned forward, letting his lips brush over hers. "That's what I missed the most when I was away."

"We'd better make the most of the silence then." She pulled him towards her, but they jumped apart when someone coughed behind them.

"What's going on here?" The sparkle in Jane's eyes was a contrast to the stern expression on Sarah's face.

"Sarah. What are you doing here? It's unusual to see you out."

"Jane persuaded me. I wouldn't have bothered if I'd known I'd see such filth."

Mr Marsh jumped to his feet. "Please, forgive us. We thought we were alone."

"So it would seem." She looked down her nose at Nell. "You should know better at your age."

Jane put a hand on Sarah's arm. "That's enough. They're an engaged couple and the park's empty. They were just unfortunate we came across them."

"Yes." Nell cleared her throat. "How was Betty yesterday? Is she still making progress?"

"She is, but only because of Betsy. I worry that she's spoiling her, but I can't say anything."

"There'll be time for that later."

"That's what I thought. How's that young niece of yours?"

"She's settled in well enough. Thankfully, Elenor and Leah have taken to her."

Jane shook her head. "They are so alike, especially her

and Leah. If you didn't know better, you'd swear they were sisters."

Nell coughed as she gasped for breath. "J-Jack and his brother were the image of each other."

"That must be it."

Sarah's eyes hadn't left her. "How old did you say she was?"

"Erm ... she'll be sixteen at the end of this month. Why?" Nell's body trembled as Sarah stared into the distance.

"No reason. Something popped into my mind, but it's gone again. It doesn't matter."

I was married eighteen years ago, if that's what you're wondering. Go home and work it out.

They stood in silence until Jane looked at the sky. "We'd better be heading for home. We don't have a handsome man to escort us if it gets dark. Good day, Mr Marsh, Nell..." She leaned into her. "And check who's around you next time."

Nell's cheeks burned as Sarah nodded and they headed towards the entrance.

"I'm sorry about that. Of all the people..." She retook her seat but looked up when Mr Marsh didn't join her. "What's the matter?"

He stared out over the lake. "It was something your sister said. It had crossed my mind, too, but I told myself I was being silly."

"She said nothing of importance."

"She said that Edith and Leah look like sisters."

A pain shot across Nell's chest. "There are plenty of cousins who look alike..."

"They're both remarkably like you, too, with those dark curls and deep brown eyes..." He turned to face her. "*Are* they sisters?"

"No, of course not. How could you even think that?"

He strode to the lake and back. "You've been acting strangely ever since I arrived. You're not the same person you were over Christmas and New Year."

She tried to laugh. "Everything's different at Christmas, especially with all the eating and drinking ... and mistletoe."

His face was stern as he stood over her. "You once told me that you didn't want there to be any secrets between us. If you had an illegitimate daughter, I've a right to know."

"Illegitimate! Of course I didn't. I would never... No! You've got it all wrong."

"But she's your daughter?"

Tears welled in her eyes as she gazed over the lake.

"Elenor, tell me." He lifted her face to look at him. "Is she your daughter?"

She trembled as his eyes bored into her. "Yes ... but she wasn't born out of wedlock."

"Then why are you ashamed of her? So ashamed that you gave her to another woman to bring up without anyone in the family knowing." He paused to compose himself. "There's only one reason for that."

"No, there isn't. I promise. It wasn't like that. Let me explain..."

"Damn you, Elenor. I don't want any more excuses or lies." He marched to the lake, then turned on his heel. "I knew from the day I met you that you encouraged men with your flirtatious ways, but I still fell for you. I tried to tell myself I was different. That you'd change and be honest with me, but I'm not, am I? I'm just another fool who fell under your spell."

"You're not..." Tears streamed down her cheeks. "Please don't be angry with me. It was all a long time ago, and..."

"It doesn't matter when it was. You told me once, there'd be no more secrets, but now I find out about this. I can't trust a word you say."

She rocked backwards and forwards on the bench, unable to stop her sobbing. "It wasn't like that..."

"I don't want to know... Now, stand up. I need to get you home."

"I-I can't go like this."

"You don't have a choice. I still have to pack my bag for tomorrow and I'm seeing Mr Grayson tonight."

Her handkerchief was wet as she wiped her face, but as soon as she pushed it into her handbag, he set off towards the gate, pausing only to check she was following him. He stared straight ahead as he walked, speaking only when they arrived outside the house.

"Please don't contact me again. You bring me nothing but heartache."

"Let me explain..." She reached for his hand, but he pulled it away. "I've told you, it's not what you think. Maria knows the truth. She'll tell you..."

"What, next time I'm in Liverpool when you've had plenty of time to concoct a story?"

"We don't need to. It's the truth."

"I'm not interested any more. Good day, Mrs Riley."

Nell leaned against the wall and screwed up her eyes as he left. *I can't go in like this. Why did Rebecca have to move?*

Rebecca!

She raced after him and pulled his arm. "If you won't believe me or Maria, ask Rebecca when you visit Mr Grayson. She's the only other person who knows the truth, and she's no idea we've had this conversation."

He stared at her but said nothing.

"Please. Edith was born in wedlock, and my husband was her father. Rebecca knows why I had to give her up. Tell her I want you to know. If you hate me once you hear the truth, then I'll understand."

CHAPTER SIXTY

Nell's shoulders sagged as she walked down Merlin Street, towards home. She checked her watch before she opened the door. *Five o'clock. The girls will be here soon. Then Edith.*

Maria smiled as she went in. "How was Rebecca?"

"Missing us." She paused and looked at the table. "What's going on?"

Alice appeared from the kitchen with a large cake. "It's Edith's birthday."

"I know, but what are you doing?"

"This is the first year she's been without her mam, so I thought we'd have a tea party for her. Show her she's part of the family."

"That's very thoughtful." *More thoughtful than me.* She sighed as Alice went back into the kitchen.

"Rebecca hasn't cheered you up, then. Perhaps this will." Maria handed her a letter. "Alice thinks it's from Mr Marsh. Is it?"

Nell caught hold of the chair. "Yes."

Alice reappeared. "I told you it was. I hope it's to say he'll be back shortly. I've never known you so upset about him going away, and we could do with you smiling by the time Edith gets home." She rearranged the plates on the table before disappearing again.

Maria tutted as Nell stared at the envelope. "Don't just stand there. Take it to the front room and find out what he has to say."

"What if it's telling me he never wants to see me again? I'll ruin the party."

"It can hardly put you in a worse mood than you're in now." Maria spun her by the shoulders. "Go."

Nell's heart was racing as she took a seat by the fireplace and sliced open the top of the letter.

Dear Elenor

I've lost count of the number of nights I've been unable to sleep since I last saw you. The way I shouted and made you cry has tormented me. You were clearly distressed and yet I couldn't see beyond my own humiliation.

You'll know by now that I spoke to Mrs Grayson about the events of sixteen years ago, and I want to believe her. Really, I do.

I can't exist as I am at the moment and need to see you, even if it's only to apologise for the way I behaved. I'll understand if you hate me for what I said, but please don't turn me away when I come to call.

I expect to be in Liverpool two days after this letter arrives, and I can only pray that you'll forgive me.

Your ever loving

Thomas

Nell sat back in the chair, her eyes focussing on nothing as she stared out of the window. *He wants to see me. But only to say he's sorry.*

She didn't move when Maria knocked on the door and let herself in.

"What does it say?"

"He'll be in Liverpool the day after tomorrow and wants to speak to me."

"That's good, isn't it?"

"I'm not sure. He says he's sorry for upsetting me, but I'm not raising my hopes that it will come to any more than an apology. I suspect he's only trying to purge his guilt."

"It might be more than that. Rebecca said he seemed to understand when she told him."

"There's a difference between understanding and forgiving." She closed her eyes as the front door opened and Leah popped her head round the door.

"What are you doing in here? Are you sad again?"

Nell pushed herself up. "No. I'm finished with that. Now wash your hands. Alice has made a birthday tea for Edith."

"Is she home?"

"Not yet, but she won't be long, so hurry up and we can surprise her."

Edith stood by the table; her mouth open as she surveyed the food Alice had laid out. "Is this for me?"

Alice smiled. "It is. Happy Birthday."

Edith rubbed a hand over her eyes. "I've never had a birthday tea before, or a present. Mam would try her best, but she only had the money Dad gave her, and he wouldn't waste it on me."

Nell put a hand on her shoulder. "I'm sorry."

"It's not your fault..."

A knot twisted in Nell's stomach. "It can't have been easy for you. You should sit at the head of the table seeing it's your day. Uncle George won't mind."

Edith grimaced. "Shouldn't we wait to ask him? I don't want to make him cross."

Nell paused as the front door closed. "He's here now."

Billy was the first in and he gasped when he saw the table. "A birthday tea!" He rubbed his hands together. "We don't get these very often."

"It's a special occasion." Alice smiled at Mr Wood as he joined them. "It's not every day you're sixteen, and Edith's not had an easy few months."

"I'm not complaining. Can't we have one for every birthday?"

George eyed the food. "You'll have to put another couple of shillings into the tin if we do."

"Come on, let's not get serious. Dad, do you mind if Edith sits in your chair?"

He studied his daughter. "As long as she doesn't eat too much."

"Thank you." Edith grinned as she sat down. "You've all been very kind."

Nell watched Edith smirk at Elenor and Leah. *She may be sixteen but she's still a child. My child. It's time I treated her the way I treat the other two.*

~

Nell stood up from her seat by the fire and checked her reflection for the umpteenth time.

"I can't decide whether I want the clock to hurry up or stand still. I just want this afternoon to be over."

Maria sighed. "Sit down, he'll be here in five minutes, however quickly it seems to pass."

"What do I say to him?"

"We've been over this. Just be yourself."

"It's easy for you to say. I don't know how he'll be with me, or whether I'll even see him again."

"Do you want to?"

"Yes." She stared at her hands. "I've grown very fond of him. I know what I did with Edith was wrong, but am I to be punished for it for the rest of my life?"

"It wasn't your fault."

"It wasn't anyone else's." She sat down and put her head in her hands. "Why can't we go back to how we were at Christmas? I've missed him."

"If you feel like that, I'd be surprised if he doesn't feel it more."

"You didn't see how angry he was..." Nell's head shot up at the sound of the familiar knock on the front door. "He's here."

"Go and let him in, then."

"I can't."

"Yes, you can." Maria pulled her up and pushed her into the hall. "Take him into the front room like we said. He needn't speak to me, if you don't want him to."

Nell took a deep breath as Maria disappeared into the

living room and closed the door behind her. *This is it.* She shuddered as Mr Marsh knocked again.

I'm coming. She forced a smile as she opened the front door. "Mr Marsh."

"Elenor." His face was pale, emphasising the dark circles under his eyes. "May I come in?"

She nodded and stepped to one side as he removed his hat.

"Thank you for seeing me."

"It's the least I can do." She took his cloak and hung it up, before showing him into the front room. "We won't be disturbed in here. Did you have a good voyage?"

His watery eyes held hers. "How could I, knowing how we'd parted?"

"I'm sorry."

"It wasn't your fault. I was the one who caused the scene. Will you forgive me?"

Nell shrugged. "Does it matter if I do or not?"

"It matters to me. I don't want you to hate me."

"I wouldn't do that." She counted to three. "Do you hate me?"

"I wouldn't be capable of it. You might infuriate me, but I could never hate you. I love you too much."

"Even now?"

"Mrs Grayson told me about the terrible time you had when Edith was born."

Nell shrugged. "I realise I shouldn't have done what I did. Edith's the one who suffered."

"It's easy to say that now, but you'd lost a son. You were bound to be upset."

"It was hardly Edith's fault."

"Melancholy makes people do things they wouldn't otherwise."

Nell wandered to the window. "I was so sick when I was in the family way with her, it stopped me looking after him. Jack was away, and Maria and Rebecca didn't live as close in those days. They didn't know I was struggling until it was too late. I hated myself for neglecting him. If I'd just asked someone for help. Anyone..." She wiped a tear from her cheek.

"You weren't to know."

"If I'd had another boy, it might have been different. Jack had been so proud of me giving him a son, so to replace him with a *girl*... I dreaded him coming home."

"I'm sure he understood."

"He said he did."

Mr Marsh rubbed a hand across his eyes as Nell fumbled for a handkerchief.

"I was such a terrible mam. I couldn't bear to be with her. Goodness knows I tried, but I never felt any love for her. When I found out my sister-in-law was suffering from melancholy because she was barren, it seemed like the ideal solution..."

Mr Marsh's brow creased. "I thought Edith had brothers."

"She does, but they came afterwards. No one knows why her mam suddenly delivered three sons after five years of nothing."

"These things happen."

"The sad part was, Jack and I never had that second son. It was the one thing I wanted when Jack was taken from me, a son that looked like him. But it wasn't to be."

"Did you keep in touch with your sister-in-law?"

"We did at first, mainly by letter, but as Edith grew up, she didn't want me to have anything to do with her."

"And you didn't object?"

Nell buried her face in her hands. "Every time I saw her, she reminded me of my son... Does it make it worse to say it was a relief that I didn't have to visit them? I feel so terrible about it now..."

Mr Marsh wrapped his arms around her. "Come here." He held her until her tears stopped.

"I'm so sorry I doubted you. When Mrs Grayson told me what happened, I was furious with myself, but there was no time to tell you. I needed to be on the ship at seven o'clock the following morning."

"I knew that..."

"But after everything you had to deal with, all I could do was jump to the wrong conclusion and chastise you for it."

She wiped her face on the back of her hand. "You weren't to know."

"But I didn't stop to find out. And not for the first time. Please forgive me."

"As long as you forgive me."

"There's nothing to forgive." He kissed the top of her head and tightened his hold.

"Does that mean you still want to see me?"

He lifted her face to his. "I still want to marry you. If you'll have me."

She bit her lip. "I-I cancelled the wedding we'd booked. You told me you didn't want any further contact with me."

He shook his head. "I was a fool."

"I should put this on again, then." She reached into the pocket of her dress and pulled out the small box containing her ring. "I was going to give it you back."

"What would I do with it?" He took the gold band from its holder and slid it onto her finger. "There's no one else in the world I'd want to wear it."

For the first time in weeks, Nell laughed. "I was only expecting an apology, I hadn't dared dream of anything more."

"I've dreamt of nothing else." He leaned forward to kiss her, but Nell pulled him away from the window.

"Not in front of the neighbours. They've already seen enough."

CHAPTER SIXTY-ONE

Rathbone's tea room was busy when Mr Marsh ushered Nell inside, and he smiled at the waitress as they arrived.

"I reserved the table in the corner. The name's Marsh."

"Certainly, sir. Walk this way."

The red-and-gold flock wallpaper still captured Nell's attention as she took the chair Mr Marsh held out for her.

"Why didn't you tell me we were coming here?"

"I wanted to surprise you. And remind myself of one of the happiest days of my life when you accepted my marriage proposal."

She stroked her ring. "It seems a long time ago now. So much has happened."

"Will you tell Edith the truth?"

"No!" Her head jolted upwards. "You won't say anything, will you?"

"Not if you don't want me to."

"I don't ever want her to find out. She'd be bound to hate me if she did."

"Then your secret's safe with me."

"It's funny, but for the first time in my life, I feel some affection for her, and I'm actually looking forward to getting to know her better."

"I'm glad."

Nell gave a grateful smile as the waitress offered her a menu, but she looked at Mr Marsh before accepting it.

"Have you already ordered?"

He grinned. "I thought we'd have the same as last time we were here, if you're happy with that."

"More than happy."

He nodded to the waitress. "Two full afternoon teas, then, please."

Nell settled back in her chair. "You've thought of everything. It's as well I told Maria not to do me any tea."

"I mentioned it to her myself. I was hoping we could think again about a date for the wedding."

She smiled. "I have already, but with you having to do another voyage, it's looking like June."

"It seems a long time to wait, but you're probably right. Why were we both so quick to cancel everything...? Don't answer that. I already know..."

"It's only a month later, and looking on the bright side, the weather should be nicer."

"And at least I'll be able to speak to the vicar with you on Sunday."

Nell giggled. "He won't know what's going on."

The family were still having tea when Nell arrived home, and she joined them at the table and poured a cup of tea.

Maria raised an eyebrow. "No Mr Marsh?"

"He's meeting Mr Grayson later, so needed to hurry. He's here all week, though, so he said he'll call tomorrow."

"Have you had a pleasant afternoon?"

"Yes, thank you. We went to Rathbone's again, and..." she glanced around the table to get everyone's attention "... we've chosen another date for the wedding. Wednesday the fourth of June."

Maria smiled as Leah clapped her hands. "I'm so pleased for you. Hopefully, Rebecca can sort a dress out for you in time."

"I'll speak to her, but it doesn't need to be anything fancy."

Edith studied her. "Does that mean you'll be moving out?"

"We'll be moving..."

"We?" Edith's forehead creased.

"Well, yes. Elenor and Leah will obviously come with us, and I assumed that with you being my niece, you'd come too."

"Really!" Edith's face brightened, and she grinned at Elenor.

"If you'd like to."

"Yes. As long as Mr Marsh doesn't mind."

"He was the one who suggested it."

Billy glanced at his mam and dad. "It means we'll have loads of room here. I'll be able to have the small bedroom to myself."

Maria sighed. "I understand that you can't all live here, but it won't be the same without you."

"We won't be going far..."

"Actually..." Alice nudged Mr Wood. "You had an announcement, too."

"Ah, yes." He cleared his throat. "I've been offered the chance to run my own tailor's shop. It's an opportunity too good to miss, so I've accepted"

George offered him a hand. "Congratulations. You'll be your own boss, will you?"

"I will."

"But you'll still live here?" Maria's eyes flicked between him and Alice.

"It's in Wales."

"Wales!" Maria shrieked as she grabbed George's arm. "Did you hear that? He's taking Alice away. To another country. We'll never see her again..."

"Mam." Alice put a hand on Maria's. "We'll come to visit. You can easily get there in a day using the railway."

"A day! Aunty Rebecca moved too far away for my liking..." She stared at Mr Wood. "I knew you were a bad influence."

"Enough." George banged a hand on the table. "Alice is a married woman. It's not up to us." He looked at Mr Wood. "When will you move?"

"Next month."

Billy grinned at his mam. "So, there'll only be the three of us left?"

"No." Maria swivelled to look at Nell. "If Alice isn't here, there'll be plenty of room for you to stay."

Billy's face dropped. "So I won't get my own room?"

"We'll be rattling around the place if everyone moves out. It would be a waste of Mr Marsh's money, too."

Nell's cheeks coloured. "I-I'll have to speak to him. He seems keen to find somewhere of our own..."

"As he's every right to do." George got up from the table. "There's room for you here if you want it, but if not, we'll manage. We can always take in a couple of boarders."

Maria's eyes were wide as George looked at Billy and Mr Wood.

"Are either of you coming?"

They both stood up and disappeared into the hall as George raised a hand. "We'll see you in the morning. Don't wait up."

Nell linked Mr Marsh's arm as they strolled around the lake in Princes Park the following afternoon.

"So, you're happy to move into Merlin Street?"

He smiled at her. "As long as we're married, I don't mind where we live. It's not as if we'd be on our own if we moved out."

"Edith was pleased to be included in our plans. She gets on well with Elenor and Leah."

"So, it won't make much difference having Mr and Mrs Atkin and Billy with us."

Nell grimaced as she looked across the lake. *Don't you believe it.* "At least it means there's no rush to find anywhere to live and we can always move later if it doesn't work out."

"Exactly. I'm surprised about Mr Wood, though. Where in Wales is he going?"

"A place called Cardiff. Not that I'm any the wiser. It sounds a long way away, though. Maria's not happy, as you can imagine."

"I hope it works out for them. When are they leaving?"

"They're not sure yet, but it will be before the wedding. They'll travel back for it, though. I've checked."

"That's good."

She looked up at him. "What about your family? Will you invite them?"

He paused before he answered. "I've not told them I'm getting married."

"So, they know nothing of me?"

"As far as they're concerned, I'm still sailing around the world, and rarely set foot onshore."

"Will you write to them?"

"I probably should. I'll send a letter to my eldest brother once we've confirmed the date with the vicar."

"Do you think he'll come to the wedding?"

He shook his head. "I doubt it. He'd need to miss two days at work, which he probably can't afford."

"That's a shame. Perhaps we could visit them once we're married."

"I should have a new job by then, so I won't have time myself."

"It sounds like you're avoiding them."

He stared at the gates as they approached. "My dad destroyed any relationships I may have had with the rest of the family."

"Isn't now a good time to heal them?"

"You've clearly never experienced family feuds."

"I have, actually. Maria wouldn't speak to my sister Jane for years after she married a Catholic. In the end, she practically forced her to move to Ireland to be with his family."

He raised an eyebrow. "Mrs Read?"

"See, you'd never know if I hadn't told you, would you?"

"No, but I can sympathise with Mrs Atkin. A Protestant marrying a Catholic is quite unforgivable."

Nell rolled her eyes. "Mr Read was very nice, and with hindsight, I can see why my sister fell for him. I tried to tell Maria she should be less judgemental."

He sighed. "It's something I need to work on, too."

"Anyway, when Jane was widowed and came back to Liverpool, Maria was furious. It took them a long time to be on speaking terms with each other, let alone be in the same room, but they don't do too badly now. Perhaps you should clear the air with your family."

His head nodded slowly. "Maybe I should, but only once we're married. Hopefully, they'll be more civilised if I take you with me."

CHAPTER SIXTY-TWO

Three months later

For the second time in her life, Nell stood at the top of the aisle and linked her arm into George's.

"You're sure you want to do this?"

She nodded. "I am, and thank you for everything. Things would have been very different if you hadn't been kind enough to support me."

"What else was I going to do?" He patted her hand. "Shall we go?"

She turned to her three daughters, who fidgeted behind her with bunches of flowers. "I think we're ready."

The organ struck the opening chords of the "Bridal Chorus" and Nell glided towards Mr Marsh, her eyes fixed on the back of his dark grey suit, as he stood beside Billy. He only looked at her when she was at his side.

He was as handsome as Nell had seen him, but she

wondered if there was a tear in his eye when he smiled. He returned his attention to the vicar as he began.

"Dearly beloved, we are gathered together here in the sight of God..."

Nell sneaked a glance at him, but he stayed focussed on the vicar.

"Wilt thou have this woman to be thy wedded wife...?"

"I will."

His face was tense as the vicar repeated the same text to Nell, but he finally relaxed when she gave her reply.

Billy handed the vicar the ring, and her heart pounded when Mr Marsh slipped it onto her finger. *That's it. Please be happy for me, Jack.*

As soon as the service was over and they stepped out of church, Rebecca gave the orders to throw the confetti.

"Congratulations!"

"Thank you." Nell smiled at Jane and Sarah. "Where's Betty?"

Jane pointed. "Behind you."

Nell turned to see her niece talking to Alice. "There you are. It's lovely to see you with a smile on your face."

"It's a lovely day, that's why. And I get to be with Alice again. We need more family events."

Nell chuckled and looked up at the blue sky. "I'll call later in the week if it stays like this."

Sarah tutted. "You'll still be gallivanting, then, even though you're a married woman?"

"I'll still be visiting family and friends, if that's what you mean. Besides, not much has changed, except that Mr Marsh will be with me of an evening."

"And you'll have an extra wage."

Nell gave her a sweet smile. "There is that. Perhaps you should try it..." She was distracted when more confetti landed on her and she turned to see Leah collecting it from the ground to throw again.

Nell laughed. "That's enough. We'll be here all day if you carry on."

"But it's fun."

Nell smiled at Edith as she joined them. "Will you keep an eye on Leah once we've gone? The carriage is waiting for us."

"Are we going in a carriage, too?" Leah bounced on the spot as Mr Marsh nodded.

"We'll take the first one and then you two can follow with Alice, Elenor and your Aunty Maria." He offered Nell his arm. "Are we ready?"

Nell waved to the guests, and once Mr Marsh had helped her into the carriage, and the door was closed, he ran a finger down her cheek.

"Mrs Marsh. I never thought I'd say that. How are you feeling?"

"Strangely calm, considering everything that's happened. What about you?"

"I have to keep pinching myself to make sure it's not a dream."

She squeezed his hand. "I can assure you, it's not." She gave a final wave out the back of the carriage as it pulled away, but as the church faded into the distance, Mr Marsh turned her to face him.

"You look wonderful." He ran a finger through a ringlet that hung over her cheek.

"You're rather handsome yourself. Who'd have thought we could turn out so well?"

He kissed the end of her nose. "It's a shame Captain and Mrs Robertson couldn't join us today. We wouldn't be here without them."

"It is, but she's away from home so much, there wasn't a chance we could arrange the wedding to fit their schedule."

"Well, when you see her again, you must send her my most sincere thanks. She's helped make my life complete." Mr Marsh grinned. "Imagine. If Mr Ramsbottom could see us now..."

Nell grimaced. "Don't. He's..."

"That's enough. I don't want to hear about him." He cupped her face in his hands and leaned forward to kiss her. "You're mine now. That's all that matters."

After an extended drive around Toxteth, George and Maria were waiting for them by the front door when the carriage pulled up outside the house. Mr Marsh offered Nell a hand as she stepped onto the footpath.

"Welcome home, Mr and Mrs Marsh ... and congratulations!" Maria clasped her hands together. "I'm so pleased for you."

Mr Marsh shook George's hand and bowed to Maria. "Thank you both for making me feel like part of the family. It means a lot after all these years on my own."

George nodded towards Maria. "She's delighted you're here, especially now Alice and Mr Wood have left us."

"I am. Are you coming in? The guests will be here any minute."

Mr Marsh smirked at Nell. "Only if you let me carry you over the threshold." Without waiting for a response, he swept her up, and with Nell holding onto his neck, he carried her into the living room.

Nell reached up to peck his cheek. "I hope you'll be happy here."

"I'd be happy anywhere with you." He set her down on the floor and wrapped his arms around her. "I've dreamt of this moment for so long." His kiss lingered before he pulled away. "I only wish we didn't have another few hours before we can be alone."

The table was almost bare by the time Billy banged on the side of his tankard to call for attention.

"Ladies and gentlemen. As best man, I'd like to propose a toast to the happy couple. May they have many long and happy years together. Mr and Mrs Marsh."

The guests raised an assortment of drinks. "Mr and Mrs Marsh."

Mr Marsh held up a hand to quieten them. "May I propose two toasts? First, to my wonderful wife. Mrs Marsh. I'd like to thank her for making me the happiest man alive."

"Mrs Marsh."

"Second. Will you raise your glasses to our wonderful hostess, Mrs Atkin? We wouldn't have had such a wonderful time without her."

Shouts of Maria and Mrs Atkin rang around the room before Billy banged his tankard once more.

"Before you carry on with the party, I've a few messages to read."

"Really!" Nell's eyes brightened as she eyed the envelopes in Billy's hands. "How special."

Mr Marsh kissed her hand.

"Firstly, a card with a rather nice picture of a bride and groom." Billy held up the card to several oohs from those around them. "It says, *To my dear Mrs Riley and Mr Marsh. Many congratulations on your marriage. I look forward to hearing all about it once we're back in Liverpool. Our very best wishes, Captain and Mrs Robertson.*"

Nell gasped. "Did that arrive today? How did she manage that?"

Maria grinned. "No, it arrived last week, but Alice guessed what it was and put it to one side."

"How lovely."

Billy tapped the side of his tankard once more. "The next is a telegram."

The oohs grew louder.

"*Dear Mrs Riley, I'm glad you finally found happiness. Keep in touch, Clara.*" Billy cleared his throat. "Short and sweet there, but if you're paying by the letter..."

The guests laughed as he counted them up.

"Seventy-one! She must either like you, or be rich, or both."

Nell chuckled. "You've no idea!"

Billy unfolded the last message. "Another telegram. A long one too." The oohs reached fever pitch. "*Mrs Riley what are you...*" The colour fell from his face as he read the rest in silence. "Actually, this one isn't for public reading."

He pushed it back into the envelope. "It will keep until later."

The booing from the guests faded into the background as Nell swayed. *Please don't let that be from who I think it is.*

Mr Marsh held her elbow. "You've gone very pale. What was that about?"

"I-I don't know."

"Do you know who it was from?"

She watched Billy disappear into the front room. "How could I?"

"There are not many people who would send you a telegram. Let me get it from Billy."

"No ... don't. Please. I don't want anything spoiling today."

"Was it from *him*?"

"Honestly, I don't know." She led him to the corner of the room. "If it was, he would have sent it to cause trouble. I told you when you came back from Australia, if there was one person in the world he wouldn't want me to marry, it's you. There's a chance he found out about today..."

"Does he still carry a torch for you?"

"I doubt it. I've not seen him since that afternoon when I was with you."

"So why write after such a long time?"

Nell ran her fingers up his chest. "Do we have to talk about him? I chose you as my husband." She felt his heart pounding as she gazed up at him. "Perhaps it's time to encourage the guests to leave."

"There's no need." There was a glint in his eye. "I took

the liberty of arranging a room at the Adelphi for the night. There'll be a carriage picking us up in half an hour."

"The Adelphi..." A shiver ran down Nell's spine.

"I know you've been there before, but I heard it was the best hotel in Liverpool, and it's not every day you get married."

"No." *Of all the places, though.* She glanced around the room. "If we're going to leave, we'd better start thanking everyone for coming ... and tell Maria." She hadn't gone two steps when Edith bounced up to her.

"Aunty Nell, you'll never guess what."

"What?"

"Alice and Mr Wood have asked me to go to Wales with them."

Nell blinked several times. "I'm sorry. What do you mean? To visit?"

"No. Mr Wood needs a tailoress to finish off the garments and they've offered me the job."

"But ... but you can't. W-what about your work here?"

"We're not going until Saturday and so I can tell work tomorrow and pick up my wages."

"D-do Elenor and Leah know?"

Her face dropped. "Not yet. Leaving them will be the worst part. Alice said they can come and visit. You can come too, if you like."

"That would be nice." She rubbed her forehead. *Why is this happening today? In fact, why is it happening at all? When I've finally made my peace with her...*

"Are you all right?" Edith studied her. "I thought you'd got over your funny turns."

"I'll be fine. And you will, too. Alice will take care of you."

Edith grinned. "I know she will. I'm so excited. Let me tell the others. They've gone outside."

Maria wandered over to Nell as Edith skipped into the hall. "What was that about?"

"She's going to Wales with Alice."

Maria's mouth fell open. "Just like that?"

"On Saturday. She said she'll tell them in work tomorrow."

Maria placed a hand on her arm. "You look upset."

"It's come as a shock, that's all. After everything she put us through ... and when I finally want to spend time with her..."

"Will you stop her?"

"How can I? I'm her aunty, remember. Why would she take any notice of me?"

Maria squeezed her fingers. "You'll see her again."

"Maybe, but will I ever get to know her? Elenor and Leah will be sorry to see her go, too." Nell shook her head. "She's completely thrown me. I was about to find you to tell you we'll be leaving shortly. Mr Marsh has booked us into the Adelphi for the night."

Maria gasped. "I wish someone would take me there, even if it is only for afternoon tea."

Nell smiled. "Maybe one day. Now, I need to say goodbye to everyone. I'll let you know when we're ready to go." She slipped into the front room and headed straight for Billy, pulling him to one side. "What did that telegram say?"

His cheeks coloured as he reached into his inside pocket. "Read it yourself."

"Shield me, then. I don't want anyone to see me." Her hands trembled as she unfolded the small sheet of paper.

> MRS RILEY WHAT ARE YOU DOING – YOU MUSTN'T MARRY HIM – WRITE TO ME – PLEASE – OLLIE.

She took a deep breath and screwed it up. *I'm sorry, Ollie. Not this time.*

"Thank you for not reading it out."

"I'm sorry I was almost too late."

"It's not your fault, but please, not a word to anyone. If Mr Marsh asks after it, tell him I told you to throw it onto the range."

"Will you write to him?"

"Absolutely not, but I don't want Mr Marsh to know I've seen it."

"Do you want me to get rid of it for you?"

Nell shook her head. "I'd rather do it myself. I want to watch it burn."

Alice laughed as Nell sidled into the kitchen and casually opened the range.

"Are you after something else to eat?"

"Not at all. It was all lovely. I just had a few bits in my hand and thought I'd get rid of them." Her heart pounded as the paper caught fire, but she continued to stare until the flames engulfed it. *Farewell, Ollie. You're not ruining my life any more.* She closed the door and took a deep breath as she turned to Alice.

"I believe you've asked Edith to join you in Wales."

"We have. We used to get along so well, and when Mr Wood said he needed a tailoress, she was the first person I thought of."

"You're enjoying it, then?" Nell tried to keep her voice level.

"We are. It's very different to around here."

"I'm not sure Elenor and Leah will be happy about you taking their new friend."

"No, that's unfortunate, but they can come and stay whenever Leah's not at school."

My children leaving me... It serves me right. "I'll come with them, if you have room."

Alice didn't have time to answer before Mr Marsh disturbed them.

"Your carriage awaits, madam." He grinned at her, but Alice interrupted.

"Where are you going?"

"The Adelphi! Just for tonight. We'll be back well before you leave."

"How lovely. I'll see you tomorrow. We can discuss arrangements for a visit then."

Mr Marsh ushered her through the remaining guests, and when they finally reached the front door, Nell called to her daughters. Leah was the first to arrive.

"We're going away for the night, but we'll see you in the morning."

"Where are you going?"

"To the Adelphi."

"Really! Can I come too?"

Nell laughed. "Not tonight. Maybe one day you'll find a husband to take you."

"Ugh. I don't want a husband."

"I'm sure you will one day." Nell smiled at Edith and Elenor, who stood behind their sister. "Be good for Aunty Ria."

"We will."

They stepped to one side as Mr Marsh ushered Nell into the carriage and she waved to them as he took his seat.

"They're growing up now. They won't need me for much longer."

"I doubt that very much. You still rely on Maria."

"I suppose so. Don't tell her though."

He stared out of the window as the carriage pulled away. "I'm more concerned about learning how to be a dad. I've not had a meaningful conversation with any of them."

"That will come when you move in. As long as you're not too harsh with them, you'll be fine."

"Aren't fathers supposed to be stern? They won't learn how to behave otherwise."

Nell sighed. "I've done my best and they're not bad girls."

"Maybe Edith and Leah aren't, but I don't like the way Elenor speaks to you. I'd say she needs a firmer hand."

"You don't want them to hate you, though. It's a fine line between disciplining them and becoming a tyrant. Don't forget, they've never known a father before."

"They've had Mr Atkin."

"George is firm with the boys but less so with the girls. He leaves things like that to Maria."

"Then it will be a new experience for us all." He smiled

at her. "I'm so looking forward to spending the rest of my life with you. We've so much to be thankful for."

"We have. I hope I remember how to be a good wife. I've been a widow for as long as I was married to Jack, and I'm used to being my own person."

"I'm sure you'll do fine." Mr Marsh put an arm round her shoulders. "After everything we've been through over these last nine years, I doubt there's much else that could come between us."

She leaned into his embrace. *If there is, I'm sure you'll find it...*

THE NEXT INSTALLMENT...

The Daughter's Defiance

Would you abandon your husband for the sake of your daughter?

Liverpool 1895: In the five years since her marriage, Nell's daughters have grown from children into young women. But to their stepfather they're a part of her life he'd rather be without.

Elenor has been a source of irritation for years, and with little respect for her mam, their relationship has always been difficult. But when her world is turned upside down, there is only one person she can turn to. Nell is determined to protect her daughter from her husband's wrath, but when he learns of her transgression, their relationship is tested to breaking point.

Still incensed by the way she was treated, Elenor is only too happy to help when her younger sister Leah runs into problems of her own. But her intervention causes more problems than it solves, and leads to life changing consequences.

With the family at loggerheads, Nell is forced to take sides. Will she support her daughter or her husband when compromise is not an option?

To get your copy visit my website at:
https://valmcbeath.com/windsor-street/

If you're enjoying the series, you can sign up to my newsletter at the address below:

Visit: https://www.subscribepage.com/fsorganic

I aim to send out one newsletter a month, and you'll receive details of new releases, special offers and information relating to *The Windsor Street Family Saga,* and my other series, The *Ambition & Destiny* Series. Occasionally, you'll also receive details of other offers relating to historical fiction.

AUTHOR'S NOTE AND ACKNOWLEDGEMENTS

When I started this series, my aim was to tell the story of Nell's life as one of the few women to work on the transatlantic steamships of the 1880s. It must have been incredibly hard to be a working mother at that time, and I wanted to highlight that such work was available, and to give a suggestion of what it may have entailed.

As the storyline developed, however, it felt necessary to include many of the other problems faced by women in Victoria-era England.

You'll know by now that my family sagas are inspired by family history research and that despite the fictional elements of the books, all information relating to the family, such as births, deaths, marriages, occupations, and addresses, are true. As I write each book, however, the thing that constantly strikes me is what ordinary women had to endure.

In the last book (*The Companion's Secret*), there was a brief story line to show Rebecca's frustration with Mr Grayson. It was a fictitious event but reflects what married women could expect from life. With no means of earning their own money, there was no way to escape from controlling or uncaring husbands. In the book, despite Rebecca's brief bid for freedom, she had little choice but to go back to Mr Grayson. The fact they moved away from Toxteth Park in this book was based on fact, but I wonder if he forced her to move away against her will. I'll never know the answer, but there's certainly a possibility he did.

Betty's story showed another side to women's struggles. From the 1911 census, I know she had at least six children who survived early childhood (some will come in the next book but won't be a focus). She also reported losing four others who had previously lived. With long gaps between each live birth, I decided that a series of miscarriages, were also likely. What a desperately sad life she must have had.

As far as Nell is concerned, her time at sea was over by 1884, but looking further into the records, I realised there was still more to explore. The introduction of her daughter Edith was as much a surprise to me as to anyone else! She was an accidental find when I was checking some of my research. It started with the 1911 census, which showed that rather than the two children I knew she had, Nell actually had three children still alive, and one who had died. This set me on a trail of looking for the living child's existence.

It took me a while, and I've still only found Edith (not her real name) on three documents, but at least I now know a little more about her. The first record was of her baptism. I'd missed it originally because her surname had been spelt incorrectly. It wasn't a transcription error; the handwriting was perfectly legible, but the details about her parent's names and address matched the details for Nell and her husband, so there can be no mistake it's her. The misspelling, and the fact she never appeared on any census data with Nell, started me wondering if she'd been brought up elsewhere.

The second document is the census of 1891 (taken just after the end of this book). At the time, she was living with Alice and Mr Wood in Wales and was working as a tailoress - hence her announcement to Nell at the wedding breakfast. It was interesting that on this census, she used the same surname as Nell. That made me think that if she'd been adopted, it must have been to a brother of Jack's, so her surname would have stayed the same.

There is one other document I've found, which will become apparent in the next book, but after that, she disappears from all records. And believe me, I've looked!

Nell's relationship with Mr Marsh was a long time in the making. As far as I can tell, she met him shortly after she became a stewardess (as detailed in *The Stewardess's Journey*) and they worked together for most of that year. After that, as far as work was concerned, they appear to have gone their separate ways, and only married nine years after they met. Why they took so long, I've no idea, but it didn't strike me as a love at first sight relationship!

If you'd like to find out if Nell and Mr Marsh enjoy their happy ending, you can get your copy of *The Daughter's Defiance*, the final book in the series, visit:

https://books2read.com/TDD2

I've got into a routine now of asking my husband Stuart and friend Rachel to read early drafts of the books, and once again, I'd like to extend my thanks for their support. I'd also like to thank my editor Susan Cunningham for her excellent work and my team of advanced readers for final comments before the book was published.

Finally, thank you to you for reading. I hope to see you for *The Daughters Defiance!*

Best wishes

Val

ALSO BY VL MCBEATH

The *Windsor Street Family Saga*

The full series:

Part 1: *The Sailor's Promise*

(*an introductory novella*)

Part 2: *The Wife's Dilemma*

Part 3: *The Stewardess's Journey*

Part 4: *The Captain's Order*

Part 5: *The Companion's Secret*

Part 6: *The Mother's Confession*

Part 7: *The Daughter's Defiance*

The *Ambition & Destiny* Series

The full series:

Short Story Prequel: *Condemned by Fate*

Part 1: *Hooks & Eyes*

Part 2: *Less Than Equals*

Part 3: *When Time Runs Out*

Part 4: *Only One Winner*

Part 5: *Different World*

A standalone novel: *The Young Widow*

Eliza Thomson Investigates

A Deadly Tonic (A Novella)

Murder in Moreton

Death of an Honourable Gent

Dying for a Garden Party

A Scottish Fling

The Palace Murder

Death by the Sea

A Christmas Murder

To find out more about visit VL McBeath's website at:

https://www.valmcbeath.com/

ABOUT THE AUTHOR

Val started researching her family tree back in 2008. At that time, she had no idea what she would find or where it would lead. By 2010, she had discovered a story so compelling she was inspired to turn it into a novel.

This first foray into writing turned into The *Ambition & Destiny* Series. A story of the trials, tragedies, and triumphs of some of her ancestors as they sought their fortune in Victorian-era England.

By the time the series was complete, Val had developed a taste for writing and turned her hand to writing Agatha Christie style mysteries. These novels form part of the *Eliza Thomson Investigates* series and currently consists of five standalone books and two novella's.

Although writing the mysteries was great fun, the pull of researching other branches of the family was strong and Val continued to look for other stories worth telling.

Back in 2018, she discovered a previously unknown fact about one of her great, great grandmothers, Nell. *The Windsor Street Family Saga* is a fictitious account of that discovery. Further details of all series can be found on Val's website at: www.vlmcbeath.com.

Prior to writing, Val trained as a scientist and has worked in the pharmaceutical industry for many years. In 2012, she set up her own consultancy business, and currently splits her time between business and writing.

Born and raised in Liverpool (UK), Val now lives in Cheshire with her husband, Stuart. She has two daughters, the younger of which, Sarah, now helps with the publishing side of the business.

In addition to family history, her interests include rock music and Liverpool Football Club.

FOLLOW ME

at:

Website:

https://valmcbeath.com

Facebook:

https://www.facebook.com/VLMcBeath

BookBub:

https://www.bookbub.com/authors/vl-mcbeath

Printed in Great Britain
by Amazon

44694443R00283